the
Double
Shadow

Also by Sally Gardner

I, Coriander
The Red Necklace
The Silver Blade
Tinder

the Double Shadow

SALLY GARDNER

Indigo

To Jacky, the mistress of memories, with all my love.

In the flicker of memory's smoky light
Down corridors of forgotten places
I saw the door we should not open
That brought us to
The wasteland.

Ezra Pascoe's diary, 19 May 1943

WASTELAND

Once there was a girl who asked of her reflection, 'If all I have is fragments of memories and none of them fit together, tell me then, do I exist?'

There was no answer, only the silence of the room and the hum of the green light that oozed from the television in the corner. She had no idea how long she had been standing there, maybe an eternity. Her name, her age, beyond recall. All she knew was there would be no tomorrow if she couldn't work out the riddle of yesterday. She wondered often if she was going crazy, but it was hard to remember what crazy looked like. In the apartment, on the windowsill before her, lay a dead butterfly. Its wings and its beauty disturbed her. It was familiar, it had an echo of another time.

Softly, she sang a few words, her breath misty on the cold night-time glass, her reflection the only silent proof of her existence.

> *If you go down in the woods today*
> *You're sure of a big surprise.*
> *If you go down in the woods today*
> *You'd better go in disguise.*

She was certain there were more verses but, like so much, they twinkled on the brink of things lost.

High up in a dark tenement block, the girl looked out of the window to a wasteland. In the middle stood one building. A picture palace. She imagined that once it must have been fabulous, with its mirrored facade built of thousands of reflective squares. How it came to fall into such decay was a mystery. As so much here was. The girl could see that the movie house had three grand silvered steps leading up to diamond-paned glass doors. Now all smeared with the grime of neglect. The place looked haunted, having scared away every other building that might have kept it company, leaving it isolated. There, at the very edge of the world, the other buildings formed a protective circle, shoulder to shoulder, arm in arm, joining with rows of tall houses and one black tower to make an impenetrable wall, a mix of apartment buildings and tenement blocks whose fronts were laced with a spider's web of fire escapes, water tanks and balconies. Behind this barricade she could see skyscrapers turning their Venetian-blinded eyes away. There was no way out. This was landscape with no colour, no trees to break the endless monotony of grainy black and white, just the ever-present eerie hum of the green light. It was this light that, in the darkness, filled her nightmares. Perhaps it was the sound of crazy, perhaps it was the end. How was she to know?

The wasteland was a rippling sea, its tides rushing in on waves of things remembered, sucked out by waves of things forgotten. Here, once, a city stood. All that was left was rubble. Here, once, a burning airship fell from the sky. Then the tide changed again and the wasteland was awash with mud and barbed wire, an empty pram that no one would ever collect. The flotsam and jetsam of memories.

It was now night in this eternal day, but there was no time here, no clocks to mark the passing hours. The dark a false promise of a future that would never come.

Snow started to fall, thick, fluffy, playful flakes. The girl watched a magic of sorts unfolding as the wasteland began to turn white.

From an adjoining room, a man said, 'Do you want tea?'

She didn't answer.

'I always like my tea strong, builder's tea, proper tea,' he said. 'I know it's sweet enough when the teaspoon stands upright in the mug. Made two cups. I always make two cups. Made one for Bernie after they blew his arm off.'

The girl heard him come shuffling into the room. He was wearing a dressing-gown over a soldier's shirt and trousers of the Great War, his calves still wrapped in putties, his boots muddy. Carrying his tea to the armchair he sat down, quietened by the green flickering light from the television.

If he talked at all, he talked only of tea, toast and the trenches. He said he'd seen ghosts on the wasteland, seen the dead of Passchendaele rise, young men again.

The girl, too, had seen things on the wasteland, been tempted to go out there and investigate. But she was afraid the boy might not find her. She had searched one apartment, one tenement block after another. Now and again it struck her like a body blow that perhaps the boy wasn't there. Only the child, and she would be happy never, ever to see her again.

Then something strange happened. The sign over the front of the picture palace lit up. It read:

Vervaine Fox starring in *The Night of the Tiger*

She turned to the man in the armchair.

'Look, look,' she said. 'The picture palace is coming to life.'

The soldier said nothing, his tea untouched, the spoon still standing upright.

Now the girl stood in front of him, trying to get his attention. 'Come and see, just once, look out.'

Still the soldier sat, hypnotised by the light from the television. She went back to the window. The picture palace had undergone another transformation. No longer derelict, its mirrored face reflected the snow, shimmering with a glamour that made her long to be a part of it.

She saw a man throw open the double doors. The foyer glowed, honeypot golden, the light spilling on to the carpet of virgin snow, all crisp, all even.

The girl's heart beat faster.

A white tiger walked through the foyer, out of the picture palace, and moved languidly towards the apartment block. The closer the mighty animal came the more the girl felt alive, the more she was aware of a sensation beyond herself, within herself, a stirring, a clue of what yesterday might have been.

This majestic creature, conjured from an alchemist's book of spells, walked with measured steps, its paws leaving a map of prints in the snow. The girl felt certain that if she were with the tiger she would be safe. Safe was not anything she remembered, safe was nothing she knew, except for a snapshot of brown stripes against white fur.

She left the apartment, closing the door carefully behind her so as not to disturb the soldier in his slumbers. The corridor was deserted, green light seeped from under each of the many front doors. She looked down the thirteen storeys of the stone stairwell and started walking. On the ground floor, by the entrance, she stood gazing at the white tiger, fascinated by its beauty. It prowled back and forth, weaving between long-deserted swings and roundabouts, stopping every now and again, its blue eyes seeing right into her.

She will never find the boy, it's been too long, she's sure it's been too long. Only the child is waiting for her and she wishes she would leave her alone.

She pushes open the door. Snow flurries into the passage-way and turns to water on the concrete.

She will follow the tiger, come what may. His tracks make stepping stones across the wasteland to the picture palace. The man is waiting, watching.

He bows to Amaryllis. 'I'm Silas. It's good to see you again.'

Again?

At the top of the grand staircase stands an apparition dressed in a satin evening gown, a rippling waterfall of fabric.

The girl has seen her before. She has a name.

The white tiger prowls around this goddess of the silver screen.

Suddenly there is a noise, a sharp shaking of a door, a

clattering of brooms and brushes, and from a small panel in the mirrored foyer a young man tumbles backwards into the light.

'I'm Ezra Pascoe,' he says, scrambling to his feet. 'Do you remember me?'

'You're the cake boy,' the girl says.

A BASIC EDUCATION

The year 1937

Miss Amos sat, shaken, in her study. A bluebottle buzzed round the wood-panelled room. It was lined with framed photographs of row upon row of identical-looking girls, a paper chain of pupils down the years. Solemn faces in dull uniforms, supervised by teachers who never aged. The room smelled of beeswax and boredom, time measured by the footsteps of frustrated young ladies.

Miss Amos was the perfect picture of an uninspiring headmistress. Dressed in different tones of drabness, she had lardy skin given to moles. Tortoiseshell-rimmed glasses were the only definition in her featureless face.

Clarrington School offered a basic education; nothing that might lead any of the young ladies to aspire to ideas above their station. They were taught only what was required to become good wives and mothers, without the inconvenience of learning the facts of life. Matron gave a wholesome talk on cleanliness being next to godliness and this was considered to be more than enough. As for the nitty-gritty, they could always observe Mr Willis's sheep in the neighbouring field.

The reports of Amaryllis Ruben's behaviour from her

previous school and a child therapist in Switzerland had been dismissed by Miss Amos as codswallop. This was a simple matter of a widowed father who had overindulged his only child. Yes, it was a misfortune for the girl to lose her mother at such a young age, but Miss Amos believed, with the conviction that would please a saint, there was little that a routine of exercise and discipline couldn't cure. Better the girl be broken on the wheel of education than on the wheel of life, for in her considered opinion a wilful young woman was of no value to a man. Miss Amos had corrected many a headstrong girl, reshaping her in the image that the school prided itself on. Tame, malleable girls. The backbone of the Empire, wives for the nation, bearers of sons for the future.

It never occurred to Miss Amos that grief and a lie lay at the heart of Amaryllis's troubles, that she was a girl walking on thin ice, a girl for whom there was no solid ground. Neither was she aware that her pupil was extremely clever – and extremely lonely.

Advancing on the bluebottle with a fly-swat in her hand, Miss Amos had to acknowledge that the wretched girl had defeated her. Amaryllis's catalogue of crimes had led the headmistress to wander into a puddle of thought, muddy and unclear as it was, about the nature of original sin.

The first of her misdemeanours, as Miss Amos called them, had occurred shortly after Amaryllis had arrived at the school. The girl had made a tidy sum of money giving midnight lessons in the dormitory on the art of lovemaking. This had only come to light when a junior had fainted after being shown a collection of Parisian 'Naughty Nudes' from the 1900s. The idiot creature had fallen off her bed and broken her arm. On coming to she had given the game away.

Amaryllis had said, without an ounce of embarrassment, that she had found the postcards in an old shoe box of her father's. As for the facts of life – that was simple: she had sent away for a copy of Marie Stopes's book on married love. Much more informative than Mr Willis's sheep.

Thinking of it now made Miss Amos shudder. The misdemeanour was serious enough to get the new girl expelled and she would have been had it not been for the charm of her charismatic father.

The second misdemeanour was of more significant proportions. Amaryllis had burned down the Biology Laboratory. On purpose, so she said, to see if an experiment with a magnifying glass would work.

On that occasion, Miss Amos and the school governors had been forced into forgiveness by the size of Arnold Ruben's cheque. His gift enabled the building of new Science and Art wings. But Amaryllis's latest escapade could not be classified as a misdemeanour. It was impossible to keep her at the school a day longer.

Last night, the headmistress's call to Mr Ruben had been put through to a Mr Silas Molde.

'I regret to report . . .' Miss Amos could hardly bring herself to say the girl's name, '. . . went missing on a school trip to London.'

Mr Molde remained calm. He asked her not on any account

to involve the police or the press. Miss Amos, shocked by his casual tone, was stunned into silence.

What, asked the remote voice at the end of the line, did she intend to do when Miss Ruben returned to school?

Miss Amos didn't hesitate. 'She will be expelled.'

There was a silence that seemed no more than a click of a pen cap.

'Is there . . . a sum of money that might make you reconsider?'

Miss Amos pursed her thin lips and beads of sweat formed above them. The school motto stared down at her.

> *To serve one's country, to do one's duty,*
> *to obey the word of the Lord.*

'No, this must be the end of the matter.'

There was a long pause in which the line crackled and Miss Amos was on the point of thinking she had been disconnected when Mr Molde said in a disinterested tone, 'A car will be sent for her tomorrow.'

'But,' said Miss Amos indignantly, 'what if she doesn't return?'

The phone went dead.

That morning, just after assembly, a handsome man in evening dress entered her study unannounced, followed by a dazzling beauty of a woman. Full lips, hair perfectly coiffured, she was wearing a silver dress, a mirage shimmering into a mermaid's tail. The vision, for there was no other word to describe her, quite discombobulated Miss Amos.

The business card the man handed her read:

Maurice Sands
Entrepreneur

Miss Amos turned the card over.

'How can I help you?' she asked.

'Brought the wanderer back.'

His accent was so unexpected she hardly listened to a word he was saying.

'The wanderer?' queried Miss Amos.

'Oh, come off it – Amaryllis.'

Miss Amos, unused to being addressed in such a familiar tone, was quite at a loss as to what to say when the bluebottle noisily made its entrance into the room and headed straight for her. Flapping her hands, she tried in vain to swat it away.

The young woman was gently swaying back and forth.

'This is Miss Ruben,' said Maurice Sands.

Miss Amos was still unable to join together the dots that would make this goddess form a picture of a humdrum schoolgirl.

'What is your name?' she asked.

The goddess burped. 'Amaryllis Ruben,' she said.

And finally the drawing was complete and the full outrage of the situation hit Miss Amos so hard that she started to tremble.

'Do you realise, Mr Sands, that Miss Ruben is just sixteen years old and a pupil of this school?' She made to lift the phone. 'I am going to call the police and have you arrested for the abduction of a minor.'

'I think,' said Maurice Sands, taking a cigarette from a gold case, 'you will find that to be very ill-advised. I am sure Mr Ruben wouldn't be pleased if you involve the police. He doesn't like scenes.'

'Are you threatening me?'

'I suppose I am,' he said, blowing a perfect smoke ring.

Miss Amos let go of the receiver.

Amaryllis, still swaying slightly, suddenly burst out laughing.

Maurice Sands, despite himself, began to laugh too.

'The girl is drunk,' said the headmistress, stating what had been obvious from the start.

'High-spirited,' said Maurice Sands. He put his arm round Amaryllis. She turned and vomited all over him. He jumped back, horrified. 'You little cow! My dinner jacket's ruined . . .'

'Oh, whoops-a-daisy,' said Amaryllis, ghostly pale.

'I think you should leave,' said Miss Amos, forcefully ringing a hand bell. Help was most definitely needed.

Maurice Sands was mopping his dinner jacket with his handkerchief when Matron entered, followed by a maid.

'There has been an accident,' said Miss Amos. 'If you wouldn't mind showing Mr Sands the cloakroom?'

Maurice Sands stopped at the door and turned to Amaryllis. 'Better behave yourself. You wouldn't want me telling Daddykins what a naughty little girl he has, would you?'

Miss Amos waited until the door was firmly shut and, returning to the safe fortress of her desk, never for a moment thought to ask what Mr Sands had meant. She felt there was no more proof needed: the girl was a bad lot. With a deep intake of breath she began her well-prepared and seldom-used speech. Miss Ruben was a disgrace to the school. Before Miss Amos reached the *coup de grâce*, that Amaryllis was to be expelled, she had already picked up her silver tail and left the room.

Miss Amos was about to run after her and demand that she hear her out, but realised that what was left of her dignity would be lost. Instead she crossed the bare boards to a discreet cabinet and took out an old bottle of Christmas sherry, as sweet and sickly as cough mixture. She poured a generous glass and downed it in gulps.

Amaryllis stood in the clotted-cream-painted dormitory. On each of the regimented beds with their thin white covers sat a woebegone bear stuffed with the aching love of a neglected girl. She hated this place, this rich-man's orphanage. Her mind now crystal clear, she tipped the contents of her locker unceremoniously into her trunk.

Matron, having seen off Maurice Sands, was overflowing with an anthem of righteous anger. Amaryllis heard not one word of what was said. She had long ago learned not to listen; if you listen you can be tripped up. If you don't, you won't be. She was conscious only of an unholy din and Matron's cracked red-postbox lips going up and down. Finally, the woman, nearly beside herself with rage, grabbed hold of Amaryllis violently and shook her for all she was worth.

'Take your hands off me,' said Amaryllis.

The girl's unblinking violet eyes pierced right through her. Matron, recognising a force beyond her control, let go.

'You will come to a bad end. Girls like you always do,' she shouted as Amaryllis dragged her trunk out of the dormitory, her silver mermaid tail trailing after her.

Down the hushed corridors she went until she reached the main staircase. Bump, bump, the noise reverberated in Miss Amos's study. She shuddered and poured the last of the sherry. Amaryllis hauled the trunk to the entrance hall with its imposing front door and into the blinding sunlight. In the middle of the gravel drive, right outside the headmistress's study, she sat upright on the trunk and waited. Her head throbbed. All she wanted was to lie down in a darkened room with a cold flannel over her eyes. If it hadn't been for the fact that every girl in the school was watching her from behind the mock-Tudor windows, she may well have given in and slumped, but knowing she had an audience, hungry for drama, she felt it was her role to oblige. Standing up, she stretched, and as a curl of thick black hair came loose from its prison of hairpins, she emptied the entire contents of the trunk on to the drive. From her sewing kit she took a pair of scissors and for the next hour she cut up, with great care, her gymslip, her skirt, her tunic, her cardigan-that-couldn't-be-worn-without-a-blazer, and every other item on the uniform list from Harrods, making sure each piece was small enough to be of no use to anyone.

By the time the Bentley arrived every shred had been returned to the trunk. Longbone, the chauffeur, enquired if there was any luggage.

'None,' said Amaryllis imperiously. But seeing the eager eyes of disbelieving girls and the mortified face of the headmistress peeping out from behind Victorian lace curtains, she said to the chauffeur, 'One minute.'

Returning to the trunk, she opened it, a magician performing a final trick. She had saved a box of matches from the nightclub. She struck each one in turn and dropped them in the trunk. Only when it had caught light did she return to the Bentley.

'Home, to the old mausoleum,' she said, 'where no doubt the fatted calf has been killed for my arrival.'

'Your father's abroad, miss.'

Amaryllis sighed. She turned and looked back up the drive. Her trunk was burning bonfire-bright, framed by dark rhododendrons. She rested her head on the back of the leather seat, closed her eyes and tried not to think about Maurice Sands, or what he had done. No, that memory she would wipe from her mind.

If you don't think about it, it can't hurt . . . but hurt it did.

THE GIANT CENTIPEDE

Amaryllis's father had bought Warlock Hall shortly after his marriage. The Black Tower, the central architectural feature, dated from the seventeenth century and the house, a tumour of bricks and mortar, had attached itself much later. The result was an argument of a building, irritated and at odds with its foundations.

The tower was said to be haunted by the daughter of the Earl of Fairfield who had been walled up there for refusing to marry a man she didn't love. Amaryllis's father, who was fascinated by the supernatural, felt somewhat cheated that the maiden had given up her moonlight strolls by the time he came to own the hall.

Then again, Arnold Ruben hadn't bought the place for its beauty or its history. What had sold him the property was the extensive land which came with the house, and here, in the Garden of England, he had settled.

He had, to a certain extent, modernised the inside of the house, putting in *en suite* bathrooms and a better heating system, but the most extraordinary thing he did was to build a picture palace. His folly looked like an alien spacecraft sitting in the middle of the ancient bluebell wood. It was, in fact, a masterpiece of Art Deco design, built from thousands of mirrored squares that reflected the woods in a dazzling infinity. The Black Tower and the picture palace, divided by centuries, were united as symbols of the foibles of rich men.

The first weeks after Amaryllis returned from school the house was a film set waiting for 'Lights, camera, action!'

It was the damp, solid silence of the old place that Amaryllis couldn't stand. It seemed to possess its own internal weather, clouds of thwarted conversations. She could feel her father's displeasure as it blew, with hurricane force, across the Atlantic towards her, materialising in endless telegrams about what she could and shouldn't be doing.

His assistant, Clifford Lang, read them out to her in a cut-glass, cocktail voice. He was unbearably proper, and she had disliked him ever since he'd first arrived over seven months ago. Her only comfort was that Silas seemed to like him even less than she did.

Although Silas was not related to Amaryllis in any way, he had been more present while she was growing up than her father had been since she lost her early memories. She could retrieve nothing of the first eight years of her existence. All she remembered dated from the time she woke up in a clinic in Switzerland. The doctors in charge of her case told her father the amnesia was due to a brain fever. The psychiatrist believed it was a combination of the illness and the trauma of losing her mother. Arnold and Silas knew the truth, but Arnold refused to face it.

He had given Amaryllis an album of photographs in the hope that the images might rekindle her memories. The black-and-white pictures were of a child who looked like her: a small stranger having a birthday party; dressed for dancing classes; holding her daddy's hand. Yet none of the images meant anything to her except for one of Silas and her father in his workroom. It was the only picture she didn't want to look at, but why, she couldn't say. No one could explain to her where the past had gone. For three months she stayed in hospital, lost and confused, haunted by the child she couldn't remember.

Her father paid cursory visits, unable to accept that his beloved daughter didn't recognise him. Finally, in desperation, he had taken her home, hoping that familiar surroundings might reawaken the past. They didn't.

Her innocent love for him was gone, forgotten. She understood that he was her father, nothing more. Guilt drove Arnold further into his work. Guilt gave his work an urgency it had never had before. He told himself all would be fine and dandy.

But even Arnold Ruben hadn't managed to keep his little daughter small forever. She had grown up without his permission, and secretly she knew that wasn't allowed. The older Amaryllis became, the wider the river between them.

On her expulsion from Clarrington School, Silas employed a governess, Miss Bright, to take over her education. Amaryllis had nothing against the woman except a determination that she was not going to be told what to do by her father, Silas, Miss Bright, or that righteous prig, Clifford Lang. She stayed in her bedroom, surrounded by film magazines and copies of

Vogue, filled with pictures of perfect young women. What she longed for was someone to talk to.

The face that stared back at her from the mirror was no longer that of Daddy's little girl, whoever she had been. She knew this time she had gone too far, that the rickety bridge over the river was washed away.

'So this is me,' she said to herself, and the more she looked the more abandoned she felt.

Her skin crawled and four baths a day made her feel no cleaner. She could still smell Maurice Sands and it made her retch.

It had all started as nothing more than a silly dare.

Clarissa Bodminton-Bow, a podgy girl with the biggest breasts in the class and an obsession with food, said to Amaryllis, 'It's frightfully rotten, I've finished all my tuck. I'm ravenously hungry. Will you sneak out with me to the village shop? If you do I promise I'll invite you to my summer ball, honest injun I will.'

Amaryllis had gone along mainly out of boredom and a desire not to be the only girl in the class not invited to Clarissa's seventeenth-birthday party.

They had arrived in the village to see, outside Mrs Purdie's sweet shop, a bright-red sports car which glowed against the dreary row of rundown cottages. Clarissa was quite taken with it, but more taken with its owner, a man with the look of a pocket full of promises. He had appeared to be enchanted with Clarissa's yah yah questions, so much so that he bought them both ginger beers. As luck would have it, it was warm enough in the sun to drink them sitting outside on a wooden bench.

'Let me introduce myself. My name is Maurice Sands, and yours . . . ?' he asked, turning to Amaryllis.

'Gosh, we would be in so much trouble if we were caught,' Clarissa said, greedily sucking up the remains of her pop. Amaryllis said nothing.

'Would you like some chocolates?' he asked Clarissa, who, certain she had met her sugar daddy, went back into Mrs Purdie's shop clutching half-a-crown.

When she had gone, he turned to Amaryllis and, lighting a cigarette and blowing a perfect smoke ring, said, 'I know a thing or two about faces and, if you don't mind my saying so, you have that indefinable something – a beauty the camera would love.'

Amaryllis hadn't thought much of him. His clothes, his car – they were all too new, too brash. Granted he was good-looking in a slick sort of way, rather like a matinée idol. Well, at least he knew how to flatter and that wasn't all bad. They were interrupted by Clarissa, waddling back with a box of chocolates.

He whispered to Amaryllis, 'Why don't you call me when you're next up in town?' and slipped his card into her pocket.

On the way back to school, Amaryllis had made her first mistake. She had told Clarissa what he had said.

'Oh gosh, what are you going to do?'

'Nothing,' said Amaryllis.

That might have been the end of the matter if it hadn't been that Clarissa, green with envy, kept on asking, 'Are you going to ring him? Go on, I dare you to ring him. Get his address and Mummy will invite him to my party. Oh, gosh, wouldn't that be exciting?'

Amaryllis knew perfectly well that Lady Bodminton-Bow would do no such thing and that Clarissa would be mortified if he turned up at her ancestral home, even in his red sports car.

Perhaps it was that, or just boredom that made Amaryllis climb out of the dormitory window late one night and walk into the village, where from its only telephone box she rang the operator and asked for a Mayfair number. A woman with a grating, unplaceable accent answered the phone.

The line was not good and Amaryllis was on the point of hanging up when the woman said, 'Who do you want?' and Amaryllis, with butterflies in her tummy, said, 'Maurice Sands.'

'Who?' came the reply. 'I think you have the wrong . . .' then she stopped and Amaryllis thought she heard her say 'Darling, this must be for you.'

It was on the school trip to London that Clarissa, who had been Amaryllis's biggest champion, said spitefully, 'Personally, I don't think you should have done that. He was frightfully common, you know, not one of us. I've quite gone off him.'

At South Kensington, Amaryllis, with remarkable ease, slipped free from the giggling gaggle of girls from Clarrington School.

Everything had gone according to plan. Maurice Sands was waiting outside the tube station in a taxicab, its meter running. They'd had fun, hadn't they, she and Maurice? London was so exciting, so vibrant. Splendid shop windows, the noise of the cars, the newspaper sellers shouting, the jostle of the crowds.

Maurice had taken her to Selfridges and bought her a dress, then to Madame Gigi's beauty parlour. Wasn't that just wild? Having her hair all pinned up as if she'd had a marcel wave. Then they had cocktails at the Ritz.

'Roach, who is this gorgeous creature?' asked a well-dressed man, coming up to their table.

Amaryllis, by now slightly tipsy, asked, 'Why did he call you Roach?'

'Stupid old fossil, he always gets my name wrong.'

They had gone to a party, all the divine young things were there; life was a whirl, a laugh, full of daring adventure. This was the best night ever. More champagne and green, gold-tipped cigarettes. There was a man with a fish in his cocktail glass. Laughter, faces, flamingoes in the garden; really silly flamingoes, all pink, and the world spinning round and round.

'I feel sick,' she said.

'Don't worry, I'll look after you.'

Suddenly she wondered what she was doing there.

He had taken her upstairs to a bedroom, laid her down on the bed. She'd closed her eyes to stop the room turning, spinning out of control. Her head was throbbing. Through half-opened eyes she saw a huge centipede with hundreds of white-gloved hands going all over her body, going into places they shouldn't. A nursery rhyme was spinning in her head.

Pat-a-cake, pat-a-cake, baker's man.
Bake me a cake as fast as you can.

The centipede was hurting her, almost crushing her. One of its hands was over her mouth, she couldn't breathe, she couldn't scream, then she remembered nothing . . . nothing . . . just the rhythm of the rhyme.

Put it in the oven for baby and me.

When she awoke, Maurice was sitting in a chair holding a cigarette, a bottle of champagne by his side.

'Clean yourself up, doll,' he said, 'you look a mess. I'll send for a maid.'

She had been sick in the loo, then stood staring at her face in the mirror. Her bright-red lips were smudged, mascara had run down her cheeks. Her face was a grotesque carnival mask. The maid with cold indifference had put her back together again.

These memories, all jagged, spiked her. In the silence of the empty house it hadn't happened. But she knew it had. She'd never felt pain like that before.

'Stop it, stop it,' she said to herself. 'It's a mistake, just a mistake. It will be all right, it has to be all right . . .'

She remembered Maurice forcing her to drink more champagne before taking her downstairs to a marbled hall where she heard a woman shout, 'Christ, Everett, you'd better get her back before they call the police.'

Everett. Why did she call him Everett?

Flicking through her movie magazines, Amaryllis paused at a striking picture of Vervaine Fox, the great Hollywood legend of the silver screen, posing with a white tiger. She cared little for the film star, it was the tiger that caught her attention. She took her nail scissors and carefully cut it out. Just the sight of the great animal's wise expression comforted her like nothing else had been able to. She knew one thing – if that tiger had been with her he would have torn the giant centipede limb from limb, white-gloved hand from white-gloved hand.

BAKE ME A CAKE

Five weeks passed before Arnold Ruben returned home. On the day he was due to arrive, the house instantaneously woke up to the urgency of now. Life was being artificially pumped back into Warlock Hall with an almost frantic energy, as if everyone realised that the place had been dying from lack of purpose.

Amaryllis remained in her bedroom, removed from all the hectic activities. She felt she could congratulate herself on not having attended one of Miss Bright's lessons so far, and for avoiding Clifford Lang altogether. Silas, too, had been away for the last few days.

Amaryllis was lying on top of her bed, surrounded by a whirlwind of clutter that she had forbidden her maid to tidy, when there was a knock on her door.

'Yes, who is it?'

The door opened. Before she could say anything Silas walked in, removed a few items from a chair and sat himself down.

'If this is about Miss Bright . . .'

'No, it's not,' said Silas. He looked very serious indeed. He handed her a business card.

Amaryllis felt sick. 'Where did you get this from?' she asked.

'I went to see your former headmistress to ask about the mysterious man who took you back to the school. How did you meet him?'

'I don't want to talk about this,' Amaryllis said.

Silas studied her with his intense dark eyes.

'I met him with Clarissa Bodminton-Bow outside Mrs Purdie's sweet shop.'

'Then what?'

'I went with him as a dare, just a silly dare.'

'He bought you clothes, took you to the Ritz and then to a party. What did he want in return for his generosity?'

'I don't know what you mean.'

'That's rich coming from you. Where was this party?'

'I wasn't paying much attention. They had flamingoes in the garden.'

Silas sighed and leaned forward. 'You danced all night?'

'Yes, that's right.'

'And nothing else?'

'No,' she said, 'no.' Panic and nausea overwhelmed her. 'Are you going to tell Daddy? I know what I did was wrong. But can't that be the end of the matter?'

Silas got up. 'You don't want to turn out like your mother, young lady. That would be a terrible waste.'

'My mother? What do you mean?'

'She had a head full of parties, cocktails and men. Very little else. You are a clever girl, too clever to go down that road.'

'Please, Silas, don't tell Daddy. I beg of you. Could it be your birthday present to me?'

He closed the door behind him.

Amaryllus rushed into the bathroom and was sick. Sitting on the cold tiled floor, she started to count. Her period was late. She couldn't be pregnant . . . that would be the worst thing ever.

After lunch Amaryllis's maid brought her a parcel from Bergdorf Goodman, the department store in New York. It was a tea dress, white Irish linen, the finest lace, a dress for a little girl. The one thing she knew she wasn't was a little girl, not now, not any more.

'Mr Ruben wants you to wear it for his return.'

With great care the dress was taken from its tissue paper, the crisp linen shaken out and hung up. She waited until the maid left.

'I hate it!' she screamed at the empty bedroom. Suddenly filled with rage, she threw it on the floor and kicked it across the turmoil of her room. 'I am not a doll!' she shouted.

Then, calmer, she undressed and put it on, deciding that if she didn't go out into the sunshine she would go mad. Amaryllis slipped quietly through the house and hesitated outside the kitchen. She could see all the servants gathered together for a briefing from the head butler. The pantry door was ajar and Amaryllis spied a walnut-and-coffee sponge cake, all fluffy, pleased as punch with itself. Without a second thought, she took it, plate and all. She walked purposefully out through the kitchen garden, weaving her way towards the Wendy house.

The Wendy house was Edwardian and made out of wood that once had been garishly painted. Nearly forgotten, it had been left to decay.

Her father had taken her to it shortly after she returned from the clinic in Switzerland. He had talked all the time, telling her how frightened she had once been of the hissing geese.

'Why?' she had asked.

'Don't you remember?'

The trouble was that she hadn't. She had stared, baffled, at the Wendy house, its rosebud curtains bunched together in the window. Then she had pulled her hand free from her father's and, shooing the geese out of the way, had run towards it. Her father had watched her, puzzled. At the door she had looked back. He had lit a cigarette and the smoke put a gauze between them.

The downstairs room was decorated with rose wallpaper. There was a small chair by the fireside, and a table laid with a china tea set. A toy tiger sat in one of the chairs. Upstairs she found a bed, just big enough for her to sleep in. She was about to leave when she caught sight of a butterfly flapping against the window. She lifted the latch and pushed it open. The butterfly danced away. In the sunlight she could see her father's face, full of anticipation.

'Now do you remember?' he called.

She didn't answer. Careful to close the window, she stood taking in the miniature house and all it contained. It couldn't be hers. Surely she would never have forgotten it?

Not one bit frightened of the geese, she had walked away from the place of which she had no memory back to the stranger she called Daddy.

Her father had asked, 'Aren't you going to bring your tiger with you?'

'My tiger?'

'You remember – you must remember your beloved toy tiger?'

'Perhaps,' she had said, 'the fairies have snatched your real daughter away. I'm just made up, so you won't be too lonely without her.'

He hadn't answered, neither had he taken her hand. She had never asked to go there again.

The air smelled sweet, of rosemary and thyme. She kicked open the small door, reminded of the sin of not remembering. All the furnishings and toys had long gone, belonging to a different age, a different child. Her dress caught on a rusty nail and ripped. What did it matter? She crawled into the damp house, staining the perfect Irish white linen. She was Alice after she'd drunk the potion; her legs poked out of the door. She tore the sponge apart, sinking her fingers into the sweet creamy coffee filling, devouring it, her mouth covered in the deliciousness of it. She wiped her hands on the white lace of her dress. At last, fit to bursting, she could eat no more.

She lay still, watching as an army of ants carried away the crumbs. Her heavy eyelids closed, her worrisome mind quiet at last.

She drifted into dreams. A huge baby was sitting in her toy pram. Its head and arms were made of flesh, the rest of its body was of shell-pink porcelain. One of its legs had come off and, try as she might, she couldn't get it back on again.

The doll-baby said, in a wheezy, squeaky voice, 'That's what happens if you run away with a centipede.'

Amaryllis woke with a start. Someone was calling her name. All she could see through the window was a pair of stout, thick-stockinged legs anchored in sensible shoes. She saw with relief it was nobody but Cook, who, to Amaryllis's amazement, was addressing her with none of the deference to which she was accustomed.

'I want my cake back,' said Cook.

Sighing, Amaryllis pushed out the empty plate, then lying down again and yawning, said, 'I've eaten it. You will just have to make another. Oh, for goodness' sake, go away, don't you have . . .'

She didn't finish what she was saying. She was dragged by her ankles out of the Wendy house, firmly grabbed by the arm and made to stand up.

Nancy Pascoe was a handsome woman with intelligent grey eyes that could weigh up more than flour and butter.

'You are going to make the cake, not me.'

'Who do you think you're talking to . . . ?'

'The girl who stole my coffee-and-walnut cake and, I see, has ruined a brand-new dress.'

'I could have you fired for your impudence. Where is your respect?'

'I have none, not for a thief,' said Mrs Pascoe, her gaze unblinking. 'Now, if you had asked me for a piece of cake, that would have been a different matter. But you didn't, did you? So you will be making another one, and there's no arguing, young lady.'

She turned and walked back towards the kitchen.

Amaryllis realised she had met her match. This plain-spoken woman meant every word she said.

Following the cook, she was reminded of the nursery-rhyme book she had loved when she was little, with its pictures of rosy-cheeked women baking jam tarts for knaves to steal. A small part of her tiny and near-forgotten self was tempted to tell Mrs Pascoe everything.

Pat-a-cake, pat-a-cake . . .

The song came back to her. She longed to forget.

At the pantry door she hesitated as Mrs Pascoe took her by the hand, holding it as tight as she would a wooden spoon.

Cook's office had windows that looked out on to the white-tiled kitchen. Inside the room, on a scrubbed wooden table in neat bowls sat the ingredients for a cake. Mrs Pascoe closed the blinds so that the room was no longer in view of the other servants, then going to the door, stuck her head out and told the laundrymaid she would be needed and asked that Mrs Popplin, the seamstress, be sent to her straight away.

Mrs Popplin, her face red with permanent disapproval, studied Amaryllis's dress.

'What do you think?' asked Mrs Pascoe.

'It looks to be ruined.'

'That is as plain as the nose on my face, but what can be done to salvage it before Mr Ruben returns?'

Mrs Popplin thought better than to state the obvious. She said, 'I'll see what me and my needle can do, I can do no more than that.'

That afternoon, Amaryllis, wrapped in a huge apron, had her first cookery lesson. Mrs Pascoe, for all her bristle, was a gentle teacher.

'Do you have children?' asked Amaryllis.

Mrs Pascoe nodded, pouring them cups of tea while they waited for the cake to cook.

'Yes, two. Olive, my eldest, is working at Mrs Marshall's in the High Street, and Ezra, who you must have seen around here, is to leave school and work as a mechanic under your father's chauffeur.'

'Oh, yes, I know. How old is he?'

'Just turned fifteen. Old enough to bring home some money.'

'Do they bake?'

'Yes. Bake, clean, polish. They have little choice in the matter.'

They are lucky, thought Amaryllis, for in the warmth of that kitchen, in the strength of Mrs Pascoe's arms, in her determination that Amaryllis would bake a cake, she glimpsed for the first time what love could be, how safe it could make you feel. Like the sponge mixture, it took hard work to make something so incredibly light, something that tasted of air.

She thought of the difference between that and her father's love, which paralysed the future.

'You should be proud of yourself,' said Mrs Pascoe, when she took the cake from the oven.

Amaryllis dared not look in case the sponge changed its mind and sank. She kept her eyes tightly shut until Mrs Pascoe, laughing, gently kissed the top of her head.

'You are a daft cabbage leaf. Look, you baked a cake.'

Amaryllis returned to her room. Her dress was hanging up, looking as good as new. Only on closer inspection could she see where a panel had been added and the torn lace almost invisibly sewn together.

It was the kiss more than the cake which had startled her troubled soul. It was a kiss of forgiveness. A kiss she doubted her father would ever give her.

THE SEVERED HAND

Often Ezra Pascoe would wonder what might have happened if his mother hadn't insisted on taking Amaryllis into the kitchen that day. When he was older he realised that it must have started then, while butter was being rubbed into the flour. Unknown to him, his future became mixed with Amaryllis's, so that by the time the oven door was opened, the spell had been well and truly baked, his destiny altered by the making of a cake.

That evening, after Amaryllis's cookery lesson, Nancy Pascoe left the under-cook in charge of the kitchen at Warlock Hall. The Pascoes sat down for high tea and Ezra listened as his mother told Father about Mr Ruben's daughter. She described how Amaryllis had been expelled from school, and how she had stolen the cake.

'What that girl needs is some good, wholesome love. It's not suprising she doesn't know where she stands. One day Mr Ruben is full of wind and bluster, the next it's sunsets and cucumber sandwiches.'

'I suppose,' said his father, 'if you have that much power you can do what you like, send men over the top, have them killed by the dozen, and no one bats an eye.'

'Father,' said Mother gently, 'best not to think like that, love, it doesn't help.'

Father rolled his tobacco, his hand shaking as he lit the match. Ezra and Olive silently collected the plates from the table. They knew what was coming. When Father got all shaky, it was a sign that he was on the verge of one of his turns.

On Saturday, Father was still in what he called the bunker – the garden shed. Here he dug a trench while in his mind the shrapnel flew around him. Nothing anyone said or did could make the battlefield and the ghosts go away. Mother would take him food and wait until all was quiet on the western front of his memory. Then he would emerge, pale and ill, his head splitting with blinding pain. This unacknowledged problem meant Noel Pascoe was unemployable and Mother had to earn the money for their daily bread.

This time, Noel's turn had lasted two days and he had yet to reappear.

Ezra, rushing down the stairs that morning into the small kitchen, was bitterly disappointed to find his mother had forgotten to leave out two pennies for the Saturday Cinema Club. It was the last time he would go with his best friend Len to the Rio for, come Monday, he would be a working man.

'You haven't seen it?' he asked Olive.

'Seen what?'

'My pocket money.'

'No, Mother must have forgotten. She did the washing before she went to work. She had to be there at five this morning.'

'Why?' asked Ezra.

Finishing her tea by the kitchen door, Olive looked past the vegetable patch at the garden shed from which their father could be heard, loud and clear.

'Get down, get the bloody hell down!'

'Because,' she said, turning to Ezra, 'Mr Ruben has a house party arriving. Mother said that Vervaine Fox has been invited. Think on that, Ezra, a real film star coming to Warlock Hall.' Then, as an afterthought, she added, 'You'd better get the washing in, otherwise Father will be shouting like that all morning, thinking it's the enemy.'

'Could you lend me tuppence for the cinema?'

'No, I need my money.'

'Just tuppence.'

'Never a lender or a borrower be,' said Olive, smugly.

Ezra sighed and, scraping his chair on the stone floor, sat down at the kitchen table, resting the side of his face on his hand, well aware that he was too old to be complaining.

Olive had left childhood behind. At seventeen she had a job at a "costumier", and was walking out with Wilfred Jones.

'Personally,' she said, washing up her teacup and putting it on the draining board, 'I don't think those films do you any good. They just fill your head with rubbish.'

She dried her hands on the tea towel and put on her coat. Looking in the mirror over the fireplace, she adjusted her new hat.

Ezra watched her with a deep sense of regret. Once he had a big sister who looked after him, told him stories; a tomboy who climbed trees and could beat him at conkers. Now, standing in the morning light, was this unfathomable sister of his, all grown up, with a new hat to wear and a spotty young man to kiss.

Olive, catching his eye in the mirror's reflection, asked, 'What do you think?'

Ezra blushed. He wasn't going to say what he was actually thinking. Instead he said, 'That I'm going to have to live all my life not knowing what happened in *The Severed Hand*.'

'No, silly, about my hat.'

'It looks all right. It's a hat, that's all.'

Olive sighed. 'Boys,' she said. 'A breed apart, that's what you are. Don't forget to bring the washing in.'

The latch on the front door clicked shut behind her. Ezra wondered about going down to the garden shed and risking enemy fire by asking his father for the money. He took the laundry basket outside and put it down by the thorn-filled roses. He could hear his father shouting, 'Jesus, they shot his head in! The bastards!' and changed his mind.

He quickly took the clothes inside and hung them in front of the range as he had been taught, thankful that at last his father was quiet. Ezra hated these turns. He never said it, but they frightened him. He didn't know who the man in the shed was, he was so different from the quiet and gentle father he loved.

Without anyone in it, the cottage was creaky-silent, as if it were about to fold in on itself, like the washing. He decided to wait for Len outside.

'Is your father having one of his turns, dear?' asked Mrs

Calthorpe, their neighbour, her arms folded under her ample bosom.

Ezra kicked a stone and said nothing.

'Sad, that, for your mum,' she continued. 'My Bert said it took some of the weaker ones that way.'

Ezra didn't even bother to look up. Mrs Calthorpe could talk for hours about her husband, Bert, who, according to her, had single-handedly won the Great War. He was the oracle on all things military.

Mrs Calthorpe sighed. 'Your poor mother, having to cope with all that.' She gestured in the direction of the garden shed. 'I told her, he should be locked away.'

Ezra hated her and her smug, childless face.

He went to find another stone worthy of being a football, and reflected that the only hope he had of getting into the Saturday Cinema Club was if Len's dad had been a bit more generous than usual, and hadn't drunk all the family's housekeeping money.

'Oh, look,' said Mrs Calthorpe, leaning foward on her garden gate, her eyes squinting. 'Isn't that Tommy Cutler with your friend Len?'

Ezra spun round, his heart already sinking. There was Len with a giant of a boy in short trousers, who everyone called Tommy Treacle on account of the treacle toffee his mum made him every week.

'Not right in the head, that one,' continued Mrs Calthorpe, as if it were a revelation that would never have crossed Ezra's mind.

'I mean, poor Mrs Cutler, and they say he's still growing but his brain stopped at six and forgot to keep up with the rest of him.'

Ezra wanted to shout at her, 'Oh, shut up, you old bat!' But he gritted his teeth and stared, mortified, down the road.

'As I said to your mother, that's what you get for your sin.'

Not this again, thought Ezra. Mrs Calthorpe was sucking at her dentures with relish.

'I mean, Tommy could never have been old Fred Cutler's son because of the injury he got at Wipers. Lost both legs and more besides I wouldn't wonder.'

Tommy Treacle, seeing Mrs Calthorpe, went galumphing up to her gate and to Ezra's delight, brought out his pet mouse, Houdini.

'Hello,' said Tommy. 'Would you like to hold my mouse, Mrs Calthorpe?'

'No, I wouldn't,' she said, and returned to the safety of her cottage.

Tommy turned to Ezra. 'Why is she so full of stinging bees?' and both Len and Ezra burst out laughing.

'I know this was meant to be a special day and all that,' said Len, 'but Mrs Cutler asked me to keep an eye on him.'

'That's me, Tommy Treacle, that's who I am.'

'We know,' said Len, then dropping his voice to no more than a whisper, he added, 'Mrs Cutler also gave me sixpence, a whole blooming sixpence, and as Dad hadn't . . .'

'Mother forgot, too.'

'Can I always come with you?' Tommy asked Ezra, putting the mouse back in his pocket.

'No, I'm afraid not. This is the last time I'm going to the Cinema Club.'

'Why? asked Tommy Treacle, his face melting, his eyes filling with tears.

'Because I'm starting work.'

'Why?'

'That's a good question.' And it occurred to Ezra that Tommy wasn't unlike his father. Both suffered from a form of gentle lunacy that had more honesty to it than Mrs Calthorpe and her poisonous tongue.

The morning was still freshly risen as they set off down the lane for the walk into town.

By the time they arrived at the Rio, the queue already straggled right round the cinema, as if the Pied Piper of Hamelin had blown his pipe and assembled a jumble sale of children. Tommy walked straight to the front of the queue as usual, and Ezra and Len followed sheepishly.

The doors opened and the two usherettes stood back to let the stampede for seats begin. Beside the box office, Mr Grant, the Rio's manager, kept order.

Ezra didn't see Amaryllis Ruben with her friend Clarissa Bodminton-Bow, though Amaryllis saw him, and made sure she and Clarissa sat behind the boys. Since Wednesday, when she'd baked the cake, she'd been thinking about the mystery of happy families and she was determined to know Mrs Pascoe's son, as if he alone might be able to explain how they worked.

There was another reason for her being there: the noise was loud enough to drown out the worrying thought that she might be pregnant.

Ezra and Len were sitting behind Tommy, who, no matter what, always sat plumb in the middle of the front row. Amaryllis leaned foward and tapped Ezra on the shoulder. He looked round and was amazed to see Mr Ruben's daughter sitting there in a white linen coat and a soft hat that framed her face. She looked like a film star who had fallen from the screen and landed among these scruffy, ragtag and bobtail children.

Ezra, lost for words, was only capable of mumbling, 'Good morning, miss.'

He was distracted by Tommy Treacle standing up and shouting loudly, 'I want to spend a penny.'

Ezra leapt over the seat to get to him before he decided to undo his trousers then and there.

'All right, we'll find the lav first,' he said firmly.

Amaryllis watched Ezra guide the huge boy towards the exit.

Clarissa was complaining. 'Mummy would be so cross if she knew I was here. You mustn't ever tell her – after all, I didn't tell her you'd been expelled.'

'Oh, do stop whining,' said Amaryllis. The lights went out.

By the time Ezra and Tommy had returned to their seats, the programme had started with a newsreel of the *Hindenburg* disaster. Mr Grant felt that it was his duty to educate his young audience. Ezra watched, his eyes glued to the screen, as the enormous silver lozenge came into view over New York. The huge airship hovered above the ground, waiting to make its historic landing. Suddenly, inexplicably, the zeppelin was consumed by flames and tumbled to earth, leaving only a pile of twisted metal.

Len leaned towards Ezra and whispered, 'I tell you, you'd never catch me going up there, in the clouds. I'm sticking to the ground.'

Then, at last, it was time for the long-awaited conclusion of *The Severed Hand*.

Except, it wasn't. It was a cowboy film starring Ken Maynard, the Singing Cowboy, and Tarzan, his trusty horse, who always saved the day.

A cry went up.

'We want *The Severed Hand*.'

Answered by another cry: 'We want the Singing Cowboy.'

A flapping sound came from the projection box as the reel of film slowed down and stopped. The house lights went up. Mr Grant, the cinema sergeant-major, came back on the stage, red with rage, all pretence of liking the little urchins gone.

'If you don't all behave your miserable selves, there will be no feature film.'

'We want *The Severed Hand*.'

'You'll get what you're given,' said Mr Grant.

The film started up again. Ezra had seen this film several times before and resigned himself to never knowing the outcome of *The Severed Hand*. Some children started rocking back and forth on the seats as though they were on horseback, others were firing at the screen with imaginary guns. Any kissing was greeted with groans. Finally, Ken the cowboy got the girl. The End.

'At least it's not "To Be Continued",' said Len.

Afterwards, there was a general scrum. Tommy Treacle, now in the role of the white-hatted cowboy, rushed, as he always did, for the stairs that led down to the foyer, with Ezra and Len close on his heels. Tommy, guns blazing, pushed past the waiting Red Indians, all of whom moved swiftly out of his way. All except one chubby squaw. With a flourish Ken Maynard would have been proud of, he shoved her aside and then – disaster. He hit an unseen boulder and both boulder and cowboy tumbled down the rest of the stairs. Tommy Treacle landed on top of Amaryllis.

While Ezra and Len hurried down the stairs to pull Tommy off Miss Ruben, her friend stood there screaming about a mouse. Tommy saw Houdini making a break for the open prairie and as he scrambled to his feet, dug his knee hard into Amaryllis's stomach. He stood up, bawling like a baby.

Mr Grant was horrified by the scene before him. Arnold Ruben's daughter, ghostly pale, was being helped by the Pascoe boy. Lady Bodminton-Bow's daughter was wailing that she wanted to go home.

Len crawled along the floor of the foyer and managed to catch Houdini. He took the mouse back to Tommy, who was now sitting at the foot of the stairs with brown treacle toffee dribbling down his chin.

Ezra wondered what to do. He felt he couldn't leave Miss

Ruben, she looked so ill. Then Arnold Ruben walked into the foyer, his face frozen with rage.

'It wasn't my idea, Mr Ruben,' said Clarissa, whimpering.

Mr Ruben said nothing.

Amaryllis looked at Ezra and smiled defiantly. She didn't care what her father had to say. She could feel the cramps in her womb, the pain of her coming period, and she knew she would be able to start again, blood-washed, clean and pure.

THE UNSPOKEN TRUTH

Arnold Ruben sat at the wheel of the Bentley driving the two girls to the Bodminton-Bows' country estate. Amaryllis knew her father's furious silence was filled with unspoken words she couldn't help hearing.

Clarissa was sobbing into the soft, cream-leather upholstery of the car.

'I didn't want to go, Mr Ruben,' she kept repeating. 'I swear it wasn't my idea. What will Mummy say?'

What Mummy had to say took fifteen minutes while Amaryllis waited alone in the car.

When father and daughter arrived back at Warlock Hall, Arnold announced in a clipped voice that he wanted to speak to her immediately.

The drawing room had been specially designed by Eleanor Bilderbeck of New York in white and silver: white sofas, white figurines and silver crystal chandeliers. In the light of this bright spring day it had the sterile quality of an elaborate funeral parlour, the impression made more vivid by vases of white lilies, their heady smell overwhelming and sickly.

Arnold lit a cigarette, inhaled and, an enraged dragon, blew the smoke through his nose.

'Can you tell me, young lady, what you were thinking of?'

'I wanted to see what it was like going to a real cinema . . .'

'Why,' he interrupted, 'when we have our own picture palace, here in the grounds, do you choose to flaunt yourself in front of children who have none of your privileges?'

'I wanted to be a part of . . .'

Her father wasn't listening. He said bluntly, 'Who is Maurice Sands?'

Amaryllis felt her stomach lurch and the cramps of her period made her long to sit down.

'I told Silas. I met him outside Mrs Purdie's sweet shop and . . .'

'And what? You just took it into that butterfly brain of yours to run away with him?'

'No, it wasn't like that. It was a dare . . . a silly dare.'

'Who dared you?'

'Clarissa. And I wasn't going to . . . but then she went on and on.'

'Oh dear, and you had no ability to see that what you were doing was wrong? That by going off with a strange man you were putting yourself in danger, just because you couldn't say no to a dare?'

Amaryllis bit her lip. Never, ever had she seen her father this angry, not even after being expelled from every school she had attended. He had taken it all in his stride. Her father was as sturdy as a brick wall, whatever she did just bounced off him. But not this time. This time the cracks were beginning to show and it frightened her.

'Do you have any idea of the type of man you ran off with?'

Amaryllis hadn't given the subject much thought. Too many other things about that sleazy night had filled her with disgust at herself.

'This man Sands is obviously a playboy, a ladies' man. A man who tries to exploit young girls. This is the kind of person you think it's proper to associate with? Have you no moral compass? You might consider my reputation, even if you care little for yours.'

Amaryllis's eyes stung with tears, her pride wounded beyond all hope of repair.

'Exploit? What do you mean?' The lump in her throat made the pretence of indifference difficult.

'Just what I say. He put you in a compromising situation that he ... that could be used against me.'

Suddenly it seemed as if her period might not be the release from the nightmare she'd hoped for. Was there more damage?

Amaryllis felt her heart beating fast. A part of her longed to tell her father what had happened, just as she had wanted to tell Mrs Pascoe. She had drunk too much, been taken advantage of. But to say the words out loud was impossible. They were unspeakable. They were to be buried deep within her.

'Parties like the ones Maurice Sands attends are not the kind of parties a respectable girl should ever be seen at. I suppose,' continued Arnold, stubbing out his cigarette in a silver ashtray, 'that occasionally you lift your gaze from the pages of *Vogue* and *Tatler* and take notice of world events?'

'Yes ... sometimes.'

'So you are aware of what is happening in Germany? That

there is a policy of Aryanisation of the economy and, without any justification, Jewish businesses are being closed down? People like Lady Bodminton-Bow will tell you with enthusiasm this man Hitler is a jolly good egg for building the autobahns and getting unemployment down – just the kind of man we need to be Prime Minister here.'

'It doesn't affect me,' she said. 'All I want is to go to London, be a debutante and have a season.'

Arnold looked at Amaryllis. Was this his daughter, his one and only child? How was it possible for her to be so vacuous, to not realise that the world was about to ignite? What had they taught her at that school?

'Are you really as empty-headed as you appear?' he asked.

'Clarissa is having a ball in three weeks . . .'

'Lady Bodminton-Bow,' interrupted her father, 'has made it quite clear to me that her daughter will not be inviting any Jewish acquaintances.'

'But we're not . . . we . . . we've never practised . . . Ruben . . . it's just a name.'

'A name that no one noticed until you decided to become a common trollop, then your name – my good name – began to be examined more closely.'

There was a knock at the door and Clifford Lang entered.

'Sorry to disturb you, sir, but Sir Basil Stanhope is on the line.'

'Ask him to hold on.'

His assistant quickly left the room.

Arnold looked despairingly at his daughter. 'You have caused me quite enough trouble. After the debacle this morning I've decided to cancel the house party. You are to stay in the grounds. You have a very capable governess in Miss Bright and you will attend lessons come what may. You will associate with companions I choose for you. Your day will be strictly regulated. You will read improving books – all magazines are forbidden. When I see in your character some change for the better, then I will reconsider what is to be done with you.'

Amaryllis couldn't stop the tears.

'I'm nearly seventeen, it's my life, and I want to go to the ball,' she said, feeling the blood rise to her face. 'You can't tell me what I can and can't do!'

'But I can. So there's a thing.'

That afternoon, without saying goodbye, her father left. It was Silas who came to see her.

'Where has Daddy gone?'

'To London to dine at Claridge's with Vervaine Fox and then, on Monday, to give his lecture at Imperial College.'

'A lecture? What about?' asked Amaryllis.

'The memory machine.'

NOT THAT KIND OF MAN

Arnold's father, Herman Rubenstein, had been an unforgiving man.

Herman, and his brother, Kurt, their name truncated at Ellis Island, had emigrated to New York from Germany in 1892. Herman, three years older than his brother, decided they should open a hardware store in Brooklyn. Kurt had other plans and after a fearful row with Herman he left New York, having bought, sight-unseen, a farm in Texas. Several weeks later he arrived in the middle of nowhere to find tumbleweed blowing through a ghost town. The farm he had been sold was nothing more than a derelict shack and a few acres of scrub.

Herman opened his hardware store in Court Street, and married Frieda. Two years later, Arnold was born. He was to be their only child. His father already had a reputation as a skinflint.

'I, unlike some wastrels, know the value of every dollar I own, and how hard I've worked to make each one, so I ain't prepared to go giving it away.'

Herman had no interest whatsoever in his son, seeing him as a wimp, a mummy's boy. Arnold never felt anything for this tyrannical man other than loathing. Even when grown up he would tremble at the memory of his father's dreaded footsteps on the wooden stairs, the creak of the bedroom door and the click of his belt buckle. He learned to stay silent when he was beaten as it caused his beloved mama too much pain.

Arnold was saved by his natural optimism, a belief that things would get better, that one day he would make a fortune, buy his mama a mansion and take her away from Brooklyn.

'All the boy has is a head full of schmaltz,' said Herman. 'He takes after my good-for-nothing brother.'

The happy memories of his childhood were few and all of them Arnold shared with his mother. Their modest outings took on mystical properties. He replayed them over and over again in his imagination. Best of all was their weekly visit to the movie theatre. It was here they were free to lose themselves in someone else's story. In the smoky darkness of glittering dreams, he wished with the passion of an innocent child, for whom the word 'impossible' is meaningless, that he might invent a machine that would make memories stay alive for ever and ever. There would never be a need to return to the real world. He and his mama would star in their own movie; he would be its director and in his Utopia, memories of his father would lie on the cutting-room floor.

He studied at the library, reading all the science books he could get his hands on, determined to find a way to make his dream a reality.

Arnold was twelve when he first met his Uncle Kurt. He had never imagined he would know anyone, let alone have an uncle, who could afford a suite at the brand new Plaza Hotel.

Kurt Ruben was the polar opposite of Herman. He was a man to whom luck had taken a shine, with a suntanned face of a million smiles, a man full of passion and generosity.

'If you could do anything with your life,' he asked his nephew, 'what would it be?'

'I want to build the first memory machine.'

Kurt hadn't thought the boy was capable of such an original idea.

Afterwards, on the long walk home, Arnold questioned his father about what his uncle did, but his father was too mildewed with jealousy to reply. It was Frieda who whispered something about oil and, as they crossed Brooklyn Bridge, the young Arnold realised that in the home of the brave, in the land of the free, a dream was a guiding star.

Arnold won a scholarship to Harvard where he majored in the sciences, but his beloved mother became ill soon after he graduated, and he decided there was no question of taking up his research post. Instead he went back to their mean apartment above the miserable shop to look after her.

How thin and frail she had become. It was painful for her to move and her hands, always so elegant, so full of comfort, had become like birds' claws. Never had Arnold felt such rage as when he found her lying on top of the bedcovers, in her day clothes.

'Look at you, *Liebling*,' his mother said, holding out her hand towards him. 'All grown up and so strong, so handsome.'

'Why aren't you in bed, Mama?'

'I haven't the strength to get undressed, and your father is too busy to help me.'

'How long have you been up here?'

'Oh, not long. Don't be angry with him, he just isn't that kind of man.'

'He isn't a kind man at all,' Arnold replied. 'He's a monster.'

Arnold went down to the shop and politely asked the only customer to leave, then bolted the door.

'What do you think you're doing?' shouted his father, unbuckling his belt. 'You're not so grown up that I can't give you a good hiding.'

Just hearing that click nearly paralysed Arnold, but the thought of his mother gave him courage.

'You're not going to hit me ever again, do you understand?'

His father backed down without a fight. Defeated, he slunk into the stockroom.

'What use is your money if you won't call a doctor for your wife?' asked Arnold, still with a belly full of fire. 'You disgust me.'

'Doctors aren't cheap,' Herman mumbled. 'If you want to waste your inheritance, you go ahead.'

Herman had never before heard Arnold speak to him like this. His son was, after all, a man to be reckoned with. Herman would never say so to anyone, but the day his son stood up to him, he almost wept with pride.

The doctor came and Arnold made sure his father paid every one of the bills. The money was handed over as if it were flesh being peeled from Herman's raw body.

Frieda recovered slightly, and she and Arnold had one glorious summer together. He rented a cottage on Shelter Island, the sea air did her good and it looked as if she might make a recovery of sorts. Then in October 1916 she took a turn for the worse. Her last days were spent in the apartment over the store. The laudanum stopped working and the pain became intolerable.

On 28 October, she begged her son to put her out of her misery.

That night he sat with her, and at three in the morning, able to bear her screaming no longer, he put a pillow over her face. It was as simple as wringing the neck of a sparrow. Then, holding her hand tight, he told her of his plans, as tears rolled, salty and bitter, down his face.

After the funeral, Arnold wanted to get the hell out of there. But crushed by grief, and haunted by the part he had played in his mother's death, he stayed to sort out the business. It was a self-inflicted punishment.

'It will all be yours when I'm gone,' said his father. 'You can't walk away from it.'

Arnold's only comfort in those dark, lonely days was an interest in the occult. He thought it might be a way to contact his mother. He was bitterly disappointed. Most, if not all, the clairvoyants he consulted were fraudsters and charlatans, making money from heartbreak. It was this more than anything else that revived his interest in inventing a memory machine.

For six miserable months, Arnold worked in his father's

store. In April 1917 came his chance to break free. America declared war on Germany, and he joined up to fight in France.

'Do you think I care?' Herman shouted. 'I don't, you schmuck, I can look after myself.'

Twelve-and-a-half years later, all the money Herman possessed was lost. Ruined by the stock market crash, Herman's bare-wire pride would not allow him to ask his son for a dime. By the time Arnold realised something was wrong, it was too late. Herman Ruben had walked under a trolley car.

MISS BRIGHT'S
DILEMMA

Miss Bright stood in the empty school room at Warlock Hall, lost in thought. She was a prim, neat woman who never for a moment imagined the post of governess would be as difficult as it was proving to be.

Up to now she had lived a secluded life. Her one true love had been killed in the Great War. His letters, and there were many, were tied up and kept in a cigar box along with a packet of his favourite cigarettes, a lock of his hair and, the greatest of treasure of all, a photo of them both on their engagement. He, in uniform, was eighteen; she was seventeen. They had but kissed before death embraced him, and all her life she had mourned his loss, had seen it as one long abandonment. She had never married and, like many poor but educated women of her day, had taken to teaching.

She had been interviewed for the position at Warlock Hall by Silas Molde. He had about him the most unsettling quality she had ever come across in a man. His dark eyes had a way of looking at her that made her feel she had been X-rayed rather than interviewed. She was quite taken aback when she was offered the post. On paper – if not in reality – it was ideal: a large house in the country, one young lady to teach and chaperone.

The Bentley had been sent to collect her from her poky flat in Earl's Court and she had sat back, enjoying the luxury of the drive and the happy prospect of what lay ahead. That was before her first meeting with her reluctant pupil and now, after two weeks sitting in the musty, unused school room at the top of the house, doing crossword puzzles and reading Agatha Christie novels, she had lost all expectation of her pupil ever attending one of her lessons.

Miss Bright's only hope, or so she thought, was to have a word with her employer on his return. *Jane Eyre* was one of her favourite novels, and she had imagined Arnold Ruben as a sort of Mr Rochester, even more so when she heard that he was due to arrive with a house party, among whom would be the star of the silent screen, Vervaine Fox. But two days after his arrival, she still hadn't met him, and the Saturday had started with her finding that, somehow, she was locked in her bedroom. When at last help arrived she learned Miss Ruben and her frightful friend Clarissa Bodminton-Bow were missing, causing the whole household to go into a state of high anxiety. Where on earth could the girls be? Had they been kidnapped? When they were finally discovered at the Saturday Cinema Club in Bishop's Norgate, Miss Bright tendered her resignation.

Mr Ruben turned out to be not at all like Mr Rochester. He was charm itself. Her forlorn efforts to explain her reasons for wanting to leave were swept aside; she was offered a bonus, almost double what she was receiving, if she could induce Amaryllis to attend her lessons. Miss Bright left Arnold's study resigned to her fate, holding a letter Mr Rubens had written. It was to be read to Amaryllis.

Outside the study stood Mr Molde.

'Silas – good – just the man I want to see,' she heard Mr Ruben say.

Mr Molde, his eyes never leaving hers, went in, closing the study door firmly behind him. Involuntarily, Miss Bright shivered. The man made her flesh creep. The way he looked at her; that, and his ability to silently appear when least expected, unnerved her. The incident that had nearly caused her heart to stop altogether had occurred in the walled garden. Not so very far from the round brick ice-house which stood at the far end of the garden were the picturesque remains of an eighteenth-century greenhouse. It had once been used for cultivating pineapples. Miss Bright had been engrossed in taking a photograph of it when Silas Molde materialised from nowhere. Oddly, he seemed equally nonplussed to find her there.

There were other things about Silas Molde that didn't seem to quite add up. To start with, never had a man looked less like the name he owned to. Then there were the times she had seen, as she closed her bedroom curtains at night, his stocky figure walking purposefully towards the woods, and, being an early riser, she had on more than one occasion seen him emerge from the woods the following morning. And there was all the strange talk among the servants about the memory recordings. Quite what they were no one was willing to say, but she had overhead Mrs Popplin telling Mrs Pascoe that you got paid good money for doing it and she was thinking about volunteering. Mrs Pascoe had answered that she wouldn't touch it with a bargepole and some had suffered dreadfully from headaches afterwards.

Miss Bright sat down at her desk and reread the letter her employer had given her, wondering how she was ever going to persuade her pupil to attend lessons. The door opened and Amaryllis walked in. The sight of this wretched girl convinced Miss Bright that she couldn't take any more, no matter the size of the bonus Mr Ruben had promised.

'I would rather return to a bedsit in Earl's Court than stay here to be tormented another day by you,' said Miss Bright, picking up her notes and putting them away. 'You locked me in my bedroom this morning, and I've received not one word of apology from you.'

'I am sorry, I shouldn't have done that,' said Amaryllis. 'I promise I won't do it again, honest injun.'

Miss Bright looked at her, astounded. She had not been expecting this. The girl was so unpredictable. In the whole time she had been there, Amaryllis hadn't said more than two or three words to her, let alone a whole sentence. Miss Bright thought through her situation carefully, then taking a gulp of air she started to read aloud the letter Mr Ruben had written. She could clearly see the look of disillusionment on Amaryllis's face when she reached the part about Ezra Pascoe taking classes with her.

'Ezra Pascoe,' she repeated with disgust. It was one thing to observe him at the cinema, quite another to share classes with him. 'When?'

'Starting Monday morning,' said Miss Bright. She continued reading. Mr Ruben ended his moralising, well-meaning, apple pie of a letter saying Ezra hadn't any of the advantages that his daughter had, and perhaps by spending time with him she would realise how lucky she was.

The girl was silent, deflated. For the first time Miss Bright caught a glimpse of who Amaryllis really was under her spoilt facade. The two of them had more in common than she had thought. Girl and woman, each saw in the other a reflection of their own fears of abandonment. They both understood what a dangerous cliff face it was to live on.

Then Amaryllis said, 'Shall we do a deal?'

'A deal?' Miss Bright replied nervously. 'What kind of deal?'

'In the mornings, I will come on time to each and every one of your lessons and I will do all that is asked of me. In the afternoons, in return, I may do as I like.'

'Your father does insist you have lunch with Ezra Pascoe.'

'All right, after lunch then, and I will be as good as gold.'

It had started to rain. 'And if I agree, what then?' asked Miss Bright, allowing the roles of teacher and pupil to reverse themselves.

'Then,' said Amaryllis slowly, her violet eyes never letting go, her voice solemn, 'we will get along just humdingerly.'

By late afternoon Amaryllis, bored and deeply worried, had

called Clarissa to tell her all that had happened, and how silly her father had been about the ball, but the call was answered by Lady Bodminton-Bow, who shouted down the telephone, as did many who were unused to such a contraption.

'I told your father that I believe you are a very bad influence on my daughter, that you are morally corrupting. I do not wish her to associate with you any more. The friendship is at an end.'

Before she could reply, Lady Bodminton-Bow yelled so loudly that Amaryllis had to hold the phone well away from her ear.

'I have finished with this device. What do I do with it, Alfred?'

Then the line went dead.

Seeing the rain had stopped, Amaryllis, wearing a coat and galoshes and wrapped in a sense of injustice, went for a walk in the grounds. She wanted time to think.

She was emerging from the woods when she spied Clifford Lang some way off, hurrying down to the lake with his raincoat collar pulled up high and a trilby on his head.

By the wooden-slatted jetty, a silvery wet tongue poking out over the lake, she was suprised to see another man, smoking a pipe, waiting. Her father was very strict about who came into the grounds. The man, like Clifford Lang, was wearing his hat pulled down, hiding his face. Amaryllis knew intuitively that she mustn't be seen by either of them. The two men stood and talked. She saw Clifford Lang hand the man a brown envelope. He didn't look at it, but put it quickly inside his breast pocket before hurrying away. Clifford stood for some time staring at the lake before turning back towards the house. Amaryllis, curious but terrified of discovery, stayed where she was until he was gone.

TEA AND TRENCHES

It was late on Saturday afternoon when Ezra's father emerged, shell-shocked and blinded, into the soft rain of a fading day, to find he had made the miraculous journey from the battlefields of the Western Front to his garden in the rolling, bosomy hills of England. Three cups of tea from a china mug and half a packet of Woodbines, smoked one after another, restored him to his old bewildered self.

'What day is it, lad?' he asked Ezra.

'Saturday,' said Ezra, putting a plate of fried eggs and mashed potatoes before him. The eggs, two of them, had to be runny and the mash creamy smooth.

'Just how I like it, and good builder's tea. I like strong tea. Don't want gnat's piss. Saturday, you say? What did you do today?'

'I went to the Cinema Club with Len,' said Ezra, drying the frying pan and putting it away.

'What happened in *The Severed Hand*?'

'They showed the Singing Cowboy instead.'

'Darn it,' said his father in a bad cowboy accent. 'Someone stole your movie, boy, I think you've been well and truly done. Call for the sheriff and have Mr Grant arrested.' They laughed together.

'So we'll never know. That's a pity.'

Noel Pascoe knew all about films. Before the Great War he had been the projectionist at the Rio. He was good at his job, had a knack with machines and reels of broken film. After the war, full of patriotic fervour, Mr Grant had given him his job back. A country for heroes. Jobs for our brave lads, lest we forget. Except Mr Grant forgot quickly enough, like so many of his countrymen who had never fought, never been in the trenches, never smelled gangrene, never seen the flies, never waded through the mud and the blood, never heard grown men cry for their mothers, wives, sweethearts, caught on the barbed wire, left there, wounded, wrung out, to die before they had even learned to live.

When Father had had his first 'turn', as it became known in the family, he was showing a Charlie Chaplin film. He came out of the projection room and started yelling at the audience to get down, bloody well get down, if they didn't want their heads shot off.

He was fired on the spot. All he was good for was working in the garden, growing vegetables for his family, and keeping the house tidy.

'I'm a neat man, that's the one good thing you can say about me.'

Mother, putting her arms around him, said, 'I wouldn't swap you for all the tea in China.'

And she meant it.

'He's a brave man, a very brave man,' she explained to Ezra and Olive, when they were growing up. 'He was given the

Victoria Cross and will never say why, but what I know is you aren't given a medal like that for putting out the cat. So I think we owe him a lot of respect. None of us know what we would do if we were called upon to fight.'

High tea was the time of day Mother liked best, when all her chicks came home to roost. Behind an array of china, accompanied by the sound of tinkling cups, she held court, making sure everything was as it should be. Tonight she had some news for Ezra.

'You made a very good impression on Mr Ruben, helping Miss Ruben when she fell. He wants you to take lessons with her, from this coming Monday.'

'But what about my job in the garage, and the money?'

'You are to work with Mr Longbone after lunch, and you will be paid as agreed.'

'That's just plain daft,' said Ezra.

'Make the most of it,' said Father, 'That's my advice.'

'It's the whim of a rich man,' said Mother, getting up to refill the teapot. 'These lessons may last a week, they may last a day. Just try to get on with Miss Ruben.'

At nine o'clock on Monday morning, Ezra, washed, scrubbed, smelling of Pears soap and wearing long trousers, was taken by the butler through the servants' quarters and up the imposing staircase. Above it was a huge glass dome. Looking over the bannisters, the marbled hall seemed a long way down. The school room was in the attic but, even so, it was twice the size of the classroom at Ezra's old school. It had a blackboard, a table for the teacher and two desks placed next to one another. The room was lined with bookshelves and had that faintly neglected smell of mothballs. He waited alone, wondering, as he had all weekend, why Mr Ruben had singled him out. He had come to the conclusion that it must have been Miss Ruben's idea. Still, it didn't make much sense. Yet here he was, wishing he wasn't.

Miss Ruben seemed much older than her sixteen years and reeked of sophistication, her hair and clothes immaculate in every way. She entered the classroom and looked at Ezra in disgust, which puzzled him, and for the first time ever he felt self-conscious about what he was wearing. His trousers and jacket were baggy, Father's hand-me-downs, altered that Sunday by Mother. His shirt was patched and darned, and somewhat frayed at the edges.

All that morning Amaryllis ignored him and Ezra felt a huge sense of relief at the thought that perhaps he need have little to do with her.

By the end of the lesson, Miss Bright was delighted to have found in Ezra that rarest of things: a pupil who was hungry to learn.

'I have one of these for each of you,' she said, taking from her desk two diaries. 'Write in them anything you want – ideas, or stories even.'

Amaryllis sighed and, getting up, collected the book, put it on her desk and, with a toss of her hair, pointedly left it there. She stood by the door.

'Thank you very much,' said Ezra as he took the thick, brand-new diary. 'Can I really write anything in it?'

'Oh, give me strength,' said Amaryllis sharply. 'It's not exactly the crown jewels.'

'Please, Miss Ruben—' said Miss Bright.

Amaryllis interrupted her. 'Lessons are finished for today, aren't they, Miss Bright?'

Her governess, conscious of their agreement and the prospect of a pleasant afternoon of freedom, nodded.

Ezra was still hovering uncertainly when Miss Bright said, 'Silly me, I nearly forgot. You are expected to have lunch with Miss Ruben.'

'I would rather not,' said Ezra, truthfully.

'My sentiments completely,' said Amaryllis.

On the landing outside the classroom, she turned to him. 'Don't go thinking this was my idea. It wasn't. I don't even like you, boy. You're just another of Daddy's experiments.'

'I don't know what you mean,' said Ezra.

'It doesn't matter whether you understand or not, boy.'

Lunch was served at a long table in the main dining room, Miss Ruben at one end, and Ezra far away at the other. They were waited on by two butlers. Bright red and awkward, Ezra never had felt more uncomfortable than he did in the thunder-filled silence that lunch time. There was so much cutlery, so many different plates. He remembered nothing of what he was served. In the distance Miss Ruben pushed her food round and round her plate and ate, as far as he could see, little, but her violet eyes watched intently everything he did. At one-thirty on the dot, lunch finished, Amaryllis put down her napkin and without so much as a goodbye, got up and left the room.

The garage, in the converted stable block, had a comforting smell of engine oil and petrol. Henry Longbone was in charge of Mr Ruben's cars: a Bugatti, a Bentley, a Rolls-Royce, and a Ford used as a runaround by his staff. To Ezra the cars looked almost alive, each possessing its own unique personality.

Henry Longbone, Arnold Ruben's mechanic and chauffeur, was a kind man who was very fond of the Pascoe family.

'Well, lad, what do you think of them? Beauties, aren't they?' he said, wiping the oil from his hands.

Ezra's first job was to wax and polish the Bugatti.

'Until you can see your face shining back at you,' said Mr Longbone. 'Take your time, do it proper like.'

When Ezra had finished for the day, Mr Longbone called him to his office.

'I'm told you're only to be coming to me in the afternoons.'

Ezra nodded. He longed to say he wished he could be there all day and perhaps it was the look on his face that led Mr Longbone to say, 'Mr Ruben often gets these bees in his bonnet. I shouldn't think it will be long before you're here most mornings.'

By the time Friday afternoon arrived Ezra knew what a caged bird might feel like when he was released. Miss Ruben was subtle in her cruelty, yet the sharpness of her tongue had already injured him and there was nothing he could do to fight back. She took delight in tormenting him, seeing how far she might go before he snapped. The only thing that kept Ezra from giving up altogether was pride and a love of learning. He told himself every morning that this was the price he had to pay for knowledge. He reasoned she would always have the upper hand over him; she was his boss's daughter. There was no way round it. He would have to put up with her jibes. He walked home that Friday from Warlock Hall and, mulling it over, thought how wrong was the saying, 'Sticks and stones may break my bones, but words can never harm me'. It was a complete load of rubbish, a downright lie. Words were like knives that had the power to cut through to the soul. Stones may hurt but words, he had no doubt, were strong enough to kill.

'Well, lad,' said Father, seeing him sitting dejected at the kitchen table with Miss Bright's diary before him, 'something troubling you?'

'Girls.'

Father laughed. 'One in particular?'

Ezra nodded. All he could think of was the inevitability of Monday morning.

THE ELECTRIC
ELEPHANT

Sir Basil Stanhope was a tall man with bushy eyebrows, who always wore tweeds and bow ties, and the genial expression of a lost labrador. It was his charming wife Dorothy who attracted attention in a social gathering. She was a witty woman who shared Arnold Ruben's love of films. This had led him to be on cocktail terms with the Stanhopes.

Sir Basil, sitting at his desk, studied the report from Warlock Hall. It confirmed his worst fears. The enigmatic American was about to unleash a security nightmare. The question was, why had this very private man decided to give a lecture at Imperial College now?

Over the years there had been rumours about Arnold Ruben's obsession with memory, and about the huge sums of money he had put into his research, but the man himself had never said a word in public. Sir Basil had only recently learned of the terrifing potential of the project. Perhaps, he thought, Arnold Ruben's need to speak out was the irrational crisis of a rational man.

Leaning back in his chair, he pondered the question. There were two possible explanations: vanity, or a desire for immortality. But something didn't ring true about the whole blasted business. Vanity, perhaps, but he doubted that. Immortality? Arnold wanted his work recognised along with that of Albert Einstein and the other great scientists of the day. Why not?

On the eve of the lecture, Sir Basil set out from his office in Baker Street and, walking faster than most, made his way to Claridge's where he was shown to Arnold's suite.

'Do you want a drink?' said a deep voice from a chaise longue. All Sir Basil could see of its owner was a long, thin, white hand and a cigarette-holder containing a pink and gold-tipped Sobranie.

'No, thank you,' said Sir Basil, surprised to find the voice was that of Vervaine Fox, goddess of the silver screen. No wonder the talkies hadn't suited her. In an adjoining room, he heard Arnold speaking on the telephone.

'You have another visitor, darling,' said Miss Fox, as he replaced the receiver. Rising, she moved with lizard grace to the cocktail cabinet. 'A Martini,' she commanded.

'No,' said Sir Basil again.

Arnold stretched out a hand to greet him while turning him firmly towards the door. Sir Basil thought it was a movement he must have perfected to get rid of unwanted guests.

'Unless this is urgent,' he said, 'could it wait until tomorrow, after my lecture?'

They were standing – or rather Sir Basil was standing – in the corridor, Arnold's hand on the door to the suite. His face said welcome, his actions were all goodbyes.

'I am here to advise you against giving the lecture,' said Sir Basil quietly.

Arnold stared, bemused, at the bumbling fool of an Englishman. 'Are you drunk?' he laughed.

'Not in the slightest, old chap,' said Sir Basil. 'This is not the time to seek recognition for your life's work. Better by far that you keep the memory machine and the picture palace under your hat.'

Arnold was almost lost for words.

'The picture palace?' he repeated.

'You know what I'm talking about,' said Sir Basil briskly. 'Don't do it, that's all, old chap.'

'Darling,' came Vervaine's voice from inside the room, 'I need you. There's no ice.'

Going down in the lift, Sir Basil resigned himself to the fact that the man was determined not to listen to a word he said.

'A pity,' he muttered under his breath. 'A great pity.'

At Imperial College the following day Arnold gave his lecture, which he called The Electric Elephant, to a packed hall. He explained he was on the the brink of testing the first fully functioning memory machine. Memory would be recorded and revisited outside the confines of time in a fourth-dimensional world where the living would re-experience the past as reality. He illustrated his claims with rough film footage of what he called living memories.

Afterwards the audience was invited to ask questions.

Professor John Smithers, an eminent government scientist,

said, 'Surely this is nothing new? It has already been achieved by photography and the projected image.'

'No,' said Arnold, 'if that's what you think this is about, then you've totally misunderstood all I've been saying. I'm not talking about a moving picture on a screen. In my machine, a recorded memory of you would play in a fourth dimension; you would be as substantial and as present as you are now.'

'In order to do that, you would have to stop time, and that notion, if you don't mind my saying so, belongs to fantasy.'

'What if I told you that I have done it?'

'I wouldn't believe you.'

There was a snigger of laughter.

'Mr Ruben,' asked another scientist, James Boyle, 'are you really suggesting that the footage you showed earlier was of recorded memories, that the people they belonged to were elsewhere, and that you have made the memories exist in another dimension?'

'Yes.'

'Preposterous,' said Professor Smithers. 'This is an insult to my thirty years in scientific research. Sir, you should be producing cinema films rather than trying to convince us of this lunacy.'

'You are refusing to see beyond the straight lines of narrow thought,' said Arnold. 'I am talking about the curve of light . . .'

'You are talking rubbish, sir.'

This was greeted with more laughter.

But not everyone in the audience was so quick to dismiss Arnold Ruben's ideas.

A man with a rose in his lapel asked, 'Can you alter the memories stored in the machine?'

'Yes, there is an advantage in that we can edit out painful experiences.'

'Would it be possible to wipe away someone's memory completely and give them fabricated memories?'

'That is not the purpose of my invention, but in theory, yes . . .'

Professor Smithers leapt to his feet. 'Surely that is brainwashing?'

The chairman hastily stood up, relieved to bring the debate to a close.

'Without doubt, Mr Ruben,' he said, 'you have given us much to think about.'

On that note, and to feeble applause, the lecture came to an end.

Arnold returned, disillusioned, to his suite at Claridge's.

Next day, Sir Basil Stanhope phoned to invite Arnold to lunch. Arnold had no desire to see Sir Basil again and told him he was returning to Warlock Hall. In the foyer of the hotel, as he was about to leave, he was greeted by two plain-clothes detectives. They were there to escort Arnold to the Garrick Club. He sat between the two men in their unmarked car, furious at being treated like a criminal. Why, dammit, he was a prominent American citizen. The minute he was home he would call Ambassador Bingham. He deserved to be treated with respect, not taken against his will to a place he didn't wish to go to.

At the Garrick he was led up a back staircase all the way to the top of the nineteenth century building and into a small library.

Sir Basil rose to greet him.

'What is the meaning of this?' said Arnold, rattled. 'I tell you, I will instruct my lawyer . . .'

'I've ordered you a Black Velvet,' interrupted Sir Basil, smiling amiably. 'I thought it might be just the ticket.'

'Last night you pestered me in my hotel and today you have me hijacked.'

'Do take a seat,' said Sir Basil. 'I understand you don't wish to stay for lunch, so I thought we would get this over and done with as quickly as possible. I advised you, old chap, not to give your lecture. I think perhaps it's my fault that you didn't take the matter more seriously, believing, as many do to their cost, that I am a prehistoric relic. It's an appearance I have cultivated. It always confounds people.'

Arnold began to realise, with a sickening feeling in the pit of his stomach, how badly he had misjudged the man.

Sir Basil took a thick file from his battered briefcase. On it, in small, official-looking type, it said:

Ref. P87

M. M.

ARNOLD RUBEN

He placed the file in front of Arnold, who stared at it, bewildered.

'Who the hell are you?' he asked.

Sir Basil, as was his way, ignored the question. 'Now, old chap, to the matter in hand. We're fully aware that your picture palace is more than it seems. It is a goose hiding a golden egg. The concrete basement is where you have your laboratory. That is where Silas Molde carries out the memory recordings.'

Arnold sat stony-faced.

'You have built six prototypes of the machine and the one you talked about yesterday, the seventh, is far more advanced. The first three were rather primitive and caused very bad side effects.'

'I don't know what you are talking about.'

'I will enlighten you. I work for the government, in a department called the OSP – the Operation for Scientific Protection.'

Arnold's face remained a perfect blank.

'It is my business,' continued Sir Basil, 'to keep myself well informed about an invention which could be a threat to national security. An invention like yours has far too much potential to allow it to fall into the wrong hands.'

'This is ridiculous,' said Arnold. 'My lecture ended with a top government scientist making me look an idiot. And that was before today's papers tore the whole thing apart.'

'I sent our scientists to do their damnedest to discredit you. As for the newspapers, we issued an embargo to prevent them from writing anything other than what we gave them permission to report. It was done for your own safety, old chap.'

'My safety?'

'Are you telling me that, brilliant as you no doubt are, you have not thought through the ramifications of what you are creating? That you have been so obsessed with achieving the impossible that you fail to see what it's capable of?'

'I designed it for my personal use.'

'So why did you give your lecture? Why didn't you keep it quiet?'

Arnold looked uncomfortable. He did not reply.

'Might I suggest vanity, combined with the desire for immortality?'

Arnold remained silent.

Sir Basil took a list of names from the file and handed it to Arnold.

'All these people are in your employ, I believe?'

Arnold nodded.

'There are fifteen names on this list. Of those who sat for the memory recordings, six have received medical attention for severe headaches, one was hospitalised and two complained of amnesia. All who have taken part in your experiments can remember little about them apart from a hum and a green light.'

Still Arnold said nothing.

Sir Basil continued, 'You tell me this machine is for your personal use, yet you are taking the memories of others, without them being aware of the consequences.'

'It's not a crime.'

'I'm not so sure about that. If any of the people on this list went so far as to press charges, I would imagine they would have a very good case against you. Now, let's talk about Amaryllis.'

'What's she got to do with this?'

Sir Basil thumbed through the file. 'Here. A report from a children's hospital in Switzerland. At the age of eight Amaryllis suffered from a form of severe memory loss. She was in hospital for three months. Correct?'

'It was the trauma of losing her mother that had affected her,' said Arnold, taking a gulp from the silver tankard.

'Four years after her mother's death? When we questioned him, her doctor said that he thought there was something strange about her case, from the very beginning. Neither the brain fever nor the tragedy would account for the severity of her amnesia.'

'Wasn't the loss of her mother sufficient?'

Sir Basil once again ignored the question. 'So, what happens if someone else tries to take control of the machine?'

'It's impossible. The memories are constructed on a mesh, each mesh represents one person's remembrances which can be played time and time again. My daughter's memories form the very core of the machine. Once I activate it, all the other memories will be locked into Amaryllis's mesh. Without her the machine would self-destruct.'

Sir Basil leaned back in his chair so that its front legs left the floor and at this angle, an argument between him and gravity, said, 'Old chap, you do realise it is perfectly possible for someone else to build a replica with another person's memories at its heart? Then there would be two machines, next, three, and, as the technology advances, no doubt numerous machines. It's not beyond probability that in the future they could even talk to each other.'

'I am creating a Utopia, not a world that can be corrupted by politics and wars. My vision is for the good of mankind,' said Arnold.

'So, I believe, were gunpowder and the guillotine. Is your daughter aware of the role she is to play in your creation?'

'No, not yet.'

'Poor little rich girl,' said Sir Basil. 'So you, as an upstanding American, have rights and liberty which your daughter doesn't share. She is just the guinea pig in all this.'

Arnold stood up. 'I am not staying here to be insulted by you.'

Sir Basil took a sip from his silver tankard as Arnold marched to the door. The two detectives who had brought him there barred his exit.

'Sit down. Who is Silas Molde?'

'I met him in Paris.'

'We know all that, old chap, and we know that he is largely responsible for the work on the machine. We also know that Silas Molde died in the Great War, quite early on. We believe his family comes from Yorkshire. Whoever the man is who works for you, one thing is certain: his real name is not Silas Molde.'

'I have nothing to say on the subject.'

'We want the project mothballed for the time being and your plans handed over to us.'

'This is ridiculous! The machine is my invention. It's a free country, isn't it?'

'Yes, said Sir Basil, 'and I intend it to stay that way, without brainwashing machines becoming available to all the minor and major dictators of the world. Whatever way you wish to dress this up, you have created one of the worst security headaches we have had for a long while.'

'And what if I refuse to stop work?' said Arnold, feeling as though the ground beneath him had moved.

'Then l can't guarantee the safety of you and your daughter.'

Arnold got up to leave far less self-assured than when he had arrived.

'Is that a threat?'

'No,' said Sir Basil, 'it's a polite warning that you are in great danger.'

'Danger?' repeated Arnold.

'There are spies out there, desperate to get their hands on the blueprint of your machine. They would stop at nothing.' Sir Basil collected his papers and returned them to his briefcase, clicking the catch shut. He finished his drink. 'As always, it's a delight to see you,' he said, shaking Arnold's hand.

THE WISDOM OF
HOT-WATER BOTTLES

Sitting in the back of the Bentley as Longbone drove him back to Warlock Hall that afternoon, Arnold Ruben found Sir Basil's questions had stirred up the muddy waters of his memory.

At the end of the Great War he had been demobbed as a hero, with several medals pinned to his chest, to find the world a different place. New countries had been formed, old ones abolished; new ideas and radical thinking were changing the order of society. Arnold too had changed. When the Armistice was announced, he could not fathom why he should still be alive when so many of his comrades were dead.

The Paris he recalled from those traumatic days after the war resembled a huge railway station, a terminus for anyone trying to find their place in this reconstituted Europe. In all the confusion, amid the rumours, the fears and the Spanish flu, and with such an unbelievable number dead, it was easy for someone to disappear unnoticed into the body of a deceased man, to re-emerge with a different identity. There was no need to return to an unhappy marriage, an unforgiving family. With stolen papers, your life could begin again. He had known from the very first day Silas bumped into him that he was one of those men. He saw immediately that they were both looking for graves in which to bury the past.

They had met at a picture palace, the only place in which Arnold had ever felt safe. It was showing *The Night of the Tiger*, featuring a young actress called Vervaine Fox. For a while, as he watched the movie, the trenches, the stench of death, left him. He was lost in the glory of the star's white flesh, her large, liquid eyes, her full lips. In the musty darkness he felt his mother beside him and he recalled his boyhood vision of a memory machine. He left the cinema, wrapped in his dreams, almost unaware of where he was until he collided with a stocky, balding man, somewhat older than himself.

'Sorry, buddy. I wasn't looking where I was going.'

'Neither was I.' The man spoke English.

By now they were outside on the busy Boulevard Saint Germain and Arnold, seeing all the crowds, said, 'I'm tempted to go back in.'

The stocky man laughed, and offered Arnold a cigarette. 'I've already seen the picture ten times.'

There was no need to say why. Arnold instinctively understood that only in the velvety blackness with the flickering beam of dusty light, did life become manageable.

They walked for a while, talking about the film, and recognising that here was a man who knew as much about moving pictures as he did, Arnold invited him for a drink.

'You didn't tell me your name,' said Arnold, after the first bottle of wine was finished and he'd ordered another.

There was a moment's hesitation before his companion said, 'Silas Molde.'

Arnold didn't for one minute believe it was his real name and at the same time thought it didn't matter a monkey's toot, but he repeated it to himself so he wouldn't forget it.

'And what did you do in the war, buddy?' Arnold asked.

'I was a wireless operator.'

Arnold had been interested. The arrival of the second bottle encouraged him to tell Silas about the memory machine, drawing a rough diagram on the back of a cigarette packet.

'To extract memory,' Silas said, 'you'll need to use electrical waves to get the readings, and possibly a magnetic force field to make it operational.'

Arnold's eyes opened wide. 'Then you understand what I'm trying to do?'

'Why, of course,' said Silas. 'But without its own force field, it'll never work . . .'

The rest of the evening and way into the night, the two men talked of nothing else. Arnold returned to his hotel having agreed to meet Silas Molde the next morning for a late breakfast.

The following day Arnold had woken to the news that his uncle, Kurt Ruben, whom he had only ever met once, had died, and his will made Arnold the sole beneficiary of a considerable fortune. Overnight he had become one of the wealthiest men in America.

That day he asked Silas if he would like to go with him to New York and try to actually build the goddamn machine, and that was the extent of the agreement between the two of them.

It had been during the transatlantic crossing that Arnold met and proposed to Clementine Glenville, the enchanting daughter of Sir Richard Glenville, a Member of Parliament. It was a whirlwind romance. Arnold had adored his pretty doe-eyed bride, who possessed all the gloss of an expensive education. He had mistaken her superficial charm for virtue. Too late did he come to see that Clementine was no different from any young lady of society on the lookout for a wealthy husband. She was just seventeen and he some seven years older. It was a marriage doomed from the start for, as they walked up the aisle, neither of them had any idea of who the other was.

They had eventually settled in London where Arnold had cultivated an air of easy charm. An Anglophile American, who knew he was never going to understand the wisdom of hot-water bottles, he wore Savile Row suits and handmade shoes from Lobb's.

His fortune enabled him to discreetly set up a workshop in an old bicycle factory, and there he and Silas had started to build the first prototype memory machine.

In 1920, Amaryllis was born. Arnold saw his mother in her soft violet eyes. He wanted to cocoon her, never let the real world touch her, never make her sad. But four years later, Clementine had drowned during a family holiday on his yacht off the Isle of Capri. It was nearly a week before her body, bloated and half-eaten by fish, was caught in a fisherman's net. It was Silas, not he, who identified the body; it was Silas who dealt with the local press after one of the yacht's crew talked to a reporter. The press pursued the foolish cabin boy, only to find him stretched out on a slab in Capri's city morgue.

Arnold had returned to London, with his daughter and his wife's coffin, to face the flashbulbs of the world's press. 'The tragedy that broke a millionaire's heart' read the headlines.

The bitter truth of their marriage was lost in his grief-filled devotion to a fantasy. Only two other people knew the whole truth: Silas, whose tongue turned to stone whenever the subject was raised, and Arnold's very small daughter.

The Bentley made its way out of the city and Arnold saw in the rolling pastures a truth lead-heavy enough to drown a man. He had failed to protect Amaryllis. He had been too haunted by the shadows of the past, by the click of a belt buckle, by a soft white pillow, by the whirl of white-foamed water. But most of all he was haunted by the memory of his trusting little daughter, who, as he strapped the heavy helmet to her head, had asked him, 'Will it hurt, Daddy?'

In Arnold's world, impossible did not exist. When the machine was activated it would be as if these events had never happened. He would wipe away all the bad memories, save Amaryllis from this brutal world, make it all better. But his stomach turned at the thought of a Manila envelope locked away in his safe. It contained photographs of his daughter too repugnant to look at. For the first time since the war he felt the silt in his soul churning.

Longbone slid open the glass partition. 'Nearly home now, sir.'

Home, thought Arnold. He hadn't been home since he was a boy of ten sitting in a picture palace in New York, his mother's small gloved hand holding his.

Home was in the memory machine.

IF YOU GO DOWN IN
THE WOODS TODAY

Ezra hated Amaryllis, hated being called 'boy', hated going to Warlock Hall. Every day she became more vile. He wondered why on earth he was there, other than to be a plaything for her to torture. She took delight in humiliating him at every opportunity, especially in front of the servants. She had done all in her power to make him feel wretched. He had never in his life dreaded anything as much as the walk up those stairs to the school room, knowing she was waiting for him, a cat ready to torment a mouse. What frustrated him the most was that his position as the son of her father's cook meant he was powerless.

One day, to his utter misery, Mother told him he was no longer to work in the garage. Mr Ruben wanted him to keep his daughter company in the afternoon as well. According to his mother, Mr Ruben was delighted with the good influence Ezra was having on his daughter.

'Rubbish,' said Ezra, miserably, 'I think I would do anything rather than have to spend another hour with her.'

'She's a very troubled young lady,' said Mother. 'Try to be kind, love; her father is so busy and all she has for company is you. And Miss Bright tells me you're a very clever lad. You could, if you worked hard, go to university.'

Ezra wasn't listening. 'I hate Miss Ruben. I really hate her.'

It happened on one of those hot, lazy days, the kind of day that glimmers, dragonfly-bright in the memory.

Ezra, stuffing his hands in his pockets, went to find Amaryllis. She stood at the top of the stairs waiting for him, her hair in old-fashioned ringlets, and wearing a flowered dress which seemed too small, too . . . wrong. Wrong was the only word that came to mind.

'Come with me, boy,' said Amaryllis.

He followed her, reluctantly, up more stairs. She stopped at the small door that led to the Black Tower.

'Have you ever been up there?' she asked.

'No,' said Ezra.

'It's haunted, did you know that, boy?' She laughed. 'As Miss Bright will no doubt tell you, there is a poem about a maiden who, when the moon was full, could be seen standing on the turret, calling to her lover.'

The tower had a winding stone staircase and felt colder than the rest of the house, as if detached from it.

'No one comes up here,' she said. They reached the small room at the top. 'Look at me, I'm Rapunzel. Shall I let down my hair? Do you think my lover might come and save me?'

The garret, for that was all it was, had mean windows on every side with long views over the woods. There was no glass and the wind moaned through the stones as if the room had a voice, and all it spoke of was sadness.

Amaryllis said, 'The story goes that the maiden was walled up in here by her father because she refused to marry a man she didn't love.'

'Shall we go down now?' said Ezra.

'Her ghost has been seen up here. Does that frighten you, boy? Perhaps I'll lock you in.'

'What's wrong with you?' said Ezra, going back down the stairs, fast.

'I'm looking for Crazy,' she said, theatrically.

Ezra almost walked out of the house then. But she grabbed his arm and pulled him along the passage into a room which had a long mirror. On the top of a chest of drawers was a gramophone with a large red trumpet.

'Do you like my hair?'

'I don't know,' sighed Ezra. 'It's all right. It's hair.'

She picked up a large pair of sewing scissors from a table next to the mirror. He had begun to notice such things, certain that some items held clues to her moods. The scissors worried him the minute he spied them. It felt to him that they had been left there by design.

'I think my hair looks very babyish, not grown up, not the thing.'

'What?' he asked.

'I want to grow up, drink cocktails and drive in fast cars, all night.' Still holding the scissors she started to spin, round and round, then said, with a smile curled on her lips, 'Do you know how people make love?'

Ezra turned bright red and made the mistake of taking

his eyes off her, studying the bare wooden floor instead. The sound of the scissors made him look up. She had her back to him. Her face reflected in the mirror was filled with concentration. Half her ringlets had already been chopped off.

He stared transfixed. Her hair lay like a mantle at her feet.

'Let's go swimming,' she said, 'and we'll have music. Yes, that's what we need, music while we swim.'

Ezra, still shocked by her brutal haircut, watched as she went through the pile of records next to the gramophone, throwing one after another on to the floor, not caring if they broke. He felt unsafe in that moment, as if he were falling from a great height.

'I've found it,' she announced. 'This is the record I want to hear.' Then looking at Ezra, she said, 'You're a wimp, do you know that? A pathetic wimp. Bring the record player, there's a dear.'

Reluctantly, he carried it down the stairs, out of the house and along the gravel drive. He was aware of the sweat pouring off his brow, of Clifford Lang watching them from a window. The damned thing weighed a ton. They passed the tennis court, to the jetty, where, his arms aching, he was relieved to put it down at last.

'Well? Wind it up,' ordered Amaryllis.

She had been holding the record of 'The Teddy Bears' Picnic' as if it were an offering to the nymphs of the woods. She put it on the turntable.

'Come on, we'll swim,' she said, as the music started. She took off all her clothes.

'I don't have a bathing suit.'

'What, are you shy, boy? Never seen a girl naked before? Go on, I dare you, take your clothes off.'

Arnold Ruben emerged from the dark of his study, momentarily blinded by the sunlight. Shading his eyes, still unable to see, he was disorientated by the sound of music coming from the lake, a happy, tea-time march which belonged to the nursery, and the unexpectedness of the song bit him like a mosquito.

> *If you go down in the woods today*
> *You're sure of a big surprise*
> *If you go down in the woods today*
> *You'd better go in disguise.*

He walked towards the music. There by the lake, on the wooden, slatted jetty, sat a gramophone with a big, red trumpet, the words of the song itching at the heaviness of the day. In the heat haze before him the scene appeared as unreal as if it were from a silent movie. He seemed to see his young wife standing at the end of the jetty, her hair cut short, her naked skin iridescent against the still waters of the dark lake. He was about to call out, but his voice froze in his throat as he realised that she wasn't alone. The cook's son was there too, standing a way back from her.

Ezra had finally reached the end of his tether. He had had enough, more than enough, of being tormented by this spoilt, impossible girl. There was no need for her to look for 'Crazy'. She *was* crazy. He used a word he'd never said before, but had heard his father shout when stuck in the trenches of the garden shed, the worst word he knew, a word that would get him sacked.

'Fuck you!'

Arnold heard nothing above the jolly music; he only saw the boy running away from her. Slipping and sliding on the wooden decking, he knocked the gramophone, jogging the needle so it clicked repeatedly as the girl dived into the black, deep waters, the ripples spreading out around her disappearing figure in perfect, ever-widening circles.

Arnold Ruben sensed in that moment his past and present colliding. He watched hypnotised as the girl returned to the jetty, a Venus, a rainbow gauze of droplets streaming from her. Amaryllis placed the gramophone needle on the exact verse of the song she wanted to hear and, looking around for the disappearing boy, saw her horrified father staring at her. With a splash she returned to the cool waters.

> *If you go down in the woods today,*
> *You'd better not go alone.*
> *It's lovely down in the woods today,*
> *But safer to stay at home.*

The words chased Arnold Ruben, nibbling at his ears. He was profoundly shocked by what he had witnessed. He thought of the contents of the Manila envelope. It was too late. Time had taken his daughter hostage. Where was the child of yesterday? The child who once adored him, the daughter for whom he had built his dream?

It was clear to him now what had to be done. He must activate the memory machine.

He turned away towards the picture palace and was lost in the long summer shadows.

> *Beneath the trees, where nobody sees,*
> *They'll hide and seek as long as they please.*
> *Today's the day the teddy bears have their picnic.*

Amaryllis, knowing and not knowing quite what she had started, floated on her back, feeling the water caress her body, rushing between her thighs.

STOLEN KEYS

'Kiss me.'

Amaryllis had Ezra pinned between the dining room and the hall so that without physically touching her it would be impossible for him to pass.

'Go on,' she cooed, 'kiss me.'

In the week since the episode by the jetty Ezra felt his heart was wound up faster. There had been something so mysterious and desirable about her nakedness. It wasn't right. The little he knew of the facts of life was what his father had told him and it hadn't been that much help.

The conversation, if he remembered rightly, had been filled with coughs and 'Would you like another cup of tea, lad?' mixed in with 'Well, you see your timmy tickler becomes all . . . sure you don't want sugar in your tea?'

'All what, Father?'

'Stiff, lad. That happens because you're in love with a woman. Would you like a biscuit?'

'No, thank you, Father. What happens with the woman?'

'Look, it's simple. When you're in love, you get all aroused and that's how you make babies. I think I'll see if I can find a book on the subject at the library.'

He never did.

And that was that. It had been very awkward and Ezra had put it out of his mind. It was a conversation better not had with your parents. Len knew a little more because of the number of babies his mum had had. They came out from in between the woman's legs.

'Yikes. That sounds disgusting,' said Ezra.

'It's a bit of a mess,' said Len, remembering how he'd walked in when Elsie, his sister, had just been born.

'But how do they get in there?' asked Ezra, and Len was not much wiser than he.

'Perhaps through the tummy button?' he suggested helpfully.

Until that moment by the lake, Ezra had never seen a naked woman. Now he could hardly think of anything else.

It couldn't be right. Maybe he wasn't normal for, according to his father, this only happened if you loved someone and he didn't love Amaryllis. He hated her.

Now, as Amaryllis pressed him against the door frame, he could only hope that, if he was caught like this, Mr Ruben might release him from his daily torment and send him to work in the garage again. This could happen any moment now as Mr Ruben was due to leave, taking a small party of friends to Lord and Lady Darlow's, and they would have to walk out through the hall.

Vervaine Fox had arrived last night, throwing the house into a vortex of activity. His mother had cooked a huge dinner for twenty guests and there had been music and dancing late into the night.

'Go on, what are you scared of, boy? said Amaryllis. 'Kiss me. I order you to.'

What saved Ezra from an inescapable doom was the appearance of the great actress herself.

'My dears, how intriguing,' she said in her strange, harsh voice, pitched low for such a feminine-looking woman. The voice and the face didn't seem to match. Sizing up Ezra, she asked, 'So, young sir in the ill-fitting clothes, are you going to kiss this little vixen?'

Amaryllis was now standing rigidly upright and well away from him. Ezra saw that for the first time someone had got the better of her.

'Is this your beau?' asked the painted lady, for close up her face was heavily made up and the impression of youth somewhat lost. To Ezra at least she looked like a goddess. She smelled of exquisite perfume, heady and strong; her hair was white-blonde with a diamante-and-feather arrangement, and she was wearing a long grey satin dress with a diamond clasp and sequined shoes, a white fox fur draped casually over one bare shoulder.

'Come now,' continued the goddess in her mismatched voice, 'kiss, you two, and make up, and I won't be a tell-tale.'

Ezra knew Vervaine Fox was enjoying this little game all the more because of Amaryllis's embarrassment at being caught red-handed and up to no good. He was surprised to find, strange as it was, that he felt no thrill at seeing his tormentor get her comeuppance. Miss Fox stuck one of her long red fingernails into Amaryllis's back, hurting her enough to make her lean forward, pushing her small round breasts out towards him. Ezra, who had never looked at this girl as anything other than an enemy, was again disturbed by the sudden stirring within him. He blushed as Amaryllis had no choice but to peck his cheek.

'Call that a kiss?' said Vervaine Fox. 'I say that's pathetic. Why, don't you watch the movies at all?'

'Perhaps, Miss Fox,' said Amaryllis, shaking herself free and in doing so bumping into Ezra, 'we don't feel like kissing.'

'Vervaine's my name, honey. How many times have I told you to call me Vervaine?' She smiled, revealing perfect teeth. 'Let me give you some advice. If you don't know how to play, honey, don't roll the dice. In other words, if you don't want it, don't ask for it.'

All the colour drained from Amaryllis's face.

'Ready, darling?' came a voice from along the corridor as Arnold Ruben appeared in evening dress. He didn't seem to see his daughter or Ezra standing in the shadows. 'The show starts at five. Longbone's outside.'

Turning to Arnold, she smiled and without a backward glance was gone.

'Vervaine Fox,' said Ezra, watching them walk away. 'Vervaine Fox.'

Amaryllis said nothing.

'The great star of the silent screen,' he said.

He turned to look at her and saw in her eyes the beginning of tears.

'The very same,' replied Amaryllis, sure that he, like everyone else, was completely starstruck. Feeling her old anger rise, she was ready to resume warfare. But then she realised there had been a hint of contempt in his voice; he was genuinely upset at her distress. She felt an unfamiliar wave of remorse.

Trying to make light of it, she laughed. 'Yes, the very same, with a voice like a foghorn that no amount of elocution lessons could change, so now the talkies are in, she's out.'

'What's she doing here?'

It was the first conversation she'd had with Ezra that hadn't involved her being unbearably beastly to him. Something, she knew, had shifted. It was as if the curtain had lifted on Act Two.

'She's another one hoping to snap up my father and fritter away his fortune.'

'Crikey, that's bad.'

They heard the car leave.

'I'd better go,' he said.

'Wait.'

Ezra stopped.

'There's something I want to do.'

'No,' said Ezra, 'I don't want to see the Black Tower, or help you "look for Crazy", or go swimming naked, or . . .'

'I'm sorry. I've been utterly horrid to you.'

In the darkness of the hall, he wasn't sure if she was just making fun of him.

'See you tomorrow, then,' he said.

'I meant what I said, honest injun. Could we be friends?'

'Why now?' asked Ezra. 'You appear to hate me and I don't much like you. In fact, I don't like you at all. You make my life hell and if I never come back here again, it would be too soon.'

'I know it's my fault. Could we declare a truce? I want to show you something.'

'No.'

'To the truce or me wanting to show you something? It's really important.'

She took from her pocket a bunch of keys. A door opened and Clifford Lang stood in the hall. Amaryllis quickly hid them.

'What are you doing?' he said. 'Shouldn't you have your noses in books or some such thing?'

'We've been given the afternoon off,' she lied.

The phone rang and he went back in the room, closing the door.

Amaryllis pulled Ezra out of the house and along the gravel drive towards the woods.

'What do the keys open?' he asked.

'The picture palace,' she said. 'Silas has gone with Daddy to the Darlows'.'

'Wait, wait,' said Ezra, as they entered the woods. 'Where did you get the keys?'

Amaryllis, looking behind to make sure they hadn't been followed, whispered, 'I stole them from Daddy's study.'

Ezra put his hands up in surrender. He was going home. He started to walk away but, like Orpheus, something made him look back. She stood there, a thin, lonely figure, her head down. Ezra kicked a pebble, then walked towards her.

'When I made the cake with your mother,' she said, 'I saw

what a family could be, and I wanted more than anything for her to be my mother, to belong to a family that was safe and full of love. So I decided I would make you my friend. I wanted to be asked home for tea and things like that.'

'You have a funny way of going about it.'

'You don't understand.'

Ezra saw tears shining in her eyes. She was either a great actress or what she was saying was the truth, mad as it sounded.

'I wanted you to like me for me. Then Daddy ruined it by taking control, saying you don't have all the opportunities I have, and it would do me good. I hated him and I hated you for going along with it.'

'I don't have any choice,' Ezra replied. 'I'm paid the same as if I was working for Mr Longbone. We need the money. Olive, my sister, is earning and I have to as well. Father hasn't been able to work since the war.'

'What's wrong with him?' asked Amaryllis.

'I don't know. Mother thinks all the memories of the dead haunt him.' Ezra shrugged. 'I'll be going then.'

'No, please, could we start again? Please. I need a friend.'

'What do you want to do?' he asked, more gently.

'I want to show you the picture palace.'

They walked along a path that twisted and turned, the trees a dense patchwork of colour. Ezra, like everyone else in the neighbourhood, had heard about Mr Ruben's cinema, but nothing had prepared him for the sight of the picture palace itself. When he saw it he felt they had stumbled upon something quite extraordinary.

Amaryllis took out the keys and unlocked the foyer doors, which swung open with a whoosh. The inside of the cinema was even more spectacular. The foyer had its very own box office. The carpet design was in the shape of a sun, its rays reaching out into the far corners. At one end was a grand, sweeping staircase leading up to a gallery. On either side were doors to the auditorium. Amaryllis opened one and Ezra followed her in.

He was overwhelmed by the smell of luxury, the plushness of the carpets, the peach-skin softness of the seats, which were so wide it seemed they were designed for vast, baffled giants. It was all so different to the Rio, with its stink of stale cigarettes and mouldy sweets, its prickly upholstery, which made you itch and fidget, and gave you fleas.

'This is where Daddy shows all the latest films from Hollywood. It even has a small Wurlitzer,' said Amaryllis. 'It comes up through the floor from the basement.'

The Rio had never run to anything so grand.

Pulling aside some velvet curtains, she unlocked a steel door. It swung open.

Ezra said, 'Maybe we shouldn't.'

'The whole point of getting the keys is to see what's down there,' she said.

The steps were concrete and a greenish light in the stairwell gave the impression that they were entering a murky pond.

'Close the door behind you,' she whispered, finding a light switch on the wall.

At the bottom of the stairs was a long corridor with a small storeroom on one side and, on the other, a huge, clinically white laboratory. Strapped to the middle of the floor was a metal chair. Above, an aluminium helmet hung on wires, a green light shining from its top. Out of it came wriggly eels of grey tube. Everything was connected to a bank of zinc work stations, consisting of many dials and clocks. Behind the chair was a large screen and, high up on the wall, a huge clock that ran at a different speed from any other clock in the room. It emitted a dull noise: electric, crackling, like the beginning of a headache.

'This is where people come to sit for my father's experiments.'

'What is it?' asked Ezra.

'The memory machine.'

Ezra was only half-listening. He looked behind the screen to find nothing apart from a pile of tarpaulins and a panel of levers. One was labelled 'Wurlitzer'.

'Let's go,' said Amaryllis, her mood changing again. 'This place gives me the creeps.'

Suddenly a bright-red light flashed.

'What's that?'

'I think it's an alarm.'

They ran into the passage to see a pair of two-tone shoes descending the stairs.

A hushed voice said, 'The door's unlocked. Do you think anyone's down here?'

Amaryllis froze. Ezra pushed her back into the laboratory and dragged her behind the screen. Gesturing to her to get down, he pulled a tarpaulin over them both.

'No, I told you, no one's about. I made sure of that,' said a second voice.

'We don't need a gun, Roach,' said the first man. 'Put it away for goodness' sake.'

His voice was soothing, his words perfectly pilled.

'Shut up,' said Roach. 'I'll do my job and you do yours. Do you know how the machine works?'

'I've never seen anything like this. It's extraordinary. What's behind that screen?'

From under the tarpaulin Ezra heard the sound of a camera shutter. He could smell cigarette smoke and glimpse a man's two-tone shoes as he walked towards them.

'Nothing,' Roach said, as he turned and walked away again. 'How long is this going to take?'

'I don't know. It's much more complicated than I thought. Wait a minute, Everett, I need to reload the camera.'

Too late, Ezra became aware of the tension in Amaryllis's body. A muffled sob broke free from the moorings of her mouth.

'What the hell was that?' said the man in the two-tone shoes.

'Someone is here. I knew it,' said his companion.

'It seems we do need this after all.'

There was a click as the man cocked his revolver and, in an instant, Ezra freed himself from the tarpaulin, reached up and pulled the Wurlitzer's lever. Above them the organ rose into the auditorium, flooding it with jaunty music. The two men ran from the laboratory towards the stairs.

Ezra held tight to Amaryllis's hand and they fled into the passage. One of the men stood at the top of the stairs with his back to them. Amaryllis pulled Ezra into the storeroom and shut the door quietly. In the pitch-darkness, her heart thumping, she fumbled with the keys and, after what seemed an age, found the one that locked them in. She began to feel her way along the shelves that lined the walls.

'What are you doing?' hissed Ezra.

'Looking to see if there's a way out.'

'Yes – the same way we came in.'

Something clattered from a shelf on to the floor.

They heard the first man say, 'There's no one up here.'

Then they both jumped out of their skins.

The door handle rattled and the other man said, 'That's because they're in here.'

Amaryllis pushed herself so far back there was nowhere else to go. There was a quiet click and for a moment Ezra thought the man in the two-tone shoes had unlocked the door. Then he realised the back wall of the storeroom was sliding away, and he and Amaryllis found themselves on the other side of the shelves as the wall glided back into place.

They were in a narrow tunnel and in the distance Ezra could see a dim light. Several minutes later he kicked open a grille at the foot of some steps inside a cool brick building.

Ezra laughed with relief.

'We're in the ice-house!' he said. He turned to Amaryllis. Her face was white. 'Are you all right?'

'I know one of the men,' she said quietly.

'That's impossible. You can't.'

'I wish I didn't. You don't know how much I wish I didn't.'

'Which one?' asked Ezra.

'The man with the two-tone shoes.'

'Who is he?'

Amaryllis sank down on the cold step. 'I know him as Maurice Sands. But I think his real name is Everett Roach.'

AVOIDING ICEBERGS

The crunch of wheels on the gravel drive announced to the sleepy household of Warlock Hall that Mr Ruben and his party had returned. The head butler greeted them and they were ushered into the drawing room for late-night brandies and tisane.

Silas thought it had not been the most successful of evenings. Things were not right with Arnold. He had known and loved him long enough to guess that something was seriously troubling him. Whatever it was, Arnold was keeping it close to his chest. That in itself was out of character, for there was little Silas didn't know about the man; in fact he could say that he alone was the keeper of his deepest secrets. All except this one.

He had noticed a subtle change in Arnold since he had delivered his lecture nearly a month ago. No one else would have been aware of it, of that he was sure. As always, Arnold, a handsome man whose greying hair gave him a look of distinction and wisdom, maintained a faultless facade of elegance and charm.

Arnold's silence was beginning to feel like a betrayal. This state of affairs was a new departure; their friendship had lasted a long time, steering well clear of icebergs. Silas wondered if Arnold was in love with Vervaine. He was realistic enough to know that if he was, then he, Silas, would have to swallow that bitter little pill. Not for the first time, he felt the ache of jealousy.

Before dinner, the guests had wandered out into the garden which had the beauty that only long-established wealth can bring. Here, in a paradise of sorts, they sat on gilt chairs and listened to a private performance of *Don Giovanni*, the singers' voices fighting nature's own little diva, the nightingale.

Vervaine had revelled in the attention she received. Silas watched her performance in the role of the great tiger huntress, stalking the men of the party who remembered her at the height of her fame. She lived off flattery as others lived off food.

It was during the interval, while champagne cocktails were being served, that Silas overheard two pretty young women.

'Oh, isn't Vervaine Fox a hoot!' said one. 'Do you know what? She told me she was about the same age as me.'

'Darling, she didn't!'

'She did.'

'Well, how deluded can you be?'

'She told me she kept her figure by eating colours.'

Both women giggled.

'What colours?' asked her friend.

'Oh, reds, blues, greens, yellows.'

'Was she talking about cocktails or pills?'

This was greeted with a shriek of laughter.

'Promise faithfully that you will tell me if I ever become that old and silly.'

On his return to Vervaine's side Silas, for the briefest of moments, saw her in the light of reality. His heart went out to the woman he had worshipped for years. He would talk to Arnold. There must be a way of saving her before time turned her beauty to ashes.

Now, in the drawing room of Warlock Hall, Arnold stood with a gravestone face. He seemed impatient for Vervaine to retire.

'Darling, that was just a glorious evening,' she said, kissing him on both cheeks. 'Such a quaint idea, opera in one's own backyard.' She sighed. 'A pity that Don Giovanni took so long to go down to hell. You know, you'd have thought by tonight's performance that rigor mortis had set in before he died.'

'Quite,' came Arnold's clipped tone.

'I hope, darling, in the morning you'll be of a sunnier disposition. Maybe after a talk with Silas things will look brighter.'

Vervaine departed to bed, leaving Silas and Arnold together.

Silas closed the door and asked, 'Is there anything you're not telling me?'

Arnold wasn't listening. 'What on earth did she mean by things will look brighter after I've talked to you?'

'I want to take Vervaine with us into the machine.'

'And that's supposed to brighten things up? You've no right to go making half-baked promises.' There was an irritable silence that began to say more than words ever could. 'I thought we had an agreement. There will be the three of us, no more.'

'Yes, I know this, but – don't you love her? You can save her, no one else can. It's nothing short of your duty to do so.'

Arnold laughed. 'Love her? Are you mad? It's an amusing interlude, that's all. And save her from what?'

'From age, from time taking more of her beauty. We both know we have the power. Surely it's where she belongs, in the memory machine. I built the machine too; why shouldn't I have a say?'

'Oh for God's sake! Silas, we have more urgent things to discuss.' Arnold poured them both a brandy. 'We have to activate the machine.'

'We can't,' said Silas. 'There's more work to do. I need time.'

'Time? We are the masters of time.' Arnold laughed and downed his brandy in one. 'You might like to know that Sir Basil has a file on us.'

Silas turned pale. 'What does the file say?'

'Among other things, that you are dead.'

'Did you tell him anything else?'

'No, Silas, because I don't know anything else about you.'

Silas sat with his head in his hands, lost in thought, then said, 'Why did you never ask me about my past?'

'You wouldn't tell me the truth and, anyway, it doesn't matter. You have more than proved that you're a loyal friend to me, the best a man could hope for, and now I'm not sure I want to know. Let's leave it be, and forget about this foolish crush you have on Vervaine Fox. I can tell you that my little dalliance with her has come to an end.'

'My name is Gunter Leichman.'

'You don't have to do this. I told you, it is better left alone.'

'No, if I tell you, you'll understand why I want Vervaine to join us. I am from a Viennese family of doctors. Like you, I am of Jewish origin. I was studying to become a surgeon in Berlin, when I met and married a nightclub singer called Lottie Mertz. She was sixteen, I was twenty-four. One night I found her in the arms of another man. I walked away from the wreckage, broken. The war saved me, gave me a new name and a new country to fight for. When I met you in Paris, I had only that week discovered what had happened to my little Lottie: she had gone to Hollywood, changed her name and was the star of the film, *The Night of the Tiger*.'

Arnold stood up. 'Are you still legally married to her?'

Silas nodded.

'I wish you'd told me this sooner.'

'I wanted to see her again, be close to her, even though she wants nothing to do with me. I still love her.'

Arnold laughed ruefully. 'Look, the most important thing is what we have built together, the rest doesn't matter. But I don't want Vervaine in the machine, playing the wicked stepmother. She's jealous of Amaryllis's beauty. She'd make trouble. And I don't trust her.'

'And I don't want to be without her.'

'All right, we'll strike a deal. You can take a memory recording from her if you must. That way you can see her whenever you want. But she physically must not enter the machine. Record the memories and then send her packing. I'm going to London tomorrow to see my lawyer, and I want her gone from here by the time I get back. Tomorrow is Amaryllis's seventeenth birthday. At ten-forty-five p.m., we will activate the machine. Agreed?'

'No,' said Silas. 'No. I have had problems editing the memories. Some are so strong, it's impossible to obliterate them.'

'Impossible? Impossible bores me. We can correct these faults from within the machine. I should be back by early afternoon, and tomorrow night we will finally be able to see what we have created. And by that time, Silas, Vervaine must be gone. I mean it.'

Silas nodded. 'Pour me another one,' he said, handing Arnold his glass.

Arnold took it and turned back to the drinks cabinet. 'This man Maurice Sands. Did you find out anything more about him?'

'No,' said Silas, struggling to keep his rage in check. 'I put out feelers in all the obvious places – Soho, Mayfair – but drew a blank.'

Twenty-two hours later – too late – Arnold regretted that he hadn't told Silas the whole truth: that he was being blackmailed to hand over the plans of the memory machine in return for the negatives of the shocking photographs of his naked daughter.

TODAY IS MY BIRTHDAY

Ezra woke the next morning to hear muffled voices followed by the front door being closed. From his bedroom window he could hear his father whistling in the henhouse. Ezra washed, got dressed and went downstairs to the kitchen. His mother was at the sink staring out of the window, deep in thought.

'Who was that at the door?' he asked.

'Mrs Calthorpe.'

'Oh, no, what did she want?'

'She came to tell me that Mrs Popplin, the seamstress at the hall, died last night at the cottage hospital.'

'What of?'

'A brain haemorrhage, so they say. More likely those memory recordings. Poor woman, all she wanted was a little extra cash.' Mother turned round and looked at her son. 'You are never, ever to do that, no matter how much money they offer. You are not even to go anywhere near the wretched place. Promise me?'

Ezra nodded and poured himself a cup of tea from the pot.

'I wouldn't do anything so daft,' he said, with his fingers crossed in his pocket. It was too late. He had seen for himself what was in the basement of the picture palace.

Hearing Noel whistling his way towards the back door,

—— 112 ——

Nancy said, 'Not a word to Father. We don't want him set off again.'

It was one of those glorious mid-summer mornings when everything is buzzing with the promise of the future. A chorus of birdsong, the cow parsley growing tall, the meadows filled with wild flowers. But Ezra's mind was on other things as he walked to Warlock Hall. He felt as if yesterday had been a living nightmare, and he wondered whether he could trust his memory. Had he really been down to that basement, seen the green light, heard that dreadful hum, escaped from the clutches of two sinister men? One thing was for sure, it was a lot more scary than the *The Severed Hand* had ever been. That was pretty straightforward: a hand with no body, no conscience to bother it, climbing all over the place like a spider and murdering villains who looked like villains. But what was happening at Warlock Hall was a whole new mix of mystery.

He pulled a blade of grass absent-mindedly and a Red Admiral fluttered in front of him. He could see the Black Tower peeping over the top of the trees, the sky above it growing ominously dark, heralding a summer storm.

Ezra wondered if Amaryllis would have rethought the whole notion of his being her friend. It wouldn't surprise him. She was many things, all of which could be put together under one heading: unpredictable. Going through the green-baize door into the hall the first thing he noticed, as he always did, was that the place was cold, so much colder than outside.

Amaryllis was sitting on the top step, waiting for him. Ezra kept his distance. She stood up and came down the stairs towards him.

'Hello,' she said, with such enthusiasm that Ezra felt guilty for thinking she might have changed her mind. 'I was going to ask Miss Bright for the morning off.'

'Why?'

'Because . . . because I need to talk to you. It's important.'

Yesterday, thought Ezra ruefully, just yesterday I would have said she's doing an audition for the village amateur dramatics. Yesterday the world seemed safe, yesterday *The Severed Hand* looked like a horror film. Today it belongs to a *Boy's Own Annual*. Today feels like a continuation of a nightmare broken only by a fistful of sleep.

Miss Bright was sitting at her desk waiting, dreaming. This was the anniversary of the morning in 1917 when she had received the letter telling her of her fiancé's death, ending a part of her life that had only just begun. In the light of this unholy day she looked back at wasted years, rimmed by unnoticed tears.

When Amaryllis asked if she and Ezra might be excused from class, Miss Bright took a deep breath that sounded like a sob and said, 'Yes.'

Outside, it started to rain as they made their way past the tennis court and down, through the small gate where the geese hissed in fury, to the Wendy house. It smelled of rosemary and wet grass. There was just enough room inside for them both, and Amaryllis closed the door as the skies darkened and the rain came down. It was too cramped to sit up so she lay on the floor and Ezra did the same, their knees bent, their hands by their sides.

'There is something I have to ask you,' she said.

'What?' he asked, studying a spider scuttling across the ceiling.

'Are we friends?'

'I suppose. Yes,' said Ezra.

'Why "suppose"?' she asked.

'Because I wasn't sure if today you might feel different.'

'No, never!' she said, with such passion that it took Ezra by surprise. Unexpected as it was, he felt just the same. Yesterday they had been threaded together by survival.

'I want to tell you how I know that man, Maurice . . . Everett Roach.'

'All right. But you don't have to, if you don't want to.'

'But I do, I have to tell someone. First of all I have to ask you a question, and I don't want you to worry if the answer is "No". Do you know about the facts of life?'

Ezra said nothing.

'I won't laugh, I promise,' she said. 'I won't be horrible or make fun or tell a soul. Cross my heart and hope to die.'

'No, not really,' said Ezra, screwing up his face. 'My best friend, Len, thought it had something to do with tummy buttons.'

He was so grateful they were lying down and she couldn't see his deep embarrassment.

Amaryllis gave the talk that had made her famous in the dormitory at Clarrington School.

'That sounds much better than belly buttons.'

She rolled on her back and said, 'Last night I came to the decision that if I couldn't tell my father about Everett Roach I would tell you. But if you didn't even know the facts of life, you see, it would all be meaningless. Everett Roach raped me.'

'No!' said Ezra shocked. Even he had heard the word and knew it was something downright terrible.

Saying his name out loud made Amaryllis's stomach turn. She was unconscious of her tears, or that she was twisting and pulling the skin round her fingernails. Ezra with more strength than she thought he had, pulled her hands apart and held one of them tightly.

'I will kill him if I see him again.'

She let out a faint laugh. 'It was my fault. If I hadn't run away from school, if I hadn't drunk those stupid cocktails . . .' She turned her face towards Ezra. 'Ezra, I'm frightened that something really bad is going to happen.'

'I will protect you,' he said.

He leaned over and, to his own surprise, kissed her on the mouth, such a sweet, tender kiss that it made her cry all the more.

They lay together on the wooden floor, saying nothing, listening to the rain on the wooden roof. Amaryllis felt peaceful, her hand in his.

The rain stopped and as they walked back to the house, they saw Vervaine Fox coming towards them from the direction of the picture palace. Her face was pale and she was swaying as if she were tipsy. Stopping by the tennis court, she leaned against its wire-mesh fence.

'Are you all right, Miss Fox?' Ezra asked.

'No, I am not. Do I look all right? My head is about to explode. I need my doctor. Oh, you, boy, go and get help, quick.'

'He's called Ezra,' said Amaryllis.

'Listen, Miss Smarty Pants, I don't give a damn what your little playmate is called. Just get help. I'm ill.'

Ezra ran to the house.

Amaryllis led Vervaine to a seat.

Vervaine dropped down and dragged Amaryllis with her.

'Mirror, mirror on the wall. Aren't you a lucky girl?' she said. 'You'll stay young and beautiful for ever.'

Amaryllis tried to stand. Vervaine's red nails scratched at her bare arm.

Then she said, 'Do you know what Daddykins has planned for you?'

The word 'Daddykins' made Amaryllis's whole being tighten.

'No.'

'Well, honey, shall I tell you? He's about to freeze your life. What do you say to that?'

Amaryllis wasn't listening. She had glimpsed Silas watching them from the edge of the woods. Then the butler and Mrs Pascoe came running from the house to escort Vervaine Fox to her room and, when she looked again, he had disappeared.

Amaryllis stayed where she was, on the seat. Ezra came and sat next to her.

'What's wrong?' he asked.

'Vervaine used a word that Everett Roach used. She said "Daddykins". You don't think she knows him, do you?'

'How would she know someone like him?'

'That's what I'm wondering.'

They'd had lunch in the dining room. The places were laid as they always were, at either end of a very long mahogany table so that they were as far away from one another as was humanly possible. This used to be a blessing but today it was a hindrance. There was no hope of talking. The grandfather clock, the clink of plates, the clatter of cutlery, were all the conversation the room had to offer. The three tall windows were open at the bottom so that the usually still solemn lace curtains danced in the breeze. Ezra had never noticed the wallpaper before. Today everything had a sharpness about it that nothing prior to this moment had possessed. It was green, painted with birds and branches of trees. It reminded him of the green light.

At last the plates were cleared away. Neither had touched the food. Amaryllis got up and went towards him. Taking no notice whatsoever of the two servants, she bent down, tilted his chin towards her and kissed him, pushing the tip of her tongue into his mouth. He felt his breath being taken from him.

'Thank you,' she said, quietly. 'It's best you go now.'

He stood up, bewildered. 'Are you sure?'

'Yes. Daddy is due back this afternoon.' She looked so serious. 'Today is my birthday. I am seventeen.'

*

Ezra walked home happy as a sandboy. Now at last he knew what men and women did in private behind bedroom doors, in hotels, in houses, cottages, flats, tents, caves and places all over the world. He jumped up in the air, filled with joy. It didn't matter if his timmy tickler went up and down like a merry-go-round horse. Thinking about the deliciousness of Amaryllis's kiss, he felt a shiver of excitement.

He arrived home to find his father once more on the brink of one of his turns; his eyes had that strange stare to them, as if he no longer saw the room, only the battlefields.

Mother was sitting at the kitchen table. 'Please, Noel,' she was saying desperately, 'it's doing you no good, brooding on this. Sit down, love, and drink your tea.'

'He shouldn't meddle with people's lives. He's like all those bloated generals who sat drinking, while Tommies like us were killed. It's happening again. It will never stop.'

'Father,' said Ezra, standing at the kitchen door.

'Is that you, Bernie?' Father shouted. 'Don't be frightened, lad.'

'Please, Noel, don't leave me, not now, love, not now.'

'It's Tommy this and Tommy that . . . that's the order . . . hear it? We're going over the top, come on, Bernie, you'll be all right, lad, don't cry for your mum. I'm with you, stay close, lad . . .' He went out in another shower of rain to the garden shed.

'What set him off?' asked Ezra.

Mother let out a huge sigh and wiped her eyes. 'Mrs Popplin. Your father was Stan Popplin's best man. Stan was killed at Passchendaele.'

Ezra sat down next to her. His mother's bare arms were stretched across the kitchen table, strong loving arms that had held this family together for as long as he could remember. He saw the blue-green veins standing proud on the back of her hands, the brown liver spots: the markings and rivers on the map of a hard life.

'How did he find out?'

His mother stirred the cold tea in front of her.

'How do you think? Doreen Calthorpe couldn't keep it to herself. She had to tell all and sundry, including your father.'

'Did you sit for the experiments, Mother?' Ezra asked.

'No, of course not.'

'Vervaine Fox did today. I think that's why she was taken ill.'

'Stupid woman. I tell you, I wouldn't trust her as far as the front door. She's up to no good.'

'Amaryllis thinks she's after marrying Mr Ruben.'

'Mr Ruben is wedded to that blasted invention of his. The rich are a breed unto themselves; about as practical as . . . as caviar on toast.' And, changing the subject, she said, 'Make us some more tea, there's a love.'

As Ezra put the kettle on the words of a song went round and round in his head. One line stuck out above all the rest.

If you go down in the woods today
You're sure of a big surprise.

THE SILVER TIGER

The afternoon of 19 June 1937

It was late afternoon when Miss Bright went for a walk. She couldn't stand the feverish activity that had affected the whole house since Vervaine Fox had been taken ill. The clock in the hall had struck six, that much she recalled, also that Mr Ruben had by then returned from London and was upstairs with the ailing actress. Silas Molde looked positively washed out and a maid had reported to the butler that Miss Fox was that poorly she thought she might go the way of Mrs Popplin.

Miss Bright suspected that Vervaine Fox was another of the many who had, like herself, sat for the memory recordings. The strange, or rather the disturbing, aspect of her particular experience had been that she remembered little apart from two days of appalling headaches. Nor could she describe accurately where it had taken place, or even what the picture palace looked like. The building was out of bounds to Mr Ruben's staff. She had never dared to disobey that order although more than once she had been sorely tempted to have a look at it for herself.

Being an avid reader of detective stories, Miss Bright felt there was something curious about the memory recordings.

She asked herself what they were for and why after Mrs Popplin's death would Silas Molde make another recording? Surely he must have told Vervaine Fox about the dangers? Had he purposely decided to keep quiet?

She had passed Silas in the hall on her way out and had heard him shouting at Clifford Lang to put another call through to London, and to find out exactly what time Doctor Pincher and the private ambulance were due to arrive.

Yes, sir,' she overheard Cliffford Lang say, 'but the police are on the line, wanting a word.'

Silas disappeared into the office, slamming the door shut behind him. Yes, thought Miss Bright, without doubt Mr Molde would be the main suspect in any good murder mystery.

It had been raining on and off all day but at least now there was some sunshine. Miss Bright walked briskly, as she always did, into the grounds beyond the lawns to one of her favourite paths, which followed a stream hidden in a ravine through a copse of trees. She had reached the small bridge that crossed into the meadow beyond and was about to emerge under the darkening skies into a beam of fluorescent sunlight, when she heard the unmistakeable rumble of a large car. She paused. Officially the Daimler wasn't on Mr Ruben's land for it had pulled up in the lane on the far side of the stile. It seemed to the would-be detective rather odd to have driven such a hugely expensive car so far from the main road. The chauffeur leaned against the bonnet with his back to her, smoking a cigarette.

The passenger door opened and a smartly dressed man got

out, stretched his legs and looked around. He was of smaller build than the chauffeur, and all she could see of him was his three-piece suit with a gold watch chain hanging from his waistcoat pocket. As both men were wearing hats she was unable to see either of their faces clearly. One thing she noticed in the eerie light before the thunderstorm erupted was that the passenger wore a red rose in his lapel.

The chauffeur blew a smoke ring and said, 'What's the time?'

The man with the rose studied his watch. 'Six-thirty.'

'Good,' said the chauffeur. 'Old Frankie-boy should be there with the bird. He said getting the uniform had been a doddle.'

The sky was now nearly black. Both men got back in the car and it started to reverse down the grassy lane. Miss Bright was annoyed with herself for forgetting to bring her glasses – the numberplate was a blur.

After the car had disappeared from sight she started to walk back towards the house. Outside the gates and just off the road she spied an ambulance and once more she stopped, making sure she wasn't seen. The Daimler approached and pulled up alongside it. The ambulance driver got out and joined the passenger in the car. Miss Bright realised that her heart was beating faster and she felt genuine fear – of what, she wasn't sure. It started to rain. Giant globes splashed down as the ambulance driver quickly returned to his vehicle and started the engine. Bell ringing, it headed in the direction of Warlock Hall, closely followed by the Daimler. They sped through the gates and up to the house.

No, thought Miss Bright, this is all wrong. The man in the

Daimler must be a doctor, so why would the ambulance driver get in the car for a chat when, a few hundred yards away, someone was seriously ill? Very shady, that's what it was, very shady indeed. She followed the vehicles up the drive, but was prevented from reaching the house by torrential rain, which forced her to take cover under the porch of the games shed. It was half an hour before she was able to set out again, and there by the front entrance the Daimler and the ambulance stood waiting.

By the clock in the hall it was now five past seven, and she was soaking wet.

Miss Bright went to her bedroom, then had a bath. Lying in the hot, steamy water she began to think that perhaps she was making ordinary things more dramatic than they really were. Fiddlesticks, she said to herself. You have allowed your imagination to run away with you. And, turning on the hot-water tap again, she felt certain there was a simple reason for what she had witnessed.

She dressed and once more looked at the present she had bought her pupil; a small gesture, one she hoped might further break the ice between them.

Miss Bright closed her door behind her and made her way to the west wing. She saw the ambulance driver, accompanied by Silas Molde, carrying an oxygen cylinder up to Miss Fox's room. She was going to ask how the actress was but thought better of it. Silas's dark eyes followed her as she knocked on Amaryllis's door. There was no answer, but then she saw Amaryllis coming down the corridor towards her.

'Are you all right?' she said, seeing the girl's pale face.

'Yes,' she said, 'just dandy. Why, is there anything wrong?'

'No,' said Miss Bright, losing her confidence. Amaryllis seemed to be back to her old self.

Amaryllis opened the door. 'Come in,' she said.

The room was immaculately tidy, very out of keeping with Amaryllis's nature, and something altogether more worrying occurred to Miss Bright. It felt as if everything had been packed away in preparation for a journey. To her surprise the diary she had given Amaryllis, which had been so rudely dismissed, was open on her dressing table, with writing on the page. There was a knock on the door and a maid entered carrying a tray with two glasses of champagne.

'Happy birthday, Miss Ruben,' said the maid. 'Mr Molde thought you and Miss Bright might like this.'

'That's very kind of him,' said Miss Bright.

'Will he be joining us?' asked Amaryllis.

'No, Miss Ruben.'

'Well,' said Miss Bright, putting her hands together. 'What a treat – and a bit naughty.'

Amaryllis smiled involuntarily at her governess's genuine enthusiasm.

'Before we drink a toast, I have a present for you,' Miss Bright said, taking from the pocket of her cardigan a small box.

Amaryllis opened it with great care.

'It won't bite, that much I can say,' said Miss Bright.

There, wrapped in tissue paper, was a thin chain and hanging from it a small silver tiger.

Amaryllis stared at it transfixed. It was so elegant, and such a well-considered gift.

Miss Bright said, 'It's only silver-plated.'

'I love it, I really do! How very clever of you.'

'I spotted the magazine picture you'd taped to the inside of your desk lid.'

Amaryllis fastened the chain round her neck and looked in the mirror. She thought it was the most perfect present she had ever been given, more personal than the many and extravagant gifts which her father had lavished on her. This birthday he had promised her something out of this world. Far from a thrill of excitement, she felt a numb pain of dread. Unlike this simple gift, her father's came wrapped in unspoken reproaches.

They sat drinking champagne and Miss Bright thought how sad the girl looked.

'You should be happy on your birthday. What did your father give you?'

'I'll get my present tonight. Do you know what I wish for?'

'No,' said Miss Bright, 'what?'

'I wish he would give me a whole lot of nothing. That's all I want – nothing.'

'Of course he's going to give you a present.'

Amaryllis's violet eyes looked straight into Miss Bright's. 'What if you knew that you were going to be seventeen for ever and ever? Do you think you would want to celebrate your birthday?'

Miss Bright left, ten minutes later, saying the bubbles had

made her sleepy. Alone in her room, Amaryllis thought back to the interview she had had an hour before with her father. It had gone very badly. She had written most of it down in her diary. She found the lined, non-judgemental pages calmed her and helped her think.

Her father had told her he would give her his present at a quarter to eleven that night. She had made up her mind what she was going to do: she was going to run away. She would go and find Ezra and ask Mrs Pascoe to help her.

She took her diary and quietly closed her door. Everyone was too preoccupied to notice her leave. Only Silas saw her sneaking out through the walled garden. She looked back to make sure she wasn't being followed and was overcome by a wave of tiredness. She stopped, trying to think straight. Her memory was playing tricks. She was nine years old and her father had bought her a bicycle.

At the back of Warlock Hall was a tarmac road used by delivery vans and here she had been given her first and only lesson in cycling. It had been autumn and there was a chill in the air.

Her father, wearing a hat with his suit, held on to the back of the bike running, or rather striding, after her, and saying all the time, 'Keep pedalling, don't stop.'

'You will be there, behind me?' she'd asked.

'Of course,' he'd replied.

And pedalled she had, asking over and over again, 'Are you there?' as his voice grew fainter. At the end of the drive, before it curved out of sight, she had turned back to see him, a small dot in the distance, and realised that she must have been cycling by herself for ages. Only then did she wobble, and at the same time knew she had learned to ride a bike. Still, she stopped, got off and stubbornly wheeled it back to him, furious that he had left her on her own. She felt . . . what?

Leaning against the garden wall, battling to keep her eyes open, she saw Silas coming towards her. She remembered exactly what it was she had felt. She had felt cheated.

THE NIGHT OF THE FIRE

19 June 1937

Ezra arrived home about two o'clock that afternoon. In retrospect he wished he could have been more precise about the time, for timing would turn out to be of vital interest to the man from the Operation for Scientific Protection.

At nine-thirty, just as they were going to bed, Mother asked Ezra to check on his father. The skies were still dark with clouds, but at least it had stopped raining. Ezra could see no sign of Noel. He was about to knock on the shed door when he saw that it was open, swinging on its hinges. Inside, the trench, a wound, ran grave-deep down the middle, the earth neatly piled on either side. His father was not there. Ezra looked around. Beyond the garden, over the woods, was a particularly spectacular sunset.

There was a knock at the front door as he went back inside. Mrs Calthorpe stood on the step with her Bert.

'Have you seen it?' she said.

'I think it's Warlock Hall,' said Bert Calthorpe.

'No. You don't think, you know,' said his wife.

'Know what?' asked Ezra.

'The place is on fire,' said Mrs Calthorpe.

Ezra felt his insides turn over as an awful certainty hit him. That's where Father was, he felt sure of it. He would have seen the light in the sky and believed it to be another battle; heard the voices of the lost calling to him.

Ezra pushed past Mrs Calthorpe.

'Where are your manners?' she shouted after him.

Ezra didn't stop running. Through the darkening woods the glow in the distance guided him. He heard a sound, it rumbled dragon-loud, the very earth reverberating under him as it found its terrifying voice. The wave of noise engulfed everything, a huge explosion lit up the woods so that not one detail of bark or branch was lost. Through the trees, he could see the great house ablaze. The fire engine's bell chimed with the ringing in his ears. He didn't stop running. Gasping for breath, his lungs hurting, he pushed himself to go faster and more furiously onwards, the smell of burning filling his nostrils. All the time, under his breath, 'Our father who art in heaven . . .'

He burst out of the woods and stopped. Warlock Hall was an inferno. The staff were standing well back on the lawns, as if turned to stone by the heat.

'Mr Longbone,' he said, 'have you seen my father?'

'Yes, lad, he was here, but he went into the woods, on his way back home, I'd say.'

'And Miss Ruben?'

'I haven't seen her, nor Mr Molde, but I expect they're together. Silas Molde wouldn't leave her in all this. I managed to get the Bentley out.'

Mr Longbone was staring up at the Black Tower.

Ezra followed his gaze. There, at the top, he could see, illuminated by the encroaching flames, a woman screaming from a turret window, her voice lost in the roar and crackle of the fire god, dining so hungrily on such a gloriously combustible feast.

'Isn't that Vervaine Fox?' asked Ezra. 'Someone must save her.' He moved towards the house but Mr Longbone grabbed him. 'But we can't leave her up there, the floor is wooden, it will burn through and . . .'

'Best you don't look, lad. Believe me, the firemen have tried, but the flames are too intense. They can't get their ladders anywhere near the place.'

There was a hypnotic beauty about the magnitude of the fire. Ezra, like everyone else, watched awestruck as ravenous flames climbed the side of the tower. The floor must have burned away, for they heard a crack and Vervaine Fox fell like a stone into the core of the inferno.

From the two wings that made up the living quarters of Warlock Hall came the sound of brittle beams breaking, all the strength eaten from their wooden spines: the pop, hiss and crackle of the fire god grinding his teeth on the girders of the house. In the white heat the skeleton outline of rooms could be clearly seen. With an insatiable appetite the fire raged onward.

To Mr Ruben's staff it was becoming crystal clear that anyone still missing from their number was not going to be found alive. As the full extent of the disaster sank in, their livelihoods disappeared in the billowing smoke rising into the thunderous night.

Ezra couldn't see Amaryllis among the familiar faces. He stumbled across a confused Miss Bright.

'Are you all right?' he asked. Her face was covered in ashes and she had burned her hand.

'Terrible! Isn't it too terrible? If only they'd taken that poor woman to hospital sooner. Why didn't they when the ambulance was all ready and waiting? I can't bear to think about it. So frightening, not being able to escape . . .'

She looked as if she was about to faint. Ezra helped her to sit down on a stone seat.

'Amaryllis – have you seen her?'

'I heard something – a bang, a . . .'

'Yes, yes, but where is Amaryllis?'

Miss Bright let slip a Manila envelope from under her arm. Ezra bent down and handed it back, impatient to be gone, noticing and not noticing that it was addressed to Arnold Ruben.

'Yes . . . yes . . . I had . . .' she said, holding tight to the envelope. Her mind was filled with smoke. 'Oh, dear,' she said sadly, 'when was that?'

Ezra left the governess muttering to herself, and began to search for Amaryllis, asking the staff if they had seen her.

No one was sure. Some said they thought they had, others couldn't remember, it had all happened so fast, there had been a terrible explosion . . .

Clifford Lang was looking for the doctor who had arrived

late that afternoon to attend to Miss Fox. Many of the staff were in need of medical care.

'No,' he said, in answer to Ezra's question, 'and I can't find Mr Ruben or Mr Molde, either.'

They must all be at the picture palace, Ezra thought. But he didn't say so; he had never taken to Clifford Lang.

'There's Doctor Pincher,' said Mr Lang.

The doctor was helping his nurse into the ambulance. Her face was buried in her hands and, from where they stood, it appeared she had sustained some injuries. Before they could reach the ambulance it drove off at speed.

'What is he up to?' said Clifford Lang. He looked at his watch. Ezra could see reinforcements arriving: fire engines were belting up to the hall. He thought, they are going to have a battle on their hands if anything is to be salvaged from the wreckage. He turned towards the lake, the flames reflected in its still waters. Birds, confused by this unexpected dawn, were beginning to sing. He must find Father and Amaryllis. Past the tennis court, on the path leading to the picture palace, he caught a glimpse of his father up ahead. He was wearing his dressing-gown over his clothes.

Ezra ran after him, calling, until his father stopped and said, 'Is that you, Bernie? Is that you, lad?'

'No, Father,' said Ezra, 'it's me, it's your son.'

His father came up to him, his face covered in dirt, and putting one hand on his shoulder kissed him gently in the middle of his forehead. 'Go home, son, and look after your mother.'

Those were the last words his father said to him. He disappeared, ducking and diving in the darkness, ghosts following in his wake: the Tommy this and Tommy that, the long-gone, forgotten comrades buried in a foreign field of poppies.

'Wait,' shouted Ezra. He ran down the woodland path, trying to catch up with him, but his father had disappeared altogether.

All Ezra could think of now was Amaryllis. His father would find his own way home, he always did. In the clearing, the picture palace was illuminated. She would be there, he thought, with Mr Ruben and Silas Molde. He would have said, if his mind wasn't so rattled with fear, that the building was shuddering. He felt his heart soar when Amaryllis appeared on the mirrored steps. He called her name and started to run towards her. He lost his footing in the earth, muddy after all the rain, and fell flat on his face. He looked up to see a pair of two-tone shoes in front of him. As he scrambled to his feet, he was nearly deafened by the sound of gunfire.

Later, when there was so much of his memory he couldn't trust, he wondered if it had really happened. The two-tone shoes . . . he couldn't be sure. Time present became time past. He wasn't expecting the blow. It felt like a dead weight on the top of his head, crushing it, exploding in his brain. Oozy black tears of tar rolled down his eyes, sealing his vision. A bitter taste of dead leaves mingled in his mouth with the iron taste of blood.

*

It was about a quarter to eleven when Sir Basil Stanhope was contacted. He was at a very dull dinner party in Mayfair when the message reached him.

Getting up, he excused himself straight away. Giving his wife's arm a squeeze, he said, 'I'll make sure a car picks you up.'

This, Lady Dorothy knew of old, meant, 'Don't expect me home tonight.'

She smiled. Other men might have mistresses but dear old Basil had the secretive service.

Sir Basil arrived at Warlock Hall well after one o'clock the following morning. He had seen the blaze from a distance of three miles, but was still shocked by the sight that greeted him as he neared the house. He had been there several times socially and, though he wouldn't himself have chosen it as a home, it was without doubt a landmark, known throughout the district. Now, Sir Basil wondered if it wouldn't be known for all the wrong reasons.

The two wings of the house had collapsed and only the tower was still ablaze. The firemen had their work cut out. Clifford Lang greeted him.

'What happened?' asked Sir Basil.

'I think there were two separate fire bombs, one in the guest suite and the second on the ground floor where Mr Ruben had his study.'

'The staff – where are they?'

'I've had them taken to the village hall, sir. I thought it best they were all in one place.'

'Good. Mr Ruben?'

'He is missing, sir.'

'His daughter?'

'Missing,' said Lang.

'Is that the extent of the missing?'

'No,' He handed a sheet of paper to Sir Basil.

'Vervaine Fox?'

'Believed dead, sir. She was a house guest.'

'Silas Molde. Surely he is where he usually is, at the picture palace?'

'That is the other thing I think you should see, sir.'

Lang switched on his torch as they entered the woods. Along the path he shone the beam on a large patch of blood.

'This is where I found the Pascoe boy, unconscious, with a gash in his head.'

'Will he be all right?' asked Sir Basil.

Lang shrugged his shoulders. 'It looked pretty bad to me.'

Lang came to a halt. Sir Basil wasn't quite sure what he was looking at: it was a huge straight-sided crater, excavations for the foundations of a building.

'What, precisely, are you showing me?' asked Sir Basil.

'The picture palace,' replied Clifford Lang.

'Come off it, old chap, there's nothing here.'

'That's what I'm showing you. The picture palace has vanished into thin air.'

THE MORNING AFTER

Ezra had been taken to the cottage hospital on the night of the fire and then, on the orders of someone called Sir Basil Stanhope, transferred to Great Ormond Street Hospital. Nancy was able to have only the briefest time with Ezra before the ambulance came to take him to London.

It was hard to believe it was her Ezra she was looking at, her son, her sunshine, his face unrecognisable, all blown up with a huge black eye, and his bandaged head seeping blood.

'Oh, Mother,' wept Olive, 'it wasn't just a fall, was it?'

'No,' said Nancy, 'someone hit him over the head.'

'But why? He's never done wrong to anyone. Who could have done this to him?'

'I don't know, love.'

Nancy, her face pale, held Ezra's hand. 'Olive, love, you wait outside, that's my girl. I don't want him hearing you weep. He needs all his strength.'

Olive left and Nancy sat with Ezra.

'Just open your eyes, love,' she said, 'just once, please.'

Still Ezra's eyes, like the rest of him, were closed, shut off from the world.

Leaning forward, she kissed him and whispered, 'Don't you go dying on me, you hear me? You just keep going.'

It had gone three in the morning when Nancy and Olive arrived back at the cottage, exhausted, hoping as they had done all night that Noel might have returned. The idea that he too had been hurt, or worse, was unbearable.

The cottage was dark. Dawn was beginning to break through the trees and the whole area smelled of burning. They could still see the smoke and the red glow of the fire. Visible above the trees was the shell of the seventeenth-century tower. Opening the cottage door, Nancy knew Noel hadn't come home. She couldn't bring herself to acknowledge it, not after the night they'd just been through.

'Maybe he's in the shed,' said Olive, with a glimmer of hope, as if they both hadn't thought of it. She came back, crestfallen. 'Oh, Mother,' she said, wrapping her arms about her, 'what are we going to do?'

'What we always do,' said Nancy.

'What's that?' sniffed Olive.

'Survive.'

The morning after the fire, Nancy was up early, a routine that she was unable to break. She thought the range could do with a good going-over and that took arm muscle. Anything that involved work made you less likely to think, and thinking was the one thing she didn't want to do, not that early in the morning.

She nearly jumped out of her skin when there was a knock at the door. She stood up, wiped her hands on a cloth, patted down her apron, then slowly lifted the latch, expecting the worst in whatever form the worst came.

Standing there was Tommy Treacle.

'Is Ezra here, Mrs Pascoe?' said Tommy.

'No, love, they've taken him to a hospital in London.'

'Oh, that's bad. Is that bad, Mrs Pascoe?'

'I don't know, love,' said Nancy. 'I don't think it's good.'

Tommy looked more dishevelled than usual and, she thought, he seemed a little thinner.

'Come in, love, and I will make us both a cup of tea.'

For some strange reason she felt comforted by the sight of him and by his honest questions. She sat at the table while he ate a large slice of bread and dripping, sharing it with his mouse.

When he had finished, he said, as if he had been thinking about it for a long time, 'You need money for a big city like London.'

'Yes, love.'

'I don't know if they take mice on trains.'

'Neither do I, love,' said Nancy.

Tommy stood up and said, 'Thank you,' and he shook her hand. Nancy wanted to say, 'Don't go,' but that was daft. She watched him as, with his head solemnly bowed, he walked to the garden gate.

Nancy called after him, 'If you see Mr Pascoe, will you bring him home?'

Tommy's face lit up. 'I will find him. Me, Mrs Pascoe, me. Tommy Treacle will find him, you can trust that in me.'

Mrs Calthorpe was the next to arrive. She bustled her way into the kitchen.

'Have you heard?' she said.

'No,' said Nancy, her heart skipping a beat.

'Well, they say that Mr Ruben was killed in that fire, no doubt trying to get his daughter out, and then there is that actress Vervaine Locks.'

'Fox,' said Nancy, dully.

'The press are up there in car-loads, and the newsreel. I mean who would have thought our little village would be in the newspapers?'

Olive came down the stairs.

'Oh well, no surprise to find you here,' she said.

'Well, I never, young lady,' said Mrs Calthorpe. 'And what do you mean by that?'

'I mean,' said Olive, 'if you hadn't gone telling Father about Mrs Popplin he wouldn't have had another of his turns. You're a meddling old cow.'

'Olive,' shouted Nancy, 'stop it this instant.'

'Well, she ruddy well is,' said Olive, grabbing her coat and hat.

Mrs Calthorpe folded her arms under her bosom and jiggled them as if they were the power behind the throne.

'I only answered your father's question truthfully. It's not my responsibility that he goes losing his marbles. Goodness knows how your mother has lived so long with such a madman . . .'

And before she could finish it was Nancy who told her bluntly that was quite enough and she was to leave that minute. Mrs Calthorpe said not another word as she scuttled away, no doubt to report all that had been said to anyone who cared to listen.

'I'm going to get Wilfred and we'll look for Father,' said Olive.

She opened the door to find a man in a tweed suit standing there. Olive stared at his bushy eyebrows.

'Good morning,' he said, 'is Mrs Pascoe at home?'

'Yes. Well, you'd better come in. Mother, you have another visitor.'

Sir Basil smiled his most jovial of smiles, the one that always reassured people they were dealing with a crumbled teacake. But he could see immediately that Mrs Pascoe was not so easily deceived.

'What can I do for you?' she asked, terrified that he might be there to tell her Ezra had died in the night.

'I came to put your mind at rest. Ezra, although still very poorly, is showing signs that he will recover.'

'Thank you,' said Nancy, feeling her knees go weak.

'May we sit down?'

'Oh yes, I am sorry. Olive, love, put the kettle on.'

'No need.' Sir Basil took from his pocket a silver flask and, asking for glasses, poured Nancy a generous tot of brandy. 'I think it might do you more good than the cup that cheers.'

Sir Basil turned to Olive. 'Don't let me keep you, Miss Pascoe.'

'Will you be all right, Mother?' asked Olive.

Nancy nodded.

When she'd left, Sir Basil took out a card and put it in

front of Nancy. It read:

Sir Basil Stanhope
Operation for Scientific Protection

Nancy looked at it for a long time before saying, 'You think the fire had something to do with the memory machine?'

'Precisely,' said Sir Basil, helping himself to a measure of brandy. 'Have you ever heard of Proust, Mrs Pascoe?'

'No, who is he?'

'A French writer. There's a famous episode with a madeleine – a cake – in the first section of his novel. He is eating the cake and that is the key to memories forgotten. In the last volume, *Time Regained*, a flashback like the one caused by the madeleine is the beginning of the resolution of the story. Proust never missed a thing, a canny man if ever there was one, took note of every detail.'

'Forgive me,' said Nancy, 'but I have only read Charles Dickens. These new, fandangle writers have rather passed me by.'

'That is not my point. My point, Mrs Pascoe, is that I believe – in fact, I know now I've met you – that you are a canny woman. You don't miss much, and I wonder if you would tell me all that you recall of yesterday, in particular anything concerning Miss Fox.'

'Ezra and Miss Ruben found her in the grounds when she was taken ill, and Ezra came to the kitchen for help. Miss Fox did look awful, but . . .' She paused. 'I don't like to speak ill of the dead.'

'But what, Mrs Pascoe?'

'I never trusted her. After all she was an actress. I believe that's what they do – act.'

Sir Basil laughed. 'She was taken to her room? Correct me if I'm wrong.'

'Yes, I helped her upstairs.'

'And did you see Silas Molde?'

'Not then, but later, several times.'

'I want to know whether you thought he was acting.'

Nancy took her time before she said, 'Silas Molde isn't a bad man. I never felt him to be. I think he carries a lot of weight. Not physically, but within himself, as if he was Atlas carrying the memory machine on his shoulders. I'd never seen him so genuinely worried as he was yesterday.'

'When did Mr Ruben return from London?'

'I think about five-thirty.'

'Did you see him?'

'Yes, he went into the kitchen, he'd never done that before. The kitchen maid was quite taken aback. He walked round, inspecting it, and then he came into my office, and I asked him how Miss Fox was and he said not well. He said that I'd been an excellent cook and asked if I'd been happy working for him. I said yes. He then told me that Miss Bright had informed him that Ezra was a very clever boy and would go far.'

'Did you think that was strange?'

Nancy laughed a hollow laugh. 'So much in that house has been strange for a long time, as I'm sure any of the staff could tell you.'

'What happened then?'

'He asked if I had finished Miss Ruben's birthday cake. I showed it to him. He had been most specific as to what it was to be and how it was to look, and what was to be iced on it.'

'And how was that?'

'It was his favourite, a coffee-and-walnut sponge, decorated with coffee-butter icing. The words were the hardest part for there were so many of them.'

'What did they say?'

'"If you go down in the woods today you're sure of a big surprise." No "Happy Birthday", nothing like that. He asked for a knife and cut himself a slice and sat in my office in silence and ate it. Then he left and that was the last I saw of him. I was home by six.'

'My dear lady, Proust would have been proud of you. One last thing: did you notice anything on your walk home?'

'Yes, an ambulance passed me, going towards the hall.'

'Was it going fast, bells ringing?'

'No, I would say it was ambling.'

'That's all I need to ask you now. When your son is better I'll need to speak to him too.'

The newspapers, to begin with, concentrated solely on the tragic death of Vervaine Fox and the mysterious disappearance of Arnold Ruben.

The goddess of the silver screen has been identified only by A DIAMOND RING purchased in Asprey's of Bond Street.

Miss Fox's picture was on all the front pages with particulars about her luxurious life style, her lovers, her houses, her cars and her romance with the multi-millionaire Arnold Ruben.

Little was mentioned about the others who were missing and were yet to be accounted for: Amaryllis Ruben, Silas Molde and Noel Pascoe.

The local papers concentrated on their own home-grown heroes. Noel Pascoe had been awarded the Victoria Cross for his bravery in the Great War, and neither hide nor hair had been seen of him since that terrible night. Then there was the unexplained, brutal attack on his son, Ezra.

The village had a lot more to say on the matter. There was a feeling that something supernatural might have happened on the night of the fire, for now the area around the woods was firmly cordoned off and no one knew what it was the authorities were hiding.

Tommy Treacle told Nancy there was just a ruddy big hole where the picture palace had been.

'You shouldn't be going up there.'

'It just went whoosh, and vanished,' said Tommy.

'Did you see that, Tommy?'

'No,' he said, sheepishly. 'Houdini did, though.'

OUT OF TIME

Amaryllis remembers little of how she came to be in this empty bedroom, only a jumble of images without narrative; no beginning, middle or end. She has awoken to find herself lying on a child's bed in this bare room, a room she has never seen before. The last thing she is conscious of is the colour green, everything else is a half-rubbed-out memory. She hears a hum, a distant hum.

Was it yesterday, a week ago? Amaryllis sits up, her head aching. She is wearing a petticoat. Once, when time was still counted by the tick of a clock, she would have been able to make sense of the world. Now there is just this hurting strangeness, which has taken root in the soil of solitude.

The room is narrow and has a window at one end with a blind drawn down. On a chair next to the bed is a pile of soiled clothes. They have nothing to do with her. There's blood on them. Then she sees in their folds the muzzle of a revolver, a black, hollow eye looking for its victim.

Leaving the bedroom, she goes into a hall. It appears to be a large apartment and for a moment – just like that moment before you realise the grown ups have been lying to you all along and there is no one to trust – in that moment she has the vaguest of hopes that she can get back home. Every room is bare, not a stick of furniture, just parquet flooring, white walls and shaded windows. The only thing the kitchen has to offer is a cathedral of a fridge, empty except for a jar of peanut butter. Its label is printed with the rays of the sun.

That jar jogs her memory. She jumps away as a cockroach hurries out from its hiding place. This has happened before, just the way it is happening now. She hates cockroaches. There had been one on the night . . . a hot night . . . she can't remember . . . she is losing her mind . . . all there is is the colour green. The cockroach scuttles across the lino-covered floor and she rushes from the room, shutting the kitchen door.

In the awesome stillness of the apartment she is jolted by the rattling of keys. She turns, and stares transfixed at the front door. Someone is turning the key in the lock.

She darts into the bedroom and retrieves the revolver, knocking over the chair in her haste. It falls with a thud that echoes through the empty rooms.

Whoever it is now knows she is there.

The revolver is heavy, cold, obscenely real in a way that nothing else here appears to be. Her hand shakes.

The door grinds open.

'Amaryllis, are you in here?'

Amaryllis backs away out of the hall into the gloom of the big room. A man is silhouetted in the doorway, the dim light from the corridor throwing two shadows across the parquet floor. She can see his face. He is wearing round dark glasses and has with him a suitcase, her initials clearly marked on it.

'Oh, there you are.' He moves towards Amaryllis, slowly. 'You know me – I am Silas – Uncle Silas.'

She holds on to the gun tightly, her finger on the trigger.

'How do I know you're not an apparition? What would it matter if I fired? None of this is real.'

'Wait, wait,' says Silas. Damn it, he thinks, I thought I had taken the gun. A stupid mistake. 'I am real, so are you. Please put it down.'

She pulls the trigger and jumps back as it goes off with a resounding bang.

Silas clasps his arm. The sleeve of his jacket is singed by the bullet. Amaryllis, shocked by what she has done, lets the revolver fall to the ground. Nothing makes sense.

Silas picks it up and puts it in his pocket. He says angrily, 'Why don't you ever do what you're told?'

'Where's my father?'

That much she can remember. Her father, distant, puppet-like. Silas examines his sleeve. No damage done. None that he would feel in this world.

'I don't know. He was supposed to be with us when the machine was activated, but he never came. The time was preset, nothing could be done to stop it.'

'When was that?'

'It doesn't matter.'

But it does, she thinks, it must matter. If there is no time, where are the coat hangers to hang your days on, to fill up your wardrobe with years?

'I never, ever wanted this,' shouted Amaryllis.

'It is your birthday present. All you need to understand is that this whole world was designed for you. Unfortunately, there are some difficulties. They will soon be ironed out. For the time being, you must stay in this apartment. It is for your own safety.'

Silas goes to the corner of the room and fiddles with a television set. She hadn't noticed it before. From it comes a green, hypnotic light.

'You'll like it here, just wait and see.'

She finds herself drawn to the screen. Her mind is stilled by the green light. The more she looks at it, the harder it is to turn away.

'I'll come back for you. I'll find out what happened to your father. Everything will be all right, you must believe that. You do believe that, don't you?'

Amaryllis nods. Silas, relieved to find the light from the television working on her, disappears into the bedroom and comes out with the soiled clothes.

'Don't worry. Uncle Silas will make everything all right.'

She says nothing.

'Now that's more like it.' He turns to leave. 'Just remember what I told you.'

She knows he is watching her. She says in a monosyllabic voice, 'Everything will be all right.'

'*Wunderbar*,' he says to himself.

She hears him leave, turning the key in the lock.

Maybe, she thinks, this is a dream and I will wake up. But only if I stop looking at the green light.

It is hard, hurtful to look away. She closes her eyes; she walks backwards from it, feeling its octopus tentacles stretching away from her, losing their grip on her mind, reluctant to let go. Only when she has closed the door is she free from their clutches.

What did the man call her? What did he say her name was? All gone.

Now there are two rooms out of bounds. Here in the hall, in the no-man's-land between them, she opens the suitcase that the man left. Inside are clothes. She puts on a new, unworn, satin slip and a small red cardigan. There are plimsolls, a linen coat and a cloche hat. At the bottom of the case she sees, hidden in the fabric of other bits of clothing, a pencil, a diary and a necklace: a silver tiger on a chain. She holds it in her hand, a treasure from the seashore of another cosmos where once she had footprints that held weight. She fastens it round her neck. For a moment it is cold against her skin. Slowly, she looks at the diary, through pages and pages of empty lines. With a deep sense of disappointment, she is about to put it back when she finds, right in the middle, written close to the margin:

It's my birthday, I am seventeen. I am nearly all grown up. I told my father I am not a doll. He just said I wasn't right. I asked him, what do you mean, I'm not right?

He said I have no moral boundaries and I needed to go where no more harm could come to me, where I could heal. I asked him what this prison is made out of and he said, 'Memories.'

I wanted to scream, but that would have proved he was right.

He said it was the shape of the future. I told him, no, no, but he wasn't listening. Surely the past is there for us to remember? If there is no future but the worn out memories of others, then I will be lost. I don't want my future stolen from me.

He told me to leave and to go to my room, his face steel-hard.

I am going to fight for my freedom, come what may.

Amaryllis stares at the exuberant handwriting. They are her words but when did she scribble them down?

She decides what she is going to do. All she will take with her is the diary and pencil. They fit in the pocket of her coat. She will be an explorer, wear her courage like armour, make a map, find her way home.

It occurs to her that the diary might be the only solid thing in this theatre of memory, for nothing else has the honesty of reality, now the revolver has gone and the man with the sly name has turned the key in the lock. The idea of staying here is impossible. For a while she sits wondering how to escape. The key is still in the lock, on the outside. Carefully she pushes at it until it clatters to the floor. Lying on her belly she can see under the door. The key is just out of reach. She tries to retrieve it with the pencil. Suddenly she recoils, for on the other side are the bare feet of a child. Amaryllis quickly pulls herself away and leans against the wall, her heart beating fast, waiting for whoever or whatever it is to go.

The key slides under the door.

As she grabs it a line from a song floats in her head:

Every teddy bear who's been good
Is sure of a treat today.

Silence. Not a breath, not a movement.

Lying once more on her tummy she can see nothing. No one is there. She had imagined the little feet. Gathering her courage, she unlocks the door. The long corridor is deserted. Just metal green-shaded lights hanging from plaited hangman's ropes of electrical cable. On and on they go, into oblivion, giving out a yellow light of loneliness. Quietly, she lets the door shut, making a mental note of the number of the apartment. Eighty-seven. She starts to walk down the corridor. She looks behind her and nearly jumps out of her skin. Standing not so very far away is the child. She is about four years old and is wearing a summer nightie. She has dark hair, Shirley Temple hair, in thick ringlets. She has the sweetest of faces with bright, violet-coloured eyes.

'Mummy, mummy,' she says. 'I found your earring. Look.'

Amaryllis backs away. I am well and truly lost, she thinks.

VINEGAR AND
BROWN PAPER

July 1937 to February 1938

Tommy Treacle had gone every day to the Pascoe's cottage to ask after Ezra. Come rain or shine, there he was, his mouse Houdini in his pocket.

'Will Ezra's head get better, Mrs Pascoe?'

'We hope so, Tommy.'

'Will they wrap it in vinegar and brown paper?"

'No, Tommy, it's not that sort of fall.'

'Is Mr Pascoe home yet?'

'No, Tommy.'

'Are you sad, like my mum?'

'Yes, love, very.'

His father, Fred Cutler, who had been ill for quite some time, had died in late June and Mrs Cutler was beside herself with grief. After a while, Tommy had stopped coming.

As Nancy fed the washing through the mangle, squeezing the water out between the rollers, Mrs Calthorpe said, over the garden fence, 'She's taken it very bad, has Enid Cutler. Lost that much weight she has. But as I said to Bert, it couldn't have come as that much of a shock, what with Fred having no legs

--- 153 ---

and things. Now she's left with that half-baked lad to look after.'

Nancy was trying her best not to listen, until Mrs Calthorpe went, as she always did, a step too far.

'I see they've put your Noel on the list of those officially lost in the fire. Perhaps it's for the best,' she said. 'I should have thought it would have been quick, that's what my Bert says, anyhow.'

Nancy picked up the galvanized-iron tub, full of wrung-out washing.

'Doreen,' she said firmly, 'my business is my business and it doesn't concern you. '

She went inside and closed the back door.

She had lived all her life in the village and had never understood why people couldn't keep themselves to themselves, instead of all the nit-picking that went on, all the twitching of net curtains, all the noses in other people's handkerchiefs. But human nature never changes and there was really only one subject that anyone wanted to talk about: Warlock Hall. It had even brought tourists to the sleepy village, come to see the ruins for themselves. They had been disappointed to discover the area cordoned off, but if they had visited the teashop they would have found Mrs Calthorpe working there, happy to embellish and polish any good, fantastical notion.

Then, out of the blue, something quite extraordinary happened to the Pascoe family. In the middle of July, a few weeks before Ezra was due to return home, Nancy received an official-looking letter in a thick white envelope. She'd had to sit down after she'd read it, and only then did she believe her good fortune. In fact, she did something that Olive had rarely seen her mother do, not even when told of Father's disappearance or Ezra's injury. She burst into tears.

On the morning of the fire, Arnold Ruben had informed his lawyer that he and his daughter were going away for some considerable time. The house would be closed down and Mrs Pascoe was to receive an annuity and a grant for the education of her son.

Olive asked, 'What will happen if he can never go back to school again?'

'We will cross that bridge if we come to it,' said her mother.

Ezra had liked Sir Basil Stanhope from the first time he'd visited him at Great Ormond Street Hospital. Ezra had told him he would like his diary back, but the diary wasn't forthcoming. It had been removed from his bedroom when the government men had searched it after the attack.

When his head had stopped aching and he could see straight, the diary was returned to him. Ezra quietly flicked through the pages.

'You write well, old chap,' said Sir Basil. 'Your last entry is on the seventeenth of June, two days before the fire. May I ask you what you remember of subsequent events?'

'Nothing, really,' said Ezra.

'Very well. I will tell you something. Let's see if it brings anything back. What I'm about to tell you is a secret, do you understand?'

Ezra nodded.

'The picture palace vanished into thin air. Not one brick, not one pane of mirrored glass remains, only a big crater where the foundations were.'

'But that's impossible.'

'That's what our people said. But, old chap, I'm beginning to believe in the impossible. There is no rational explanation for what happened.'

'Do you think my father and the others disappeared with it?'

'That is one theory. Not the official theory, you understand.'

At the beginning of August Sir Basil made the last of several visits to Ezra and took with him a present. It was a Parker fountain pen. Ezra had never in his life been given something so valuable. It was marbled red, with a gold nib. The ink was not the cheap, blotchy kind he had had at school, but smooth, like silk.

'I thought if you remembered anything, old chap, you could write it down and send it to me,' said Sir Basil, handing Ezra his card.

Next day Henry Longbone brought Ezra home in style in Mr Ruben's Bentley, which the lawyer had entrusted to his care.

The whole village turned out to welcome Ezra home. He looked well, yet both Mother and Olive noticed over the following weeks how much quieter he was and more subdued. He asked about his friend Len and about Tommy Treacle, but he didn't talk about his father.

Ezra was allowed to sit a late entrance examination to Broughton Grammar School, just before term began. As it turned out, he won a scholarship, all fees paid. Before he started, Ezra and Len had been to Mrs Cutler's house to enquire after Tommy Treacle as no one had seen him about for a while.

Mrs Cutler had opened the front door only long enough to reply that her Tommy wasn't feeling well. They went again a few times, always to be told the same old story. Ezra was so wrapped up in his new school that to his shame he slightly forgot Tommy. At the end of the autumn term Ezra and Len realised Tommy Treacle had become invisible. As Nancy said later, he had been swept under the carpet of other people's consciousness, a problem no one wanted to look at.

It was in December that the village had a whole new scandal to unsettle them. Saturdays were always busy in Mrs Marshall's dress shop, even more so in the weeks leading up to Christmas. Mrs Marshall, a small, bright, budgerigar of a woman, employed two assistants, one was Mrs Cutler, the other, Olive Pascoe. Olive was her favourite by far. Poor Enid Cutler had lost the knack of selling ever since her husband had died that summer.

Mrs Marshall had said to Olive, 'It's very sad and all that about Fred Cutler, but still, in my book, it's no excuse for letting yourself go. I'm not a charity, I'm trying to run a business and there's nothing more off-putting for our lady customers than a dreary-looking sales assistant.'

Olive had told Mother about Mrs Cutler letting herself go,

but even Nancy didn't suspect that there was anything wrong with the poor woman other than grief which, as she knew herself, was hard enough to bear. The difference between Nancy Pascoe and Enid Cutler was that Nancy, despite what the police told her, never believed for a moment that Noel wouldn't be coming home, whereas there was no disputing the fact that Fred Cutler was dead and buried.

That Saturday morning, Mrs Marshall said to Olive, 'Go round and ask her highness if she will deign to come to work this afternoon.'

Mrs Cutler had been absent from the shop since Wednesday.

It started to snow as Olive made her way down the street of tightly knitted, gossipy houses. She knocked on Mrs Cutler's front door and noticed the milk hadn't been taken in, but sometimes people forget. Perhaps she wasn't well, that's why she hadn't come to work. Olive knocked again and again. It now struck her as all wrong, and she went along the small alleyway round to the back and climbed over the fence, laddering a perfectly good pair of silk stockings in the process. It was freezing and it made no sense to Olive that the sheets had been left hanging on the line. Later, she thought sadly that they looked like flags of surrender and she supposed in a way they were. They blocked the scullery window and Olive had to stand on an upturned flowerpot to look in. She saw, sticking out from behind the kitchen door, a pair of feet. Olive used the same pot to break the window, and climbed into the scullery. The smell of gas was something terrible, it stank out the whole house.

She found Mrs Cutler with her head in the oven. She ran to the neighbours and asked them to call an ambulance from the telephone box, but it was too late, Mrs Cutler had been dead some time. The police came, took down the details, then left.

It was blooming cold in the house, as if the fires hadn't been lit in ages. Nancy, Ezra and Olive searched for Tommy, but he was nowhere to be found.

'Of course,' said Olive, 'it being Saturday, he'll be where he always is, at the Cinema Club.'

The fact that he hadn't been seen there in weeks had registered with none of them.

Ezra found him just as they were leaving, in the one place they hadn't thought to look: the cellar. No one knew how long Tommy Treacle had been imprisoned there. The gas had sent him to sleep; he was half-frozen, dehydrated and smelled of dead mouse.

'We should call the ambulance and get him taken to hospital straight away,' said Olive.

'No,' said Mother firmly. 'We're taking him home and that's the end of it. Ezra, go and get Mr Longbone and that car of his, and call the doctor from the phone box. Tell him to come to our cottage as quickly as he can.'

'But Mother,' said Olive, 'surely he would be better off . . .'

Her mother interrupted her. 'They would send Tommy to one of those institutions I rescued your father from, and over my dead body will he be going there. I know what they do to lads like him. I've seen it with my own eyes.'

They drove Tommy home in the lovingly kept Bentley, Henry Longbone worrying all the time that a smell like that might linger.

'Poppycock,' said Nancy firmly.

It took the combined strength of Ezra and Mr Longbone to get Tommy Treacle up the stairs to the bedroom. There they found the cause of the pong. Houdini was dead in his pocket. By the look of the mouse it had been dead for a while.

Nancy took the poor little creature away.

'What are you going to do with that?' said Olive, holding her nose.

'Bury it by the shed.'

'Why?'

'Your father told me he remembered Fred Cutler took a white mouse to war. He still had it after they blew his legs off. He kept it and brought it home with him. When Tommy was old enough, Fred bought him his first white mouse. He told him mice were very lucky and extremely wise.'

Olive went and found a box for a coffin.

For the next ten days the doctor came and went, leaving bottles of medicine. Tommy had bronchitis. He lay like a plank of wood, too terrified to move. Every night he wet the bed, every morning he said the same thing.

'I'm sorry, Mrs Pascoe. Don't send me into the darkness again.'

A week later, Ezra went to the pet shop in Broughton and bought him a white mouse with a black patch over one eye, and a cage.

'I've got you a present, Tommy.'

'For me?'

'Yes.'

'A present for Tommy Treacle. But I've been bad.'

'No, you haven't, Tommy,' said Ezra, sitting on the edge of the bed.

'Mum said I was . . .' He stopped. 'Are you sending me home? I don't want to go back to the darkness.'

Ezra put the cage with the mouse in it on the bed.

Tommy gently let the mouse out. It bit his finger and then ran up the sleeve of his pyjamas. Retrieving it, he said, 'It isn't Houdini, is it?'

'No.'

'I tried to warm him up, but he'd gone all funny and cold.'

'There was nothing you could do.'

'Is this my mouse?'

'Yes.'

'I'll call him Popeye. He's very cheeky. Popeye's cheeky and has a friend called Olive.'

'That's right.'

The mouse was the beginning of Tommy Treacle getting better and by the time Christmas had come and gone he felt, and was felt to be, a part of the family.

The new term started and Ezra would set off for school every morning accompanied by Tommy with Popeye in his pocket. At the bus stop Tommy would wave like a concerned parent then, turning with a hop and a skip, go home through the woods that surrounded what had once been Warlock Hall. Here, for an hour or so, he'd play out the films he had seen that weekend at the Saturday Cinema Club. The rest of the day he'd spend in Noel Pascoe's old shed. At dinner time he would wash his hands and eat with Nancy before returning there. The only two breaks in his happy routine were to help make pea soup on Fridays, and to go to the pictures on Saturdays. It was Ezra who had first been allowed to see what Tommy Treacle had been up to in Father's shed. In this forbidden land where he never dared go, Ezra stared flabbergasted at the transformation.

Tommy had filled in the trench with earth and lovingly laid all the boards back, nailing each one down. He had neatly put away all Father's paraphernalia from the war, painted the walls white and – this was what took Ezra's breath away – in no childish hand, but with an originality and a quality of craftsmanship, had drawn in pencil images of his mouse in all his many positions, every detail captured. Ezra felt himself to be an explorer who had stumbled across cave drawings for the first time.

Speechless, he took Mother and Olive to see the shed.

'Did you really draw these?' asked Olive.

Tommy hung his head. 'Have I done bad?'

Mother wrapped her arms around him. 'No, love, you've healed a wound, made the place look right again. And as for the drawings, they are beautiful, Tommy, I had no idea you could draw like this. Who taught you?'

'My dad. He drew.'

After that, while Ezra did his homework, Tommy Treacle, tongue sticking out, did his drawings. Olive showed him how to write the words he wanted to put underneath them. The drawings were so light but his handwriting so heavy the marks nearly ripped the pages.

It was in February, when the snow started again, that Ezra, sitting in front of the fire, trying to work out a mathematical equation, glanced absent-mindedly at what Tommy was drawing. This time it wasn't a mouse, but what it was sent a shiver down his spine. Tommy Treacle had drawn the picture palace, not one detail missed out.

'When did you see this?' asked Ezra.

'Today,' said Tommy, 'I saw it today.'

MISS BRIGHT'S INVESTIGATION

May 1938

Miss Bright had taken a position locally at a private school for girls. She had no desire to return to London and with her new job came a small cottage. There was a garden at the back and roses grew round the front door. Finally she felt she had somewhere in which to make a life.

But the terrible night of the fire cast a long shadow and, like many of the survivors of Warlock Hall, she had suffered from recurring nightmares. Miss Bright's were always of Amaryllis Ruben. And of the dreadful photographs she had found.

Of course she had been interviewed by the men from the government, like everyone else. Being an honest woman she had answered each of their questions to the best of her ability.

When had she last seen Miss Ruben? In the early evening.

Had she ever sat for Mr Ruben's memory recordings? Yes.

Any side effects? Yes. She had experienced appalling headaches.

For how long had they lasted? Two days.

Then, holding her breath, she had waited with a thumping heart for them to ask the one question she didn't want to answer.

Had she come across anything that might be of interest to this investigation?

Instead, they had thanked her for her cooperation and dismissed her, as so many people did. After all, what would such a drab little woman know?

As she herself would say to her gals, the question is king. The men from the government might have done well to have pushed their questioning further. Miss Bright felt almost giddy with relief, for the last thing she wanted was to show anyone the pictures she had found. Some things are best kept to oneself.

At home she'd stared with loathing at the Manila envelope on the mantel shelf. She had stumbled across it while escaping the fire. In the crush of people it had caught her eye. Someone, in their haste to get away, must have dropped it.

She had picked it up with the full intention of returning it to its owner. But as its owner had been missing since the night of the fire, she had opened the envelope and tipped the contents on to her writing desk. She stared with horror, unable to believe her eyes. It was impossible to imagine who would have taken such revolting pictures; they were nothing short of an abomination. Amaryllis Ruben lying naked on a bed. It was too disgusting, it was unnatural. The girl looked asleep, or worse, drugged. Why Mr Ruben had these degrading pictures she couldn't imagine. She felt it was best all round that no one saw them, but she resisted the immediate temptation to burn them. Intuitively she felt they were connected to the mystery of Warlock Hall. Such evidence could prove vital. She decided to keep them safe until someone asked her the right question. There was, set in the wall by the fireplace, a small cupboard with a lock, and here she put the envelope under a pile of old knitting patterns and tried her best not to think about what she had seen. Nevertheless she was still troubled with nightmares and they were always the same.

In the woods surrounding Warlock Hall, the picture palace is before her, a green light oozing from it. Nearby she hears heavy breathing, someone is running through the woods, she sees him in slices, the trees making him into a flip-book figure.

He is carrying something white, something human . . . her vision is blurred . . . if only she could focus . . . Then he stops. A revolver is fired, she feels the wind of the bullet as it passes her. The man has vanished. In front of her stands a girl in a mask made of cloth. From her lips comes a trickle of blood. She is on the point of saying 'Amaryllis' when she wakes up, always disorientated, always terrified. Now she has no wish to sleep, preferring to wait for the dawn before she rests again . . .

Miss Bright was a practical woman and nothing apart from the loss of her lover had ever defeated her. She was dashed if this would. There was only one thing to do and that was to confront her nightmare by revisiting Warlock Wood, a place she had avoided ever since the fire.

One afternoon she put on a pair of stout walking boots, picked up her stick and set off.

Disregarding the notice which read:

GOVERNMENT ORDER
NO ACCESS
KEEP OUT

Miss Bright followed an overgrown path. She had no particular route in mind and only the shadow of a memory of sitting for Mr Ruben's experiment. It was mostly by instinct that she found her way back to the spot where she assumed the picture palace to be. She stared bewildered at the crater in the barren ground, unable to make her reason stand the right way up. What was reality? What was a dream? She knew the picture palace had existed. One's own eyes don't lie, do they?

The phenomenon reawoke Miss Bright's fascination with physics, a subject she had studied with her father, a professor of science. He had been ahead of his time, believing a girl should be fully educated, especially if she had a first-rate mind, like his daughter. In the sad years after the war, science was the only thing that had kept Miss Bright from falling apart. She had been accepted to read physics at Oxford. Afterwards she discovered that being clever did not mean she was employable in a man's world.

With a pair of binoculars and her Kodak Brownie 2 camera she began her own home-grown investigation. She returned regularly to the site and kept meticulous notes of the times of her visits, the weather and when the government men came.

Over the winter months she started to research the probabilities of an entire building vanishing. The more she read, the more intrigued she became.

It was in the spring of 1938 that Miss Bright came to the startling conclusion that the answer to the riddle of the disappearing picture palace must lie in a combination of the equations found in Einstein's Theory of Relativity and in Meteorological Constants. Her former physics professor, now retired, much enjoyed his afternoon teas and his stimulating talks with Matilda Bright.

'You see, dear lady,' he said, 'scientists are arguing that time has slowed down. The speed of light was always thought to be a constant. No one believed it would change.'

'If it slowed down altogether, would time stop?' she had asked, nibbling a jam tart.

'I suppose it would come to a halt, yes.' For a moment he was silent, as the full implication of this sank in. Then he said, 'Theoretically, it's not impossible. We would be eating tea into eternity.'

It had been a good spring. The woods that May were full of bluebells, it was the perfect excuse for Miss Bright to investigate further. That warm day in the depths of the bluebell woods she nearly jumped out of her skin when Tommy Treacle leapt from behind a tree.

'Your money or your life.'

He had a spotted hankie tied over his mouth.

'Is this a hold-up?' said Miss Bright, a smile of relief spreading across her face.

'Yes. It's for my mouse, Popeye.'

'Is he the head of your terrible gang?'

'Yes,' said Tommy, a little unsure.

'Then what can I give you?'

'I know,' said Tommy, 'you could let me take a picture with your camera.'

'But would that be enough to satisfy a sinister highway robber like yourself?'

Tommy pulled down the spotted hankie, his face falling. 'It's only me, Miss Bright, Tommy Treacle.'

'I know,' said Miss Bright, and handed Tommy her camera.

'What do you want to take a photograph of?'

'Mr Ruben's picture place,' said Tommy. Miss Bright felt her heart miss a beat. 'Come on, I'll show you.'

She followed Tommy through the woods.

'There,' he said.

Before her was the picture palace. Miss Bright was deeply frightened. Tommy seemed unsurprised by its appearance.

'It comes and goes,' he said. 'I've never been inside. I think it's a trap, but Tommy Treacle ain't that stupid.'

Miss Bright was regretting letting go of her camera.

'Will you take a photograph?' she whispered. 'Could you do that now?'

Tommy clicked.

'And again,' she said, going closer. It was just as she remembered it except the sign over the front was lit up. It said:

The Night of the Tiger starring Vervaine Fox

The whole place hummed; a green light oozed from its very foundations.

Through the swing doors, she caught sight of him. He hadn't changed. He was in his uniform, that smile on his face, still young, waiting for her by the box office with two cinema tickets in his hand. He was waving . . .

'Miss Bright, don't go in,' said Tommy. 'It will gobble you up.'

But Miss Bright wasn't listening. Just like the man in the two-tone shoes, she went running in . . .

'. . . and, whizz bang, she was gone. Just like a conjuring trick,' Tommy told Ezra.

'Where's the camera?' asked Ezra.

Tommy brought it out from under his jacket. 'Have I done bad?'

'No,' said Ezra. 'You were very clever.'

Ezra wasted not a moment in going down to the telephone box on the village green only to find Sergeant Bert Calthorpe bivouacked outside it, sitting in a deckchair with sandwiches and a flask.

'I need to use the phone,' said Ezra.

'Well, you can't. I put an advertisement in the local paper, to sell a tandem, and this is the number I gave for anyone who felt like buying it.'

'It's an emergency.'

'Oh, yes?' said Bert, looking around him. 'What kind, lad?'

'Please, I need to use the phone.'

'Bugger off,' replied Bert.

Ezra went home.

Nancy looked up, worried.

'Have you heard Tommy's story?'

Ezra nodded.

'Do you think it's true?'

'It is,' said Tommy, 'I swear it on Popeye's life.'

'Then we should tell the police.'

'No,' said Ezra firmly. 'We need to tell Sir Basil Stanhope. And I can't because Bert Calthorpe has invaded the telephone box.'

'There may be some simple explanation for all this?' said Mother. 'Why don't we wait a day before bothering important people?'

'No, Mother,' said Ezra. 'I really must tell Sir Basil at once.'

Nancy let out a sigh, got up, put on her hat and coat and walked with Ezra and Tommy down to the village green.

Bert was finishing off his rations.

'Sold the tandem, then, Bert?' asked Nancy.

'Sort of.'

'Then we'll use the phone – right now.'

Next morning, Ezra and Tommy went to Miss Bright's cottage, to make sure she hadn't by some miracle turned up again. No one was in. They returned home to find, parked outside the house, an Armstrong Siddeley convertible. Inside the cottage, eating buttered toast and drinking tea, was Sir Basil Stanhope.

'Have you come to take me away?' said Tommy, crestfallen. 'I haven't been bad.'

'So,' said Sir Basil, 'this is the young man who has a mouse.'

Tommy looked surprised. 'Yes, that's me, Tommy Treacle.'

'Tell me, Master Tommy Treacle,' said Sir Basil, 'did you see Miss Bright yesterday?'

'She's nice, Miss Bright, she has small breasts, not like Mrs Calthorpe next door. She has huge breasts that she has to hold up by folding her arms. She doesn't like my mouse.'

'Love,' said Mother, gently, 'just tell this gentleman what happened.'

'I clicked the camera,' said Tommy. 'I took pictures of the picture palace.'

'With Miss Bright's camera?' said Sir Basil.

'She said I could.'

'And what photographs did you take?'

'I took a picture of the man waiting for her.'

'What man, Tommy?'

'He knew her, he did. In his hand he had two tickets and he pushed open the door. I couldn't stop her. Then Miss Bright and the building were all gone.'

'Where is the camera now?' asked Sir Basil.

Ezra went upstairs to fetch it.

'No one's touched it.'

'I took the pictures, me, Tommy Treacle, that's who.'

'Tommy,' said Ezra, 'tell Sir Basil about the man in the two-tone shoes, who blew smoke rings.'

'Not all bad men wear black like they do in the cowboy pictures. But he was a bad, rotten apple. I know that.'

'How do you know?' asked Sir Basil.

'He said he would do me in if he ever caught me there again. I spied on him with my little eye.'

'What was he doing?'

'Poking at the ground where the picture palace comes and goes. And once he brought a small round man with him.'

Sir Basil smiled. 'Tommy, you have done very well indeed.'

'Can I go now?'

'Yes. One thing, Tommy. You are not to go back there again. Do you understand? You must keep out.'

Tommy nodded gravely.

'And that goes for you too, Ezra.'

'I understand, sir.'

They all got up and saw Sir Basil to his car. Mrs Calthorpe was already standing on the path, Bert peeking out from behind her.

There was something in Tommy's story that niggled at Ezra. He wished he remembered more about the night of the fire and what he must have seen, yet time had stubbornly refused to bring anything back to him from the foggy marches of his memory.

THE CAKE BOY

If this is a dream, thinks Amaryllis, then there is no waking. If she is a ghost, what is she haunting? If she is dead, why does she have a shadow?

She writes a name in her breath on the windowpane, the name she supposes to be hers; makes lists of random words she remembers on the dust of the floor; starts to make notes, about the apartment, about the wasteland beyond.

The first entry in her diary reads:

The cake boy
Treacle
Mouse
The severed hand
Wendy house
A picnic
His name is easy. No, his name begins with E, but it isn't easy. I must remember his name. That is my task, to remember his name. What about treacle, where does treacle come in?

I am working in the crack of time. There is a spot of blood on my camisole. I am investigating a robbery. Who stole my memory?

His name is Esrot.

Esau

Everett

Evert

Red sports car.

Evert

I am going crazy and I don't even know what crazy looks like, but all this feels worse than crazy.

What if there never, ever is another tomorrow? Not a real, unwritten tomorrow, just these artificial days marked by the absence of light? Well, then, welcome to my fun . . . er . . . al.

It makes Amaryllis feel better, gives her hope, of sorts, yet all the written words speak of a past she can only vaguely recall. She reads and rereads the words she has written, worried now that she might have wasted space by making a list, for this is all she owns, this one book, the only record of all that has vanished.

The next time, she draws with meticulous care a plan of the apartment, making miniscule notes about what can be seen from each of the windows and in the wasteland beyond. She stays away from the walnut box in the corner.

This is what I have discovered behind some of the apartment doors. A mesh. It is geometric. I touched one of the threads and it was sticky.

I made a note of the door and went back again to find

memories had been built on to this mesh, as solid as Sundays. The people in the memory do the same thing again and again, as if they were on a loop. They never change. I've seen many memories, mine, and what must be other people's. But I am more drawn to this one. I don't know why.

The man, all red-faced and angry, so angry that the veins stand out on his neck fit to burst, shouts at his wife. He shouts harder at the boy. The mother looks scared. I know that under the table she holds her son's hand. Once I tried to stop the man from saying those hurtful things but he didn't see me, he looked through me. That's when I realised what he said never altered. This hideous man is doomed to always say the same thing; the boy, his head bent, peeling skin off his fingertips.

'You are a schmuck, that's what you are, a spineless schmuck, just like your good-for-nothing uncle.'

'Herman, please,' pleads his wife, standing up.

The man pushes her back into her seat. 'Do you know what he is, Frieda, this schmuck? A mummy's boy, a wimp.'

It always ends with him pulling off his belt and grabbing the boy by the arm, while the mother screams, 'Don't do it, leave him be!'

Herman is the angry man.

His wife is Frieda.

The boy is called Schmuck.

It's hopeless, I'm not good at being a detective. Why should I be good at it? After all, it's my life I'm investigating, and as far as I can see there is not enough evidence. I am a film, half-ruined by over-exposure to the green light.

She is there again, the child, in a pale-primrose dress with forgetful flowers embroidered on it. She is swinging back and forth in the empty playground, the 'creak-scratch creak-scratch' a lonely sound. No one comes to take her home.

To get away from the child I take my diary, the only thing that matters, and go back to the apartment with the soldier. He asks me if I want tea, he always does, he always says he made tea for Bernie when they blew his arm off.

Usually I don't bother to answer, certain he is just a loop memory like that awful Herman. Today I say, yes, I would like some. I thought he would just carry on and ignore me. Here's the strangest part.

He comes back into the room with two cups of tea and asks, 'Are you all right, love? You're very pale.'

I say, 'Can you hear the swings?'

He goes to the window.

'I think she's waiting for you, love,' he says, seeing the child.

You could have knocked me down with a kipper. Maybe there is hope. He spoke words he has never said before. I can see his double shadow. He isn't a loop memory. He is like me.

I ask him and he pats my shoulder.

'The only way to deal with fear is not to run,' he says.

I have moved apartments again, to escape her. One block, two, three, four, still she gets closer. I'm getting good at sneaking out, just making it into the doorway of the next building, then the next one. Finally, I don't know why, I choose a building made of brown stone. This apartment is on the first floor, above a shop. No one is here, the place is empty with yellow walls and peeling lino. I sleep on the floor, feel safe. Nothing is what it seems. The swings are further away. I leave when I see a cockroach.

In the lightness of this seasonless place the child is there, right outside, skipping.

I think about the soldier's words.

Walking towards the child, I say, 'I'll take you home.'

I am standing near her. She says not one word but stares at me with those violet eyes.

My eyes.

She has vanished, the child has vanished and I'm thinking where has she gone and why is everything so big? I think I must have shrunk and I look down to find that it is me wearing the yellow dress with forget-me-lost sewn on it. The two shadows on the ground are mine and the child's. We walk together as one.

Beside me is a man with the longest legs, so all I see are cream brogues and linen trousers with sharp, pressed lines down the middle. I find myself being lifted up and the sun is so bright that the face of the man is lost under his hat.

Words come from me but I don't seem to be saying them or thinking them. They are childish words.

'Daddy, Daddy, can I have an ice cream?'

'Yes, my little princess,' the man says.

I don't know what comes next. No need to worry, the child has this all buttoned up.

I'm sitting on a chair under a big striped umbrella, near a harbour, but I know it's the wasteland, I'm not fooled, I've seen too many curious things out there to be fooled. Yet a part of me wishes that my big shadow would disappear and I could once more be my daddy's princess, right all the wrongs, so that he would still love me.

There are boats in the harbour, the water a mirrored surface spotted with white waves.

A musician is taking a break. I look at the dark piano player, wrapped in bandages of smoke.

The child nearly makes me jump out of this borrowed skin.

'Please, Daddy, make him play "The Teddy Bears' Picnic", please, pretty please.'

I study my daddy's face. It is handsome, open; a new-washed face. There is a drink, long and tall beside him. Kneeling up, I . . . the child . . . kiss him.

'I will love you forever,' she says.

He kisses me and says, 'I will love you for all eternity.'

Suddenly I'm aware of a knot that tightens like a wool ball in the pit of my stomach, and makes me feel sick. The other customers at the café stare, astonished. Walking none too steadily, Mummy arrives. She sways dangerously close to the water's edge, this pretty piece of thistledown, this near-forgotten mummy I once had. Both the child and I feel older and wiser than this tottering, beautiful drunk.

What is her name? A fruit. She is a Christmas fruit, this mummy of mine, crystalised, sugar-sweet, wearing a white linen dress, tanned like treacle toffee.

Treacle. That word again. It goes with toffee, it goes with Tommy. Tommy Treacle. But who is he? And, someone tell me, whose name begins with E? I must try and remember. Easy peasy. Why can't I find it in the library of my mind?

The child pulls me back. My tummy is aching. Mummy has a silvery tiger cub on a lead.

I try to work out how old I am when this happens. By the time she gets to our table I have guessed, by the smallness of me, no more than four. My father stands up. The chair scrapes the ground, an ugly sound.

Maybe I should look again at the green light. I'd be pleased to forget all this, but my desire to remember one name outweighs all the rest.

———

Esray. No, that wasn't his name. Esrot. Well, that makes me laugh. No one is called Esrot. I wonder what an Esrot might look like? Don't waste paper. I have to write it all down. I must, otherwise it will all be dust.

I'm sitting at the table by the harbour and a waiter brings the ice cream in a tall glass with a paper umbrella. I'm studying that glass very hard indeed. I see what is happening in the reflection on the glass. The child looks down, but I don't.

My daddy is taller than my mummy. I look like her but dark, not fair.

'What are you doing?' says my father, in that clipped Anglo-American accent he has when he refuses to lose his temper no matter what.

'Don't be grumpy. I want a drink, a Martini.' The waiter takes the order.

'No,' says my daddy.

'Oh, darling, please. I need a drink.'

The grown me can see that he is using everything to control his rage. He nods at the waiter.

She bends down and picks up the tiger cub and strokes it. 'Don't you think he is just the cutest little tiger-riger kitty you have ever seen?'

'No. I think he is a wild animal that is not meant to be in a café in Capri.'

'That's very beastly of you. I thought you would like it.'

'No, you didn't think. You never think. That is your problem.'

She lifts up the animal, all floppy and furry, its legs and tail hanging down. She blows on the tiger's belly. 'Why is Daddy being so horrid to his sweet pea?'

And I see then a tear glisten in the sunlight and roll down the fresh fields of her skin. She kisses the cub's tummy and puts it on the floor by her feet.

'Goddamnit woman, are you insane?' says my daddy,

uncrossing his legs. The steel cap on the heel of his shoe comes down hard on the ground.

'I thought Amaryllis would like to see a real tiger, claws and all.'

She sniffs. I can see she is crying. 'Wouldn't you like to stroke it, darling?' she says. She leans towards me. I smell a blend of Chanel No 5 and cocktail, a scent that will always bring this stranger home to me.

I move to get down off my seat. Now, the big me is not so sure that this is a good idea. I can see that Daddy agrees.

'Stay where you are, Princess,' he orders.

Then turning on his wife, his wife with the name of oranges, small oranges, he says, 'Where did you get the tiger?'

'It belongs to Henry Vanderbulk. He's taking it to the castle he's building in California. I went to luncheon at his villa.'

'I made it quite clear to you that you weren't to go there. I don't like the guy and I don't like the company he keeps.'

'Everything I do is wrong. Why is everything wrong? Once you loved me; don't you love me now?'

'You are being ridiculous.'

'I know what we should do. Have another baby, for Amaryllis's sake, a brother or sister. I want to have a huge family, isn't that what you wanted?'

'No. I have one perfect daughter. I don't want any more.'

'A son . . . all men want sons.'

'Well, I don't, and this is not the sort of conversation to be having in front of our daughter.'

My mother laughs, such a great infectious laugh. I had no idea I have the same laugh as her.

She is not listening to him. 'I was always told by Nanny that children were of no consequence until they were five.' She tickles my chin.

'Stop it, leave her alone,' says Daddy. 'She is not a doll. As for your nanny, if I remember rightly, she killed your baby sister by putting her into a scalding bath.'

'Why bring that up? Do you want to send me crazy? Why would you want to say that?'

'Quiet. You are making a scene.'

'I don't care. You know it was an accident. Why do you remind me of these things?'

The waiter has brought the cocktail and taking the glass she downs it in one.

'Wait,' she says, 'I want another.'

I now look into my daddy's face. Thunderstorms are descending under his dark eyebrows, his smile a crooked lightning flash.

'You are drunk,' he hisses. 'What sort of an example are you setting your child?'

'I keep telling you, she doesn't understand.'

The knot in my stomach is very bad. Me and my double shadow climb down from the chair. Mummy and Daddy are shouting at one another, they have forgotten me. Unnoticed, I walk away with the tiger cub and hide under the table where the waiters keep the plates. From here I can see all the tables in the café. They are made out of jelly and in the heat everything is wobbly and melting away. We cuddle up together. The tiger cub is sleepy and warm. I smell his fur, the child knows it's a smell of safety. I watch the tablecloth, a sail blowing in the wind over jelly-top tables. Back and forth it blows, letting in the blue, blue sea, as my eyes become heavy with sleep.

I wake up under the table. Not in the café, not with the tiger. Herman is shouting. How did I arrive here? This is a nightmare. I crawl out of the apartment, close the door behind me and run, run as fast as I can. And as I run, the song rushes into my head:

> *If you go down in the woods today*
> *You'd better not go alone.*
> *It's lovely down in the woods today,*
> *But safer to stay at home.*

I stop dead. It's come back to me, the name I've been searching for.

The cake boy is called . . . Ezra.

THE KEEPNET

August 1939

By the summer of 1939 Miss Bright's unexplained disappearance belonged to the past. The terrifying prospect of another war overshadowed the mystery of Warlock Hall, which, in the light of the present alarming situation, seemed to belong to a golden era, doomed by its own folly. All that was left standing of the once-grand house was the burnt-out Black Tower, a memorial of sorts to those who had perished in the fire.

Gas masks had been issued to all citizens and Bert Calthorpe was appointed the local Air Raid Precaution Warden. His job was to make sure every villager had blackout curtains in place. He was a stickler for drills. If one pinprick of light could be seen he felt it would represent a national threat, a guiding beacon to a Nazi bomber.

The only silver lining in the gathering storm clouds was that at long last there was work to be had near Bishop's Norgate. A brand-new munitions factory had been built on the outskirts of Broughton. Bert Calthorpe frightened all and sundry by telling them that they would now be in for it, that the factory would be a target for enemy attacks and they would all be blown to smithereens. The only hope was for everyone to build Anderson shelters.

'Even the King has one in his back garden at Buckingham Palace,' he said.

But there were many among the sleepy inhabitants of Bishop's Norgate who hoped that Neville Chamberlain could still avoid another all-out war. Too many remembered the last one and no one wanted a repeat of that. They prayed in church on Sunday: let there be peace in our time, let no bombs fall on Bishop's Norgate.

Ezra had been at his new school for nearly two years and had decided that if a war was to come he would join the RAF. On his seventeenth birthday he and some seventy-five other lads had been selected to join the Air Defence Cadets. So far Ezra had been the star pupil and he felt certain that he would be chosen to train as a bomber boy.

It was late August when Ezra, Len and Tommy went fishing. The canal was fairly smelly at this time of year, and Tommy kept asking to fish on the lake up near the ruins of Warlock Hall.

'It's all beautiful. I see fishes through the watery glass. And there's no one there, not now. Only the men in boiler suits and dark glasses, but they don't see me. They won't see us.'

Ezra loved Tommy as deeply as a brother, but he had learned not to take much notice of his elaborate stories. Often they were more to do with the films he had seen at the Rio than with reality.

The day Ezra gave in to Tommy's request was the one day Len couldn't come.

'I can't, blast it. I have to stay home with the little ones. Mum's gone and found a huge horseradish and Dad's taken the wheelbarrow to dig it up. They say they can make a lot of money from a plant that big.'

Ezra sighed. He didn't want to be reminded of Amaryllis. He had struggled not to think about her over the past two years, yet in his mind's eye she had become more vivid with every passing day.

'I don't really want to go up that way,' he said to Len.

'Then don't.'

Tommy went on and on about fishing at the lake until Ezra gave in. Weighed down by rods and a basket of food, the two set off. Tommy was as happy as a sandboy, Popeye in his pocket, a day of perfect bliss rolling out before him.

Ezra, walking ahead, surrendered to the past. The rainbow waters of the lake reflected a luminous image back to him: Amaryllis standing all naked on the jetty, diving like a silver fish through his heart.

He set up the rods and put the net in the water with the ginger beer in it. It struck him, seeing the bottles bobbing up and down, that Amaryllis and he had been caught in some strange keepnet. After years of banishing such thoughts from his mind, now they flooded back to him. He missed her. He knew that was what this was, this sadness. Simple. He missed . . . missed her smell . . . missed the way she . . . they . . . what? What had happened on that day? Why couldn't he remember?

Why was it all lost? What had frustrated him most – and still did – was that, regardless of what the doctors had said, he'd never regained his memory of that time. Angry with himself, and wrapped up in the same old thoughts that never reached a conclusion, he only gradually became aware of a stillness. The birdsong, the hum of the bees buzzing in the grasses, all the sounds of a hot day, but Tommy was unusually quiet.

'Tommy,' he shouted, 'hurry up. What are you doing? Stop hiding.'

Looking back he saw the empty path, the woods, the fence. Panic flooded him.

'Tommy,' he screamed. 'Tommy, where are you? Tommy!'

Through a hole in the fence he caught a glimpse of Tommy and pushed through after him, his heart racing.

'Tommy . . .'

Ezra stopped dead in his tracks. He was staring, fish-faced, at his own reflection in the facade of the picture palace. From under it oozed a green, artificial light. Through the glass swing doors that led into the foyer, he saw Fred Cutler as he once must have been, before he lost his legs, a beaming smile on his face. In his hand he held a white mouse.

'It's all right,' said Tommy. 'Look, it's my dad and he's got Houdini.'

'No, no!' Ruddy Nora, why couldn't he move? 'Wait, no, no . . .'

'Dad's found Houdini,' said Tommy. He went galumphing through the doors and the picture palace vanished.

Ezra stared, bewildered, at the empty crater. At his feet,

something white caught his eye. He looked down to see Popeye staring up at him.

Ezra remembered little of getting home. He supposed he must have brought back the fishing rods and basket, for they were in the cupboard under the stairs, but had he said anything to his mother, or did he just disappear into the shed?

That was where Sir Basil found him. Ezra wasn't surprised. It was as if he had been waiting for him without knowing it. Sir Basil looked grave. He examined Tommy's mouse pictures.

'The young lad has quite an exceptional talent,' he said. 'What happened?'

Sir Basil listened to all Ezra had to say, then said, 'It's not your fault, Ezra, so don't blame yourself. We know Tommy is not the first to have gone into the picture palace, as I told you when you were in hospital, if you remember.'

'I do. But you said you weren't sure.'

'Now, old chap, we are almost a hundred-percent-positive. We believe your father, Amaryllis Ruben and Silas Molde are in there.'

'What makes you so certain?'

'Miss Bright's notebooks. They are filled with details, theories and observations. And photographic evidence that proved there had been unnatural disturbances in the area where the picture palace stood. Jim Boyle has found her work to be more than helpful. A remarkably clever woman, a first-class brain – she studied physics at Oxford after the war, you know. Such a waste, a woman like that ending up a governess.'

'If they entered the picture palace so easily, what makes it so difficult to leave?'

'A good question. Unfortunately, there is no simple answer.' Sir Basil sat down near Ezra on a broken chair that Tommy had been in the process of mending. 'There are theories we are exploring but as yet we aren't sure exactly how the building comes and goes. It seems that the picture palace is a gateway – a portal, if you will – to the fourth dimension.'

In the cottage, Nancy looked worried when Sir Basil came in without Ezra. Olive had just returned from work.

'Firstly, Mrs Pascoe,' said Sir Basil, 'before we proceed any further, I must ask you and Olive to sign this, then we can talk freely.'

'Blooming Ada,' said Olive. There was an army bloke standing outside their cottage, Mrs Calthorpe was twitching her curtains and here was Mother, ashen, sweeping nonexistent biscuit crumbs from the tablecloth. 'What's happened?'

'Tommy's gone missing.'

'Oh, no,' said Olive, 'not our Tommy. Where?'

'In Warlock Wood.'

'Well, what are we all doing, standing here like a row of onions? Shouldn't there be a search party looking for him?'

'This is the Official Secrets Act,' said Sir Basil, ignoring her. 'It means that you will not tell another soul what is discussed between us. If you do go talking to anyone, I cannot vouch for your safety. Do you understand?'

Nancy understood all too well that behind this benevolent,

avuncular mask was a man as hard as nails. This was no boiled-sweet threat; he meant every word he said.

'Has Ezra to sign it as well ?' asked Olive.

'He has signed it already, while he was still in hospital.'

Mother put her hand on Olive's, then they both signed.

'Good,' said Sir Basil, collecting the papers. 'Mrs Pascoe, you have an idea of what I am about to tell you?'

Nancy nodded.

'I don't think, Miss Pascoe, you do. Without going into the science of it all, we know that Arnold Ruben built a memory machine. It was activated on the night of the fire. We don't know exactly what happened at the picture palace that night, but it seems likely that Ezra saw it all. Due to the injury he received, he remembers nothing. We believe, Mrs Pascoe, that either by accident or design, your husband was also taken into the memory machine.'

'But what is the memory machine?' interrupted Olive.

'According to its inventor, it has the capability to make a three-dimensional – some even say four-dimensional – world out of people's recorded memories. Mr Ruben hoped to create a Utopia from his own happy memories, where his daughter would be safe from another war.'

'And that's where Father and Tommy are? What about Miss Bright?'

'We know Miss Bright is in the machine.'

'My question, sir, is . . .' Nancy's voice was wobbly.

'No, Mother,' said Olive quickly, 'don't ask . . .'

'I must. What if everyone who goes in there just dies?'

'I can't tell you, Mrs Pascoe, but Arnold Ruben wouldn't have taken that risk with his daughter if he thought it might kill her. Silas Molde must be alive in order for the building to come and go as it does.'

Nancy, her grey eyes not leaving Sir Basil's, said, 'What do you want us to do?'

'I don't want anyone to know about Tommy's disappearance. It's far too explosive at this moment and we need to make some investigations. You will say that Tommy came home from the fishing trip poorly. We will send a doctor and an ambulance tonight, and you will say that he has tuberculosis and is in an isolation ward in a London hospital.'

Nancy and Olive nodded.

'To nosy neighbours you will say you can't at the moment go to see him.'

There was another question Nancy feared to ask. Beneath her courage she had a premonition that one day Sir Basil would come to claim Ezra. And that he, like Noel, would vanish. The idea of it near broke her heart.

'What if there is no way out of the machine? What then?'

MANY MEN IN HADES

Guilt plays tricks with memory. It changes fiction to facts. Silas Molde knows this better than anyone else. The truth can be so destructive, more so than a lie. What else could he have done? The memory machine was programmed to activate at ten forty-five. As for the fire, he is no fortune-teller. The present has always been troubling. What is the present? He has lost all track of real-world time. Perhaps a day, perhaps a year has passed. What he suspects is that by taking the picture palace back to Warlock Wood, hoping to collect Arnold, he has unwittingly let in others.

Silas surveys the landscape before him. This is not the world Arnold had envisaged. He had tried to warn him that memories were unpredictable. Nevertheless, Silas has grown to like the bleakness of the place, this wasteland, hungry as it is for memories that disappear as fast as passing clouds. Here he is, finally, where he belongs, master of his small world. Secretly he thinks to himself that if Arnold were here, he would have taken that role, with Silas, as always, the servant. But no more.

He smiles to himself. Why not enjoy what you spent hours in the dark working to create? This is your memory, your past, your show.

His eye catches a poster. It reads:

A film for our time
Starring Vervaine Fox
Vermont Pictures is proud to present
The Night of the Tiger

Silas feels himself to be a magician. He knows he is in one of his memories. The year is 1919, it is July. Paris is sepia. Before him once again is the Boulevard Saint Germain.

Shared memories of anywhere and anyone are always more vivid than the memories of one person's half-forgotten life. Silas tingles with pleasure. Beside him stands a tall, willowy young man wearing a badly made suit. It has begun to rain and the plane trees smell of washed leaves. Pulling up his collar the man next to him sings softly under his breath,

There are many men in Hades
Who are taken there by the ladies

Silas laughs.

'You speak English?' asks the young man, turning round to face him.

'Yes.'

'Great, have you a light?' He has an American accent. He is one of the many who have good papers on them, who could have gone anywhere and decided to stay in this city.

Silas studies this eager face, a face he came to know all too well. A young man, puppy-dog keen, with clean-cut features. He hasn't yet filled out. Money would do that, all those greenbacks would make him beefy. Still Silas finds it hard to believe how young Arnold Ruben was that day they first met.

He strikes a match, cups his hand so it won't go out. Arnold bends towards it.

'Thanks.' The young man takes a drag of the cigarette. 'Did you enjoy the film?' he asks by way of small talk.

'Yes,' Silas says, 'I've seen it many times.'

'It's good old escapism,' says Arnold.

It's starting now to rain heavily; the pavement shimmers in the dusk.

'Thanks again for the light.'

Silas thinks, this is not how the first meeting went, surely? It wasn't he who said, 'Would you like a drink?', but seeing young Arnold Ruben walking away, he realises it must have been.

They sit in Les Deux Magots and it is Silas, near broke, with only a few coins in his pocket, who finds himself buying the first round of drinks before Arnold orders a bottle of cheap wine. They talk about movies, about Vervaine Fox who Arnold says he is in love with.

Silas, reliving his thoughts, feels the flash of jealousy the careless words ignited in him. Did he really feel all that anger? He knew he did. He had just discovered what had happened to his wife, his Lottie. For a moment, to impress his new-found friend, he has a desire to tell him the truth about the actress. All that stops him are the dead man's papers in his pocket, his passport out of Europe. The conversation has moved on. Arnold is an idealist. He talks a lot about the possibilities of making a better world, where a war like the one they have just fought wouldn't ever happen, not ever, not once.

'You didn't tell me your name,' Arnold says, long after he has introduced himself.

Gauche as Arnold is, Silas can see he isn't fooled by the name he gives. It clings, limpet-tight, to its new owner, awkward and ill-fitting. For a moment Silas is convinced he has been found out, but to his utter surprise Arnold asks no further questions. This is when Silas realises that they have more in common than he thought. Both are on the run, each for different reasons.

'And what did you do in the war, old bean?' Arnold asks.

'I was a wireless operator,' Silas says. One lie, two lies, all lies.

Arnold, unused to wine, expensive or cheap, begins to talk. Silas listens. Oh, with what relish he listens. This is a golden moment.

'I'm fascinated by the fourth dimension. Time is the third dimension, the line by which we live our lives, but that doesn't mean that a fourth dimension couldn't exist.' Arnold is now leaning forward. 'We can see in front and sideways, but not behind, even though we know it's there. The same goes for the fourth dimension: not being able to see it doesn't prove anything.'

Silas is smiling, something he does rarely.

'I'm boring you.'

'No, no, not at all. Please go on.'

'I've been following Einstein. Have you heard of him?'

'Yes, oh, yes.'

'Then you must have heard about the eclipse observations by Eddington and others, which they say confirm Einstein's General Theory of Relativity. But I think the findings are flimsy. There are many in the scientific world who believe that the speed of light is not a constant, and if that's the case then time can speed up and slow down.' Arnold is perched half out of his seat as if to sit would be impossible. 'This is what I've dreamed of since I was small. You're going to think me crazy. I want to make a memory machine. I believe it's possible. Everyone is capable of time travel for a minute or so by running up and down the scales of their memories. But what if you could capture those memories like a film? Then they could be played again in the four dimensions of space.'

'I see what you're driving at. A place where time wouldn't hold the same power over us.'

'Yes, yes!' Arnold leaps up and hugs Silas. The rest of the drinkers turn to watch them before the chatter of conversation starts up again.

'Maybe you should publish your theories.'

'No,' says Arnold. 'Never. I don't want to do that. What for? Hardly anyone will read it and those who do will think I'm mad. I just want to make my machine. If I can do it, then it won't be a theory; there will be actual evidence to back it up.' He stops, pushes his hands through his hair. 'I've been in Paris since the Armistice, learning French, trying to work and study here. I haven't met one student who comprehends what

I'm doing, then I bump into you, a complete stranger and you understand.'

'Yes, I also studied science.'

'Where?'

'Oh, here and there. Only as an amateur.'

As Silas says this his mouth is dry, and he is relieved that his new friend isn't listening, seemingly lost in his own thoughts.

'I want to go further still,' says Arnold. 'I want to edit memory like you can film, cut out all the bits you don't like.'

'The war,' says Silas, 'the Spanish flu.'

'Yes, or more personal things.'

They catch each other's eye and see there a mirror, a reflection of all they both long to escape.

Silas breaks the silence. 'You can live forever in the best parts of your life, outside time, revisiting and rerunning the golden moments. Never grow old.'

'There would be no future, just the everlasting now,' says Arnold. Moving his hand with a sudden jerk, he knocks over the glass. They watch the red stain spread on the white tablecloth. Arnold laughs. 'In my memory machine the wine would be back in the glass once again, not a drop spilled.'

In the past, when Silas had remembered this moment, Arnold talking earnestly, no glass of wine had been spilled. Neither had they returned to Arnold's hotel together, singing rather drunkenly,

There are many men in Hades
Who are taken there by the ladies

What he remembers quite clearly was saying to a sober Arnold, 'To extract memory, you'll need to use electrical waves to get the readings, and possibly a magnetic force field to make it operational.'

But that conversation appears to have been edited out.

'Molde isn't a Jewish name,' says Arnold, swaying slightly at the entrance to the hotel. Silas notes that this leading question has *not* been cut.

'No,' says Silas, nervously.

'Well, there's a thing, old bean. See you tomorrow. *Bonsoir.*' And with that he was gone.

It is the next morning, and Silas supposes that Arnold must have been worse for wear, otherwise he would have questioned him more closely about his past. As he sees it now, his memory is in conflict with Arnold's, for here he is in an ill-fitting suit, holding on to the ends of his cuffs, hoping that the frayed edges would not be noticed. He asks the porter for Monsieur Ruben and is pointed to an upholstered chair where, slumped, is the young Arnold, three telegrams in his hand.

'Good morning,' Silas says.

Arnold, in a fog of preoccupation, doesn't seem to recognise him.

'We met last night.'

'What? Oh, yes, old bean, of course,' he says, barely looking up.

'Bad news?'

'No, and yes.'

Silas, seeing how white he is, orders him a cognac.

'D'you know, old bean,' says Arnold, 'I've just inherited a fortune from my uncle. Only ever met him once and the guy's gone and left me the whole caboodle.'

'What is the whole caboodle?'

'Lasco Oil. Heard of it?'

Silas has always specialised in keeping a straight face. 'With that kind of money you could build a memory machine.'

Arnold stares at Silas as if seeing him for the first time.

'Here, read them,' he says, stuffing the telegrams into Silas's hand.

The first is from Mr Kurt Ruben's secretary, informing Arnold that his uncle had died last night of a massive heart attack and that funds were being wired to him so that he could return home straight away.

The second is from Kurt Ruben's lawyer. Arnold Ruben is the sole beneficiary of Kurt Ruben's will. He has left his entire fortune to his nephew, with some words of advice: 'Believe in your dreams.'

The third telegram is from Herman Ruben. It says:

UNCLE DEAD FUNERAL NEXT WEEK

Silas returns to the porter's desk and catches sight of himself in the mirror. So this is what he looked like as a young man. He wasn't unattractive. Short cut hair, stocky build, a prominent nose, dark eyes in a bowl of a face. Still, not without charm in the right light. He asks the porter about booking a passage to New York.

Arnold says, 'Make that two first-class tickets, old bean.'

He turns to him. 'Who's the other one for?'

'You, if you want it.'

The lobby door bursts open and there is someone else, someone who was never there before. How did he come to be here, this large boy in shorts?

'Hello, have you seen my mouse?' says the boy. 'I'm Tommy Treacle.'

The memory is broken, all gone. Paris, the hotel, Arnold. Just this ungainly boy who stares up at the poster for *The Night of the Tiger*.

'Is that the picture you're showing? I've seen that one. Do you have any new films, with cowboys and Indians?'

'Go away,' says Silas, eager to return to the golden moment. He pushes the boy out into the wasteland. He'll deal with him later.

Smiling to himself, he remembers the day before he and Arnold sailed. They had gone shopping. Arnold bought a cashmere coat and brogues, and suits in soft greys that smelled of money. Silas preferred black, three-piece suits, which organised his shape into something altogether menacing.

It was during the voyage to New York that Silas and Arnold formed the bond which would never be broken. By the time they docked Silas had grown into his suits and his name, and become indispensable to the newly minted – and newly bethrothed – millionaire.

'Silas, I need you, darling,' shouts a voice, jerking him from his memories once more.

His round face becomes still. How thrilled he had been, the night of the fire, when he saw Vervaine in the memory machine. He'd believed he had achieved his greatest memory recording, more real than anything else here. That, he'd thought, is because she is a light in the hall of the memory of the masses. He had looked at her in admiration, full of wonder at his own brilliance.

Then she had turned to him and said, 'Do I need a drink after the night I've had.'

No, no, this was not what he had created. He had spent the last few feverish hours before activation editing her memories, filtering her voice, making her softer, kinder towards her Silas. Momentarily he was jolted by the harshness of her reality. His mind quavered and he had to remind himself that this was the woman he loved.

'Darling,' she'd said, as she fitted a pink-tipped cigarette into a holder, 'did you really think I would be just a memory, like some piece of celluloid? Here is where I belong, here my beauty will live forever.'

He goes up the stairs. Behind the velvet curtain is no longer the cinema screen, but grand and fantastic rooms, a montage of film sets. There are huge drapes across a window, a white piano, a roaring fire, portraits, all of Vervaine. She is posing by the mantelpiece, dressed in an evening gown, her double shadow elongated by the firelight. At her feet is the white tiger.

'Oh, there you are. I've been calling for ages. It's cocktail time, don't you agree?'

'Yes, *Schätzchen*,' says Silas. He knows now Arnold was

right. Vervaine's corrosive obsession with her reflection in the hall of mirrors that was her life has destroyed all Silas's dreams.

Now there is that ridiculous boy, who ruined a golden memory. There is no doubt in Silas's mind that what he had dreaded has happened. The boy had a double shadow. He wasn't a memory recording, he is an interloper. How many more are there who have entered unseen, their memories captured at the diamond-paned doors as they leave the real world? What effect do they have on the delicate balance of the machine?

He has to find Amaryllis. He should have brought her to the picture palace, despite Vervaine's jealousy. He hadn't thought the girl would try to escape from the apartment, for the green light should have stupefied her into a world of daydreams. But Arnold had programmed the machine with her at its heart; perhaps she is immune to the light . . .

Somewhere out there, among the tangled reels of other people's memories, Amaryllis is hiding.

TRAINING

Mother hadn't gone to the station to see Ezra and Olive off. She didn't like long goodbyes. As they walked down the garden path, Mrs Calthorpe was watching them from her front door.

'My Bert says London will most probably be flattened. Gassed, then flattened. That's what my Bert says.'

Olive turned on her. 'It's a wonder your Bert is able to to get a word in edgeways. You say more than enough for both of you.'

'Well, I never did! Never in all my life—'

'Oh, keep your stays on,' interrupted Olive.

Mrs Calthorpe slammed her front door.

Mother laughed and kissed them both at the garden gate.

'Bert says it might be over by Christmas.'

'Well, if it isn't,' said Ezra, 'we know who to blame.'

The train to London was packed with men and women in high spirits, all going to sign up. Olive had been accepted by St Thomas' Hospital to train as a nurse.

'It's a relief, I suppose,' said a young woman called Trudy, sitting with them in the overfilled compartment. 'I mean, now we know it's war, I feel we can get on with the job, so to speak.'

'Of course we can, my lovely,' shouted a man standing in the packed corridor, 'we're finally going to win the war, finish what the old boys couldn't.'

A cheer went up.

Ezra sat lost in his thoughts as Trudy and Olive chatted like old friends. Yesterday, that momentous day, 3 September, he had been in morning drill in the gymnasium when the door swung open and his name was called out. He was to be at the school gates in seven minutes. Ezra came out of the changing room to find Flying Officer Emerson standing there, his face grave.

'There is a government official waiting for you in a car.'

'For . . . me?' Ezra stuttered.

'Yes, Pascoe. Unless there is another boy in the school by that name, you are the one he asked for.'

It struck him as he walked along the shining corridor that he was filming a long farewell, leaving behind his childhood for good this time, and yet he had no reason to think this, no idea what lay beyond the grey of the outside world except a certainty that after today everything would change.

Sir Basil Stanhope leaned over and opened the passenger door of the Armstrong Siddeley.

'Let's take a drive, old chap,' he said, starting the car. 'Tell me this, Ezra Pascoe, have you ever dreamed of being more than you are?'

Hesitantly, Ezra nodded.

'Good,' said Sir Basil, 'very good. According to Mr Emerson's report, you are just the kind of young man we're looking for.

We want you to work for us. We would take over your training; you would become one of our boys.'

Ezra sat back and thought for a moment before asking, 'Is this anything to do with the picture palace?'

'Correct.'

'I wanted to go into the RAF.'

'I know,' said Sir Basil. He took a file from the map pocket and handed it to Ezra. Inside were three photographs.

Ezra looked at them and said, 'These are the ones Tommy took with Miss Bright's camera, aren't they, sir?'

The first one was of the picture palace. There was an unearthly glow coming from under the building. The second one was of Miss Bright standing, spellbound, by the mirrored steps. Through the glass doors behind her could be seen, quite clearly, a young man in uniform. The third showed the same young man. He was holding the door open for her.

Ezra felt an icy chill go down his back.

'Those photographs were taken in May sixteen months ago,' said Sir Basil. 'The man in the photo is Captain Fitzsimmons. Killed in action in 1917. He was engaged to Miss Matilda Bright. This is not a fake photograph of a ghost. These are the first photographs ever to be taken of a memory. Arnold Ruben did what we all thought impossible: he built his machine. I believe it never occurred to him what the consequences might be.'

'What consequences, sir?'

'A machine that can store memories may also wipe memories away. Think what a weapon it would be. Time would begin again, a clean slate, no madeleine to bring back what's been forgotten. I think there are many people in this mad world who would kill for such a machine, don't you?'

'Yes, but I still . . .'

'We know the machine was built round Amaryllis. She is the heart of it. Without her, the machine will implode and it won't fall into enemy hands. We are now certain that Arnold Ruben is dead. I want you to go into the machine to bring everyone back. Amaryllis may well have very little real memory left so it is vital I send in someone she trusts.' He paused. 'There is a risk, Ezra, that there may be no way out.'

'If I did this – supposing I could get in – would my family be looked after if I never returned?'

'Of course.'

Ezra was very quiet.

'I should tell you,' said Sir Basil, 'that the Prime Minister is shortly to announce to the nation that we are at war. Do you need time to think?'

'No,' said Ezra. 'My answer is yes.'

He and Olive arrived at a Victoria station crammed with people coming and going, and many lost in-between. There were huge groups of weeping children being parted from anxious parents. Some of the children were so tiny that Ezra's heart went out to them.

'Well, said Olive, 'you take care, love,' and kissed him.

'Do you know how to get to St Thomas'?'

'I'm going there too,' said Trudy. 'I know the way.'

Ezra watched them disappear into the melee, then boarded a double-decker bus to Baker Street. What he saw astounded him. Sandbags piled round important buildings, an anti-aircraft gun in Hyde Park . . . he was overwhelmed by this city he didn't know and had never visited. The headquarters of the Operation for Scientific Protection were to be found in an unprepossessing building at 85a Baker Street. The doorman viewed all newcomers with suspicion, and no one made it as far as the lift unless they knew the password. Ezra didn't.

'I'm meeting Sir Basil Stanhope,' he said.

'Never heard of him. You've got the wrong building, young man. Now, 'op it.'

'No,' said Ezra desperately, 'it's definitely number 85a,' and he showed the doorman Sir Basil's letter.

'Why didn't you say so in the first place? Heathguard Knitwear Limited. Second floor. There's the lift.'

Ezra clanked the metal gates shut and the lift rattled up inside the old building. On the second floor was a door with a frosted panel and the words HEATHGUARD KNITWEAR written on it. He knocked, even less certain that he had the right address.

'Come in,' said a voice, belonging to a secretary in her late forties. She had glasses and not the most winning of manners. She hardly glanced up from her typewriter. 'Well, what are you here for?'

'To see Sir Basil Stanhope.'

'Um . . . never heard of him. Take a seat.'

Ezra felt she wasn't the kind of woman you argued with so

he sat on a long wooden bench and took in his surroundings.

The room was very small, brown-panelled, with framed pictures of women and men modelling jumpers that were too hideous to think about.

After a while, he said, 'I think I might have the wrong place.'

The secretary looked up at him as if surprised to find him still there, then lifted the phone. 'That salesman is here.'

Ezra stood up. 'I'm not . . .'

'I told you to stay put,' she snapped.

Ezra sat down again. On the table before him lay magazine after magazine of knitting patterns. He was flicking through them when the door behind the dragon secretary opened and there was Clifford Lang. What on earth was he doing working for a knitwear company?

'Good to see you again,' said Clifford, holding out his hand. 'I know Sir Basil has done the right thing, bringing you on board.' He led Ezra down a long corridor to another frosted-glass door. 'Through here,' he said.

As far as Ezra could make out they had entered another world entirely. Here was a laboratory, the height of modernity, and several serious-looking men in white coats were working on what seemed to be as far removed from knitting patterns as it was possible to be.

Sir Basil was in his office. In fact he had hardly been home since war had been declared.

'Pascoe. You found us all right?'

'Yes, thank you, sir,' Ezra said, perplexed.

'Good, very good. You know Clifford Lang.'

'Yes,' said Ezra. 'He was Mr Ruben's secretary.'

'Actually, he was working for us. The clever chap photographed Ruben's blueprints of the memory machine. They've been very useful indeed. We kept an eye on Arnold Ruben but the man still managed to take us all off guard. It's very good to have you with us. I'll let Lang give you a guided tour, so you can get your bearings. We've rented a bedsit for you, just off Marylebone High Street. It's not far to walk every morning.'

Ezra knew that he had been thrown in the deep end and it was a matter of swimming or drowning. In the following days he was briefed on all that had been discovered about the picture palace and the fire.

He was introduced to the OSP's top scientist, Jim Boyle, who, working from the blueprints, was constructing theoretical possibilities of the whole building vanishing.

There were endless briefings. Ezra had simply had no idea how painstaking the inquiry had been.

'Pascoe,' said Sir Basil at one such briefing, 'if anything we say jogs your memory, speak up. We think Arnold Ruben was being blackmailed. We learned from Amaryllis Ruben's headmistress at Clarrington School that Amaryllis went missing on a trip to London and was brought back the following morning by one Maurice Sands. We have since discovered he is also known as Everett Roach.

'Say the name again,' interrupted Ezra.

'Everett Roach,' repeated Sir Basil. 'We found a Manila

envelope containing photographs at Miss Bright's cottage. She most probably stumbled across it as she escaped from the fire and, since they are of an unpleasant nature and involve Miss Ruben, decided to hide them. Why she didn't destroy them I have no idea. All I can say is, it's a damn good thing she didn't since they hold some vital clues.

'Unpleasant? In what way?' asked Ezra.

'They are sexually explicit,' said Sir Basil.

Ezra's stomach churned.

'The man calling himself Roach has vanished into thin air,' continued Sir Basil. 'This is not as surprising as it sounds. We can't even be certain that Roach is his real name.'

Ezra had a fleeting image of a Manila envelope falling to the ground, but he couldn't trust his memory enough to say so.

Sir Basil tipped back in his chair. 'Roach may or may not be connected with Doctor Pincher, who attended Vervaine Fox on the evening of the fire at Warlock Hall.

'MI5 is watching Doctor Pincher. He has some very interesting acquaintances – here and in Europe.

'Have you met Greg Benson?'

'Yes, sir, he's in forensics,' said Ezra.

'One of the very best in his field. He sent away to Hollywood for Vervaine Fox's dental records. They do not marry up with the teeth of the lady in the morgue.'

'Then who is she?'

'One Ethel Gilbert,' said Clifford Lang. 'She worked at the Windmill Club in Soho and was the spitting image of Vervaine Fox. She used to be hired for parties, as a spoof.

Of course, we'd interviewed a woman we were told was the nurse, immediately after the fire. She was lying, no doubt on Pincher's orders.'

'So Vervaine Fox isn't dead?'

'We believe she, too, is in the memory machine,' continued Lang. 'We've had a look at her early career in Germany. It turns out she was married, very young, to a Viennese Jew called Gunter Leichman. Leichman murdered a man in a Berlin nightclub and disappeared.'

'Believed to be among the many dead of the Great War, known only unto God,' added Sir Basil, and pushed his chair even further back so it looked as if at any moment he would go crashing to the ground. 'You'll be interested to know that Arnold Ruben didn't die in the fire.'

'You're joking!' said Ezra.

'No, old chap, I never joke much about murder. It's usually a seriously unfunny matter.'

'Murder?' said Ezra.

'Yes, that's why all of this has been so tricky. There are two murder investigations: those of Ethel Gilbert and of Arnold Ruben. Ruben was shot. Greg Benson discovered three bullets in the rubble of his study. Ethel Gilbert burned to death.'

'And seven missing-person investigations,' added Lang. 'Amaryllis Ruben, Noel Pascoe, Silas Molde, Vervaine Fox, Matilda Bright and Tommy Cutler. All are most probably in the memory machine. And then there is Everett Roach.'

Sir Basil tried, with difficulty, to relight his pipe. 'Mr Holmes up the road at 221b never had this problem.'

Ezra smiled. 'Sherlock Holmes didn't have to deal with vanishing picture palaces, sir. You don't think this man Roach could be in the machine too?'

Sir Basil's chair fell forward with a thud as he leaned across the desk.

'Yes,' he said. 'I'm afraid we do.'

DOCTOR PINCHER

December 1940

Ezra was on night duty when the call came through. He pulled on his coat and went outside to where a car was waiting to take him to Latchmere House.

Some weeks earlier, Sir Basil had learned that MI5 was tapping Doctor Pincher's telephone. It was nothing to do with the fire at Warlock Hall, but because his name had come up more than once in reports received from a double agent. Sir Basil had suggested to an associate at MI5, known to all as Tigger, that Pascoe should listen to some of the taps.

With the sugar-coated-medicine voice of Doctor Pincher in his headphones, Ezra had wondered, again, why his mind stubbornly blanked out so much of what had happened around the night of the fire. All he could be certain of was that he had heard the voice before.

He was trapped . . . where? Where was it? A small space, dark, and he was with . . . he was with . . . Again his memory was no more than a mirage, its images all but lost to him.

He had been interrupted by the arrival of Tigger.

'Anything come to mind, Pascoe?' he'd asked.

'Yes, sir. I know that when I heard that voice before, I was terrified. I can't recall why, except that I was in a small space with . . . with . . .' and then it came to him. '. . . I was with Amaryllis. Amaryllis Ruben. We were hiding. Damn it, I wish I could remember more. We were hiding . . .' Ezra stopped. 'I can't say why, but I'm certain that Pincher is somehow associated with the memory machine.'

'That's very interesting, Pascoe,' said Tigger.

As Ezra's car sped through the blacked-out streets of south London, Sir Basil was to be found at his club in Garrick Street. He had his letter of resignation in his pocket, signed and sealed. He felt completely defeated, not by the Blitz, nor even by a tangible feeling that at any moment this sceptred isle would be invaded by Hitler's forces. The Channel Islands were under occupation and Sir Basil, like every other Englishman, was well aware how hard Hitler was kicking at Britain's back door. No, he felt defeated by the general lack of interest in the work his department was doing. It seemed that no one possessed the imagination to understand the terrifying implications of the machine Arnold Ruben had built. His last hope had been the coalition government and the Prime Minister, Winston Churchill.

Now Sir Basil felt the fight to be over. His small devoted team would soon be broken up; he had already lost his wireless operators to Bletchley Park and Clifford Lang to the Special Operations Executive, and his talented protégé Ezra Pascoe was being sized up by MI5 to join the team of interrogators at Latchmere House. As the noise of the sirens filled the deserted streets, he ordered another whisky. The head waiter advised him to make his way to the air-raid shelter.

'No,' said Sir Basil. 'Leave the whisky on the table. I'll be all right here.'

The lights flickered and died. He sat there in the thick blackness of the room until they sputtered back to life. The all-clear sounded. Taking a last swig from his glass, he went down the stairs, put on his coat and picked up his tin hat and gas mask.

'False alarm,' he said to the doorman. 'Goodnight, George.'

Covent Garden was near deserted. This beloved city that he had known all his life, this great old good-time girl of a town, was broken. There was something operatic about the scale of such destruction. He walked through disconnected streets, the crunch of glass under foot. Some buildings were sliced in half, looking not unlike dolls' houses; a bed precariously perched on splintered floorboards, curtains flapping at nonexistent windows. The dust and dirt of it all. Then, in the darkness, he heard a blackbird sing.

He arrived at his house in Cheyne Walk. Having insisted that his wife and daughter move to the country, these days it felt empty, hollow. He went down to the kitchen to make some tea. He turned on the taps. No water. From the cupboard he took the bottle of Ardbeg whisky he kept for special occasions and poured himself a glass. Before he'd taken a mouthful, there was a furious banging on the front door.

'All right, I hear you,' he shouted.

Opening the door, he recognised the car, a black Morris, waiting in the road, engine running.

'Sorry, Sir Basil,' said the driver, 'I thought you might be down in the shelter.'

'No. What can I do for you?'

'Can you come to Latchmere House, sir? We have a man there by the name of . . .' The driver looked at his notebook. '. . . Doctor Goodwin . . .'

'. . . Pincher!' said Sir Basil grabbing his hat and coat. 'Well, there's a turn-up for the books.'

In the observation room that cold winter's night, Ezra studied Doctor Pincher through the glass as he waited for Sir Basil to arrive. The doctor sat in the grey room, unaware he was being watched. A single light hung from the ceiling, a cold metal table stood in front of him, a cold metal chair opposite him. Otherwise, the room was bare.

'Well, well,' Sir Basil said, as he strode into the observation room, accompanied by Tigger. 'What made you bring him in?'

'This young man,' said Tigger, nodding at Ezra. 'You were right. Those taps jogged his memory, just enough to make me think it was worth having our boys take a discreet look at the doctor's flat. What they found would have made a stone blush.'

'Tell me,' said Sir Basil. 'Tell me.'

'For a start, our dear doctor was a member of the British Union of Fascists. He believes in racial hygiene, and has very strong anti-Semitic views.'

'Anything else?'

'Oh, yes. By the looks of things he's been passing on information to a man he meets in Bayreuth.'

'Information about what?'

'Ah,' said Tigger, 'I thought you should have the pleasure of finding that out, before we have a go at him. And, Sir Basil, you know the policy here: violence is taboo.'

'Not my style, old chap.'

Doctor Pincher glanced up as Sir Basil entered the interrogation room and was relieved to see a tweed-suited, bow-tied toff. Sir Basil noted the doctor's red complexion and the smell of disinfectant, mingled with bad breath. He watched as the doctor picked invisible specks of fluff from his clothes. A pernickety man, thought Sir Basil, one who was rarely satisfied with what life had to offer him. Sir Basil's first question was no soft-shoe shine shuffle; he started as he meant to go on.

'When did you first hear of the memory machine?'

It was clear that Doctor Pincher was unprepared for such directness. He was somewhat surprised to be spoken to in such an abrupt fashion without any formal introduction. The doctor pursed his lips.

'May I ask who you are?' he said.

'My name is irrelevant,' said Sir Basil. 'Answer my question.'

'A patient, Miss Vervaine Fox, first told me about it.'

Sir Basil hadn't stopped staring at Dr Pincher. 'Tell me, why do ladies come to see you?'

By the self-regarding look that came over the doctor's features, Sir Basil felt he was on safe ground.

'They are mainly concerned about ageing. I help them.'

'In what way, help?'

'I give them vitamin injections. And some of my patients have other problems.'

'Like unexpected pregnancies, drugs – things that their husbands and families would not be too happy about?'

The doctor said nothing.

Sir Basil tried to light his pipe, always difficult in damp rooms.

'You have two passions I believe, Doctor Pincher,' he said, finally getting the pipe alight. 'The first is the opera. You went to the festival in Bayreuth between 1929 and 1937.'

'That's not a crime.'

'The second is gambling. A hobby which, along with your over-indulgent way of living, brought you near bankruptcy.'

The doctor looked decidedly less smug.

'It's very cold in here.'

'While you were in Bayreuth, listening to the works of your favourite composer . . . remind me, how many operas did Wagner write?'

'Music dramas. Thirteen in the canon. He is one of the greatest composers . . .'

'Quite,' Sir Basil interrupted, 'Whom did you meet there?'

'I met many people in Bayreuth.'

'I'm sure you did. But who was it who suggested a way out of your financial problems?'

Doctor Pincher said nothing. Sir Basil took a sheet of paper from a file. 'It says here that 1937 was a very lucrative time for you.'

'This is a damn outrage. You have no business snooping into my private affairs.'

Sir Basil slammed his hand down hard on the table. 'Bunkum! What happened on the night you were called to the house Vervaine Fox rented in Belgrave Square?'

'I had been there on many occasions. Which night in particular?'

'The night photographs were taken of Amaryllis Ruben after she was sexually assaulted.' On the table in front of him, Sir Basil put the photographs that had been found in Miss Bright's cottage. 'Here.' He tipped back in his chair, his eyes half-closed.

The doctor looked decidedly wretched.

'It was in the early hours of the morning when I arrived at Belgrave Square. I found a young girl in an hysterical state. She was very drunk.'

'Did Vervaine Fox know what was going on in the bedroom upstairs?'

'I don't know, I can't remember. Yes, perhaps.'

'What did you do?'

'I gave the girl a sedative.'

'When were the pictures sent to Arnold Ruben?'

'I had nothing to do with that. It was Roach . . .'

Sir Basil's chair crashed down on to the concrete floor, causing the doctor to nearly leap from his seat.

'Everett Roach,' said Sir Basil, leaning across the table. 'Now, he's an interesting chap. A small-time crook with a penchant for explosives. A womaniser, a thief with a list of aliases. He's served two prison sentences, one for beating up a nightclub singer and the second for blowing up a safe. He made a tidy living by blackmail, as you well know. A fair number of your patients became his victims.'

'That is slanderous! I only know he wanted to take revenge on the judge who gave him his last prison sentence.'

'Do you remember the judge's name?'

'Sir Charles Bodminton-Bow.'

'How did he intend to exact his revenge?'

'Roach planned to seduce his daughter, Clarissa, and take pictures of her looking . . . like a strumpet. By chance Roach stumbled across Arnold Ruben's daughter. May I have a glass of water?'

'It appears,' said Sir Basil, 'that you don't have anything to tell me I don't already know. I will hand you over to Scotland Yard. You will be charged with assisting in the physical assault of a minor.'

'I want to see a lawyer.'

'MI5 would like a word with you too, and they are nowhere near as polite as I am. I suppose you can comfort yourself that we no longer hang, draw and quarter traitors like you, but believe me, it won't be pleasant. And in the end you will be shot.'

'I am not a traitor! I am a physician, an upstanding member of British society.'

Sir Basil collected his papers.

'My colleague will be taking over now.'

And with that, he left.

He was followed into the observation room by Tigger carrying a tray of tea.

Ezra stood up and took a cup.

'Pascoe', said Sir Basil, his face serious. 'prove that he's involved. This is our last hope. Bring the bastard down. Use deception, use whatever comes to mind, but make sure that two-faced canary sings.'

What came to Ezra's mind was Everett Roach.

THE DOOR IN HIS MIND

'He's a grumpy old fart, my boss,' said Ezra. The doctor almost smiled. 'Tea. Drink up. No sugar, I'm afraid.'

'I didn't like that man,' said Pincher, sipping his tea. 'May I have a cigarette?'

'Yes, if you feel like answering a few more questions.'

'Will you be asking them?'

'Yes,' said Ezra, using all his training to keep his emotions at bay. He felt like throttling the doctor for his part in what had happened to Amaryllis. But Sir Basil had taught him well. Ezra had been an outstanding pupil in the art of interrogation. He always trusted his instincts and, more often than not, they were right. He handed Pincher a cigarette and a lighter. 'These are only minor questions. Where you go next will depend on the answers.'

He could see by the way the doctor's suit lost its cardboard grip on him that he viewed Ezra as a pushover.

'How old are you?' the doctor asked in a well-practised bedside manner, as if it were a matter of genuine concern.

'Eighteen and a half,' said Ezra, enjoying the look of satisfaction that came over the doctor's face.

The moment the doctor's suit visibly relaxed, Ezra knew the line of questioning he was going to take.

'You met Everett Roach . . . where?'

'At a poker game. An East-End thug with film-star goodlooks and a brain the size of a pea.'

'I think I should tell you that Everett Roach gave himself up to MI5 about ten days ago. But you know that, don't you?'

Doctor Pincher's eyes bulged in disbelief.

'Roach?' he said. 'That's impossible.'

'Doctor Pincher, we have made a deal with Roach. He promised to tell us everything and, in return, we will spare his life.'

Ezra watched as the doctor swallowed the bait.

'Roach is a liar. He is not to be trusted.'

Ezra stood up.

'Where are you going?'

'Roach gave us proof that you are a spy. I'm handing you over to MI5.'

'Wait, wait, I beg you, wait. What if I make the same deal as Roach?'

'That would depend on what you have to tell us. What was your interest in the memory machine?'

Ezra sat down again. He could see the doctor hesitating, a tightrope walker wondering if he could make it to the other side of a lie, or if the truth would be the easier option. Wavering, he stammered.

'I . . . I had been approached in Bayreuth by a man who was simply called Z. I never knew his real name, that is the truth. He was aware I had friends in high society – aristocrats, Members of Parliament – and he told me I would be paid extremely well for any useful information I could send him. Roach was having an affair with Vervaine Fox. He told me she was terrified of losing her looks and suggested she should become my patient. Then she met Arnold Ruben. Somehow she discovered that Ruben had built a memory machine. She became obsessed by the thought of a place where there was no time, no threat of ageing, where she could relive the triumphs of her youth. When she told me about it I was intrigued. I went to the lecture Arnold Ruben gave at Imperial College and saw the potential of the machine. Z offered me a great deal of money to obtain the blueprints. But he also wanted evidence that Arnold Ruben had indeed built the machine.'

'What sort of evidence?'

'I . . . we . . . took photographs, the day before the fire. We knew from Vervaine that Ruben and his man, Silas Molde, wouldn't be there.'

Something in what the doctor was saying began to unlock a memory, an undeveloped snapshot of a moment.

'What did the machine look like?'

'It was a strange affair. There were zinc work stations with hundreds of dials and in the middle of the room stood . . .'

. . . stood a chair, thought Ezra, remembering, with a helmet connected to many wires . . .

He must have said the last words out loud for the doctor said, 'If you know what it looked like, why are you asking me?'

Ezra quickly closed that door in his mind and continued, 'How did you know the machine was to be activated?'

'Vervaine eavesdropped on a conversation between Silas

Molde and Arnold Ruben the night before. She telephoned Roach. We had to bring our plan forward. The fire was Vervaine's idea. She wasn't interested in the blueprints, she just wanted a distraction while she smuggled herself into the picture palace. The following evening, Roach drove me in my car to Warlock Hall. He'd organised the ambulance. It contained the fire bombs so the driver had to take it slowly. Roach had paid some floozy from the Windmill to dress up as a nurse. I forget her name.'

'When you arrived at Warlock Hall, what then? '

'Ruben was with Vervaine. I kept him as long as I could to give Roach time to set up the explosives. One had been concealed in an oxygen tank and the other was in a doctor's bag. Roach placed the second one in the cloakroom that backed on to Ruben's study. Vervaine had given us clear details of the whole place.'

'How did you get the nurse to change clothes with Vervaine?'

'She thought it was a bit of fun for a party. The first of the bombs went off at nine, the second one a little later. Roach had timed them so that both wings would be alight but the house would not immediately be an inferno.'

'What happened to the girl?'

'She panicked when the first bomb exploded. I gave her a light sedative in a glass of wine, but it seems she didn't drink it all. She ran off.'

'Was it your intention that her charred body would be mistaken for that of Vervaine Fox?'

Ezra noted the doctor avoided answering the question.

'There was no time to look for her. The ambulance driver had taken my Daimler to the end of the drive and returned on foot. Shortly after the second bomb went off we left the house, Vervaine disguised as the nurse, and hurried to the ambulance.'

An image suddenly flashed across Ezra's memory.

'You scuttled away while people there needed medical attention?'

'Vervaine insisted. She wanted time to get inside the picture palace without being discovered. It was easier than we thought; Silas Molde was so distracted by the fire. He was far enough away not to see her slip in.'

'Wearing the nurse's uniform?'

'No, she changed in the ambulance. She told me to make sure Roach got there before the machine activated, but I knew he had no intention of going with her.'

'Did you see Amaryllis Ruben?'

'No. The ambulance headed back to London. I waited with my car as planned at the end of the drive. I was very shaken up. Roach arrived with the plans and told me Ruben was dead.'

'Did you ask him how he died?'

'Yes, I did. He said the less I knew, the better.'

'Then you went to Bayreuth as usual and handed Z the blueprints and the microfilm?'

'Yes.

'And he delivered them to his clients. Who are his clients?'

'I don't know. I believed that would be the end of the matter.

I'd told Z I was being investigated about the fire. For nearly a year I had no contact with him. But then he turned up again. His clients were insisting he gave them a report on the conditions inside the machine.'

'What happened when the picture palace reappeared in the woods?'

'What I saw I could hardly believe. The whole building materialised. A green fog descended, bringing with it the picture palace. I was terrified.'

'Did anyone see you?'

'Yes, there was this boy watching us, a big thing, retarded. Roach gave me his gun and told me to deal with him, then went inside, saying he wouldn't be long. The boy ran off. The doors swung shut and the building, Roach, everything, vanished. That was the last I saw of him.'

Ezra left the interrogation room. As he closed the door behind him the door in his memory reopened. I remember, he thought to himself, I remember.

MOUSE WINGS

I am in the apartment that the man first took me to. He hasn't come to see me. Maybe he's forgotten. I remembered to write down his name: Silas. Odd how important a name is, when there is no time to hang it on. Still, he doesn't look like a Silas to me. I try to imagine what a Silas might look like and I see him being of earth, not with eyes whose dark light pierce you so your skin feels tighter over the bone. He is no Silas.

I haven't left this apartment for a long part of nothingness. There's no point saying 'time', there is no time. I am no older, everything is frozen in this one moment. Only the past reigns supreme. In my head I am wiser, but what use is this wisdom if I stay forever as I am? No tick of the clock, no movement of hands over its face, no passing of days, months, years. No way out. A glimpse of hope is that a grain of time, only seconds, must have seeped through, for the blood on the camisole has grown bigger. I am bleeding from . . . I won't look.

I change it for a new one I've found in the suitcase that Silas brought.

I wonder if it's he who controls the memories? How did he

know I would need more camisoles, more petticoats? Had he foreseen that sometimes the blood would leak?

There is a mirror on the back of the bedroom door. I don't want to see where the blood is coming from, it will make no difference. Anyway, I don't trust mirrors. Reflections are always backwards. They are the first of all the lies we are told, the first of many.

The child who was following me has never come again. Perhaps now she will leave me alone.

I spend my days watching the walls. The light is forever changing. I make shadow puppets like my father used to. There are cats chasing birds, men with odd noses, and there is just the nothing, endless nothing.

I think I should go and find the soldier, but what does any of it matter? If I stay here, maybe Ezra the cake boy will find me.

I write down what I see from my window. I don't know what I would do if there was no more paper to write on. I was stupid when the book was given to me.

How do I know that?

Most days – what days? Most of nothing divided by nothing, that's what I'm in. Limbo, time in waiting.

One limbo ruby-red morning I woke and there it was, a circus sitting on the wasteland. It must have arrived while I was sleeping, and I wonder if they have a tiger, but I don't see any animals. I watch the garish painted caravans, the big top with its flaps pulled back, and then I see a boy, not the cake boy, in the middle of all the people, and I'm sure I know him.

Treacle, he is to do with treacle. There is a man and a woman with him and they look happy. The man is in army uniform. He has his arm around the women's waist, she is holding a red balloon. They all disappear into the big top. By the time the colours fade the circus has gone. Like the weather the wasteland is forever changing but the treacle boy is there, alone, and he is wearing wings and holding the red balloon, his arms outstretched, running about as if he's an aeroplane. He lets go of the balloon and it comes floating up and up, past my window it goes, a red sun to light a scarlet memory by.

I have forgotten all this by the time the doorbell rings. It has a silly ring, a cheerful 'Of course we are at home' ring. I am not at home. I don't want anyone to find me. I will ignore it.

Whoever it is is still ringing the bell, or else the bell is stuck. I go to the door. I am frightened. Let it be anyone but the child. When I open the door there is no one there. I look down the corridor and then I see him, a large boy with a pair of wings tied on to his back. He looks like a neglected angel.

'Hello,' I say. Perhaps he is a loop memory and he'll just keep walking away. To my surprise he turns around.

'I thought it was you,' he says. 'I told Houdini it was you. I'm Tommy Treacle. Do you remember me?'

'No. Sort of. Maybe,' I say, and he comes rushing back down the corridor. His wings have feathers stuck to them. He is extraordinary, an angel, all flapping and smiling, so pleased to see that I'm here, and he hugs me, lifts me off my feet as he hugs me.

'You are beautiful,' he says. 'You have a beautiful face and lovely eyes, deep, all-seeing eyes.'

And I am laughing, really laughing. He is like warm water in a bath after a cold day.

'You are the girl from the big house.'

'Am I?'

'Yes. You are the girl from the big house who came to the pictures. I'm Tommy Treacle and this is my mouse, I have another mouse but he isn't here.'

He walks into my apartment, opens the door to the room with the walnut cabinet in it and sits down in front of it and turns on the green light.

'You shouldn't watch that,' I say.

He turns and smiles. 'My brain is not the sieve they say it is. The green light fills in the holes, makes me remember. It helps me. I found the soldier and the Brightness. It makes them forget.'

'It makes me forget. I have even forgotten what the cake boy looks like.'

Tommy laughs, a round, giggly laugh.

'Cake boy, who is the cake boy? *Pat-a-cake, pat-a-cake . . .*'

'No!' Why am I shouting? 'No, that's not him, he is . . .' I go to find my diary. '. . . Ezra,' I say.

Tommy sighs. 'Ezra.' He says it with such longing. 'He's not here.'

'How do you know?'

But he doesn't answer. He says, 'Have you been out there?'

I shake my head. 'It frightens me.'

'It's just a cinema with different shows. I've been to the circus with my mum and dad. That's where I got my mouse wings.'

'Why are they mouse wings?'

'Dad told me they were made out of mouse feathers.'

I want to say mice don't have feathers and then I'm not even sure that is right. Perhaps they do? Why shouldn't they?

'Have you seen the man who blows the smoke rings?' he asks, 'With the two-tone shoes?'

I wish he hadn't said '*pat-a-cake*'. I don't understand why it makes me think of a giant centipede with hundreds of white gloves.

'Miss Bright knows all about mice,' says Tommy. 'There are very, very rare mice, did you know that?'

'Who is Miss Bright?'

'She taught you and Ezra and she has a world of learning in her head. There are no holes in her sieve.'

'How do you know all this?'

'Because I visit her. She finds the green light very muddling. She knows a lot about mice, though. Like Gould's Mouse which lived in eastern Australia and is ex-stinks, which means goggled up and gone forever.'

'That's sad. Perhaps it's here, a memory mouse.'

'Then there is the Preble's Meadow Jumping Mouse, which lives in America, which is a very big place for a small mouse.'

I stand there speechless and Tommy turns off the green light and takes my hand.

'Shall we go and see Miss Bright?'

He is bright. He is the brightness of the day, but who this Miss Bright is, I don't know. At the door of my apartment I stop.

'This is not a bright idea,' I say. 'I don't want to leave. There will be the double shadow.'

And he does this funny thing that makes me cry. He puts his hands very softly one on each side of my face and says, 'I have a double shadow too. Mine is made of skeleton bones and inside is a little boy with a big head that is me, when I was small. Sometimes I stay with my mum and dad, before all the sadness came, and sometimes I just watch and I'm not there. Only my double shadow knows what to do.'

I am the one who is crazy, not this boy, this treacle-sweet boy, this galumphing angel. My eyes are so blurry that I don't pay much attention to where we're going. All the corridors look the same. At an apartment door, the same as all the others, he knocks then walks in, and sitting in a chair looking out of the window in a sort of trance, is a small, thin-stick, upright lady with her hair twisted into a bun. Tommy shakes her.

'Oh, there you are, dear one,' she says. 'I have had such a lovely day. He asked me to marry him. He is so handsome, is my love, his hands are long and thin. My heart will always be tucked away inside his jacket pocket. Now, what is the lesson for today?'

'No,' says Tommy, 'no lesson. See who I've brought.'

And she looks at me and her face goes cloud-dark with worry and she starts to pull at a loose strand of wool in her cardigan.

She says, 'I came looking for you and I am trying to remember why . . . but for the life of me I've forgotten. Have we had tea?'

'No,' says Tommy, holding Miss Bright by one hand and me by his other, both of us trailing behind him. Our double shadows trailing behind us. Down more corridors we walk and I hear the Herman man, or I think I hear the Herman man, then we are in the apartment with the soldier. He is busy making tea.

'I always make tea,' he says.

My heart sinks. It must have been just that once when the loop went wrong because he is talking again, using all the same words. He stops, and as he steps into the light from the window, I see, with relief, his double shadow.

I've worked it out. Our double shadows are the only evidence that we have a future.

'Well, I never,' he says to Tommy, and smiles. 'You found the girl and the Brightness together.'

In the soldier's smile is the outline of a face I know but can't remember.

'Who are you?' I ask the soldier.

And he looks at Tommy as if Tommy knows all the answers and says, 'In the land of the lost only the jester holds a light.'

I think, yes, you are right. Tommy with his mouse wings is the guide here in this maze of memories.

This is the sanest and craziest tea party I have ever been to. We sit in the room and the soldier tries to keep his eyes away from the television in the corner. Miss Bright drinks her tea and unravels her cardigan until the whole thing is as good as undone. She rolls the wool into a ball, then from her handbag takes out knitting needles and starts knitting it up again.

'We should stay together,' I say, as if I have a plan.

Miss Bright puts away her knitting and gets up to leave. I try to stop her. Her bare arms are tissue-soft.

She turns to me and says, 'I want to tell you to be careful . . . but that isn't right . . .' She lights up. 'You will have to rescue yourself. No, no, that, too, is wide of the mark. Most disappointing. You are a riddle of riddles. You are why we are in this riddle. I can't be certain but I think the word I am fishing for is "danger". Yes, that is the very word. You, my dear, are in great danger.'

PARADOX 87

Wintry sunlight seeped through the clouds as Ezra walked to work the following day. London, even with all its injuries, still retained a grey graciousness about it. He had watched the capital burn, seen buildings fall, old brick to rubble, life to death, the demolition of a city. He'd marvelled at the indomitable spirit of Londoners, their determination to survive, come what may. Perhaps it was only in these electric days that you lived in the here and now, when your life, stripped of its excesses, was brought, thin and fragile, into focus.

It struck him as extraordinary how quickly the exception became the norm. He'd seen an ambulance man in the debris of a bombed-out house, collecting blown-off limbs as if they were vegetables from some cruel allotment, a dead baby, covered with a blanket, lying in the street. Life that once had been so precious, valued by church and state, now stood naked, unredeemable, in the onslaught of war.

At the offices of Heathguard Knitwear everyone was in a state of nervous anticipation – men from the Prime Minister's office were with Sir Basil. Ezra went to his small cubbyhole of an office and started writing down all that Doctor Pincher had jogged in his memory: the basement of the picture palace, the chair, the odd helmet, the huge clock with the whizzing hands and . . .

'Looks like you've bloody well done it,' said Jim Boyle, poking his head round the corner.

'Done what?' asked Ezra.

'Given the doctor a chronic case of verbal diarrhoea. There is even talk of turning him into a double agent. Whatever he has been saying has put a rocket up the backside of Whitehall. Look out of the window.'

In the street below were several lorries with HEATHGUARD KNITWEAR painted on the side.

'I didn't know we possessed any transport.'

'We don't,' said Boyle. 'Those are army lorries, but look at all the trouble they've gone to to make sure they look the genuine article. Impressive, I call it.'

Ezra shrugged his shoulders. 'They could be here just to close us down.'

'Bet you a pint at your local in Bishop's Norgate that we're on the move.'

At eleven o'clock everyone was called into the briefing room.

Sir Basil, his face solemn, said, 'We have been ordered to pack up our things and to be out of here by fifteen hundred hours at the very latest.'

'Oh, no!' came the response from Sir Basil's loyal staff.

'It's over then?' said Ivy Reed, the dragon secretary.

Sir Basil beamed. 'No, ladies and gentlemen, it is just beginning. We have all the funding we need to send Pascoe into the memory machine to bring out Amaryllis Ruben and the others. The PM wants the thing destroyed before it falls into enemy hands.'

A huge cheer went up.

'Well, what are we waiting for? There's work to be done, and tonight we'll be in our new official headquarters in the grounds of Warlock Hall.'

'Why so soon?' asked Miss Reed.

'First, there are reports that London is going to be the target of heavy bombing tonight; second, they see what we've been beavering away on is too damn precious to be lost. It's a miracle that this building is still standing. I'll be driving down to Bishop's Norgate with Pascoe. The army is already on site, erecting Nissen huts and laying the cables we'll need. The whole area, including the Black Tower and the grounds, will be officially under our supervision. It will be known from now on as Paradox 87 and all reports will be headed as such. So – pick up your knitting patterns and let's get out of here, pronto.'

Sir Basil and Ezra were heading out of London in the Armstrong Siddeley when the air-raid sirens started wailing, quickly followed by the sound of planes overhead, a thousand angry bees swarming over London. Then came the distant 'crump crump crump' as the bombs fell, destroying building after building, fire after fire breaking out with monstrous force so London appeared ringed in flames.

At Crystal Palace they got out of the car and stood silently watching. Only the dome of St Paul's stood heroic above the smoke.

At midnight, just after they arrived at Paradox 87, the news from London was bad. Much of the City had been destroyed.

Sir Basil's team was very subdued as it went about the work of settling in, and for the second night none of them slept. In the early hours, news came through that the weather had changed and the expected last wave of bombers hadn't arrived.

'If they had, London would have been an inferno,' said Sir Basil. 'God alone knows how many innocent citizens died last night, but at least St Paul's is still standing.'

Jim Boyle was relieved to hear the news.

'I was worried about my mother,' he said to Ezra. 'She refuses to go down the shelters. Every time the sirens go off she stubbornly makes her way to St Paul's to pray. I thought, last night . . . well, I just thought.'

The grounds of Warlock Hall in the dawning of that bitterly cold winter's day were barely recognisable; everything was decayed, dead-looking. The tarmac on the tennis court was bubbled and covered in frost, the jetty that once stuck out like a tongue into the lake had suffered a stroke and hung lopsided in the frozen water. Even the woodland paths, where not long ago will-o'-the-wisp ladies in floating evening gowns had wandered, enchanted, towards the picture palace, had disappeared. Only the Black Tower stood belligerently upright, an exclamation mark in a broken landscape.

The site of the picture palace became the main focus of attention for Sir Basil's team. Several trees were being felled to make the clearing wide enough for all the instruments that were needed to record any activity. A high fence was being erected to keep the villagers away, and a bunker was under construction.

To begin with, the personnel from the OSP, their nerves torn to rags by the nightly Blitz, found the quiet of the countryside most unsettling. The sudden eerie silence of the place made them even more edgy than usual. Even Ezra, who had grown up there, couldn't get used to the stillness. It was hard knowing his home was so close and at the same time so far away. It seemed to belong to another country, where once he had kicked stones and daydreamed. Now he felt himself standing on the edge of two worlds, hovering, waiting, and wondering if he would ever get into the memory machine, ever see the girl who was looking for 'Crazy', ever remember what he had forgotten.

Time began to drag its feet for him, stubbing its toe on the boredom of endless days when nothing unusual occurred in Warlock Wood. Ezra longed for someone to talk to, someone his own age. Everyone he worked with was far older than he was. Most had families and were beyond the stage of worrying about whether or not they would ever have a girlfriend. At least in London there had been some purpose to his days. Here he was just drifting. Until, that was, Louis Lindo was seconded to the team at Paradox 87. The sergeant had arrived in a thick snowstorm, but with him he carried sunshine and a smile that made the day feel warm. Ezra had immediately taken a liking to the Jamaican airman, perhaps because he was only two years older than Ezra, perhaps because Ezra admired his courage. It had taken a lot to leave the Caribbean and come to

England to join the RAF; a difficult journey, full of 'can't dos' that, by sheer determination, Louis had overcome. Finally, he had trained as a wireless operator. He'd been looking forward to joining a bomber squadron when, instead, he was sent to Paradox 87. The two soon became inseparable. It was Louis in whom Ezra slowly began to confide.

Ever since the interview with Doctor Pincher, frame by disconnected frame, his memory was beginning to come back to him, but still the movie refused to splice together.

Sitting outside on the steps of the Black Tower one crystal-cold morning, Louis said to him, 'You grew up round here?'

Ezra, only half-listening, nodded.

'What was the house like?'

'Small, child-sized, with stairs that led up to a room you couldn't reach unless you were seven years old.'

'That can't be right,' said Louis. 'I heard it was a mighty big house with two wings and this tower bang in the middle.' He could see by the confused expression on Ezra's face that he'd been talking about something else. Louis changed the subject.

'Ever been with a girl?' he asked.

'Once,' said Ezra absently, then he stopped. 'The house I remember had something to do with hissing geese. And the facts of life.'

'Maybe all houses do,' said Louis. 'But have you?'

'Have I what?' said Ezra.

'Ever been with a girl?' Louis repeated.

'Once. You?'

'Yes, but never the right one. I think I'll know her when I meet her. Everything will be different, the world won't ever look the same again.'

'A Wendy house,' said Ezra.

'A what house?'

'It was a Wendy house and I had completely forgotten it. Amaryllis took me there . . .'

'Amaryllis Ruben? That was the girl?' said Louis.

'Yes – no, not like that. I was younger than her and storybook naive, if you know what I mean. She asked me . . . wait, wait, this is important, if I can get this I might be able to put the rest together.' After a long while, he said, 'She asked if I knew the facts of life.'

'Did you?'

'Hell, no, I was still wondering about storks and tummy buttons.'

Louis laughed.

'She told me, without embarrassment, as if she was . . . she just wanted me to understand something . . . that's what I can't remember.'

'Leave it. It'll come back in its own time, in its own way. Just tell me, what is she like this Amaryllis, this young lady who is stopping me from joining a bomber squadron?'

'She has violet eyes, raven hair . . . oh, those are just words, they don't do her justice. I'd never met anyone like her before. I'd never met anyone I disliked more and yet liked just as much, at the same time. She's exotic, in a way, like you.'

'No, man, not me. I'm just one dumb son who decided

to swim against the tide and become battle-fodder. Even my grandma thought I might secretly be on the rum. What else happened with Amaryllis?'

'I kissed her.'

Louis laughed.

'What's funny about that?'

'You. Look, you were a young boy and she was definitely three steps ahead of you in years, in knowledge, in class. It wasn't a fair contest from where I'm sitting.'

That afternoon, having nothing better to do, Ezra tried to map the outline of Warlock Hall and its gardens. Clouds had gathered and turned to icy rain by the time he came across the Wendy house. It appeared ghost-like, its paint now completely washed away. Come the spring it would be hidden in an eiderdown of greenery. Ezra pushed open the little door, its rusty hinges groaning like stone bones. Inside there was a small fireplace and a gathering of dry wood. On his hands and knees, he lit the fire in the iron grate then lay down on the floor, his legs bent, taking in the smell of earth, the decay of wood, the crackle of the fire. Rain began to fall on the roof. Drip, drip, drip.

It was then, in his mind's eye, in slow motion, that he saw it. Sir Basil would have called it a madeleine moment.

It was summer. It was raining, the last time he was here with Amaryllis. His legs were bent, they touched hers. Was it the day of the fire? Or the day before? Did it matter? Why, he wondered, had she told him the facts of life? Why that day? She just wanted him to understand . . . to understand what?

He sat bolt upright and banged his head on the ceiling. Yes, he thought, she told me because of what Everett Roach had done to her.

'He had raped her,' he said aloud, 'and I wanted to kill him. That's all I could think about and I didn't pay attention to what else she was saying. She was saying she was frightened. She was frightened of the memory machine.'

THE GLASS CLOWN

February 1941

On 17 January, it started to snow, and the cold and the fact that the picture palace hadn't been seen since Tommy Treacle's disappearance began to affect the morale of Sir Basil's team. Ezra was on standby night and day, but there was no way of predicting when or if the picture palace would ever be seen again. On the first Sunday in February, while the snow still lay on the ground, Ezra was given twenty-four-hours' leave.

As he set off for home, Mrs Calthorpe was busy telling Nancy Pascoe about the goings-on in Warlock Wood. What they were doing up there was top secret, according to her Bert, Mrs Calthorpe whispered to Nancy across her kitchen table.

'Walls have ears. A careless word could cost lives. Bert says there are spies everywhere.' Today her excuse for popping round and talking about things that were best kept mum was a large cabbage from Bert's garden. 'For the little ones,' she said.

Nancy knew that these gifts of food were Bert's way of thanking her for having taken in the Gilbert children. The last thing Mrs Calthorpe could have coped with was an evacuee.

'It's all the ornaments,' she had said. 'They're valuable, they are. I don't want them getting damaged. I mean, they've been passed down from my great-grandmother. One of them comes from Venice, you know, the little clown made of Murano glass. I would be heartbroken if anything untoward was to happen to it.'

At the start of the Blitz, Lady Bodminton-Bow had been recruited as the Billeting Officer for the area. She had decided on a policy whereby families in Bishop's Norgate and the surrounding villages would take just one evacuee each from the East End of London.

By the time Nancy had entered the church hall on the day the children were distributed, there were only three left. Each had a name tag round its neck, and carried a small suitcase and a gas mask in a box. One was to go with Mrs Calthorpe, another with Lady Bodminton-Bow and Nancy was to have the third, a boy of two, who had been sick and was now bawling his eyes out. But the two girls, identical twins aged ten, refused to be separated. The girl called Ellen spoke up for the three of them.

'We're staying together. I told Mother I wouldn't let no stranger take our Joey, and that was a promise. You either take us all or we won't budge. Ain't that right, Elsie?'

Elsie nodded.

Mrs Calthorpe was not pleased to be spoken to in this way. 'You'll do as you're told, young lady,' she said folding her arms under milkless breasts, 'and that's that.'

'We ain't budging.'

Lady Bodminton-Bow's promise of a nice homemade cake did little to alter the situation.

Ellen, wiping her runny nose on the back of her hand, said, 'I told you, missus, we won't be parted, not for any old cherry cake.'

Nancy scooped up the toddler, took out a hanky and wiped his face.

'I'll take them all, if that's all right,' she said.

Through that autumn of 1940 and into the bitter winter of January, Nancy Pascoe became known as the last resort for unwanted evacuees. She ended up with a house filled with seven children of various ages from ten to eighteen months. By giving them all a home she felt she was doing something for the war effort and it stopped her – as much as the noise and laughter of seven children could ever stop her – thinking too much about Noel, Ezra, Olive and Tommy.

She hadn't seen her son since the day after the declaration of war. She'd had letters from him but that was all, and where he was or what exactly he was doing she didn't know. Olive had now completed her training at St Thomas' Hospital. Every day Nancy lived in dread of receiving a telegram telling her that one of her beloved children had been killed in a bombing raid.

'My Bert says there are army lorries coming and going all night at Warlock Hall,' whispered Mrs Calthorpe. 'He says there's more personnel up there than he's seen before. It looks like quite a big military operation.' She dropped her voice even lower. 'The Home Guard has been asked to patrol the fences. Poor Bert's going to have to work nights.' She paused. 'It's very large.'

For a moment, Nancy couldn't think what she was talking about.

'The cabbage,' said Mrs Calthorpe. 'I imagine it's more than enough for your lot. Would you mind if I just took a quarter? I hate to see waste.'

Nancy, swallowing a sigh, got the kitchen knife, and seeing the desperate look on Mrs Calthorpe's mean face, handed it to her.

Mrs Calthorpe cut the cabbage and taking the larger part, stood up to leave. 'Oh, I nearly forgot. Bert told me he'd seen Ezra up there.'

'Up where?'

'Warlock Hall. Didn't you know he was there?'

'No,' said Nancy.

It was already beginning to get dark and the snow was falling in cartoon flakes as Ezra walked down the lanes towards his home. The fields were blue white, the houses ships adrift in seas of snow. His cottage looked comforting, its thatched roof pulled down over its blacked-out windows, smoke curling from its chimney. In the kitchen he found his mother seated in a chair by the fire, a baby asleep in her arms, other children in a range of sizes sitting at her feet while two girls drew at the table. All were listening enraptured as Nancy read to them from *The Railway Children*. His mother looked as she had all his life. A hearth of love to warm the soul by.

Nancy, glancing up from the book, for one brief moment

thought Noel had come home until she realised it was Ezra, all grown up. Gone were the awkward angles that young men can be made of and in their place was a handsome man, who, in the flicker of the firelight looked a lot like his father. The same soft brown eyes, the same brown hair, and that smile, Noel's smile – before he went to war.

'Don't just stand there,' said Ellen, 'sit down and listen. This is the important bit. Go on, Auntie Nancy.'

Nancy spoke not one word to him, but her smile said it all and she carried on reading. Ezra pulled up a chair and Elsie climbed on to his lap, and the other children moved a little closer to this stranger in army uniform.

'What are you doing here?' asked Nancy, when she had put all the children to bed and they could, at last, talk in peace.

'Mother!' Ezra laughed. 'How come you've ended up with so many little ones?'

'That's a story and a half. But I like it. Are you working up at Warlock Hall?'

'You know I can't say.'

'I do, love. Then you're here because you're going away?'

'Yes, perhaps. I hope so.'

'Is it dangerous?'

'Mother . . .'

She sighed. 'I tell you this. Even with all these children, the noise and the chaos, never once is it loud enough to stop me longing for this war to be over and for all of us to be home again together.'

That night Ezra slept in a chair by the range. At three in the morning, he was wide awake. He had heard the planes even before the siren sounded. He woke his mother and together they got the children up.

'Quickly, the bomb shelter in the garden,' she said.

Ezra held her back. He knew it was too late. 'Under the stairs,' he ordered.

'There's not enough room for us all,' said Nancy.

'It will have to do.'

'I'm sure they're only passing overhead.'

Ezra had just managed to get everyone into the cupboard except himself and Ellen when there was an unearthly silence. The world held its breath. In that moment he grabbed Ellen round the waist and pushed her under the table, throwing himself on top of her. He felt the boom, his insides flattened by the force of the blast, then sound returned with a deafening explosion and the whole kitchen turned yellow-white as the windows blew out and the door was torn from its hinges and tossed across the red snow of the garden. Ezra, the air squeezed out of him, tried to breathe.

'We forgot about the chickens,' said Ellen, gasping.

'Mother, are you all okay?' shouted Ezra.

'Yes . . . a bit shaken, but we're . . .'

Then Ezra saw the flames. They had caught the kitchen curtains.

'Stay where you are, don't move.' He rushed to beat them out before the cottage caught fire. Through the broken window Ezra could see where the bomb had landed. The Calthorpes' cottage had taken a direct hit.

Turning round he saw a small incendiary bomb roll in through the door towards the table. Without another thought he threw it outside. For a moment the garden was illuminated as his father's shed exploded in a fireball. In all, three bombs fell on the village that night.

Two hours later when the all-clear sounded, Nancy and the childen emerged into the dawn of a winter's day unlike any they had witnessed before. Father's shed had burnt to the ground, all Tommy's wonderful drawings gone. Dead chickens lay in the snow. But these were only tiny details compared to the complete destruction of the Calthorpes' cottage. Bert had been on duty that night leaving his wife alone. She was believed to be buried under the rubble. Nancy and Ezra worked as hard as they could to find their neighbour, and more local people and Bishop's Norgate's firemen came to help. Most of them hadn't experienced a bombing raid before.

It was midday before they found Mrs Calthorpe. She was dead. She had slept through the sirens, earplugs in her ears, curlers in her hair, hairnet on her head.

Bert arrived home that morning and, his face wet with tears and mud, had dug alongside his neighbours. When they found the body of his wife, he couldn't bring himself to look.

It was Elsie who discovered the little glass clown, unbroken in the snow. Very carefully, she handed it to Bert, a sacred relic.

He stood for a long while, staring at it.

The military jeep screeched to a halt outside the cottage just as the light was failing and the snow had begun to fall.

Nancy opened the door to find a tall black airman surveying the wreckage of the Calthorpes' cottage.

'Mrs Pascoe?' he said.

Nancy nodded.

'I'm glad to see you weren't harmed. I've come for Ezra.'

Nancy stared at him. Never before had she seen such a beautiful man. The rich colour of his skin flustered her and she went red with embarrassment.

Louis, who was not unused to having this effect on people, flashed her an enchanting smile. 'Er . . . Ezra, Mrs Pascoe? It's urgent.'

Ezra appeared behind her, putting on his greatcoat. He kissed his mother. 'I have to go.'

'Bring them home, love,' she said quietly. 'Just bring them home safe.'

A DI DUTTY
DUPPY MAN DWEET

Louis rammed the jeep along the narrow country lanes. Its headlights were blacked out and the hedgerows loomed skeletal in the darkness. The snow was falling heavily and the windscreen wipers failed to keep it at bay.

Ezra was exhausted. His mind was on the bomb-damaged cottage, his mother left with the mess of everything and all those children.

'Last night,' said Louis, 'the instruments in the Observation Bunker started whirling round the dials as if they were making scrambled eggs. They sent the scientists into one merry dance. I even saw a smile stretch across Jim Boyle's crooked teeth.'

'It could just be that the bombs set them off,' said Ezra.

'That's been ruled out – the machines are still going crazy.' He paused. 'Bet you half-a-crown, you're going on a journey.'

Ezra, who had thought this moment would never come, felt white-ice fear crawl over him, the same kind of fear he'd had as a child when staring into the starry skies, terrified by the vastness of the unknown. No mirror-ball of dreams, those stars, but a reminder of how lost in eternity he was. He would get out of bed with cold feet and a frozen heart, and walk what felt like a hundred miles across the landing, seeing monsters in the dark recesses waiting to gobble him up. He would lift the latch on his parents' bedroom door and crawl under the warm silky eiderdown, safe, whole again, attached to mother earth. In the morning he would wake to find, as if by some miracle, he had been returned to his bed. This time there was no eiderdown to hide under, just the brutality of now. What if he failed?

Louis talked and Ezra was grateful for it.

'They think last night's raid was aimed at the munitions factory. One of the bombs fell in the lake and that's giving Head of Operation something to think about. The ducks don't seem too happy either. It broke the ice though. Sir Basil requested two Lewis anti-aircraft guns.'

'Do you think,' interrupted Ezra, 'there is a way out of the memory machine?'

'I hope so,' replied Louis, 'because I have my heart set on you meeting my gran when the war is over. We'll lie in the sun, drinking rum, and I'll teach you how to play the sax.'

'I didn't know you could play.'

'Sure do. I had to sell it though, and my bicycle, to get to Blighty. Got fifteen pounds and bought myself a First Class cruise.'

'That was a bargain.'

'Not really. No one was going to England apart from an eighteen-year-old idiot Jamaican who dreamed of joining the RAF.'

'Tell me about when you were young, tell me anything that'll stop me thinking I can't do this.'

'All right,' said Louis. 'Once, when I was six, I flushed Gran's best Sunday church hat down the lavvy.'

'Why?'

'It was an accident. I thought I'd see what I looked like in it. The only snag was that the mirror hung over the lav. Between the climbing-up and the balancing, it fell into the stinking pan. I thought, best get rid of the evidence, but would the blessed thing go? No, it wouldn't. When Gran caught me, I told her "a di dutty duppy man dweet".'

Ezra laughed. 'What does that mean?'

'The dirty ghost did it,' said Louis.

'Did she believe you?'

'Like hell she did.'

They'd arrived at the barracks. Ezra got out of the jeep and turned to Louis. 'Thanks,' he said.

'What for?'

'For making me laugh.'

'You'll be all right, man, I have faith in that.'

The Ops Room was in the cellar of the Black Tower. Down a tight stone stairwell was a large stone room with no natural light. This dark, dank space was the hub of all the activity that took place at Paradox 87. It had been rigged with strip lighting, which had the effect of making everyone look mauve and sickly. A combination of cigarette and pipe smoke meant the place was in a permanent fog. In the middle of the room was a large table with a model of the picture palace on it, surrounded by desks, banks of telephones and telegraph machines. In this unhealthy environment Sir Basil's team worked their magic.

'Good,' said Sir Basil. He had the ability to carry on a conversation as if you'd never been away. He looked, Ezra thought, like a walrus with his bushy but well-trimmed moustache. In a man who had trouble doing up buttons correctly, this detail was engaging.

'Just in time for the briefing,' he said, sweeping Ezra into a small room that offered the closest thing to privacy down there. 'Our friends at MI5 are taking an interest.' Tigger was already seated at the table. 'You know each other,' said Sir Basil, waving vaguely. 'All yours, Tigger.'

Sir Basil sat down and fiddled with his pipe.

Tigger held out a hand to Ezra. 'You did a first-rate job with Doctor Pincher. He's been singing louder than the nightingale in Berkeley Square.

We've already put him to good use. Our chaps at Camp 020 have invented a fictitious agent whom Roach is supposedly dealing with in London.'

'You mean,' said Ezra, 'Pincher still hasn't worked out that he was duped?'

'No, not at all. The mere mention of Roach's name is enough to make him do anything we want. This is bloody dangerous, what we're asking you to do.'

'I know, sir, and I'm ready.'

'Now to basics,' said Sir Basil. 'We've prepared your kitbag and included several pairs of these.' He handed Ezra a pair of sunglasses, something Clark Gable might wear. 'They will filter out the green light completely. There are enough for everyone you need to bring out.'

'I feel like a spectacles salesman,' said Ezra.

'The main thing is, they work,' continued Sir Basil. 'Of that the boys in the back room are sure. Jim Boyle believes it's because of the green light no one has escaped. They've lost their identities, lost the will to leave. That's why you must wear the dark glasses at all times, understood?'

'Yes, sir.'

'We've packed your diary. It might jog Amaryllis's memory. And also *The Times* from today and from the day war was declared, and pictures of Warlock Hall after it burnt down. You are nearly four years older than when Amaryllis last saw you. She, of course, is still the same age as when she went in, so we've included a photograph of you both, taken by Miss Bright. Remember, it is vital to win Amaryllis's trust. Get her out and the machine will self-destruct.'

'One more thing,' said Tigger. 'Unfortunately there isn't time to brief you on all we have recently uncovered regarding Arnold Ruben, Silas Molde and Vervaine Fox, so we've given you copies of top-secret dossiers on them, for your eyes only. They're at the bottom of your kitbag, sewn into the lining.'

'Have you eaten?' asked Sir Basil. 'You'd best do so.'

'Yes, sir. Sir, perhaps some of the lads could repair my mother's cottage. It was damaged in the raid and she's looking after evacuees – six children and a baby.'

'Of course, leave it to me. Now don't worry, just concentrate on the job in hand.'

It was still dark when Ezra, Sir Basil and Tigger left the Ops Room to go to the Observation Bunker.

Louis was waiting outside. 'Permission to accompany you to the bunker, sir?' he said to Sir Basil.

Sir Basil glanced at Ezra's pale face. 'Very well, sergeant,' he said.

The anti-aircraft guns had arrived that morning and the unit was now in position, on the lookout for bombers. Still the snow was falling, cold, bitter, unforgiving. Jim Boyle was on duty in the bunker.

'Things have started to happen,' he said. 'The picture palace has partially materialised, twice, both times like a ghost of a building. It disappeared after just a few minutes, although the dials are still showing great activity in the vicinity.' He added, rather pessimistically, 'Bet the blasted thing won't show up again now you're here.'

From the bunker's window-slit it was hard to see anything at all, harder still to imagine a building appearing there. The unreality of it made Ezra think that perhaps reality was only ever a footnote in a person's life, something most people escaped from by going to the pictures or reading books, avoiding the pitfalls of being in the present, in the now. As he stood on the brink of the unknown it occurred to him that he himself had banished memories that were rightfully his.

A tune meandered into his head and he sang it quietly under his breath.

If you go down in the woods today
You're sure of a big surprise . . .

And it came to him, a postcard of a memory.

'Look!' shouted Jim Boyle.

Before them was a phantom, an outline of the picture palace in green light. At that moment the air-raid sirens sounded. They could hear, far off, the rumble of *Luftwaffe*'s bombers.

Sir Basil cursed under his breath as the spectral building disappeared.

'The basement . . .' said Ezra.

'It's no damn good,' said Boyle. 'You can't do anything until the raid is over. Anyway, the memory machine seems to be losing power. If it doesn't fully materialise, I don't think there'll be a way in.'

'If the building isn't solid we'll have to call off the whole blasted shooting match,' said Sir Basil. 'It's too risky. Even if Pascoe gets in, he might not be able to get back.'

Ezra wasn't listening.

Beneath the trees, where nobody sees,
They'll hide and seek as long as they please.

The song went on and on in his head.

Today's the day . . .

. . . the day he and Amaryllis had hidden from Roach and Pincher in the basement of the picture palace . . . they'd escaped through a tunnel that led to . . . where did it lead to?

The ice-house. They'd come out in the ice-house.

Ezra picked up his kitbag.

'Boyle,' he said, trying to keep his voice calm, 'is it possible that just a part of the building could fully materialise, perhaps where the power is concentrated, around the memory machine itself?'

They could hear the bombers approaching, flying low. The bunker trembled slightly as the anti-aircraft guns found their target.

'Damn and blast it!' shouted Sir Basil above the noise.

Jim Boyle was looking at his logbook again, concerned he had missed something.

'I suppose it is theoretically possible, but . . .'

He didn't finish what he was saying. Ezra was already opening the door of the bunker. In a gust of snowy wind he was gone.

Outside, the noise of the Stuka bombers was terrifying. They seemed to fall out of the air, diving upon their prey then zooming up high, out of danger. Ezra, nearly deafened, ran towards the ice-house, ran like he had never run before, almost dancing to avoid the rat-a-tat of machine-gun fire. By the first clump of trees he flattened himself in the snow as another plane made its alarming dive toward him. He saw it pull up out of its nose dive as its engine cut.

Ruddy Nora, thought Ezra, unable to move, it's going to come down on top of me. But the plane was hurtling, ablaze, towards the lake, where it exploded in a fireball. All around the snow glowed orange.

Getting up, he saw that Louis was running after him.

'Go back,' he yelled. 'Go back!'

His voice was drowned by the sound of another plane. Ezra was nearing the walled garden but the Stuka was upon him, over him as it dropped its load. Ezra felt his whole body leave the ground. For a moment he might have been made of nothing. Flames danced along the snow-laden garden wall, then there was a roar as they reached the ammunition stored in the ice-house. The explosion illuminated everything. He was suspended, floating among the debris of brick and bark. He felt an unpleasant jerk, the pull of gravity, as he hit the ground. Another plane approached, this one lower than all the rest. As bullets jiggered around him, he looked back. There was a dark shape in the snow. A fallen branch? He prayed that it wasn't Louis, that he'd got back to the bunker.

Ezra struggled to his feet again. A hundred yards away, the ice-house was a smouldering ruin. Disorientated, he was uncertain which way to run when suddenly the earth opened up and swallowed him whole. He wasn't sure if he lost consciousness. He became aware of the dark, of how intense darkness can be. He waited a moment to see what was hurting and was surprised to find he was all right.

Like a blind man he felt about him. He'd fallen into the tunnel. Shouldering his kitbag, Ezra started back towards the site of the picture palace. The earth above him was beginning to give way and he fought a rising panic, fearing he'd be buried alive. Then, through the smell of wet clay, came another smell, of rust and celluloid, of reels of film. Ahead of him a shaft of red light illuminated what had been the entrance to the basement storeroom. The sliding door was hanging from its track, buckled by the blasts. The tunnel began to collapse, and an avalanche of earth rolled towards him. He ran the last few yards. The basement vibrated with the presence of the memory machine. He knew exactly where he was.

At the end of the corridor was the flight of stairs that led to a small door, smaller than the one he remembered. He turned the handle and pushed hard. The door gave and to his surprise he fell into a broom cupboard. Breathless, he leaned heavily against what seemed to be a solid wall – and found himself tumbling backwards, accompanied by a percussion of brushes, brooms and buckets.

And here, in the pink glow of the foyer of the picture palace, staring down at him, bewildered, is Amaryllis Ruben.

AFTER THE BALL

The air-raid warning sounded again just a few hours after Ezra left with Sergeant Lindo, and once more the cottage shook to the terrifying noise of bombs exploding nearby.

Nancy looked down at the small faces of six scared children and one screaming baby, and said, 'It's all right, it's all right.'

Oh, please, dear Lord, may nothing happen to Ezra. 'All right' is a downright lie, she thought, to keep a flame of hope alive, but in the dark under the stairs it was the only weapon she possessed.

The only weapon, that is, until Bert Calthorpe started to sing at the top of his voice, drowning out the noise.

> *After the ball was over,*
> *Mabel took out her glass eye,*
> *Put her false teeth in the water,*
> *Hung up her wig to dry,*
> *Put her peg leg in the corner,*
> *Hung her tin ear on the wall,*
> *And the rest of her went to bye-bye,*
> *After the ball.*

'And again!' shouted the children. Even the baby had stopped his screaming. By the time the sirens called the all-clear, there was no one there who would ever forget the night that Bert Calthorpe sang his heart out.

After the destruction of his cottage and the death of his wife, Nancy had said he was welcome to stay with them. She was, if truth be told, grateful for the help, for there had been little water or electricity to speak of in the Pascoes' cottage since the bombing, and what there was came in fits and starts.

While Nancy was busy tucking in the children, Bert built up the fire, swept the kitchen floor and had the teapot and cups on the table, all ready and waiting.

Sitting down together, Nancy said, 'You're a very practical man, Bert. Doreen was lucky to have a husband like you.'

Bert said nothing.

Nancy turned the teapot three times before pouring, mainly out of habit and a notion that it made the tea that bit stronger. It was, she thought to herself, the mundane, the ordinary that took on a near-religious quality when life was this butterfly-fragile.

'I hate to think what the missus would have said,' said Bert, 'if she knew where she'd been taken. She wouldn't like it, not one jot, being left at the cottage hospital in a make-do mortuary. A particular woman, was my missus.'

Their conversation was peppered by the sound of ambulances and fire engines whirling past, their dimmed lights searching out the moth holes in the blackout curtains, throwing motes of brightness into the darkness that was only held at bay by a candle in a jam jar.

'The weather hasn't helped,' said Nancy kindly. 'They couldn't get Doreen to the funeral parlour in Broughton because of the snow.'

'I don't want to see her again,' Bert said abruptly.

'You don't have to if you don't want to. I'll go to the cottage hospital in the morning if you like, and sort it out.'

'You would do that for me?' asked Bert, amazed.

'Yes, of course.'

'I want to tell you something,' said Bert, his face darkening. 'It might upset you.'

'Bert, say whatever you like.'

He took a deep breath. 'I was never anything in the Great War. Never made sergeant, never got any medals, I was just a plain foot soldier and a ruddy coward. I was lucky not to have been put against the wall and shot. Noel, on the other hand, was a lion. Brave – the bravest man I'd ever known. Not only that, but he had dignity. He never bragged about how he came by his medal. I should have had the guts to tell my wife to shut up, that I was nothing, ruddy nothing, in the Great War.'

'Bert . . .' protested Nancy.

'No, no, let me finish. I've never spoken of this and I know Noel won't have told you. I don't suppose you know how he came to have that medal of his?'

Nancy shook her head.

'I thought not. It's a story about a hero and it went round those stinking trenches like wild fire. Noel's officer, a piece of stuck-up toffee on a stick, ordered Noel and his men to retake some useless trenches we'd lost months before. Noel went out there fighting, but it was hopeless. Cannon fodder they were. He got a lot of his wounded men back to their trench. There was a young lad of sixteen who Noel had taken under his wing. Bernie, his name was. Bernie'd fallen on the barbed wire in no-man's-land. His arm was blown off and the more he tried to move, the more the wire cut into him.The officer ordered he should be left there to die, said it was too dangerous to try to get him back. Everyone could hear him screaming, calling for his mum. Noel was having none of it. He told the officer where he could go. Then he took off his tunic and climbed out of the trench, no gun or anything, just a white handkerchief on a stick. He started to walk, his arms spread wide. Everyone thought he was a proper goner but the Hun didn't fire. Noel, with his bare hands, freed Bernie from the barbed wire and carried him back to the trench. The lad was losing so much blood, he didn't stand a chance. Noel had tea brewed for him, strong with sugar, and helped him take sips, all the time telling him he was nearly home. Bernie became very peaceful and he died quietly in Noel's arms. The officer said he would have Noel court-martialled for disobeying an order. Noel stood up, looked the man straight in the eye and said, "It's Good bloody Friday, sir, the day Christ made the greatest sacrifice for mankind. I wonder if He would have bothered if He came back now and saw the things we do in His name." They arrested Noel then and there. It caused such an uproar in the trenches that he was quickly released. He was given the Victoria Cross for his courage. Never said a word about it to anyone. I'm ashamed of my wife, of what she used to say to you, going on about him being off his rocker. I'm ashamed I never told her to shut up. I'm ashamed of my cowardice. Noel didn't give me away, though he knew the truth. Now tell me to bugger off, tell me you never want to see me again.'

Nancy had tears in her eyes. 'Lots of us live secret lives, telling ourselves the story of what might have been. You're not a wicked man, Bert.'

And in the dark, she hugged him.

Early next morning, Nancy was up and dressed. She woke Bert, who had slept by the fire in an armchair he had salvaged from his cottage. It was burnt in parts and smelled of smoke. Stuffing was leaking from the back. It seemed to Nancy that the chair and the glass ornament were all that was left to Bert from what was fast becoming his former life. And that morning, Bert, for the first time since he married Doreen, felt a lightness of being.

'While I'm gone,' Nancy said, 'you'll need to keep the fires going. Make sure the little lad eats his porridge. Oh, yes, another thing – the water pipe outside is frozen solid.'

Bert was busy making notes when there was a knock on the front door.

Nancy braced herself as she lifted the latch. For a moment she couldn't for the life of her make out who the young man standing before her was.

'Mrs Pascoe, it's me, Len,' he said.

'Why, Len,' said Nancy, 'I hardly recognised you in uniform.'

She was almost overwhelmed with relief that it wasn't someone come to tell her that Ezra had been injured or worse.

Len was as drainpipe-skinny as ever.

'Come in, love,' she said.

'I've got some leave and Mum told me about the air raid and all, and I wondered if I could help.' Seeing Bert, he said, 'Sorry about your wife, Mr Calthorpe.'

'Thanks, lad.'

'I have a motorbike. I could fetch anything you need.'

Nancy grabbed her coat and hat. 'Do you think you could take me to the cottage hospital?'

Len drove with great care down the snowy lanes, the motorbike skidding only occasionally. Nancy kept her eyes closed and told herself, what will be will be. At least it saved a long walk.

When they arrived she straightened herself out, pulled down her coat and adjusted her hat.

'Shall I wait for you, Mrs Pascoe?' asked Len.

'No, love. If you could help Bert, that would be grand.'

His reply was lost in the roar of the bike.

The cottage hospital was tiny. Before the war it was a sleepy place where nothing much happened, but today the usually empty corridors were lined either side with trolleys full of wounded men, some looking close to death. Nancy's heart sank as she seached the faces, terrified of finding Ezra there. She stopped abruptly when she saw Louis Lindo. His leg was badly injured and there was a huge gash on his right side. His face was covered in lacerations.

'Sergeant Lindo,' said Nancy, 'do you remember me? I'm Ezra's mother.'

Louis managed a weak smile.

'Good to see you, ma'am.'

She took his icy hand and watched as one line of trolleys was moved to waiting ambulances.

'Where are they going?' she asked one of the army orderlies.

'They're being taken to London, to St Thomas' Hospital. The trolleys on this side . . . no hopers,' he said bluntly and disappeared down the corridor.

Louis was drifting in and out of consciousness.

Nancy hesitated, checked no one was watching then wheeled Louis's trolley to the other side. She noticed that the chart at the foot of the trolley had a red line penned through it. Quickly she stuffed it in her handbag and hoped no doctor would appear before Louis was safely in the ambulance.

'Try to stay awake, love,' she said, 'please.'

'Are you an angel?' Louis asked.

'No, love.' Though she thought an angel or two might be handy in this particular situation. Nancy stayed, holding his hand, determined that he should get into one of the ambulances. As they neared the door a nurse looked at the foot of Louis's trolley.

'Where's his chart?' she asked.

'He didn't have one,' Nancy lied.

A doctor was called. He lifted the blanket covering the shivering Louis and said, 'He's in the wrong line. He should be moved to the left.'

'No,' said Nancy firmly. 'He must go to St Thomas's. I'm a relative, his distant aunt.'

The doctor, deeply puzzled, took her aside.

'Your name?'

'Pascoe. Mrs Noel Pascoe.'

With rising panic Nancy could see the ambulances were getting ready to leave. 'You have to send him to London, you must. He is going to live,' she said, passionately.

It was then that an angel of sorts appeared in the shape of Sir Basil Stanhope.

'Oh, at last,' said Nancy, as if she had been waiting for him for ages.

'My dear lady, is everything all right?'

'No,' said Nancy quickly. 'Sergeant Lindo's transfer papers are lost and this doctor thinks he should be kept here.'

'Is that the last of them?' shouted the orderly down the corridor.

'No,' said Sir Basil firmly. He could see, sticking out of the top of Nancy's handbag, a corner of Louis's chart. 'Doctor, I am here to make sure every one of my injured men is given the best possible care. The sergeant must be transferred with the rest.'

'But, sir,' said the doctor.

'Do I make myself clear?'

'Yes, sir,' said the doctor.

Louis squeezed Nancy's hand and said, softly, 'Thank you, Auntie.'

'Why him, in particular?' asked Sir Basil when the last of the ambulances had driven off.

'Because he's Ezra's friend. And because he has a lovely smile.'

Sir Basil laughed. 'You are a wicked woman, Mrs Pascoe. But you should have hidden the chart a little better. Would you like a lift home?'

'No, thank you,' said Nancy. 'I have to see what's happening to the body of my neighbour, Mrs Calthorpe. Her husband wants her taken to the funeral parlour in Broughton.'

'I doubt that it will happen today,' sighed Sir Basil. He looked at Nancy's exhausted face. 'I will see what I can arrange. It might take time. It's a bit of a mess up at the base,' he added.

'Is Ezra . . . ?'

'All went according to plan,' he said, and smiled.

Relieved, Nancy watched him leave. She had to wait the best part of the day for the undertakers, but to keep herself occupied, she wrote to Olive, telling her to look out for a rather special young RAF sergeant.

When the undertakers did arrive, they came not in a hearse but in a Victorian funeral carriage pulled by an old farm horse.

'Sorry,' said said one of the men. 'It was all we could muster, petrol being so scarce.'

As the carriage slowly made its way back towards the small market town Nancy fancied she could hear Doreen Calthorpe in the wind, still complaining.

She walked home, tired and hungry, knowing her day was far from over, what with the house to clean, clothes to wash, beds to be made, children to be comforted, seven hot-water bottles to be filled and a grieving Bert to deal with.

She opened the front door expecting an avalanche of children to come rushing towards her, but all was quiet and peaceful. She stood stock-still, her hat in her hand, wondering what on earth had happened. Someone had had the presence of mind to hang a curtain across the hallway to keep out the cold. Lifting it, she found Bert and Len busy. Len was hanging nappies on the clotheshorse near the fire; Bert was standing over the range stirring a pot from which came a smell that made her mouth water.

'I was just about to go and look for you,' said Len. 'Then one of the children came down wondering where you were, but they're all asleep now.'

'What have you both been up to?' said Nancy, staring in amazement at the parlour and the kitchen. 'The place is spick-and-span.'

'Everyone helped, even the smallest. They all had their jobs, all except the baby,' said Bert.

Nancy sat down, quite overwhelmed. Beside the chair clucking sounds were coming from two cardboard boxes.

'Goodness knows how they survived,' said Bert, bringing her a cup of tea. 'Len found the cock and a hen under the shed door. They're thawing out nicely.' A smile flickered across Bert's face. 'It's a rabbit stew with dumplings, if you're wondering.'

Nancy looked at Len.

'I borrowed Mr Pascoe's old hunting gun,' he said sheepishly. 'It just needed a bit of work, then I went out to find supper. There are two more hanging in the larder.'

A COCKROACH
IN PARADISE

Ezra Pascoe's arrival from the broom cupboard, extraordinary as it was, couldn't compare with the enormous shock to Silas when Everett Roach had appeared wreathed in smoke, a genie conjured from Aladdin's lamp. Silas cursed himself for once again believing Vervaine's lies.

'We mustn't give up,' she had pleaded. 'Arnold will be waiting in Warlock Wood for us.'

Too late, Silas had discovered it was not Arnold she wanted but Everett Roach. It was not the first time she had so deceived him. Vervaine immediately cast off the role of the tragic diva and took on the new role of romantic heroine whose long-lost love had at last returned to her.

'I knew you would come,' she'd said, draping herself around Roach.

A smile of smoke crept from his lips.

Silas sees him as a cockroach in the Garden of Eden, more poisonous than the snake. He hasn't come here for Vervaine, of that Silas is certain. For all his pretence at love, Silas suspects Roach's motive is far less honourable. He has discovered him down in the control room with his camera.

Roach's excuse is that he enjoys taking pictures and, indeed, has made something of a career of it. Silas suspects someone on the outside wants to see what the inside of the impossible looks like.

'What are you doing?' Silas asks him on the third occasion he finds him there, focusing his lens on the dials.

'Nothing, my old fruit gum. Clever, your boss.'

Silas is repulsed by him. He has started to plan how to remove Roach from the picture palace. Finding him alone upstairs, lounging in a leather armchair, smoking, Silas asks, 'Why don't you go, and take all those pictures of yours back to whoever it is that wants to see them?'

'If you think I believe you would let me do that, my old fruit gum, you must think I'm a right nitwit.'

Silas's dark eyes turn steel hard. 'What are you here for? What do you want?'

Roach, watching a smoke ring break apart, says, 'The Jew's daughter, she's here, isn't she? I'd like to see her. I have unfinished business.'

Pure hatred oozes from Silas in the form of a cold sweat.

'What business? You've never met her.'

Roach laughs. 'That's where you're wrong.'

Silas remembers the business card Miss Amos gave him and feels sick to the pit of his stomach.

'Maurice Sands,' he says, slowly. 'It was you who abducted Amaryllis.'

'I'm surprised a clever fellow like you missed that one, my old fruit gum.' Roach lifts a Martini to his lips.

'You have the pictures, what else are you after?'

'The question is,' says Roach, 'why would I want to go when I can spend all eternity with the love of my life?'

'Shall we stop playing games?' says Silas.

'You see, this is a tricky business, what with the old girl. I don't want her clinging to me all the way back to Wednesday, if you get my drift.'

'I will take care of that.'

'I need to get into the apartments and see what's in them – without losing my memory. Is that possible?'

'Yes,' lies Silas.

It isn't possible. Not without the glasses, of which, as far as he knows, Roach is ignorant.

'If I were to help you, will you tell me what has happened to Arnold Ruben?'

'I haven't a clue, my old fruit gum. Anyway, what do you think the old girl would say if she knew what you had in mind? She's not all fur coat and no knickers. I can tell you this for nothing, she won't be best pleased with her Silas when she finds lover boy gone, will she?'

Silas is nearly trembling with rage.

'Let me worry about that.' He can hardly bear to hear the cockroach say another word. 'And I will make it safe for you to take pictures in the apartments.'

'What's the sudden hurry?' says Roach.

'The truth is,' says Silas, 'I'm not sure how many more times I can take the machine back.'

'I'll do this for you, my old fruit gum, I'll think about it. You never know, if you set it up, I might even be tempted to take a walk out, stretch the old limbs, get a few racing tips. Are you a gambler?' Roach takes a pack of cards from his pocket. 'I always carry them, never know when they might be needed. Now, pick a card.'

'Why?'

'Just pick a card.'

Silas, his hand trembling, picks the Knave of Clubs.

'Spot on the money, my old fruit gum, that's me to a tee. Pick another.'

Silas picks the Queen of Spades.

'That's the old girl in the boudoir. And the last.'

Furious, Silas picks the third card and turns it over.

'Predictable, that's what I say. The cards never lie. You are the Joker. Do you know, in most games, the Joker is the first to go.'

'What do you mean by that?'

'An observation on the situation. As I said, you do what you have to do and I might well feel like getting a breath of fresh air. No promises, mind you. Is that a deal?'

Roach, his long legs in front of the fire, watches as Silas walks away, and laughs. He'd found where the Joker had hidden the gun. It took a crook's nose to sniff it out and now it's sitting snugly in his pocket, loaded, ready and waiting like a good-hearted tart.

Why should he leave, he says to himself. What's to be gained? Nothing but a whole lot of trouble. The disadvantage of staying is the old girl. She isn't easy. She makes demands and her devotion irritates him. Yes, he thinks, it would be good not to have her dead weight hanging on him. But then again, there are so many compensations here. If he was to go back . . . there'd been all that talk of war. It might not have happened. Or it might actually be happening, right now. No, he isn't that thrilled by the idea. And that's without taking into account a lot of awkward questions about blackmail, explosives and murder. All right, given a fair wind, a lot of money and a good lawyer, he could most probably wriggle his way out. But then there's Pincher to consider and he's a different kettle of fish, he wouldn't hesitate to shop him to save his own skin. No, best to stay put, he thinks, and be the king of the castle, do time here rather than time in jail, where he stands to lose his good looks. When he finally comes out of this, he will be perfection personified and ready to resume his career.

This is what Roach thinks, leaning his head on the back of the chair.

Vervaine is taking direction from Cecil B. DeMille in a film for which she had once auditioned, but was never to make. Silas has edited this memory, it is his love poem to her.

'Darling,' Vervaine asks the director, 'does the tiger have to be in every scene?'

The tiger lets out a roar and Vervaine moves cautiously away.

'Darling, remind me, what am I thinking at this moment?' She addresses her questions to DeMille, who is sitting in his director's chair.

'You are triumphant, you can take your revenge.'

Silas is pulled up short. No, no, that's not how this golden memory goes. He feels his love poem soiled by cheap melodrama. The bile of jealousy rises in him. Had he given Arnold Ruben his life only to be rewarded by the inventor's magic tricks? The twist of memory, the truth lost? What is truth? All is in disguise, nothing is what it appears.

'Profile, darling,' shouts the director. 'Roll camera.'

Silas watches as Vervaine comes alive. The lens on her face a lover's embrace, the perfect all-seeing eye, the eye that adored and devoured her, the only eye that ever understood her. She says nothing, her face tells the story.

The tiger leaves her and paws at the picture palace doors, demanding to be let out. He lopes towards the apartment blocks, his double shadow lengthening in the snow.

A memory can't have a double shadow but the tiger does. Why did Arnold choose to make this one memory more powerful than all the rest? Silas wonders now, as he often does, if Arnold has betrayed him, has tampered with the memory recordings. It nags at him, this thought, a maggot in his subconscious. Has the memory machine started to reprogramme itself without him noticing? It isn't possible, Silas repeats to himself like a mantra, it isn't possible. Yet the worm of doubt eats deeper into his brain.

Silas has restarted the machine. He waits. At any moment Warlock Wood should appear. The wasteland shimmers as if it is suffering from double exposure; images overlapping, vague outlines of woods, then, snowblind white. Finally he has to acknowledge he is losing control over Arnold Ruben's creation.

The tiger returns, leading Amaryllis across the wasteland and into the picture palace. Why, thinks Silas, why? He watches anxiously as the tiger leaps up the mirrored staircase to the gallery, prowling this way and that, his menacing presence trapping Vervaine where she stands.

Silas is horrified to see the change in Amaryllis. When he left her in the apartment her face had life to it. Now she is pale, there is an unhealthy translucence about her skin. It dawns on him that in his desire to find her father he has unwittingly put her life in danger, whenever he returned the machine to Warlock Wood. Time, tick-tock, drip-drop, undetectable seconds depleting her strength.

In the dim light at the back of the foyer, Silas sees one solitary smoke ring glide upwards, a warning.

Amaryllis is staring at a cupboard from which comes a rattle of brooms combining with the machine's hum, purring from its electric throat. The mechanical orchestra builds to a high-pitched whine, a jazz haze of a racket, before it spirals helter-skelter, a cacophony of noise crashing to the bottom. Accompanied by a drumbeat of buckets, and a roll of broom handles, a young man tumbles out of the utility cupboard. He lands in the foyer, his skin aglow with health and reality.

Silas recognises Ezra Pascoe. Is it possible that so much time has passed? He has grown up, no longer a young boy. Clearly he has brought with him the future. He has about his person the tendrils of time, connected to hours that are still seconds-warm. Silas doubts he will be like the others, who, with the simplicity of sheep, have been seduced by the green light.

Silas wants to ask him: is Arnold Ruben alive? And if he is, why isn't he here? But he can see the young man has a mission. Silas supposes it is to take Amaryllis home. It mustn't happen, can't happen. Ezra has come in the wrong way, the machine hasn't captured his memories. The sealed, timeless Utopia will be rocked.

Amaryllis is staring down at the young man.

'I'm Ezra Pascoe,' he says, scrambling to his feet. 'Do you remember me?'

'You're the cake boy,' she says.

He hesitates, then smiles. 'Yes, I suppose I am.'

Everett Roach walks purposefully towards them. He is holding the revolver.

'That's no use to you here, Roach. For God's sake, put it away,' shouts Silas.

The machine once more makes a high-pitched whine, its crackly hum a deafening sound, rising octave by unbearable octave.

'What the hell is the Pascoe boy doing here, Silas?' shouts Vervaine above the din, 'tell me that.'

'Well,' says Roach, pointing the revolver at Amaryllis, 'we meet again.'

There is a look of pure terror on Amaryllis's face.

'Put the gun away, Roach, you're frightening her,' says Silas. 'It's all right, Amaryllis, he can't hurt you here.'

She grabs Ezra's hand and runs towards the doors.

Everett Roach cocks the pistol and takes aim at her, but the tiger leaps down the staircase and knocks him to the ground. The pistol goes off and in that instant Silas finds himself in a memory he'd long tried to forget. A mirrored ceiling is shattering, silver rain pouring down upon the young actress and her lover.

Vervaine's shriek brings him back. 'Stop that noise, Silas! Stop the noise!' Silas watches as the young man follows the girl and the tiger across the thick, white, untouched snow of the wasteland and, for the first time in nearly thirty years, he weeps. Still the ever-present hum, the monotonous sound drones on. Even when the machine is silent, Silas hears its magnetic waves. They seem to be repeating: save her, save her, save her.

With razor realisation, he understands too late what he and Arnold Ruben created: a monstrous masterpiece of machinery. He knows this just as he knew, when he looked into Ezra's eyes, that Arnold Ruben is dead, and he is on his own.

WHY ARE YOU WEARING
THOSE GLASSES?

The logbook has a grey cover. Written in the right-hand corner is the word 'Confidential'. In the middle of the front page is printed 'The Monthly Logbook of Paradox 87'. Under that, in smaller type, the date: 'February 1941'.

On the first page are a set of instructions on how to keep a logbook. On the left-hand side are lines with the hours, the day, the weather and so on. On the right-hand side of the page is a space for short bits of commentary.

Ezra starts to write:

This is the first entry in the first of my logbooks. A note to myself: I am using the pen that Sir Basil gave me.

The time is . . . I haven't a clue. My watch shattered when I was blown off my feet. The whole logbook and all it stands for appear redundant. What do you write when time is no longer the ruler of your days?

It is dark. A deep, green dark, not a night-time dark.

Weather: bitter cold, still snowing. I am wearing the dark glasses.

I see no other person on the way to this apartment where Amaryllis lives. It is in a tall building that looks like all the others that ring the wasteland. Her word, not mine. Thirteen flights of stairs we walk up, Amaryllis, the tiger and I, then along huge empty corridors. I am aware of the green light seeping from under each of the many front doors. There is an unhealthy silence in this place. By that I mean it sounds as if someone is holding their breath and has been for a long time. I can still hear a green hum, like the one in the picture palace. I feel as if I am wading against the tide.

I tell you this much – this is unlike anywhere I have ever been, literally. It reminds me of the old gangster films at the Saturday Cinema Club. We used to love them, Len, Tommy and I.

I suppose it's someone's memory of New York. I don't know if New York looks like this, having never been out of England. I keep thinking James Cagney is going to come knocking on the door. Crikey. No one would believe me if I told them where I was.

I have not taken off the glasses. I am tempted. I mean, I wonder what it would all look like without them.

I can confirm that Everett Roach, Silas Molde and the actress Vervaine Fox are here. Roach has a revolver and a mind to kill Amaryllis. As far as I can see there is nothing wrong with his memory. I asked her if he had tried to kill her before. She didn't answer.

Vervaine Fox appears as she always has done, with a voice that makes you long for silence. Silas is the unknown one, he looks worried, or perhaps it was just the sight of Roach with the gun, or seeing me again. There is no sign of my father, Tommy or Miss Bright. I ask Amaryllis if they are here. She says maybe. I soon realise this is what she says to most things she can't remember.

Who am I talking to? Myself? Yes. I think that is who this logbook is for. It has no lines for the notes I need to take.

I wonder if I am dead?

I can take no credit for our escape from the picture palace. It was due to the white tiger. Ten feet long. No, I am not exaggerating, I've never seen an animal so big. It is extraordinarily beautiful: white with brown chocolaty markings and blue-sky eyes. It belongs, I think, to Amaryllis. The tiger knocked Roach off his feet. We didn't dilly-dally after that. We made a run for it, out on to the untrodden snow. Ruddy Nora, it is cold in the wasteland.

Amaryllis is dressed in the flimsiest of clothes, a red cardigan which she never seems to take off. She is very thin, thinner than I remember, but then I don't know if I trust my memory completely.

Jim Boyle would be pleased to know that his theory about time is right. Amaryllis is the same age as on the day of the fire. Once, when I was younger, when I hated her with a passion, I had a fantasy of being the eldest. Now I am and it just feels wrong, as if time has been stolen from her. Which I suppose, when you think about it, it has.

Blast it! I don't know about these dark glasses. They hurt my eyes.

The tiger must have been to her apartment before because he knows where she lives. Only when we open the front door does he walk away from us, back down the bleak corridors to be lost in a green haze. Inside the apartment the rooms all have parquet flooring and are bigger than I would have imagined. Or maybe it's because there is little to no furniture in them to make them seem smaller.

Finally, there is something I can log in a rational way. There are two bedrooms, one bathroom, one kitchen. The bathroom is tiled black and white. The main room has nothing in it apart from a walnut cabinet from which an eerie light illuminates the room. I feel as if I am in pond water. One of the bedrooms has a small bed, the other a wrought-iron double bed. Behind the door of the room with the small bed is a mirror. A suitcase sits in the middle of the room with a diary on top. It is the same as the one that I was given by Miss Bright. I was ridiculously excited at the sight of it, something that appears to hold gravity, that belongs to a world where I could keep a proper logbook.

'Do you have any pencils?'

This is nearly all she has said since she first asked me if I was the cake boy.

'Yes.'

'Good.'

Then she says, 'Why are you wearing those glasses?'

I go and get a pair for her from my kitbag. She looks at them and laughs.

'Do you think the green light won't get you if you wear these?'

'Yes.'

She says nothing.

In this room with the suitcase, her room, she has decorated the walls with a collection of slips and bodices. There is nothing else. The kitchen and the bathroom are tiny. Green water comes from the taps. Everywhere is bitterly cold. No heating. Not even a paraffin heater. Why is there no heating? I am frozen to the marrow.

Amaryllis says, 'You can stay here,' and she shows me to the room with the wrought-iron bed.

I tell her I don't need such a big bed.

She just walks away. I put down my kitbag.

Before she closes her bedroom door, she says, 'Don't look at the green light, even with the glasses on. If you do, you'll become like the others.'

It is cold in this room, ruddy cold, and it is still snowing outside. The bed has very thin sheets and one blanket. I think I will sleep in my clothes. The bed is damp. Hell's bells, I am so goddamn tired and the ruddy bed is damp. Tomorrow I am going to find Father, Tommy and Miss Bright, and get everyone back to civilisation. The sooner this is over the better.

I wake in the night . . . wrong, I wake in the dark to see Amaryllis standing at the side of the bed, watching me.

'What are you doing?' I ask.

'I am very cold,' she says. She has on the thinnest of

petticoats and that red cardigan. I lift up the thin covers, letting in an Arctic draught as she climbs in. She lies rigid beside me. I too am pretty rigid. I hear her teeth chattering and I think, this is stupid. If we're ever to get warm, we'll have to share each other's body heat and wearing clothes isn't going to help.

'What are you doing?' she says, when I take off my shirt. I tell her I am going to make her warm. Her face looks terror-struck and I remember what Roach did to her.

'I'm not going to do anything but put my arms around you to warm you up, and rub your back to get your circulation working.'

She laughs at that, a mirthless laugh. I hold her freezing body next to mine, she seems colder than death and her feet are like blocks of ice. I lie there and finally I fall asleep.

I have no idea how long we have slept. When I wake she is on her side facing away from me and I am curled around her, holding her tight, my hand resting on her breast, and it feels far from wrong. She is already awake.

'You talk in your sleep,' she says.

I move my hand away. She puts it back.

'I'm warm,' she says, 'warm for the first time since being here.' Then she turns to face me. 'I waited for you. I had given up waiting. I thought I would all but forget you – and here you are.'

'It took time to work it all out and how to . . .' I don't finish what I am saying.

She kisses me gently on the mouth, a little kiss. I daren't

move. I would love to kiss her back, fill her mouth with my tongue.

'Your name isn't easy to remember,' she says.

It is an effort to get out of bed and leave her.

She smiles at me.

I wash my face and wait until I feel calmer, under control. I have only ever slept with one woman, that's all. We met at the cinema, watching Charlie Chaplin in *The Great Dictator*. We were both laughing and afterwards we went for a drink. I walked her back to her flat and she asked me up.

I was all fingers and thumbs. I felt like a complete fool. It lasted less time than a sneeze and I thought she would kick me out on my ear.

Instead she said, 'Stay.'

We made love again as the bombs dropped. Even now I find it funny to think that we didn't notice that half the bedroom wall had been blown away.

It was the postman who shouted up to us next morning. 'You all right up there?'

'Never better,' she called back.

I never saw her again. She was killed a week later in another raid.

I go back into the bedroom. Amaryllis has gone. Hurriedly, I get dressed.

She is in the main room, looking out at the wasteland. It is still snowing and on it is a field hospital from what has to be the Great War.

We watch together for a long time until it becomes unbearable.

We can hear the men call for their mothers, wives, lovers. Their cries wound me, just by listening.

'Perhaps we should go and find the soldier,' she says.

'What soldier?'

'The one who makes tea for Bernie.'

My father. Oh God, we are looking at his memories. Now I know what he relived again and again in the shed. These are the ghosts that haunted my childhood and robbed my father of his sanity.

SOMEONE SWITCH
OFF THE LIGHT

No date.

No time.

Weather: Still snowing

The act of recording is meaningless. The hours feel less and less important.

Amaryllis stays with me again. It is just as cold as the darkness before, and the darkness before that. We cling to each other for warmth. She has always gone when the light comes, so whatever heat this bed has to offer also vanishes.

Much about her has altered. All that I took for arrogance is no longer there. Instead, her violet eyes see all and say little. I ask her if she remembers going down to the basement of the picture palace.

'No.'

It strikes me then that Amaryllis has never asked after her father, or about what is happening in the world she has left.

'I brought some cuttings, and a newspaper,' I say.

'I know,' she said. 'I read them. There is a war on and our men were evacuated from Dunkirk. There is talk of invasion. My father is dead, isn't he?'

'Yes,' I say. 'I am here to save you.'

'That's really awfully kind of you,' she says, in a put-on stage voice. Then she smiles gently. 'Better you save yourself and get the others out, if you can. There is nothing you can do for me.'

'You're wrong,' I say emphatically. 'You're wrong.'

She is quiet for ages and I think perhaps she is asleep when she says, 'My father built this machine and made me the heart of it. Why would he do that?'

Ruddy Nora. It's a good question. If my head wasn't hurting I think I could answer it better. This headache started the minute I arrived. See how addicted I am to time? One minute. What does that mean? Nothing. But I seem to lack any other ability to measure what is passing or not passing. It is hard to think straight when your head is splitting open and there are heavy clouds over your eyes. One thing to note: I can't be dead if I feel pain like this.

I say I want to protect her. I know it sounds feeble.

She says quietly, 'I think this machine has a mind of its own.'

That's not possible. We are both silent.

She says, 'You still have all the full stops in you, don't you?'

'What does that mean?' I push myself up on my elbow to look at her. 'I will help you get out.'

It sounds less convincing, the words shallower.

She turns her back to me. She says, gently, 'Lie down, you are letting winter in.'

I have not seen her this morning. I sit on my bed, steel bands tighten round my head, squeezing my brain. I try another pair of the glasses, but it makes no difference. Then another. Just the same. I try to stop thinking about it.

'Mind over matter, old boy, and all that jazz,' as Sir Basil would say.

I should go to look for my father, and Tommy and Miss Bright, but I stay stuck to the bed. Everything is skew-whiff. I can't let this defeat me. I must try to do something, so I take everything out of the kitbag and at the bottom I unpick the first of the three layers. The file in layer one relates to Arnold Ruben. I push through the pain to read it. I have to stop when my vision goes cockeyed. I am lying down when the door opens. Amaryllis looks as if she is made from thistledown. One puff of wind and she would be gone. She's wearing another petticoat, a cardigan, a thin linen coat and a cloche hat. She has plimsolls on her feet. She is so unsuitably dressed for this weather.

'Haven't you anything to keep you warm?' I ask.

She shakes her head. 'Just the petticoat and the things on the wall.'

I give her my coat. It drowns her.

She smiles. 'I used to be bigger than you, now you have overtaken me. I am stuck at seventeen . . . for ever after. Without the happy.'

She doesn't wait for me to recite my well-rehearsed lines about saving her.

'Do you want to see the angry man?' she asks.

I wonder if a walk would help clear my head, and I put everything away carefully in the kitbag, and hide it under the bed.

For some reason I think the tiger will be waiting for us. I am disappointed that he isn't here. I think of asking Amaryllis where the tiger has gone, but even my own voice sounds like a meat grinder. These corridors are so bleak.

We finally stop outside one of the doors. It is the same as all the others. She listens. We hear raised voices. She opens the door and we go in. I am expecting a poky flat with a green light.

I am completely speechless. Never have I seen such grand rooms; they are swimming-pool-big. Out of the windows is a view I have seen only in films. It is New York. The suite has a bedroom and another small room as well as this grand sitting room. There are white flowers in glass vases. Through one of these I see a thin, terrified-looking woman sitting on a sofa. Beside her is a boy. Both are caught in a goldfish bowl.

A waiter is clearing away the remains of a meal on a trolley. A man in a perfectly cut, off-white linen suit follows the waiter to the door through which we've just come. I am about to introduce myself, sure he will be wondering what we are doing there.

Amaryllis laughs at me.

'This is a loop memory,' she says. 'Whatever you do, whatever you say, they can't hear you. Look, they don't have double shadows: that's how you can tell.'

The man whose hand I had tried to shake has a suntanned face of a million smiles. He has gold rings on his fingers and a gold chain on his waistcoat and is wearing cowboy boots. Amaryllis points to the other man in the room, the one in a black, cardboard suit.

'That is Herman, his wife is Frieda, and the boy is called Schmuck.'

The boy is about twelve. He is in a cheap, shiny suit and his hair is plastered down on his head.

Herman, Amaryllis tells me, the angry man, beats his son with his belt. 'I have tried to stop him but I can't.'

She doesn't lower her voice and not one of the players in the scene seems at all bothered. It is as if we are invisible.

'I know who the boy is,' I say. 'And far from being a schmuck, he was, perhaps, one of the most brilliant men of his time. He's your father.'

I meant to say it with more of a bedside manner, and I would have done if my head wasn't so bad.

'I think I know that,' she says.

I have just read the file on Arnold Ruben. Why is it so hard to remember the other man's name? The angry man's voice is shooting red-hot wires through my eyes.

'I'm pretty sure,' I say, 'that is his uncle, Kurt Ruben.'

'The angry man calls him schmuck too,' she says. 'He doesn't look like a schmuck, does he?'

Now I just watch. I long for somewhere to lay down my head, for someone to switch off the light.

'If you could do anything with your life,' says Kurt to the boy sitting awkwardly with his mother, 'what would it be?'

'I want to build the first memory machine, sir.'

'What would that be like?' asks Kurt. You can tell he is impressed with this small lad.

'A waste of time, what else,' shouts the Herman. 'Don't encourage the boy to be more stupid than he is.'

I had looked at the file just before coming here but for the life of me I can't work out when this is happening. 19 . . . 07? Whenever it is, it's a past long gone and yet it feels tangible. Real sunlight fills the room, rose-pink.

Frieda looks at her son anxiously. 'Answer the question,' she says gently.

'W-well, sir,' young Arnold has a stutter, 'it would capture your memories and be as real as you sitting here.' You can see he is nervous, twisting in his seat, picking at his fingers. 'Then we would be able to live in all the best parts of our life.'

'In other words,' says his uncle, 'alchemy.'

'Memories,' interrupts Herman. 'All a load of baloney. What would you do with the memories you want to forget?'

'You tell me,' says Kurt. 'You tell me.'

Herman isn't in a listening frame of mind. He says, 'You never had any sense, you were always chasing dreams. I, unlike you, know the value of every dollar I own, and how hard I worked to make each one.'

'You know the value of zilch,' replies Kurt, 'not even love. How do you think I come to be staying in the best suite at the Plaza?'

'Probably because some other dope is paying.'

Kurt laughs. 'There, brother, you are wrong. It took all my courage to walk away from you. I left New York with every penny I owned . . .' he's talking to the boy now, '. . . and bought, sight-unseen, a farm in Texas. I arrived in the middle of nowhere to find tumbleweed blowing through a ghost town and one saloon with a barman who had drunk the place dry. The farm was nothing more than a derelict shack and a few acres of scrub. The barman told me I'd been sold a load of bull crap.'

'Bull crap just about sums it up,' says Herman.

'That farm turned out to be sitting on top of liquid gold. I own one of the largest oil companies in the United States, Lasco Oil. If I can give you any advice it would be this: believe in your dreams for a dream is a guiding star. Fate smiles kindly on the open-hearted and has no interest whatsoever in a clam who is too tight even for his own chowder.'

'I am still your elder brother and I demand respect,' says Herman, getting to his feet.

'Well, you'll not have any from me,' replies Kurt. 'From what I hear, the hardware store is the same as it was the day I left, just with fewer customers. Most folks prefer to go elsewhere rather than deal with a skinflint like you.'

Herman seems to have grown into a Goliath, out of

proportion to everyone else in the room. I think my headache
is affecting my vision.

Amaryllis reassures me. 'This is the clearest moment of
the memory. It often happens that one part of a loop memory
gets bigger or smaller or just fades away, depending on how
important it is.'

Herman takes a swing at Kurt. Frieda puts her hand over
her mouth to stifle a scream but the boy watches intently. His
uncle ducks, then with one punch fells Goliath. Frieda, crying,
holds her son to her. While Herman lies dazed on the ground,
Kurt takes an envelope from his inside pocket.

'Don't ever let my brother know you have this. Keep it for a
rainy day, understand?'

Frieda nods.

Two men come in from the other room. They are huge and
look like they could kill you with one squeeze.

'I'm about to teach you . . .' says Herman, when they take
him, each holding him under one arm, and throw him into
the corridor.

Freida follows hurriedly. Only Arnold turns back to smile at
his uncle.

We walk along the corridors. My head is so bad I'm losing
my vision. I have no idea if I dreamed the next part or if it
happened, but we are on Brooklyn Bridge. I know it from the
photos I've seen. Frieda, Herman and Arnold are walking
home. We are following behind. I hear Frieda whispering
to her son, then they become nothing more than a sepia

postcard. It fades and I'm back in the apartment, blind.
Amaryllis helps me lie down. She takes off the glasses,
her cool hand is on my head, and at last the light is
switched off.

WHEN I WAS FOUR

Ezra is ill. Maybe it's due to the machine or maybe it's the glasses he wears. I don't know what to do. He is sleeping, not an easy or peaceful sleep, but full of groans and measurements of pain. I put my hand on his head, stroke his soft, warm skin, feel life beating in it.

He has a future.

I am sure that I do not.

I longed for him to be here and now that he is I am baffled. Baffled by how much older than me he is.

How much more grown up than me he is.

How handsome he is.

His chest is smooth, with thirty-six hairs on it, I counted them. And straight hairs in his armpits, with a birthmark on his chest on his right side. I know all this because I undressed him and put him to bed, then spent a long time studying him. I wondered about taking off his trousers. Thought better of it.

He must have woken when I was out of the room for he'd

kicked the rest of his clothes off. I walk in to find him naked, his arm across his eyes, fast asleep and peaceful at last.

I have never seen a man like this before, not in the flesh. I turn to leave, then stop and turn round again, intrigued. He looks, in the moonlight, beautiful. I thought only women looked like that but there is no other word to describe him. He has noble feet and very long legs, his skin is silvery. Outside the window it has started snowing. He stirs and pulls the covers over him, and calls my name in his sleep.

I curl up beside him and he wraps me in his arms. I lie there feeling all of him and dare not move; for fear of what, I don't know. In the night I wake. He is looking at me. I kiss him, this time hard on the mouth, he kisses me back, his tongue touches mine. I feel as if someone has lit a sparkler and I am on fire. I am aching. He pulls himself away from me, now fully awake.

'No,' he says. 'No.'

I can see that 'No' is causing him a lot of trouble.

'It's all right,' I say. 'I want to.'

'No, it's not right.'

'Why not? I don't understand.'

'Because it means nothing without love, and I want it to mean everything.'

I feel like saying he is being an old fuddy-duddy and then I wonder if he thinks I might become pregnant. The thought is so silly that I laugh.

'What's so funny?' he asks.

'I won't have a baby, not here, where everything is in limbo.'

'I'm not worried about that,' he says.

'What then?'

'I'm worried that I'm falling in love with you and you are not in love with me.' He says it so simply.

I am stumped by that. Love. Goodness, isn't that what time is all about? Love and how long it will last? Ezra is still in too much pain to answer such a thorn-filled question. I can see his head hurts.

He holds me, but I feel him colder. The fire has gone out.

I turn my back to him and we sleep, his hands around me, and I place them on my breasts. I haven't been hungry once since being here, now I am starving. Not for food, for him. Is that love? I don't know. Perhaps I don't know what love is.

When I wake the light is bright, the snow has gone. I close the curtains to try to keep the room dark while Ezra is still sleeping. I walk into the hall and hear a low growl coming from the corridor.

Without thinking about it – which I regret – I open the front door.

The child is standing there with the white tiger cub. I see in its double shadow that of a full-grown tiger and I want to close the door, go back to the bed, curl up beside Ezra.

But before I can do anything I am sucked into the child. Everything is bigger and I am lost. My double shadow is all that is left of my older self.

I think we are on a boat. I'm not sure but as always the child seems in control. The floor is carpeted and the air is cool. It is a boat. I feel it swaying, the gentle lapping of the water. All the doors are tall, wooden, with numbers on them.

Outside one we stop and call, 'Mummy.'

There is no answer. I would rather we didn't go in. In fact I'm sure we shouldn't go in. The tiger cub pushes on the door and it swings open. The grown up me wants to say, and can't, look, if you are going to do things you shouldn't, lock your door, rather than let the four-year-old me just wander in on you like this. But I am not in charge, the child is. She has other plans, this younger me. In my mind are the chalk outlines they put down in movies after someone has been murdered and the body removed. I see the room now, everything outlined in chalk, the scene of a crime.

This is the moment before the moment you wish you could take back all that is about to happen. The moment your life could have turned out differently.

Inside the cabin there is a semicircular bed raised on a platform with mirrored steps. The portholes look out on to a bobbing blue sea. I am very relieved because my mummy, the lady with the name of small oranges, doesn't seem to be here.

But the child stays put.

What I see, she sees. The only difference is I want to get the hell out of here. The small child, confused, determinedly sticks to the ground.

'Mummy,' she says again. 'I found your earring, look.'

And in her hand is a diamond big enough to see the child's anxious face in.

There is a man; his back is to us. He has very suntanned

skin and blond hair. He is moving on top of a woman who is groaning. She has red-painted toenails. Well, that's all we can see of her.

The room is a mess with champagne bottles on the floor and an ashtray full of pink and gold-tipped cigarette butts. On the table near the bed is a syringe.

I don't want to know, never ever, who the woman in the bed is. I want to scream: let me out, stop this, stop this now.

The child is crying too, 'Mummy, Mummy, look, I found your earring.'

The man stops moving. He turns his head in our direction.

'Get lost,' he says. 'Just go away.'

'Oh, Christ,' says the mummy, 'what's she doing here?'

The child runs from the cabin. I can feel her heart – my heart – racing. Only the cub runs happily behind us. We rush out on to the deck; the sunlight is blinding-bright. There are three people there. I can make out their shapes. A wind-up gramophone is playing.

I see them now. One woman and two men. The woman has very short hair, almost mannish. She is topless, her swimsuit rolled down. Flat-chested, she looks like a blood-sucking vampire to me. One of the men is lying on a towel, the other sitting upright in a deckchair.

He says, 'Darlings. Kiddywink alarm.'

'Oh, really. We're not babysitting that spoilt brat,' says the vampire. 'Darling, do something, for heaven's sake. Ring a bell, get help. I am quite allergic to those small fingers, they just give me the creeps.'

The man who is lying on the towel glances up lazily. 'She's let that tiger out again.'

The deckchair man rises to his feet and looks towards the harbour. 'This will set the cat amongst the pigeons,' he says. 'I'm sure that's Ruben's motor launch heading this way. Someone'd better go and warn Clementine.'

'I am not moving, darling,' says the vampire.

Deckchair-man rings a bell. A butler appears, thin and tall, with a face that gives little away.

'Better tell Mrs Ruben that her husband is back,' he says, as he takes another cigarette from a silver case and taps it before putting it to his mouth. He squints his eyes and lights it. 'Oh, James,' he calls after the butler, 'Martinis all round.'

What about me, I want to shout, what about the four-year-old me? Are you just going to ignore her? I have a tiger cub, that's not safe. I could fall through the rail into the sea. Maybe I should ask for a Martini, that might get their attention. No, make that a double, make that a treble, make it a gallon.

The child sits down. We sit down, away from the group of adults, the tiger cub beside us. Even I feel like crying. I am four. Why does no one do anything? The only comfort is my shadow of the older me and it is the older me who wants to protect the child from all this.

The three of them are gossiping about Mummy.

'Perhaps we shouldn't be discussing this in front of the child,' says the deckchair man.

Finally someone with some sense. No, this is not what I should be hearing, most definitely not.

'Darling, the child is quite unaffected by what her mother does,' says the vampire.

'Clementine should be more careful,' says the man lying on the towel. 'I mean, all this sleeping around and the addiction to you-know-what, it simply isn't good for a girl's complexion.'

The vampire adds, with a certain amount of glee, 'And she was once so-o beautiful.'

'I tell you,' says the deckchair man picking up the tiger as if it's a kitten, 'she should never have married him, he is such a bore. She only did it for the moolah. The only thing he seems to care for is the child.'

The man on the towel watches as his friend takes the cub to its cage under an awning.

The butler comes back with the drinks, and a stern-faced woman in an apron, who speaks a language I don't understand, takes my hand. There are seagulls circling overhead. I am marched back to my cabin, put in a cot and the door is shut and locked.

All I want is to be out of the child.

It is night and I have been asleep. I wake to hear my mummy's voice. She picks me up from the cot. She smells of cocktails and Chanel No 5. I am so sleepy that I'm not sure what she is doing. I know she is very unstable on her feet because we nearly fall over.

'Whoops-a-daisy,' she says, steadying herself.

She is wearing an evening dress and her face is covered in tears. She is holding me tightly.

Up on deck the yacht looks deserted. I see, under a striped awning, the remains of a meal, chairs left in disarray. Two have fallen over. Music floats across the bay. A necklace of lights dances in the dark.

My daddy is standing with his back towards us, watching as the group I had seen earlier climb into the motor launch. I hear the engine start.

'Where are they?' Mummy shouts when Daddy comes towards her. 'You sent them away. Why do you always do that? I hate you. Call them back, I need them.'

'Why do you need those leeches? They're not your friends, darling. And I know they despise me.'

'I don't care. I despise you too. You bore me, you're nothing. Nothing!'

Daddy says quietly, 'Give me Amaryllis.'

'Don't touch me!' She is screaming.

The sight of my daddy is the only safe thing that has happened. The child's arms go out towards him. I am all in favour of that but Mummy isn't letting go. She runs, laughing, to the stern of the yacht. 'Aren't we having fun,' she says to me, sobbing.

'Put me down, please, Mummy,' says the child. Mummy isn't listening.

'Bring them back,' she shouts at my daddy. 'Bring them back or I will throw her into the sea.'

Me? Is she talking about me? I am her child.

I don't want to be here. Why am I here? Oh God, no, no. I know what's going to happen. Stop, please stop, someone rescue me. Please, someone stop what's going to happen. I beg of you, memory machine, stop now. I will believe in fairy tales, I will believe in happy-ever-after . . .

My mummy, my drugged, deranged mummy, is now climbing with me in her arms over the yacht's rail, and the waves are churning waterfall froth behind the boat, spraying us with a fine mist.

Daddy is walking very slowly towards her. He says quietly, 'Give me the child and let me call for a doctor.'

'I don't want a doctor. I want my friends back.'

I feel us fall. My stomach lurches and I am holding with all my strength to the rail, my mummy clinging to my little legs.

'Help me,' she screams. 'Help me!'

Daddy is here. She lets go of one of my legs and holds her hand up towards my daddy. His two strong arms grasp hold of me, just me, and with a scream my mummy has vanished into the dark frothy whirlpool.

He is crying. I feel his tears. The crew have the boat out and one of them dives into the sea. I hold on to my daddy as if he is a lifeline. Behind him I see Silas Molde.

'Forgive me, my darling,' Daddy whispers softly in my ear. 'I love you too much to lose you.'

It's all gone. The yacht, the whirlpool, my father. I am in a corridor with the green light. I can't stop crying. The full-grown tiger is sitting beside me. My sobs are so loud I feel they are breaking waves of drowning grief.

Ezra is here. He kneels beside me, gathers me in his arms.

'What's happened?' he says.

'Tell me,' I weep, 'what is love?'

ANGOSTURA BITTERS AND ICE

I want to tell Ezra what I'm doing in the corridor, why I'm crying about my sweet orange of a mummy who went bob-bob-bobbing away in the briny, salty sea. But I can't. There is a huge sob at the heart of me. It echoes through my body, it is in every breath I take. It brings back the long-forgotten thing, the centipede. I know who he is now, because I've seen him again: he is the man with the gun.

Ezra holds me gently, rocks me. He helps me to my feet and we go back to the apartment.

Just inside he stops and asks, 'Can you hear the sound?'

I hear only the hum of the green light. I'm so used to it that I hardly notice it any more.

He tells me the noise is worse in the apartment than it is in the corridor. 'It's a high, twisting spider of a noise. It's everywhere, all out of tune. It ends as abruptly as it starts, without warning, just to begin over again – time recorded in musical shadows . . . listen, listen, you must be able to hear it, it paralyses me.'

He holds the side of his head. I can see the weather inside his head. It's very bad again, the storm clouds gathering in his brain. I help him to lie down. The room is bitterly cold and snow is falling.

He tells me when the light comes back and the noise goes away, he's going to get us out of here, '. . . before all this topsy-turvy racket takes away my sanity.'

I ask him, has he experienced a memory here? He says, no.

Everyone else has, why not him? I feel panicky. He has no double shadow. Maybe he isn't real, maybe he's just a trick. The thought is unbearable. It is the darkness that I fear the most.

Ezra never sat for a memory recording. I think about the soldier. He belongs here. His memories are wounds that ooze out his past.

Ezra sleeps in fits and starts. I climb under the covers with him and put my arms around him, mostly to reassure myself he is real. I listen to his heartbeat. I like the sound, the pulse of blood. No matter how slow it goes, it is still a heart waiting to speed up again when time floods back upon him.

When he wakes he asks me what I remember of the real world.

I want to tell him about the man with the gun, but I can't bring myself to hear the words rattle around my head.

'I remember a house,' I say, 'a small house, my legs sticking out in the warm summer sunshine. A cake that I ate until I could eat no more.'

'My mother found you in the Wendy house,' he says. 'You had stolen the cake she'd baked that morning.'

I have to think a long time about that. I tell him I remember the smell of rosemary. Even in his pain I see a smile cross his face.

He says, 'That's what my boss would call a madeleine moment. Proust. A French writer, a philosopher. A memory triggered by a detail.'

I am half-listening because the rosemary has led me to wonder if there were geese. His right arm lies across his eyes. Drowsily, he says there were. This is my story, this is my life, I should know it and I don't. Yet I know about Everett Roach. This place is a cruel trick, I think. What use is editing the past, if all it does is make the well of forgetfulness more terrifying. What was my father doing?

Ezra says his mother pulled me from the Wendy house by my legs, took me to the kitchen and made me make another cake. I'm perplexed, why would I do that? Why would I steal a cake? He says it's not important, but I think it is. Perhaps it is the reason for everything.

When the light comes back the snow is still falling. Ezra tries to pull himself out of bed but I can see he is in a bad way. His face is ashen but he is determined to try to find the soldier and the others. At the front door he falls over and lies unconscious on the parquet. I pull and slip and slide him back to the bedroom. It takes as long as it takes to get him there. He wakes up near the bed and crawls under the covers begging for darkness, begging for silence.

I drape my petticoats in front of the window, and soak a camisole in the green water and rest it over his eyes. Why is this happening? Why to Ezra, no one else? How can he hear so much when I only hear the hum?

I sit with him, watching through the patterns of lace, the snow falling. I know that there is fighting again on the wasteland. I see the flashes of gunfire. I see grey snow, blood-red snow, white snow that clings in spongy clumps to the barbed wire. It is a flip book of a horror film.

I am at a full stop. I can't make sense of what to do next. The tiger is outside, growling. It may be the child wanting to get my attention. She wants to gobble me up in the gingerbread house of the past. I won't go there.

I close my eyes as I open the front door. I have decided that if I don't see the child, she can't see me. It's foolish, I know. Peek-a-boo, who are you? It is only the tiger with his cub double shadow. He lopes to the bedroom. Ezra is crying out in pain.

I stand by the door. The tiger paces back and forth, then he says, 'I will fetch the mouse-winged boy.'

Did I imagine he spoke, or in my panic did I give him words and in these words did I hear my father's voice? It matters little. It makes me feel there is some hope. The tiger leaves. All I hear now is silence.

When the mouse-winged boy arrives, he is very serious. He says the tiger sent him. The boy puts his big head near Ezra's, then gets up and sighs.

'We need the soldier and the Brightness, I'll bring them here.'

He sees the glasses sticking out of Ezra's kitbag and takes
three pairs. I tell him to leave them, that they made Ezra ill.

'They won't work on Ezra,' he says, 'because he's fighting
the machine. The machine has a mind of its own.' And he
says it's because Ezra didn't go through the diamond doors.

'Why should that make any difference?'

The mouse-winged boy looks puzzled, as if it was so simple
it was almost silly to have to answer.

'The machine sucks in memories, but not if you come
in through the broom cupboard.' Then he says, 'Ezra is my
brother, and in his head an elephant storm of thunder is
raging through his mind.'

The mouse-winged boy looks so sad. As he leaves he says, 'I
saw my mum today. Her mind was full of shadows. She laid
her head in the oven to cook.'

It must be the weather for mothers.

'I saw mine too,' I say. 'She wanted me to fall into the dark
water with her.'

The mouse-winged boy puts his arms around me and says I
am made of the bones of a ghost.

I want him to run and flap his mouse wings, I want him to
laugh. He doesn't do any of these things. A leaden mouse tail
of sorrow has attached itself to him.

He comes back with the soldier. I have never seen
him out of his apartment. He is dressed just the same as
always, except he is wearing the dark glasses and looks like
an extra in a film waiting for the director to shout 'Action'.
I swear that the boy's wings have drooped. He is holding

the Brightness's hand and she, like the soldier, is wearing the dark glasses.

'It's nothing short of a miracle!' she says. 'Amaryllis, I can think straight.'

The soldier, too, looks more full of himself, less stuffed with the past.

'Where is he?' asks the soldier.

I show them into the bedroom. The soldier has tears in his eyes. They roll down his face from under the dark glasses.

The Brightness puts her hands over her ears. 'Where is that noise coming from, that terrible din? Can you hear it? It ricochets round the room.'

I tell her to take off the glasses. She does. 'Can you hear it now?' I ask.

Confused, as if being chased by forgetfulness, she quickly puts them on again.

'The noise is high, very high. It crackles, runs away with itself,' she says. 'It's full of chattering voices, all speaking peppery words that make no sense. I believe it to be a lullaby, to keep us numb, but it's angry and confused. It sounds bitter.'

The mouse-winged boy says, 'Now the machine is frightened of you too.'

'Perhaps the noise won't be so bad in my place,' says the soldier, and he and Tommy lift Ezra off the bed. His head lolls forward. He looks dead. He can't be dead, dead is a place the machine won't let you go to.

We take him to the soldier's apartment where we put him in a chair. He hasn't moved. I kneel beside him, hold his hand, and I know he isn't a memory, he isn't a trick. I know he is flesh and blood.

The soldier is busy making tea and says nothing, not a word, about Bernie.

He helps Ezra to drink.

When the light outside fades, Ezra comes to. He looks at the soldier incredulously.

'Do you know who I am?' he asks.

The soldier nods his head. He is crying again. 'You are my son, Ezra.'

The soldier hugs Ezra, kisses the side of his face.

'I thought I would never see you again,' says Ezra.

The soldier – Ezra's father – says, 'You shouldn't be here, lad.'

My eyes prick with tears. I turn away. Never have I seen such a demonstration of love. Then I had what Ezra called a madeleine moment. I was making a cake and it was then, for the first time that I saw what love could be, how safe it could be. Like the sponge mixture, it took hard work to make something so incredibly light, something that tasted of air. That mixture is what Ezra is made up of: love. Never had my mother hugged me like that, and after her death my father too forgot how to make a sponge cake. They were both made half-baked, they could only mix cocktails with Angostura bitters and ice.

Ezra listens. 'It's gone,' he says in disbelief. 'The noise in my head, the noise of the walls, the furniture, the noise of everything has disappeared.' He tells them he's come to take them all home.

'Home,' says Ezra's father. 'And is that where my Nan . . . Nan . . . Nancy is?'

Ezra nods.

'And my daughter . . . no, don't say a word, son, it's coming back, it's falling into place . . . my daughter, Olive?'

'Yes, Father.'

WE ARE AS INFINITE
AS THE STARS

Why is this happening to me? I know more about the
machine than anyone here except Silas Molde, yet it is Tommy
who states the obvious: the machine is trying to shut me
down. I am a sickness in its belly, a stone in a cog. Why did
anyone suppose Tommy to be stupid? He seems to have more
wisdom in his little finger than many a plain-spoken man.

Hell, I thought I would bring everyone out. Now here I am
– this 'I will rescue you' idiot – paralysed by a pain in my head
that I have never before in my life experienced. I seem only
able to function in ditches of silence, hoping the noise won't
find me.

Quite funny, really, when you think about it – when I can
think about anything. Miss Bright all prim, wearing the
glasses, announces it would be proper if Amaryllis stays with
her rather than go back to the old apartment.

No, that is not a good idea at all, not one little part of it.
I need Amaryllis. What am I saying? I should be the hero,
instead I am useless.

Tommy saves us from being parted by saying there is nothing proper about anything here, and if Amaryllis is in danger she needs to be with Ezra.

Miss Bright remembers. Strange that the glasses work for her and Father. She suggests we all stay together but Tommy says he knows of an empty apartment for us, and he will stay with the Brightness; Father likes to be alone. I think Amaryllis is right – Tommy is no one's fool.

I have given up with the glasses. There is simply no point.

I am standing by the window in the small kitchen where Father makes tea for Bernie. I don't realise he's behind me because I can hear people talking in the other room.

He says, very quietly, 'Son, none of us know how we will react when we are sent over the top. I have seen men who boasted of being lions shit themselves with fear. I have seen men who shat themselves with fear at the thought of going over the top being lions. You, my lad, are brave, brave enough to come in here. Brave enough to take us home.'

I turn and look at him.

'It's the headaches,' I say.

'That is the battle you have to fight ,' he says. 'That's the going over the top. When it comes to it you'll do what's needed.'

I have never heard him talk like this, so simply. God knows what he must have lived through, what he must have seen to make him dig that trench in the shed for the ghosts of battle to keep him company. Here he is as I have never seen him, free of the barbed wire.

Amaryllis and I leave, agreeing we will all meet when the light comes back. Once out in the corridor, the sound shadows my every movement, runs after me, stands in front of me like a solid wall of mechanical clamour. Father is right, this is the battle.

Finally, darkness falls. We are in an apartment on the fourteenth floor where there is no noise, no loop memory playing. It is completely unfurnished apart from a mattress in the middle of a high-ceilinged room. By it is a silver candle holder, such as you might imagine Scrooge using, and one single match. I light the candle. It burns with an eerie green flame. The windows, like all the windows, have the same view of the snowy wasteland. They have no curtains.

Amaryllis brings all our clothes from the old apartment and we make a molehill, piling them on top of the bed.

For some reason I'm suddenly awkward. Perhaps it is because there is not one other stick of furniture here, just the mattress. We stand either side of it, looking down, and then, fully dressed, we burrow under the clothes. I rub her long back, gently.

I feel the shape of her breasts firm against me. I have only one rational thought: I want to kiss Amaryllis, to taste her sweet mouth. I feel her feather-soft lips on my neck.

'Can I tell you something?' she says. 'I have been thinking a lot about the cake.'

I tell her quickly that it isn't important. She says it is, it made her remember what love could be. I'm holding my breath. I don't understand, and she tells me about the kiss my mother gave her and I'm glad that she doesn't remember what Roach did.

We just hold each other in that silence, a long silence and I think she has fallen asleep though I am wide awake.

Then she says, 'I ran away from school. It was a dare and Everett Roach . . . I saw him again when you fell out of the broom cupboard. In my mind's eye he's a giant centipede with hundreds of white-gloved hands.'

I want to kill Everett for this and more besides. I am glad it is dark, that in the green candlelight she can't see my face clearly.

'It may be best to forget,' I say.

'No, no, it is because of what he did to me that I searched you out. I wanted to belong to a family that would make me feel safe . . .'

I take her in my arms and kiss the top of her head. She clings to me.

She says, 'I want you to make it better, to show me what love is, what loving can be.'

She starts impatiently to unbutton my shirt, pulls it off over my head.

'Wait, wait,' I say, 'not so fast.'

She is not listening.

I want her more than life. Still, I get out of bed. I need to think. Ruddy Nora, the room is freezing and I am not. I look at her in the candlelight. She pushes the covers back, she is wearing a camisole, nothing else. She is dazzling, her flesh white as snow, the dark mystery of her pubic hair. She watches me as I undress. She asks me if it will hurt, and I say no, but if it does I will stop.

'If you change your mind, we will just hold each other.'

I get back into bed and she kisses me with such a longing, with a kind of desperation.

'Let's take it slowly,' I say. 'We have all the darkness and all the light to get this right.'

She relaxes into me. I feel the heat of her body against mine. She is light and her skin velvety-soft. I kiss her lips, her face, her neck.

I pull away from her and look into her violet eyes.

'Are you sure?' I say.

'Yes. Every bit of me burns with yes.'

We lie wrapped up in each other. Never did I imagine that to make love could be to feel the same passion returned, until every part of you explodes into the moment. We are as infinite as the stars.

I feel her trembling, hear her heart fluttering. The room is dark, the candle nearly out.

'I think,' she says, nuzzling into me, 'I know now what love can do. It has the power to make you whole again.'

'Yes, I believe that too.'

She is quiet for a long time.

'When the centipede did what he did to me, it hurt like hell.'

I say that I want to kill him.

'But it was my fault,' she says, 'I should never have done that, never.'

I hold her tight and tell her she was not in the wrong, and I tell her most of what I know about Everett Roach, but not about the photographs, or that he killed her father. I think it is bad enough that she remembers what she does.

She kisses me, and thanks me for telling her the truth.

The thought of Everett Roach makes me ask, 'If a person was shot through the heart, would he die here?'

'No, not here. Only when he got back to the real world where there are clocks that weigh time and death.'

I think about the revolver in my kitbag.

I lie there for a long while.

'Amaryllis,' I say, 'when we get out of here I want to marry you.'

She kisses me on the lips and says, 'I would like that.'

And again we make love.

MORAL MACHINERY

I wake up, Ezra's arms around me, and I don't think I have ever felt this happy or contented, not even once. He opens his eyes and looks into mine and I know what he is thinking and I am thinking the same. As silly as it may sound, I hear birdsong, fat wood pigeons cooing, a cuckoo and a wren.

Slowly, he gets up, neither of us much wanting to be apart. He is naked. I watch him walk towards the window. Sunshine fills the room so that he looks golden. He has a glorious body, all of it designed just to love me.

'It's unbelievable,' he says. 'Look.'

The picture palace has disappeared. Outside are the grounds of a grand mansion. It is a glorious summer afternoon. Huge poplar trees throw dark regimented shadows on manicured lawns.

Ezra turns to me, asks if he can see me naked.

I smile. I say, 'No'.

He kisses me and says, 'One day, when you are my wife, can I?'

'Of course,' I tease. 'You have to have something to look forward to, otherwise where would all the mystery be?'

At that he throws back his head and laughs.

He goes back to bed and soon falls asleep. Below I see the tiger prowling, waiting. I am certain he wants to show me something. I get dressed and pick up my diary which I never leave behind. It's too important. It has my record of all this written in it.

I run down the hard stone stairs to the ground floor and arrive at the corridor that leads to the swing doors. Outside is a meadow, the grass is hip-high, blocking the door itself. I struggle to push it open. The heat is the first thing I feel, the warm sunshine of a long summer afternoon. The meadow is filled with poppies, thousands of long-stemmed, red poppies, a sea of them swaying in the breeze. In the distance are the eternal lawns of England's pleasant pastures green. The tiger is lost from view in the undergrowth.

Ahead there are two young ladies, their parasols shading their faces, meandering through their social calendars, making up their dance cards, ignoring butterflies and poppies alike. I have an unreal sensation – though what here is real is hard to know – that I am at an open-air cinema watching a film. All the colour has faded, everything is in black and white. The scene is set.

A man's voice, a voice with a German accent but recognisable as that of Silas Molde, announces, 'Prototype One, Test 31, Subject: Clementine Ruben.' Then he says, 'This is the home of Sir Richard and Lady Glenville and their beautiful daughter Clementine.'

The film judders. It is stretched, it looks like a home movie. Silas continues, reading from a script and reading it very badly indeed.

'The Glenvilles have opened their grand Georgian house and gardens to the public for the annual fete, where the common man might mingle with the aristocracy of England.'

The voice stops and the film is now subtitled. Rhoda, the eldest of the girls in the picture, is the one with the most to say. Her mouth never stops moving. She has a long, plain face made longer by silly ringlets. She is looking as pleased as punch with herself. Clementine is the prettier by far. I just write down what is on the screen, it isn't hard to follow. Here it is. Not much of a story, or so I think.

At the bottom of the screen it tells us in flowery words that Rhoda is engaged to be married to a soldier, a hero of the Great War.

'You met my Harold at the Roystons' fancy-dress ball in Henley last week. Such a pity I couldn't be there.'

The camera is now on Clementine's face. It seems to linger there and I see that something about the word 'Harold' has upset her.

Subtitle again, Rhoda speaking.

'He said you were a real wow in the Columbine costume – quite the belle of the ball.'

Still Clementine says nothing.

'So, spill the beans. What do you think of my debonair fiancé? Aren't I just the luckiest girl in town?'

Big exclamation mark.

'Yes,' says Clementine.

At last, I think, she speaks

There are no words on the screen but you can tell that Rhoda is so full of good news about her forthcoming wedding that she is oblivious to what is troubling her friend. More silent words stream from Rhoda's mouth. One can imagine, even without subtitles, that she is busy boasting; the perfect boarding-school bitch.

Still Clementine has little to say. What a miserable part, I think, and I'm somewhat bored by the film. I can't see the point to it all. Finally, the endless babbling brook that is Rhoda is diverted by two old otters, maiden aunts who take her away, moths rising from their hats in dust-filled clouds of grey.

The camera follows Clementine. The camera, you can see, loves Clementine. I wonder where she is going, all alone and quiet without a word to say for herself. She's not going back to join the party, no, she walks towards a gazebo.

And she sits there on the step, lost in thought. This is a very slow film indeed. Suddenly Clementine nearly jumps out of her skin. From behind the gazebo a man with a bushy moustache appears. The villain, no less, I think.

She says, in the subtitles, 'What are you doing here? Go away, just leave me alone.'

This is more than Clementine has ever said before. The man, you can see, has no intention of leaving. His words are not in flowery writing but plain hard script.

'Now, listen here. We need to talk about the other night at the Roystons' ball.'

'I don't want ever, ever, to talk to you again,' says Clementine. She moves with great agility to avoid him but he grabs hold of her. He looks angry, very angry indeed.

'Tell me, what is a fellow to do? I don't go around looking for these things, you know.'

'You raped me.'

What were the words on the screen? Oh, lordy lord, no. This isn't the charming, innocent, home-made film I thought it might be. This is an early memory recording taken by Silas. This is what actually happened to my mummy.

The man is not listening to what Clementine has to say; he is busy justifying his actions. His words are quite quotable:

'No matter how much a fellow may respect a girl like you, it's an effort when all's said and done for him to keep his thoughts from straying. Especially when she exposes so much of her body . . .'

'I hate you,' says Clementine. She is pulling like mad to get away from him, a fawn caught in a trap.

'You must agree,' he says, 'you were very provocatively dressed in that outfit, doing your damnedest to aggravate the sex tendency.'

'No, I just wanted to dance, nothing more, just dance. You dragged me away against my will.'

My poor mummy is shouting, she has large angelic tears in her eyes but he isn't moved by this, not one jot. There is a point to be made and he is going to make it. The point is written large, in subtitles, for all women who have been blinded by false promises, for all young girls taken against their will, for all the hurt that will not heal, for the daisy chain of broken lives.

'That is by the bye,' he says. 'I have trouble enough keeping myself clean for Rhoda's sake without you throwing a monkey wrench into a chap's moral machinery.'

She is now fighting him with all her strength and he slaps her hard across the face.

The camera pulls out. There is Rhoda. Has she seen what has happened? Has she heard what her hero of a fiancé has done? If she has, she betrays not one flicker of doubt.

'Darling, why didn't you tell me you were here? I've just spotted your car parked in the drive.'

He lets go of Clementine who is holding the side of her face. He walks towards Rhoda and kisses her on her cheek, just a small peck. A mark of respect, no doubt.

By the look of things his fiancée has decided it's best to ignore the fact that her best friend has just been slapped across the face and is crying.

The camera pans away to show the sweep of the grounds. On the lawn a marquee is set, the flaps are up and village children wearing paper hats run back and forth with squeals of delight. They are playing musical chairs. Sir Richard arrives to make his speech to the common man.

The camera now is back on Rhoda. She takes Clementine's hand and hisses at her, 'Oh, do stop being so sensitive. You're making such a fuss about nothing.'

Now I understand what went wrong with my sweet orange

blossom of a mother. She never found her Ezra to make the hurt go away. And she never stopped looking until all that hurt sent her crazy. They vanish, the three of them, into the dark shadows of the past. All that is left is the sound of the end of the reel. Flick, flick, flick.

THE SHADOW MAN

Silas can no longer sleep. He feels he is being watched. He is aware of someone behind him, looking over his shoulder. Once he even imagined he saw Arnold's reflection in the mirror, only to find it was his own face staring back at him. He is not certain of anything any more.

Silas goes over and over Arnold's calculations, looking for a way of letting Roach out without allowing more fatal time to seep back in. Finally, he comes across a note written in pencil by Arnold at the bottom of one of the many formulae. Silas reads it again and again.

The Control Code will enable us to come and go if necessary without letting time in. No need to write it down, old bean, we both know it's dead simple.

A code. There was a code, thinks Silas. How could he have forgotten? Perhaps his memory is going too.

All alone in the control room he feels fear creep in upon him, a dread that he had never in the world of time ever experienced. Studying Arnold's spidery handwriting, he thinks about the man he loved – kind, generous to a fault – who had accepted him without question.

It was he, Silas, who had found out the probable cause of

Clementine's addiction to drink and drugs, a discovery he had made when he took the first memory recording. Arnold didn't understand why she couldn't just pull herself together. The marriage was not just cracked, it was irreparably broken.

After Clementine's death, Amaryllis had became locked into herself, without much to say except to ask occasionally where the tiger cub had gone. It had been Arnold's decision to take Amaryllis's memory recording. He had become obsessed with the idea of wiping away the night on the boat. The experiment had gone disastrously wrong. Silas sighs into the darkness. He had tried to warn Arnold that the developing brain of a child would be uncharted waters.

'Let's wait,' he had pleaded with him. 'You suffered badly with headaches and so did I.'

'They were nothing, old bean. And Clementine had no side effects at all. We have to do this immediately so Amaryllis is at the core of the machine. Her earliest memories must be there. Then we can edit out the painful ones and replace them with a collage of good memories so that she will never know the truth of her mother.'

He remembered – oh, how could he forget? – Amaryllis was eight. Her red dress was embroidered with little dancing figures and had a white yoke collar. It was a favourite of hers, bought in a shop in New York. She wore bright red shoes and white socks; her thick hair cut in a waved bob. She had solemnly held her father's hand, proud to be a part of his work. She showed no fear when they sat her in the chair, didn't even cry out because the helmet was so heavy.

She cuddled her toy tiger and asked, 'Will it hurt?'

'No, princess,' said Arnold.

When it was over she got up, white as the collar of her dress. She looked straight at her father and then at Silas and asked them who they were.

Silas remembered Arnold laughing until he realised that this was no laughing matter. Amaryllis possessed not one memory of the past. The next day she had been sick with a very high temperature. It was feared she had meningitis and she was rushed to hospital. Arnold couldn't believe his machine was in any way responsible for his beloved, perfect daughter being so ill, but Silas was in no doubt. Her headaches were so terrible that finally she was moved by private plane to a clinic in Switzerland.

It was that which broke the bond that had tied father and daughter so tightly. That and the fact she had no memory of him. Arnold couldn't bring himself to see her in such a state, or to accept his part in yet another tragedy. Three months she was in hospital and Silas visited her many more times than Arnold did. When she came home she still had no memory. She accepted that Arnold was her father, that Silas was known as 'Uncle'. She was indifferent to Arnold. The deep love she'd had for him was gone for ever.

Arnold found his daughter so altered, he sent her to boarding school. Silas can hardly remember how many she had been to by the time she started at Clarrington School for Girls.

There it is again, thinks Silas. Someone is behind him, he can feel it. He swings round.

'Who's there?' he shouts. The big iron door he keeps locked eases open. 'Roach, is that you?'

There is no reply. Then he sees a shadow disappear up the stairs.

Don't think about it, he tells himself. Concentrate on the work in hand.

Silas nearly jumps out of his chair when Roach saunters into the control room.

'Look what I've found, my old fruit gum.'

Silas stands up, shaking. Roach is clutching Ezra Pascoe.

'I went out to stretch my legs and there he was. He can hardly string a sentence together, says he's looking for Amaryllis. Aren't we all, I tell him. And do you know what he says?'

'Can't he speak for himself?' interrupts Silas.

'No, he can't, on account of the noise. What bleeding noise? Can you hear any noise?'

Silas examines Ezra. He has a high fever. That shouldn't be possible, not here.

'Were you like this when you arrived?' Silas asks him.

'No,' is all Ezra can manage to mutter for he is having trouble seeing straight.

'He's not well,' says Silas.

'That's stating the obvious, my old fruit gum. He's losing his marbles.'

Silas examines him again.

'I am drowning,' says Ezra.

'When did you last see Amaryllis?' asks Silas.

'Now, that's more like it, that's the kind of question he should be able to cough up an answer to,' says Roach.

Ezra stays silent.

Silas follows Roach as he takes Ezra up to the foyer. Vervaine stands at the top of the stairs staring down at the young man.

'I've brought a new mouse for you to play with, Cattykins.' Roach turns to Silas. 'Leave it to us, my old fruit gum. We'll squeeze the juice from this particular lemon.' He clicks his fingers, a habit he has, one of many that Silas can't stand. 'Oh, and a couple of your Martinis wouldn't go amiss.' Silas watches as Roach drags Ezra up the stairs and wonders how all of this has come about, that he should have ended up as nothing more than a butler to Vervaine Fox and that crow of a crook, Everett Roach.

Silas stays in the foyer. Outside a green vaporous fog has settled ominously over the wasteland. This, he thinks, is all wrong. He notes too that the barometer has changed and the pressure in the atmosphere is heavy. He wonders if this has anything to do with Ezra Pascoe. Has he caused the machine to corrupt? If he'd come in through the picture palace doors like everyone else his identity would have automatically been captured and processed, but he came through the basement into the core of the machine, which Silas is now certain is contaminated. This is how it reacts, by taking control. Of course, he thinks, it explains why Ezra has a terrible headache, why he has no double shadow. The machine is trying to get rid of him; he is a contagion.

Silas watches with a growing sense of apprehension. There

is no longer a collection of half-remembered planets and half-forgotten stars to light up the graphite darkness of the abyss, only the green dragon-eye of a malign moon shines down, recording all it sees. It is this moon more than the fog that convinces Silas that he is right: the memory machine is reprogramming itself, and the thought fills him with an unspeakable horror. One by one, the lights of the memories in the surrounding apartment blocks are switched off.

When the next lightness comes Silas is standing on the mirrored steps of the picture palace. The fog is denser. It has changed colour. No longer a vibrant green, it smells of decay. Suddenly he is aware of something moving through the fog towards him. He calls Amaryllis's name. There is no answer. Sensing whatever it is getting closer, he rushes back up the steps. Inside the picture palace, his heart racing, he slams shut the glass doors, fumbling with the keys as he locks and bolts them. Taking deep breaths he tries to calm his tattered nerves.

He removes his glasses, wipes them carefully, puts away his handkerchief and slowly places the glasses back on his nose. He peers through the glazed doors and sees what it was he was so afraid of. From the marshy fog his own shadow is emerging. But Silas is safe, or so he thinks. Unable to help himself, he starts to laugh, hysterical with relief.

He turns round and his mouth falls open, his eyes bulge from his head, the keys clatter to the floor. He feels his bowels move. Here, right in front of him, stands the shadow man. He is made up of particles of dust, floating in beams of light from an invisible cinema projector. This featureless three-dimensional shadow possesses the faint odour of unwashed flesh mingled with overheated celluloid. Silas runs as fast as he can up the staircase. The shadow man follows him and outside the door of Vervaine's suite, Silas turns and attacks him, seeing with relief the dust-filled particles disperse, spreading out across the gallery in thin, smoky tendrils.

Roach opens the door. 'What the bloody hell are you doing?' he says. The smoke whirls past him into Vervaine's ivory salon, pulling Silas in its wake. 'Is this some kind of joke? '

Roach stops as the door slams shuts and the shadow man remodels himself into his former shape. With the arrival of the apparition, all the noise in Ezra's head miraculously stops. Everything is blissfully silent.

Ezra says not a word about this; better, he thinks, to act the part of one persecuted by pain-filled noise.

Vervaine backs away so fast from the shadow man that she knocks over some of her beloved silver-framed photographs.

'Who . . . what . . . the hell is this?' says Roach, daring to go nearer, poking his finger into the the shadow man and pulling out whirls of smoke.

'It . . . arrived,' says Silas.

'Arrived? What do you mean?'

'There is something wrong with the machine . . .'

'You can say that again, my old fruit gum, it looks like you've got yourself a ghost for a companion. At least, Silas, you'll no longer feel lonely.' Roach laughs at his own joke. 'Maybe a face to identify it would help, or even a chain it could rattle.'

With one push the shadow man throws him hard against the wall.

Roach, now less cocky, staggers after Vervaine who is edging her way towards her bedroom door.

The shadow man is at the end of the room with his back towards them. When he turns round he is no longer featureless, no longer made of dust. He is solid. He steps into the limelight and as the lights in the room begin to fade it is Vervaine, not Silas, who lets out a scream.

Ezra is the only one able to watch this without one ounce of fear. For him it is simple. Anyone who can stop the noise cannot be all bad. He is looking at the face of a kind young man, not unhandsome, dark hair parted in the middle, wearing clothes from another era. He has an air of optimism, yet, for all this, he is scaring Vervaine witless.

'Silas, would you like to introduce me?' says the shadow man. He speaks with a German accent.

'Gunter Leichman,' Silas mutters.

'You have missed out a few things: Gunter Leichman, an honourable man, a good man, a man who hoped to improve the world. Before love sent him mad.'

Ezra feels this cool voice, like ice water, bring down his fever.

Behind Gunter Leichman is a smoky screen, as if in a lecture hall. A photograph appears of Berlin before the Great War. It is replaced by another image, of a nightclub, The Green Dragon. This is followed by a risqué postcard of a buxom young woman lying, half-naked, on a fur rug.

Roach laughs, a nervous laugh. 'Here, do you remember that ditty?

> *Would you like to sin*
> *With Elinor Glyn*
> *On a tiger skin . . .'*

'Shut up, you fool,' shouts Vervaine.

'This is Lottie,' Gunter says, unmoved by Roach's outburst. 'She is sixteen. She has a beautiful body and a terrible voice, and I love her. I worked hard, harder than ever before, at the University of Berlin. You see, I had won a scholarship to study medicine, but after a couple of years I switched to physics. I had become fascinated by the work of a man called Einstein, who . . .'

'I buried you!' shouts Silas. 'I buried you. You are an outtake!'

'No, Silas. I am in you as you are in me. Do you think you can control memory? Don't you know it is the wild card, the Joker, that trips us up, daily making us remember what we would rather forget? Like the gunshot in The Green Dragon nightclub?'

Vervaine is looking terrified.

'What's rattling your cage?' says Roach to Vervaine. 'Come on, this is just ridiculous. Smoke and mirrors, nothing more.' But he is doing his damnedest to unlock the bedroom door.

'You can't leave until I let you,' says Gunter. 'Vervaine, would you like to tell us who Lottie is?' Vervaine says nothing. He continues, 'Because of the political situation I was to return to Vienna where my family lived, but when I told them of my marriage to Lottie they disowned me. With the last of my money I bought two one-way tickets to America, determined that we would start again. I went to tell my Lottie. That night at The Green Dragon I found her in the arms of another man. I borrowed a gun, drank a bottle of schnapps, then to my eternal shame, went back to the nightclub and shot the man. Didn't I, *Schätzchen?*'

'Stop it, stop it!' Vervaine shouts.

'I ran away, I had no choice. I lived, hiding like an animal until during the Great War I stumbled across a dead man whose shoes fitted me, whose papers gave me another country, another compass to live my life by. I became Silas Molde.'

'Let me out of here,' screams Vervaine. 'Just let me out, you bastard!' Picking up a vase she throws it at Gunter Leichman. It passes right through him.

'Tell them, Ezra,' he says, 'who Lottie is.'

'Lottie Mertz went to Hollywood,' says Ezra. 'She found work as an actress and became known as Vervaine Fox.'

'Full marks,' says Gunter Leichman. 'By the time the war was over a film called *The Night of the Tiger* had made my Lottie a star.'

CRAZY SEEMED A
GOOD CHEST OF DRAWERS

I am sitting among the poppies, the tiger licking my face.
How do you break the circle? The sun blinds me and the
scenery changes once more. I am at Warlock Hall.

A pane in the study window flashes gold. The tiger and I walk
towards it and enter the room through the French windows.
Daddy is seated at his desk. I know this is a loop memory. I can't
stop or change it. All I can do is watch. There is so much I want
to ask him but it is no use, in this now of all nows.

He looks at me and is not looking at me.

He says, 'If you are seeing me, my darling, it is because I
can't be with you. I want to apologise for the pain I caused you
when you sat for the memory recordings. Princess, believe
me, never in a million years did I wish to harm you.'

My father's voice is becoming stretched, distorted. The
machine is trying to close him down before he says any more.

'This . . . world is . . . my gift . . . to . . . you, with . . . love, a
. . . world . . . of perfect . . . memories.'

He has tears in his eyes. I never saw this side of my father.

I only remember him stiff, aloof. It makes me wonder why the love that I must have had for him when I was little didn't return. We were trains going in opposite directions, running on parallel lines. He was too stubborn to reintroduce himself to me, and I too lost to know where to store all the confusion in my head. Crazy seemed a good chest of drawers.

I know he is a memory. I know this, still I can't help shouting, 'What on earth made you think I would prefer to be here? I would rather have taken my chance in the world. Why meddle with the past? Even if I had forgotten it, why not leave it be? I would rather live through fire and war and have my own memories in a future that was rightly mine than be in this nightmare of your creation!'

The image of my father begins to disperse, fading into the green leaden fog. He, like the room, is lost in its vapours. The study, the house all gone, just the fog: thick, mouldy and full of ghosts, a muttering miasma of memories. The light is going and for a dreadful moment I can't see the tiger. Have I lost him? How will I ever find my way back to Ezra?

One thing I am certain of is that this fog has at its very core an evilness. It wants to destroy all that my father and Silas worked to create. It rises and falls, its waves filled with sovereigns, treasures of the past. In the encroaching darkness all the lights from the apartment blocks are going out.

No longer do I wonder if this eerie fog is made up of shadows of memories. I know it is. I hear Herman's voice in there and a small boy whimpering; I hear my orange-blossom mother calling to be saved. There is an electric noise, the high whistle of things remembered, the wailing for all that is lost. I hear Ezra's voice, it tugs at my heart. The tiger, luminous, burning bright in all its whiteness appears. We walk together through this foggy sea of muddled memories, back to where Ezra is sleeping.

Ezra's father opens the door. His face is pale under the glasses. Behind him are Miss Bright and Tommy.

'Where is Ezra?' he says. 'Where is my son?' He rushes past me and looks down the stairwell.

'I left him, here, asleep,' I say. 'Please, don't tell me he has gone.'

Tommy comes out into the corridor and points. 'The green fog,' he says and I see, streaming from under each door of every apartment, a green vapour that rolls down the stairs and out on to the wasteland. In it are all the murmurings of the loop memories. 'It's all nearly over,' he says.

I go inside and sit on the floor of the apartment. In my head a clock has started to tick and I know whatever is going to happen will not be long in coming. I'm not afraid of the darkness any more, it's only the blood in all our veins. It is the life force.

The tiger lies down beside me. He puts his big head on my lap and I smell the wild plains in his fur, I smell freedom.

Tommy sits next to me. I am forming a plan. There is a big moon, bigger than any I can remember here, and it makes me think that a gateway back to the old world might open. It has started already with the purr of the tiger and the tap-tap of Tommy's fingers on the parquet floor, with the tick-tock of the clock.

Perhaps I have become a fortune-teller, because I know who is at the door before he even knocks. Ezra's arms are around me, he kisses me, I am awake in him.

Silas is standing in the shadow of the doorway. He looks sheepish. He asks if he may come in.

'Please listen, everyone, this is very important. You must do as I tell you,' he says, as he walks into the apartment. 'You have no reason to trust me, that I know. The machine has already started to malfunction and the fabric of this world is eroding. When the lightness comes, I will try to take you home. The thing is, there is a control code. It's so simple, yet it's gone from my mind.'

'A simple code,' says Miss Bright. 'Numerical? A date, for instance?'

I say, 'My birthday.'

Silas stares at me.

'Of course. The day of activation.' He covers his face with his hands.

'How could I have forgotten that? Amaryllis's birthday. What is happening to me? I'm losing my mind.'

Ezra's father puts his arm round Silas's shoulders. 'There's going to be a tomorrow when the sun comes up, a tomorrow where my Nancy is waiting for me, at home.'

Home. What a strange word that is. My home is so newly discovered that still I haven't got the measure of it. My home is Ezra, the lock on my front door is the tiger.

Without a word being said, we leave the apartment. Silas is behind me, or so I think. The tiger and the others are three floors below. Ezra and I are one flight down when he remembers his kitbag. I run back up to the apartment to get it. Silas has it in his hand. He looks past me to see if Ezra is there.

'No,' I say, 'he's waiting on the landing.'

'If you go with the others,' says Silas in this new voice of his, 'you know what will happen?'

I nod. 'Are you going to try to stop me?'

'No,' he says. 'It's your choice.'

There is something different, kinder, about this Silas whom once I called 'Uncle'.

I hear Ezra's footsteps on the stairs. He comes into the room. 'What's keeping you?'

'I was just making sure you have left nothing behind,' says Silas, handing Ezra his kitbag. Silas turns to look at me with his dark all-knowing eyes. 'Once we are gone from here,' he says, 'there is no turning back.'

I know now that no one will ever read this.

THEN THERE
WERE THREE

On the whole Everett Roach has always been in control of his life. Luck he counted as a close personal friend, without a phone number, but one that he was able to call on when in a tight spot. For the first time he discovers the line is down. Whatever happened when the shadow man barged his way in, he brought with him a whole baked-bean can of trouble.

It started with the fog. Even before the arrival of the unwanted guest, that fog was a thug. Roach thinks maybe the time has come to take Silas up on his offer.

'Where do you think that . . . thing . . . your old mate Gunter . . . has taken Silas and the kid?' he asks.

Vervaine is at the cocktail cabinet, filling a large glass with ice.

'How the hell do I know?' she says. 'For another trip down memory lane, I guess.'

'Well, then, we're all right, aren't we?'

Vervaine takes a large swig from her drink. 'In what way, "all right"?'

She finishes her drink and returns to the cocktail cabinet.

Yes, definitely time to skedaddle, thinks Roach. 'Silas recorded your memories before the fire, right? And anyway, you never saw what actually happened in the room with Ruben, did you?'

Vervaine laughs. 'Oh dear heaven, you really are the dumb blond here, darling, not me. The minute you strolled through those glass doors downstairs, this machine . . .' she stretches her arms wide, '. . . clocked you in and sucked your memories from you.'

'Hold on, hold on, what are you saying?'

'I'm saying, if Gunter takes them back to Arnold's study on the night of the fire, whatever you did, Silas and the Pascoe boy will see it all.'

Roach takes a deep breath. Something isn't smelling that rosy.

Ignoring it, he says, 'You can win Silas over, Cattykins. If anyone can, it's you. He'll always dance to your tune. He's devoted to you.'

'Not any more,' says Vervaine, 'not any more. He's devoted to the memory of his little Lottie.'

'Cattykins, you look a millon dollars. Much better than that plump bird on the tiger skin.'

'Thanks,' she says, picking up the Martini bottle. 'This is sticky. It wasn't sticky before.'

'Pour me one,' says Roach. He too has noticed the stickiness, as if nothing has been cleaned for ages.

'Tell me what you did,' says Vervaine, 'while I was playing Florence Nightingale.'

'Come on, Cattykins, we agreed we would leave it.'

She laughs. 'It looks as though that might not be possible. I need to know exactly what it is Silas might see. I want the truth.' Her cocktail has an unpleasant taste to it.

Roach has to think carefully about his reply.

'Cattykins, the truth is something I have a little trouble with.'

'How about making an exception to that golden rule? I need to know if there is any chance of getting out of this alive.'

'All right, no need to be melodramatic. Old Pincher went to Ruben's office, told him you couldn't be moved. Ruben wanted you gone. That might harden you a bit to what comes next.'

'My heart is steel.'

'Pincher took you out to the ambulance and I waited as agreed for the first fire bomb to go off. I was about to go down to Ruben's study, but the girl – er, Ethel – woke up. I thought she just might start screaming so I locked her in the tower. Then it was a rush, I can tell you, to get to the study before the second of my little beauties blew my socks off, so to speak. Ruben was by the French windows. He had the plans, everything.'

'Then what, Prince Charming?'

'I shot him. I didn't want him giving the game away. We had all we needed.'

'You shot him. Just the once?'

'Three times. I had to make sure, didn't I? Blew his brains out. Not pretty.'

'A pity. He had a first-class mind.'

'Well, that's the truth. What does that do for us?'

'It means, my beloved moron, there is no way Silas will let you or me out of here, ever.'

'We still have the revolver, remember?'

Neither of them has noticed what is happening around them. It's only as Roach stands up to refill his glass that they see the green fog seeping under the curtains.

'How the hell is that getting in?' says Vervaine.

The curtains billow as if someone is hiding behind them.

'Maybe it's that shadow man,' whispers Roach, his mouth dry. 'Or Silas, listening to all we're saying.'

'Go and look.'

'No, you, you're the one with a heart of steel.'

'Just do it, Everett,' says Vervaine, her voice hammer-hard. He walks slowly towards the curtains.

'What if he has a gun?'

'Everett, do it.'

His heart is thumping, big bass-drum time, as he pulls back the curtains. There's no one there.

'We need to calm down,' he says, 'we need to think straight.'

He makes sure the window is tight shut, only to find that the glass doesn't seem to stop the luminous fog from leeching through. It crawls on to the carpet with a dead weight that no fog should have.

Vervaine's drink drops from her trembling hand and the fog rolls forward to swallow it up. She edges closer to the bedroom door, the green vapour clinging to the floor just an inch or two above the carpet. Slimy green tentacles spring from it, latching on to whatever crosses its path as it creeps ever closer to them, making the grand salon mildewed and mouldy.

Roach follows Vervaine to the bedroom, then suddenly he feels her red nails sink into the sleeve of his suit. They stare, both frozen to the spot. The bedroom's extravagantly ruched drapes are festering with a glutinous fungus to which the green fog hungrily attaches itself. It is claiming every part of the room. A smell of gangrene hangs in the air.

'What are you doing?' shrieks Vervaine. Roach pulls up his sleeves and rolls up his trousers. He has been careful to hide the revolver in the dressing table. There are three bullets. One for the girl, one for the boy, and finally, one for Silas.

'Leave this to me. I know what I am doing.' He puts his fingers into the stinking vapours. They are blood-warm and revoltingly sticky. He feels around inside the drawer. 'It's not bleeding well here. It has to be. Where's the gun?'

'I don't know,' says Vervaine, shaking, 'but anyway, it won't work here.'

In rage and frustration Roach lifts up the dressing-table mirror and throws it with all his might into the middle of the room. The fog leaps up to greet it and devours it whole.

'Stop it,' shouts Vervaine. 'Just look at yourself. You are covered in mould.' They run from the bedroom slamming the door shut. It creaks open again behind them.

Vervaine desperately tries to brush the fog from her satin dress.

'It's all over me,' she screams. 'Get it off, get it off.'

Roach feels it crawl up his legs. They hurry to the door to the gallery. It is locked.

Then they hear the whispering. The fog is filled with unfathomable words. They watch as the armchair in which Roach sprawled by the fire, lazily demanding cocktails, begins to disintegrate. It groans then splinters as it melts, protesting, into the acid vapour.

'We've got to get out of here, now!'

Vervaine is crying. It is something he has never seen her do before, not for real, nose running, tears. If he wasn't terrified before, he certainly is now. Frantically he pulls with all his might and the door flies open. They fall in an undignified heap on the floor of the gallery. The door slams behind them, the key turning in the lock. Roach helps Vervaine to her feet. She is nearly hysterical. Once I'm out of this horror film, he thinks to himself, and my address book is up and running, and luck is on my side again, I am going to get as far away from Vervaine and all this mess as possible.

They are both overcome with relief to find that the foyer and the mirrored stairs are all as they should be. They can see the fog out on the wasteland, but it shows no inclination to materialise inside. Perhaps, thinks Roach, what happened in the salon belongs to the headless horses of terror that occasionally ride through one's worst fears.

Vervaine has not let go of him.

'What's that?' she says.

The floor judders beneath them.

'Oh, no. Christopher Columbus!' says Roach.

They hold on to the gallery rail as the building begins to shake.

Vervaine screams, her voice bounces off the walls, and she collapses to the floor, her arms wrapped tight round Roach's leg.

It stops. All is still. For a moment neither can believe what they are seeing. The fog has gone and beyond the glass doors, miraculously, is Warlock Wood.

'What are we waiting for?' says Roach. He shakes Vervaine off his leg and charges down the stairs, two at a time.

'Wait,' she calls. 'Wait.'

Roach stops abruptly. The tiger is there, teeth bared.

Roach backs away, cautiously.

'All right, big boy, take it easy.'

Silas comes up from the basement. He is holding the revolver.

'Gunter, my darling,' says Vervaine, 'please let your *Schätzchen* go. That is all I beg of you, please, for the love of me.'

Silas smiles. 'For the love of you? For the love of you, you are staying. But Roach is leaving.'

'No,' shouts Vervaine.

The tiger keeps her pinned to the stairs. Roach is standing at the door.

'Sorry, doll, but the future is calling.' The doors, he finds, are locked. He turns to Silas. 'You couldn't open them for me, could you, my old fruit gum?'

'Of course,' replies Silas. He lifts the revolver and takes aim.

'What are you doing?' shouts Roach. 'Don't be daft.'

'This one is for Arnold Ruben, the greatest man I ever knew.'

Silas fires, straight at Roach's head. Roach, his eyes wide, puts his hand up to the hole in his skull and realises he is still alive.

'It doesn't work! It doesn't even hurt!'

He is still laughing when Silas pulls the trigger again. The revolver is aimed at his genitals.

'This is for what you did to Amaryllis Ruben.'

'Bang bang, I'm still here, my old fruit gum. Now stop messing about and let me out.'

'Certainly,' says Silas. 'When I have fired the last of these three bullets.' Turning towards Vervaine, he points the revolver at her heart. 'I have been hurt, cheated and double-crossed by you, the woman I married. So this is for you, for the part you played in Arnold Ruben's downfall, this is my Valentine, sent with all my love.'

The tiger goes to Silas's side.

Vervaine says not one word as the bullet enters her heart.

Roach starts laughing, laughing, laughing. 'It's nothing, the bullets do nothing! You're not dead either!'

Vervaine doesn't move from where she has slumped on the mirrored stairs. She doesn't say a word as Silas throws open the picture palace doors.

'Come on, Cattykins,' says Roach, 'we can get out of here.'

She looks at him. She is icy calm. 'You are a fool if you

think you can leave,' she says. 'Don't you see there is no way out?'

Roach isn't listening. He is pushing through what seems to be a membrane between him and the outside world.

'That's right,' says Silas, 'just push a little harder.'

Only when he was outside on the first of the mirrored steps did Roach realise for a second, maybe more, that Silas's aim was deadly. Luck, that fickle friend, wasn't waiting for him. He fell down on to the mossy earth, dead.

'Well, Lottie, do you want to join your lover?' Silas asks Vervaine.

She stays where she is.

'Answer my question.'

'No. No, Gunter, I don't.'

Tommy is the first out of the basement. Silas has been quite clear about the order.

'Remember,' says Silas, 'no looking back, none of you, that is what we agreed.'

'It worked!' shouts Tommy, his mouse-wings flapping as he pushes open the picture palace doors and punches his way through the membrane.

The old soldier follows, Miss Bright is next. Ezra, holding tight to Amaryllis's hand, leads her towards the door.

The machine is beginning to shake.

'Quickly,' says Silas.

Ezra feels Amaryllis's hand leave his.

'I told you, don't look back,' says Silas.

It's too late. Ezra has turned round.

'I can't come with you,' says Amaryllis. 'It's no good. Either way, I'm dead. I don't have any chance of life. You can't save me.'

'That's not true. Come on, just come with me.'

'You don't understand.'

She takes off her red cardigan and slips down the straps of her camisole. It falls to her waist and then he sees, under her bare breast, the dark crimson star of a deep wound.

It is Vervaine who says to Ezra, 'Everett shot her on the night of the fire. Silas brought her back in here and the machine saved her from death. You saw it all, that's why Roach tried to kill you too.'

Amaryllis kisses Ezra. He tries to wrap her in his arms so they never will be parted. She slips free from him.

'Go, go now. Be strong for me.'

'I'm staying,' says Ezra. 'I love you. I am not leaving.'

'If you stay,' says Silas, 'this machine will erode before I even have a chance to try to save her. If you stay, you will not destroy the machine, only help it to evolve into something even more dangerous.'

The woods are beginning to fade, so are the others. Amaryllis knows it is nearly too late.

'Go, please,' she begs. 'This is breaking me. Go.'

Some moments are longer than other moments. Some moments last an eternity in the mind, every detail remembered, regretted, relived, over and over again. A past full of what-ifs.

The tiger decides Ezra's fate. He runs at him, his huge head bent low, and throws him with all his might through the membrane, into the real world.

Ezra fell to the ground, Orpheus returned from the underworld to a bluebell wood.

COUNTING US OUT

I don't know if Ezra got back to Warlock Wood. Silas is concerned that he might have left it too late. I want to know what would happen then.

'Arnold would have been the man to ask,' he says.

'He is dead,' says Vervaine. She is sitting at the top of the mirrored staircase. She looks terrible, her dress stained, her make-up running.

She asks Silas, 'What am I going to do, darling?'

He shrugs his shoulders. 'Stay where you are, here with me, 'til death us do part.'

She laughs. 'Which one of us is sicker, you or me? Let me raise an empty glass to the three of us here in perpetual purgatory.'

'You and I don't have that long,' says Silas gently.

'Well, that's a cheering thought. So we are all dead.'

'Not Amaryllis, I hope. She is a different matter altogether and one you are going to help me with.'

'Why?'

'To make amends, and because, my dear Lottie, there is no alternative.'

I don't know what Silas means by that. What I do know is that the tiger is very agitated. I stay seated on the bottom step listening to Silas and Vervaine, and wonder how these two could ever have loved one other, for they seem as far away from each other as it is possible to be in such a small space.

We look out at the wasteland. The first of the apartment blocks is beginning to crumble. This is it.

Slowly I find my feet and holding the soft pelt round the tiger's neck follow Silas down into the basement.

'This,' he says, 'is the control room where we made the memory recording when you were little.'

'I know that.' I say, 'You washed away my memory. I now know a lot of what happened. I didn't understand, I thought I was crazy.'

'I am profoundly sorry.'

Silas is a kind man. Odd to say that, when I've seen him kill someone. But I feel released, knowing that Roach is gone. At least in the real world he is dead, he can harm no one else and, if he is still here, then he is only a loop memory.

I walk around the control room. The dials are spinning. I ask Silas why.

Silas looks so tired. 'The machine is corrupted,' he says.

I stare up at the big clock that once spun so fast, to find it is ticking slowly, determinedly.

'I think it is counting us out,' says Silas. 'It's waiting for the fog to gain the strength it needs to destroy us completely.'

'Did Ezra start that?'

'I'm not sure. Perhaps he escalated it by coming in the wrong way.'

I say, without thinking about it, 'You need to sleep, Uncle Silas.'

He smiles at me.

'That's what you used to call me when . . .'

'When I still remembered everything.'

He looks broken. He says, in his defence, that neither my father nor he realised the true capabilities of the machine.

'I think it was out of our control long before we activated it. You see, it was such an extraordinary project, a dream come true. Your father had all the money to do whatever was needed. Prototype after prototype we built. And we became so carried away with what we could achieve, that we never stopped to ask why we were building this monster in the first place.' I touch his arm. 'I have failed. Failed Arnold and, worst of all, failed you.'

'But you killed Roach. He raped me.' I say the unspeakable words and they lose their power in being heard, in Silas knowing the truth.

'I suspected, but not until far too late.'

We sit without words. Sometimes words have no value. They are the noise of a babbling brook that keeps a truth well hidden from us.

After maybe forever, maybe only an itch, he says, 'While the machine was still functioning, I revisited my memories of when I was a medical student.'

He tells me that long ago, before he was married, he had studied to be a doctor. He wanted to be a surgeon until he became fascinated with physics.

'But that is all by the bye. I think the bullet may have hit a renal artery, but I can't be sure. A surgeon would remove it through your back. If it hit your spleen, then there is little I can do. I won't know until I examine you. I'm planning to anaesthetise you, patch you together, and prevent you from bleeding with a tiny clamp. The one that I use for the smallest of wires. If it works it should give you an hour, perhaps more, to find help.'

'If it doesn't, I am dead?' I say.

'Yes.'

'I will take that chance. What will happen to you?'

'When you are gone, the machine will destroy us.'

'You, the tiger and Vervaine.'

'Not the tiger.'

'I don't understand, why not the tiger?'

'At first I didn't know why the tiger had a double shadow, why Arnold had made it so powerful, but I realise now it is the programme on which he worked the hardest so if all else failed the tiger would act as your guardian in his place. I lied to myself, refusing to accept what I knew all along to be true, that Arnold was dead. The tiger doesn't exist outside this machine. Your father was sure he would never be needed, so he gave him no words.'

I kneel down and wrap my arms around the tiger's head.

'The tiger is but a poor compensation,' says Silas.

'No, you're wrong. He says more, without words, than ever he could in a language I might understand.'

So here I am again, waiting, me and the tiger, in the weightlessness of nothing, of no time and too long to think. I wonder what Ezra is doing, I wonder if he returned home, I wonder if he is all right. I miss him. I long for him. He is the unattainable future from which I am adrift.

I stay in the foyer. There is nowhere else to go. Outside around the wasteland, the apartment blocks one by one surrender their memorised foundations and tumble in on themselves to disappear into the waiting fog. I feel the vapour growing in strength, I can even hear it hum. The edge of the world is visible, huge mesh fishing nets waiting to catch memories. All that is left now in this pea-green soup is the Black Tower which even this fog cannot destroy. A stubborn thing, that tower.

Then Silas, from the middle of what I have named hospital-ward time, time that runs on slow motion, calls for Vervaine. She walks down the stairs, her stained dress trailing. She says not one word to me.

Still the tiger and I wait. At first I don't notice it, not to begin with. I wonder if I might have grown, for the tiger seems smaller and, bit by bit, he appears to be regressing in size, in years, unwinding like Miss Bright's cardigan, until at last he is as small as a newborn cub, and I hold him in my hands, studying the perfection of him with a sense of utter bewilderment as he vanishes altogether.

I think life and death are one. There is only a collection of years, as meaningful and meaningless as we wish to make them. We are but a sneeze between the two.

Silas had waited for the tiger to dissolve, for in that long loneliness of loss, he came to take me down to the basement. Vervaine is simply dressed, she is almost beautiful, far more fragile without the war paint.

Before I lie on the zinc table Silas gives me a letter. It's addressed to the lawyer I must see if I survive.

I climb up, take off my red cardigan and lie down. In the overhead light I see a butterfly, fluttering. I don't know where it has come from.

Silas says, 'Are you ready?'

I nod.

And there is the riddle of endless darkness, the darkness we all fear. I don't see the light.

MY EYE THE CAMERA

1943

I think we must have seemed like aliens when we emerged
from the bluebell woods into the warm sunshine.

Tommy in his battered mouse wings jumped up and down
with joy as he shouted, 'We're back, we're here, we're home!'

What I remember most was the birdsong, the hum of bees,
the extraordinary colours, an overwhelming beauty better by far
than anything I remembered. We stumbled from those woods,
passed the lake, and in front of us were the green lawns of
what once had been Warlock Hall. We all felt drunk as time
suddenly flowed in upon us and rooted us to the earth.

We stood, the four of us, somewhat bewildered by what we
saw, the scene was so surreal. Gone were the Nissen huts.
Instead, in front of the Black Tower, long prefab buildings
had been erected. On the lawns were men in dressing gowns,
some in wheelchairs, others sitting on benches, accompanied
by nurses.

Then people began to run towards us.

'It'll be rich,' said Father, 'if they tell us we're trespassing.'

*

We had been given up for dead and the site of Paradox 87 requisitioned as a convalescent home for wounded soldiers. We'd turned up on the very day Sir Basil wrapped up the operation. He was about to drive back to London. Instead he ordered the area to be immediately cordoned off and all the patients temporarily transferred. The place became eerily all ours.

It was mid-May 1943. That took some getting used to. For Father, Tommy and Miss Bright, it was far worse: the war hadn't even started when they entered the picture palace. We stayed there a month in all, each of us being fully debriefed. Numerous medical, psychological and scientific tests were performed on us in order to discover how it was possible that we hadn't aged, not by one single day.

The other enigma that baffled the teams of specialists was Tommy. All his old medical records stated that he had the mental age of a six-year-old and that this brain was unlikely to develop any further. Yet something extraordinary had happened to him in the memory machine. Tommy himself explained it very simply.

'My brain was all tangled up in a big knot and the green light untangled it.'

He was still Tommy, still seeing the world in the way that only Tommy saw it, but with a wisdom and an intelligence that he had never possessed before. While we were there Miss Bright taught him how to spell his name and, for the first time, he began to read.

The doctors wanted to do more tests on him. This made me very angry. We had all been through quite enough. I told them they were to leave him alone.

'He's not a human rabbit,' said Father.

'No, I'm not even a human mouse,' Tommy added helpfully.

Father, too, had benefited from the green light, but the doctors didn't realise it, mainly because his medical records had mysteriously disappeared.

After a month we were allowed to return home. Each of us had been given an official story to explain to the startled villagers the reason for our sudden reappearance. Tommy had been recovering from tuberculosis and Father had lost his memory. I thought Father's story sounded too far-fetched.

'That is why it will work, old chap,' said Sir Basil.

Miss Bright and my stories had at least a ring of truth to them: we had been away on war work.

The day we went home was what Father called a Red-Letter Day.

Sir Basil volunteered to drive us back to the cottage.

'Why waste petrol, sir?' said Father. 'We're only down the road.' He had been given a new suit of clothes; we all had.

Father had spent time spit-and-polishing his boots, he brushed and Brylcreemed his hair, shaved, even put on a dab of cologne. I thought he looked as if he were going to church on a Sunday.

'Or to a wedding,' said Tommy.

We walked through the bluebell woods to Bishop's Norgate. There, beyond the meadow that led to our cottage, was Mother.

She was in the garden hanging out the washing. When Father saw her he started to run. Tommy and I stayed put.

It was as if I was seeing it through the lens of a camera, a sensation that had been with me ever since I'd returned. Mother dropped the basket and Father wrapped her in his arms and lifted her off her feet. She was laughing, her head thrown back so that her hair, which she always wore pinned up, tumbled down.

I heard her say, 'You've come back to me.'

'Yes,' said Father, 'the ghosts have all gone.'

Mother had tears streaming down her face. 'I can see that, love.'

From where I was filming this with my eye of a camera, they looked like a happy ending, waiting for the credits to roll and the full orchestra to play.

I left the next day. I knew Mother would suspect something wasn't right with me if I stayed any longer. I lied, said I was needed back at work, which wasn't true. I had, in fact been given three weeks' leave.

Sir Basil didn't seem that surprised to see me. He had moved the OSP back to London, to temporary accommodation off Piccadilly.

I was seen as a hero inside the organisation. For the life of me I couldn't think why. The last thing I felt was heroic. It struck me I had done little to nothing, except suffer some of the most appalling headaches I'd ever known, been as good as useless and failed to bring Amaryllis out of the machine. I was angry with myself. I just wanted everyone to stop the hero bit. And then they said I was in line for a medal for bravery. I refused it.

I threw myself into my work. There was a lot to be done. I was determined that Hitler should never make a machine like Arnold Ruben's. The idea was truly terrifying. My job was to trawl through all the intelligence to see if there was any indication that the Nazis had started building a machine. The hope was that they didn't have the resources to fund such an experimental idea. Then in July we received a signal from an agent on the ground saying that something big was being built in a factory east of Berlin. Sir Basil asked for more information in order to determine what it was.

'I don't like the sound of it one little bit,' said Sir Basil. 'What are your thoughts, Pascoe?'

'We know that Z passed on Arnold Ruben's plans,' I said. 'Roach was sent to photograph the interior, but personally I think the plans to the machine are more than enough.'

'I agree. Plus, they have clever chaps over there who I'm sure, once they'd established the principle of Ruben's machine, would make a version they could claim for themselves. I've sent a report to the PM. I'm waiting for a reply.'

All this time I had clung to the words Silas had said to me: '. . . a chance to save Amaryllis.'

It was a box of matches and, when all seemed dark in my head, I would strike one and for a moment there would be the smallest glimmer of hope.

Late that summer I received an invitation to a wedding. I

had to read it twice to take it in. Mother sent an accompanying letter – she knew I would be completely dumbfounded. And I was, in a way, and in a way, I wasn't. Tommy had met Milly, who was working as a land girl on a farm near Bishop's Norgate. According to Mother she had two passions in life: one was Tommy, the other was mice.

I was given leave to go to the wedding. Sir Basil arranged for me to borrow a motorbike, a BSA M20. It felt good to get out of the big smoke and all its dreariness and to see the green of the countryside, to feel free.

I arrived home to find the cottage in a happy state of chaos. The first person I saw as I walked up the garden path was Louis Lindo. I knew all about what had happened to him on the night I entered the memory machine.

I was so pleased to see him, yet I felt like a time traveller, as if I'd met him in another world.

'Ruddy Nora, Louis, you did it, you're a pilot!' I said.

'Yep, I have my wings.'

'You should never have followed me that night.'

'It was the best mistake I ever made,' Louis said, laughing. 'I wouldn't have ended up at St Thomas' and . . .'

He didn't finish what he was saying because Mother came out of the front door.

'There you are,' she said, as if I had just been down to the village shop. 'Come on, we're going to be late if we don't get a move on.'

Three evacuees were still living with them. The twins were to be bridesmaids and Joey, the pageboy.

I looked out of the kitchen window to see Father at the bottom of the garden with his trousers rolled up, digging. My heart sank.

'You're not going to the wedding like that, in a boiler suit?' said Mother.

'No,' I replied. 'What's Father doing?'

'Oh, I don't know. Now go and get changed, for goodness' sake, and wash your face, it's covered in soot. Well, don't dilly-dally, go.' I was on the landing when she shouted up, 'And see how Tommy's doing with his tie and all.'

I washed in the old china basin. The cold water felt good. I went upstairs and from the small bedroom I could see Father still digging away. I was thinking, oh, please, no, not one of his turns again, when Tommy walked in.

'What do you think?' he said.

His shirt buttons were done up wrong and the tie was in a sloppy knot, but, apart from that, he looked a picture.

I gave him a hug, rebuttoned his shirt, retied his tie and put the rose in his buttonhole.

'You look like Clark Gable,' I said.

A smile spread across Tommy's face from one end to the other.

'That's me, Tommy Cutler.' He was quiet, then he said, 'It's a pity Mum never saw me like this.'

'Yes.'

'She just got cooked. Life does that to some.'

'It does indeed,' I said.

'I've got two mice in my pocket, one for Milly and one for me.'

He took them out. Each was wearing a small ribbon, one blue, one red.

'She likes mice, does my Milly. She likes mice and she loves me.'

'That's the right way round,' I said. 'Do you love her, Tommy?'

'My heart is so full of love that if it were a balloon it might just burst.'

'What is Father doing?' I asked. He was still digging.

'Don't worry,' said Tommy, 'he is all fine in the head and the ghosts never bother him now.' Tommy lowered his voice. 'They belong in the you-know-what.'

Downstairs the family was assembling in an orderly fashion. Or as orderly as is possible for the Pascoes.

'Where's your father?' said Mother, adjusting her hat in the hall mirror.

'Here, love,' said Father, carrying in two crates of ale.

'Where did you get those from?'

'The bottom of the garden. I buried them before the war, didn't I? Hello, son,' he said, giving me a hug. 'Glad you're here.'

Milly was tiny, pretty and perfect for Tommy. They held their mice while Miss Bright took the wedding pictures.

We all sat in the garden, eating and drinking ale. Everyone started dancing and later there was singing. Olive was holding Louis's hand.

'We're engaged, Ezra,' she whispered.

'Well, I'm glad someone's going to make an honest woman of you, Sis. You couldn't have chosen better.'

'I had to snap her up pretty darn quick,' said Louis, 'before the Yanks got here.'

'Don't be silly,' said Olive, resting her head on his shoulder. 'There is only you, Louis, and you know it.'

'So when are you getting married?' I asked.

'The minute this blasted war is over.'

I left next day with a rather sore head. I thought I would bike straight back to London, but I didn't. I walked into the woods where the picture palace had once stood and spent a long time looking at the crater. I lit another of those matches and hoped with all my heart that Amaryllis would find a way back to me.

WHITE RICE
ON BLACK VELVET

I was informed on 12 November 1943 that, if the order was given, I was to film the bombing of the Nazi memory machine.

What worried me most was an irrational fear that it might have an impact on Ruben's original machine. I asked Jim Boyle that very question.

'Stranger things happen in science than man can ever imagine,' he said. 'It's not beyond the realms of probability.'

This was not a comforting thought. For a start it took up too many of my dwindling supply of matches.

On 18 November, I felt I would explode if I didn't get out of the basement in which we worked. I'd had the Intelligence Officer there for two days, briefing me about the target and the camera I was to use. He must have thought I was stupid because, although I understood what he was saying first time round, he had a voice that stayed on the same note and could send an insomniac like me to sleep after his first sentence. That day I had an unexpected call from Miss Bright. Sir Basil had felt her talents shouldn't be wasted and she was doing something very hush-hush at Bletchley. She had two days' leave and invited me for lunch at the Criterion in Piccadilly Circus.

We talked, skirting round the main topic until finally Miss Bright said, 'Do you ever wake up wondering where you are and if you are back there, not in this world at all?'

'Often,' I said. 'Time is still something I have a problem with.'

'I lost my fiancé in the Great War. Just one kiss, that was all, then he was killed. At least in the memory machine I was with him as much as I wanted. He never said anything different, just the same words, the same actions. Amaryllis called them loop memories. But there I was, with him again, feeling the love we had for each other.' She stopped and looked at me. 'How are you getting on?'

'Oh, you know, all right,' I lied, unconvincingly.

'In other words, dreadful.'

I smiled. 'Stiff upper lip and all that jazz, as Sir Basil would say.'

'Amaryllis was quite a remarkable young lady,' she said.

'Yes.'

'If it is of any comfort, I know what it feels like. The memory machine gave me back moments, but the grief never goes away.'

As we parted, she said, 'Take care of yourself.'

I watched her as she put on her gloves. She gave my hand a squeeze and was gone, disappearing into the drabness of a foggy November afternoon.

I knew I wasn't alone in having lost someone I loved. Half the world was grieving for the other half. Still, that thought never brought me much comfort. It belonged with the 'Have a drink, snap out of it, old chap,' approach to life.

What I knew was this: no matter what happened to me in this world, I was never again going to meet anyone like Amaryllis. She was simply unique. Not because I loved her, but because she had an aura about her, a magic that many claim and few possess.

When I returned to the office I found pandemonium.

'Where the hell have you been?' asked Sir Basil.

'Out to lunch.'

'This is no time for ruddy lunch.'

'I near as damn it live in the smoke of this office. I do need to breathe occasionally.'

'Well, you can breathe all you want. You're off on ops tonight.'

I was handed a pile of clothes, which included a big fur-lined flying jacket. I checked all my equipment and was driven, as Sir Basil put it, 'hell for leather' up to the airfield. It was pitch-black when we arrived. I heard the noise of the planes before I saw them. They rumbled like prehistoric birds yearning for the sky.

I climbed aboard the Lancaster.

The skipper turned and said, 'So you're the spare bod we've been waiting for. Welcome aboard. You nearly missed the flight.'

Then he returned to what he was doing.

I only fully realised what I'd let myself in for when the skipper said, 'Keep your parachute on. If we go down it would be nice at least to know someone got his home movie.'

This was greeted with general laughter.

He gave the thumbs-up to the ground crew and we were hurtling down the runway, engines roaring, the whole plane rattling. We were off with such a force, as if the sky longed to embrace us, wrap us in its clouds. I was inside the body of a flying iron giant. The smell of metal, fumes and oil mixed with the potent scent of fear.

By the time we were over the Fatherland the flak was bad – at least, I thought it was bad. A searchlight suddenly burst through the cloud cover.

'Pretty quiet tonight,' the skipper said over the radio to the Squadron Leader. He signed off and we flew east towards our target, accompanied by twenty-nine other Lancs. This was one bomb that had to find its home.

Ruddy Nora, I was cold, and my fingers felt as if they had turned to ice. What had been easy equipment to operate on the ground was a lot harder up here.

Through my headphones, I heard the skipper say, 'We're going in. No idea of the reception committee that might be waiting for us.'

We ducked under the clouds. The first of the Lancs had dropped incendiaries and markers for the bomb-aimer to line up on. It was an extraordinary sight, white rice thrown on black velvet. Pinpricks of fire broke out everywhere. Then we saw the red markers.

'Hold it steady, skipper,' said the bomb-aimer, looking at his radar screen. 'Steady . . . steady . . . bombs away.'

I forgot about everything and just kept filming. What happened next was not what anyone had expected. A huge green bubble suddenly rose above the target. It hung there and such was its magnetic field that the plane literally shot upwards.

'What the hell was that?' said the skipper. All his instruments were going crazy.

'Let's get out of here,' said the flight engineer. 'I don't like the look of it.'

'How are the gunners?'

'Still here, skipper. A bit dazed.'

I didn't stop filming. I couldn't. I asked if we could circle it again.

'Are you mad?' said the skipper.

'It's important, we need the footage.'

He took the plane round once more. The flight engineer slid open the side window for me to get a better angle.

The bubble was still hanging there ominously: a green luminous light, a bauble from an ogre's Christmas tree. As we passed over it for the second time it imploded with such force that we were sucked for a moment into its vortex. The skipper fought to pull the plane out of its nose dive. I held tight to the camera, to everything. We rolled over, and for one second through the open window I saw the ground, the next second, the sky. Everyone was deadly quiet until at last the great bird started to gain height and level out.

'Feel sick?' asked the navigator.

'No,' I said.

'You look a little green.'

'We all do,' laughed the skipper.

I thought that night I had seen the inside of hell's mouth.

I arrived back in London at six in the morning. The film was immediately whisked away. I was dozing in my chair when I was called into Sir Basil's office to be told that we'd definitely blown the thing to kingdom come.

'Now go home and get some sleep.'

'One more thing, sir. Was there an explosion in Warlock Wood?'

'Yes, Pascoe.'

'What kind of explosion?'

'Intelligence reports describe it as a green ball of light, very bright. It sucked back in on itself and vanished. It was on a much smaller scale than what you witnessed.'

'Any debris?'

'Nothing,' said Sir Basil. 'We've cordoned off the area. The chaps at the convalescent home are not best pleased. We said it was an unexploded bomb from the Stuka raid. Still, the villagers will tell you, there are odd goings-on in Warlock Wood.'

'It's all over then,' I said.

Sir Basil leaned back in his chair and stared at me. 'I don't know.'

I asked for permission to go down and inspect the site.

It was snowing when I arrived. There was nothing to see. I stood under an oak tree thinking that half of me never made it back through the membrane of the memory machine into this world. I know at least my heart rebelled. It decided not to leave Amaryllis, come what may.

I go to Warlock Wood quite often. I never know what I hope to find there. I think it's like visiting an unmarked grave. I find myself telling her what I'm doing. Two years later there isn't any sign of where the picture palace was, unless you know exactly what you are looking for. I do. I can pinpoint the place I lost Amaryllis for ever.

THE LAST MATCH IN THE BOX

VE Day, 8 May 1945.

It's all over, the war. I can hear the celebrations from my
bedroom window. Everyone is outside shouting, car horns
are hooting, there is singing in the street, impromptu parties,
flags and streamers. The whole of London is having a party,
but I am sure there must be millions like me who prefer to be
alone.

I live these days in a bedsit near Onslow Gardens, off Old
Brompton Road, a high-ceilinged room with long windows
looking out on to a communal garden. It has a small kitchen
in an alcove. Down the hall is a bathroom that I share.

I had a call at the office from Miss Bright. She phoned to ask
if I was all right.

'No,' I said.

She understood. 'At least it's finished.'

'Yes, that's true. But have you seen the newsreels? Do you
think Arnold Ruben was trying to save Amaryllis from all
that?'

'It's an unanswerable question.' Miss Bright paused. 'I've been thinking, Ezra. The machine wasn't all bad. It gave you back your father and mended Tommy's mind. And it gave me the strength to live in the present.'

I had nothing to say. I could only listen to the crackle on the line.

'What are you going to do?' she asked. 'I mean today, VE Day.'

'Go home, stay in.' I thanked her for calling. In the background I could hear cheers and singing. 'Go and join in the party,' I said.

'Write it down, Ezra, tell your story – but don't expect anyone to believe you.'

That made me smile as I replaced the receiver.

I had my hat and coat on, determined to slip away, when Sir Basil produced a bottle of bubbly. The last thing I wanted was to be in the office with happy, chatty people. I would rather be at home or, better still, in Warlock Wood. I wanted to tell Amaryllis that it was over.

Sir Basil shouted down the stairwell as I was on my way out. 'Pascoe, a word.'

Slowly I went back up the stairs. I had nearly got away without being noticed.

'In my office,' he said. 'Take a seat. Where are you off to?'

'Just back to my bedsit.'

'I wanted to say that you have been a great credit to the team.'

'Thank you, sir. May I go?'

'No. Glass of champagne?'

I could see I wasn't going to get out of there so easily.

'Ever heard of a young lady called Alice Riddle?'

'No, why?'

'I just wondered if the name rang any bells.'

'No. Should it, sir?'

'She was shot, been very ill.'

'That's bad luck.'

'Yes. It was a miracle she survived. I got to hear of her through a doctor friend of mine, who worked at that convalescent home they built at Warlock Hall. He asked if I could arrange to have her flown on a military plane to Switzerland.'

'Why Switzerland?'

'There's a clinic there where she'd been treated before.'

'Does she make a habit of getting shot?'

'It happens in war.'

Finally it sank in. She was one of Sir Basil's agents, and I had an awful feeling he was setting me up with a date for tonight.

'She wants to open a tiger sanctuary in India,' he continued.

It must have been obvious that I wasn't paying much attention.

'Pascoe, did you hear what I said?'

'Yes, sir. Sanctuary. India.'

'Good. She has the money to do it and . . .'

'Sir, what is this about?'

'It is about you, Ezra, it is all about you.'

I shrugged. 'I don't understand, sir.'

'No, I can see that. I suggest you think about what I've told you, and put that very good brain of yours to work. The party begins at six. My house. Don't be late. You are to be there, do you understand me? No excuses.'

I have a wind-up gramophone, which always makes me think of Amaryllis, and a boxed set of records, Rachmaninov's Piano Concerto No 2. I take great comfort in the music. It rolls along with all my memories.

I must have fallen asleep for I wake with a terrible start. Someone is ringing the front-door bell. The room is shockingly bright from the street lights outside and people are shouting. I am so disorientated that for a moment I think something awful must have happened. Oh, of course, VE Day. Blurry-eyed I go down to the hall and open the front door to find Sir Basil standing there.

'It's nine o'clock,' he says, somewhat put out. 'You were supposed to be at my house at six. Go and spruce yourself up, old chap, or we'll miss the fireworks.'

Fifteen minutes later, wearing a clean shirt and hoping I look spruce enough, I get into the Armstrong Siddeley.

'No mean feat getting here,' says Sir Basil, parping his horn. 'Everyone in London is out and making merry. Most of them pissed as newts.'

'Why did you come, sir?'

'Do you know, Pascoe, the trouble I have gone to? Are you just stubbornly refusing to see what I'm telling you?'

'I don't think so, sir. You want me to meet this young woman called Alice Riddle?'

'Correct.'

'But why, sir?'

'Well, if you haven't cracked that, you're in the wrong job.'

We are nearing the river when I realise there is one last match in that box of mine. I find I am trembling. I daren't light it. After that one is gone, there are no more.

'Has she been away a long time?' I say.

'You can ask her yourself.'

We pull up outside his house in Cheyne Walk. The place is jewel-bright. The windows are wide open and voices spill out on to the street. It is quite a struggle to get past all the guests and up to the drawing room.

She has her back to me. Her beautiful red dress is cut low and on her skin there is a mark, a small star-shaped scar.

I have the strangest sensation that the half of me that never made it through the membrane is rushing back upon itself. The room, the people, fade away. The camera in my eye is gone. I am no longer adrift, I am back in the moment, in the present, with a future.

I strike the last match.

She turns to look at me, her violet eyes dancing, my heart on fire.

the Double Shadow

IN BRIEF

A girl stands looking out onto a wasteland. Who is she? Where is she? She can't quite remember anything but fragments, and what she sees confuses her. A dead butterfly. The ruined picture palace returning to its former glory. Silas. A white tiger. Do these pieces of memory mean she doesn't exist? Is she crazy? Who is the uniformed World War One veteran watching the humming machine in the corner? Why won't the child who follows her leave her alone? And what of the boy she's looking for? Can that really be him – tumbling out of a broom cupboard into the light?

Sixteen-year-old Amaryllis Ruben can't remember her life before the age of eight, nor her dead mother. She also has only a hazy recollection of what actually happens during the evening she spends with Maurice Sands (or is his name Everett Roach?). But she knows it was bad – disappearing with him for the night is enough to get her expelled from school and sent back to Warlock Hall, her family home. She's alone there for several weeks as her father is away, and on the day of his return, angry that he's sent her a childish dress all the way from America, she steals a cake baked for him and sneaks off to her old Wendy house to eat it.

This selfish act propels her into the life of the Pascoe family. In particular that of Nancy Pascoe, the cook, (who forces her to bake a replacement cake), and her fifteen-year-old son Ezra. Through them she sees what a normal, loving family is like. But life for the Pascoes is not quite the idyll she imagines. Noel, Ezra's father, is shell-shocked following his experiences in the First World War. He's unable to work, and his 'turns' send him out to his shed to dig trenches, sometimes for days.

Arnold, Amaryllis's father, also experiences the horrors of the war first hand, but his family background is quite different. Brought up in New York, the son of an abusive father, he is left a fortune by his uncle and uses it to buy Warlock Hall and erect a magnificent picture palace in its grounds. But there's a secret in its basement. Arnold has been using his fortune to pursue his great dream – building a memory machine designed to capture good memories and help erase the bad, with Amaryllis at its heart.

His work is not without its problems, even with the help of his trusted friend and aide, Silas Molde. The unpleasant side-effects suffered by those who offer to record their memories – headaches and even death –

are nothing to Arnold, compared with having accidentally wiped Amaryllis's memory at the age of eight, leaving a chasm in the relationship between father and daughter.

Ignoring the advice of his close acquaintance Sir Basil Stanhope, Arnold goes to London to give a lecture on his invention. He's devastated when his claims regarding time travel are dismissed by the scientists, who are also unnerved at the machine's potential to alter people's memories and brainwash them. Arnold insists the memory machine is a private project, but Stanhope reveals he works for the government and that at a time of uncertainty Arnold's research poses a national security risk. He refuses to listen – his experiments will continue.

In the meantime, Ezra helps Amaryllis when she's accidentally hurt by Ezra's friend, Tommy Treacle, during a clandestine trip to the cinema. As a thank you Arnold insists Ezra attends lessons with Amaryllis and her new governess, but the two get on very badly and Ezra dreads their time together.

After weeks of torment Amaryllis calls a truce and persuades Ezra to visit the picture palace with her. When they sneak downstairs to see what's kept in the basement, the real purpose of Amaryllis's visit, they realise they're not alone just as they discover the memory machine. Everett Roach is also inside, and he has a gun. All looks lost but they manage to escape through a side entrance.

Roach is working for enemy agents and wants blueprints of the memory machine. He tries to achieve this through blackmailing Arnold with photographs of Amaryllis naked, but manages only to hasten Arnold's decision to save her from her memories by activating the memory machine the next night – her seventeenth birthday. Amaryllis is aware of what's going to happen, and is unhappy but accepts her fate, having shared a kiss with Ezra.

On the night of her birthday Warlock Hall is firebombed resulting, it is thought, in the death of Arnold's actress friend Vervaine Fox (revealed to be Silas's youthful bride). Silas, Arnold and Amaryllis disappear. As does Ezra's father Noel.

Tommy Treacle becomes part of the remaining Pascoe family following his parents' deaths, and his skill for drawing reveals that although it was thought the picture palace had completely disappeared on the night of the fire, it comes and goes in Warlock Woods. Miss Bright, Amaryllis's governess, discovers it one day, sees her dead lover inside and follows him, as the picture palace vanishes. And Tommy goes inside sometime later, when out for a walk with Ezra, summoned by a vision of his father and his favourite pet mouse.

Meanwhile Amaryllis is coming to terms with her new surroundings, trapped in the memory machine with Silas and her fragmented memories. A child who has the same eyes keeps following her around like a ghost, and soon Amaryllis realises that the girl is her younger self, and that the girl's memories are hers. Eventually she comes to understand her parents' backgrounds, how they became the people they were, and what happened on the day of her mother's death. She also meets Noel, Miss Bright and Tommy and they exist as best they can.

When the Second World War breaks out Ezra is recruited into Sir Basil's Office for Scientific Protection. Sir Basil explains that Arnold Ruben was murdered on the night of the fire, and that the dead woman everyone thought was Vervaine Fox was in fact a woman employed to impersonate her. The real Vervaine was a close friend of Roach, and entered the memory machine in an attempt to stay young. Sir Basil believes she's still inside the picture palace with Silas, Amaryllis and several others, including Ezra's father and Everett Roach. It is a matter of national security, and Ezra is the only man who can help.

Ezra remembers the second entrance through the ice house, and manages to get inside the picture palace as it reappears during an air raid. He finds Amaryllis and they reaffirm their love, but because he hasn't entered through the main doors the memory machine doesn't recognise him and makes him ill, sapping his strength in an effort to destroy him. Eventually, with Silas' help, Roach is killed as he leaves the building and Tommy, Miss Bright, Noel and Ezra are able to escape the picture palace just before it disappears.

But Amaryllis, shot by Roach on the night of the fire, can't leave because her injury will kill her outside the picture palace. Silas, who trained as a doctor, says he can perform an operation which will help her temporarily, but back in the woods she will have only an hour to get help if she is to survive. Silas knows he and Vervaine can never escape.

Back in London and despondent without Amaryllis, Ezra returns to work with Sir Basil. The German version of the memory machine is discovered, and Ezra accompanies the bombing mission sent to destroy it. That night it's reported that the site of the picture palace has exploded in a ball of green light. Ezra knows that any hope of anyone coming out of it ever again has gone, and mourns the loss of Amaryllis.

On VE Day Sir Basil invites Ezra to a party. There is someone he wants him to meet. A girl with violet eyes, who has been in hospital in Switzerland and wants to open a tiger sanctuary . . . He sees the woman and realises it's Amaryllis. His future has been given back to him, and his heart is on fire.

FOR DISCUSSION

🎞 Do you agree with Miss Bright's sentiment that because the memory machine changed Tommy and Noel for the better, it wasn't all bad?

🎞 Tigers, cakes and butterflies recur through the novel. Discuss their relevance.

🎞 The song *The Teddy Bear's Picnic* plays an important role in the novel. Have you read any other books where a familiar piece of music is central to the plot?

🎞 Did remembering her mother's death help Amaryllis? Was her father wrong to try and shield her from bad memories?

🎞 Where/what is the wasteland?

🎞 Discuss the relationship between fathers and their children. Are they more or less important than the children's relationship with their mothers?

- Did you learn anything about either the First or Second World War through reading this novel?

- During their trips to the cinema the young Arnold and his mother 'were free to lose themselves in someone else's story.' How important is this aspect of cinema to the novel?

- Is Silas Molde a bad man?

- The author takes us backwards and forwards in time, piecing together the characters' lives through their memories. What do you think of the novel's structure?

- The first chapter is dreamlike in tone. How quickly were you able to identify the key moments in Amaryllis's life which appeared in this chapter?

- The death of Arnold's uncle, and his subsequent inheritance, allowed him to pursue his dream. Can a great fortune buy you anything?

- The name Silas means 'of the forest', Ezra means 'helper' and 'Warlock' is another word for wizard.

Discuss the importance of names and how they relate to what happens to the relevant characters and places. Are there any other names, of people, buildings or places that you think are particularly fitting?

⊛ At the heart of this story is scientific experiment and time travel. Does that make it a work of science fiction?

⊛ Is the Wendy house at Warlock Hall the only place Amaryllis is happy?

⊛ The author, Sally Gardner, says in her acknowledgements that she was influenced by TS Eliot's poem *The Wasteland*. What themes does her novel share with the poem?

⊛ Nancy tells Bert 'lots of us have secret lives.' How many of the novel's characters have lives which are lived completely in the open?

⊛ If you could only keep one single memory, what would it be?

SUGGESTIONS FOR FURTHER READING

Sally Gardner acknowledges the following books as having been influential when she was writing *The Double Shadow*:

The Wasteland – TS Eliot
The Thirties: An Intimate History of Britain
  – Juliet Gardiner
The Blitz: The British Under Attack – Juliet Gardiner

Other works that may interest you:

The Time Machine – HG Wells
We Can Remember It For You Wholesale – Philip K Dick
False Memory – Dean Koontz
I Capture The Castle – Dodie Smith
Swanns Way (Remembrance of Things Past: Volume 1)
  – Marcel Proust
Atonement – Ian McEwan
Generals Die In Bed – Charles Yard Harrison
The Time Traveller's Wife – Audrey Niffenegger

ACKNOWLEDGEMENTS

I am grateful to the historian and author Juliet Gardiner for her invaluable books *The Thirties: An Intimate History of Britain* and *The Blitz: The British Under Attack*, and for the time she kindly took to answer my many questions on the period between the world wars; to Tim Nuthall MBBS for his expert advice on medical matters; and to The Cinema Museum in Kennington, London for the guided tour. For anyone interested in the history of the picture palace and the arts and crafts of film-making, it is an Aladdin's Cave of wonder.

My greatest thanks go to Jacky Bateman, to whom this book is dedicated, for keeping track of continuity and pulling me back to the path of the plot whenever I threatened to stray; to the poet Anthony Suter for introducing me to *The Wasteland* by T. S. Eliot and the music of Pierre Boulez, the *Dialogue de l'ombre double;* to my agent, Catherine Clarke for her unfailing enthusiasm; to my editor, Fiona Kennedy, who had the grace to let me finish the book I wanted to write before sharpening her pencil, and to all the team at Orion for their hard work.

During my research for this book I had the privilege of meeting Tony Iveson, DFC. A 'Bomber Boy', Tony's memories transported me back to the Second World War. My heartfelt thanks to him and to all the other young airmen who fought for this country in the dark clouds over Europe.

Sally Gardner
Suffolk
June 2011

Also by Sally Gardner

THE RED NECKLACE

Paris, 1789.

While the aristocracy dine, dance, gossip and gamble their way to disaster, the poor and starving dream of revolution.

Enter the boy Yann Margoza, destined to be a hero; Têtu the dwarf, his friend and mentor; Sido, unloved daughter of the foolish Marquis de Villeduval; and the sinister Count Kallikovski, who holds half the aristocracy in thrall to him.

The drama moves from Paris to London and back, as the Revolution gathers momentum, and the hope of liberty and the dream of equality are crushed beneath the wheel of terror.

Too many secrets, too many murders, and the blade of the guillotine is yet to fall . . .

'a story that has everything – murder, mystery, passion and even magic' *The Times*

THE SILVER BLADE

Paris, 1793.

The blade of the guillotine falls on the neck of the King himself, and the spirit of the French Revolution lies in tatters. The Reign of Terror has begun.

Yann Margoza is helping desperate people to escape to England, where Sido, the girl he loves, waits to hear from him.

But Yann's past haunts him. He is in grave danger, and so is Sido. For under the streets of Paris, in the catacombs, the howl of a great beast can be heard. And a boy with angelic looks and an evil heart is ready to do the bidding of a man who has made a pact with the devil.

A thrilling tale of secrets, of locks and keys, of murder, revenge and romance, written with the vividness and passion that made *The Red Necklace* such a fantastic success.

'Gardner occupies a unique place in children's literature, which *The Silver Blade* assures . . . An enthralling and wholly original novel, *The Silver Blade* is a must-read for a new generation.'

The Times

I, CORIANDER

I am Coriander Hobie.

I was born in the year of Our Lord 1643, the only child of Thomas and Eleanor Hobie, in our great house on the River Thames in London. Of my early years I remember only happiness. That was before I knew this world had such evil in it, and that my fate was to be locked up in a chest and left to die.

This is my story. This is my life.

'an extraordinarily beautiful and gripping tale, but what astonishes is Gardner's prose . . . This is a classic new novel by an author who has written a rich fairytale for our times.'

Amanda Craig, *The Times*

'a suspenseful masterpiece' Publisher's Weekly

'A glorious, beautifully written novel . . . This story entranced me from page one and didn't let me go until the last sentence.'

The Bookseller